M000202575

Young

Babylon

Young

Babylon

Lu Nei

Translated by Poppy Toland

This is a work of fiction. Names, characters, organizations, places, events, and incidents are either products of the author's imagination or are used fictitiously.

Text copyright © 2008 by Lu Nei

Translation copyright © 2015 by Poppy Toland

All rights reserved.

No part of this book may be reproduced, or stored in a retrieval system, or transmitted in any form or by any means, electronic, mechanical, photocopying, recording, or otherwise, without express written permission of the publisher.

Previously published as 少年巴比伦 by Beijing "October" Arts & Literature Publishing House in China in 2008. Translated from Chinese by Poppy Toland. First published in English by AmazonCrossing in 2015.

Published by AmazonCrossing, Seattle

www.apub.com

Amazon, the Amazon logo, and AmazonCrossing are trademarks of Amazon.com, Inc., or its affiliates.

ISBN-13: 9781477829998
ISBN-10: 1477829997

Cover design by David Drummond

Library of Congress Control Number: 2014921448

Printed in the United States of America

On the road to Zhongnan Mountain

The sky brightens and dusk falls away

He doesn't know that the birds at Zhongnan Mountain

Only sleep this one night of the year

—*"Zhongnan Mountain," Zhang Xiaoyin*

CHAPTER ONE
PESSIMISTS HAVE NOWHERE TO GO

Zhang Xiaoyin and I were sitting by the side of the road.

"Lu Xiaolu, tell me a story from your past," she said.

I was thirty and I hadn't sat on the curb—or the curbstones, as they call them in Shanghai—for a long time. Sitting like that made me feel like I was still pretty young. I told Zhang Xiaoyin to go buy me a milk tea, and then I'd tell her a story. I love the milk tea they sell at the roadside. Just like I love Shanghai's upmarket districts, where the curbs are relatively clean and the flavor of the milk tea is just as it should be. In the city where I grew up, water flooded from the gutters and ran down the sides of the streets, and no one sold milk tea on the street, only soy milk, which tasted like bean dregs. Nothing about that place was particularly great, but I lived there for many years all the same.

Zhang Xiaoyin is an underground poet. She posts her poems on internet chat sites, where they attract a stream of comments. I've posted comments, too, most of them just praising her writing. When we first met, she was really into walking—she used to walk everywhere. She'd steam along Zhongshan West Road, and I'd stagger after her feeling geriatric. Once we moved in together, her passion for walking abated almost overnight. She'd be walking along for no time at all before her hand was in the air and she was slipping into a taxi.

When I was her age, there weren't many taxis on the streets and I never had much money in my pocket, which made them a real luxury. When I went out with girls back then, I'd look at them and say very sweetly, "How about a walk then? We can look up at the moon together." Those girls knew exactly what was what, and in a fraction of a second they'd have hailed a taxi and climbed inside. Others would be pushing their bikes along, and when the date was over they'd jump on and ride off, never needing to be escorted home.

That was the beginning of the 1990s, when I was nineteen and living in a place called Daicheng, near Shanghai. The '90s passed in the blink of an eye, but my twenties felt like a never-ending maze. That's just the way it is sometimes: real time and time as you experience it seem like they're happening in two different latitudes.

I have a weakness for girls who like walking, and it was on Zhongshan West Road that I asked Zhang Xiaoyin if she wanted to be my girlfriend. She said yes. After we got together, she was no longer interested in walking with me. That particular weakness had been crushed, but things weren't too bad. Zhang Xiaoyin might have lost her passion for walking, but she still had her passion for writing poetry—and girl poets are my other weakness.

Naturally you can't expect a girl to write poetry and cook, be clever and beautiful, and be an avid walker to boot—that's setting the bar too high. I don't have any special requirements for a girl, as long as she's good-natured.

"I don't want to hear you talk about my nature," Zhang Xiaoyin told me. "My nature's just fine. I just want to hear stories from your past."

Zhang Xiaoyin belongs to that post-'80s generation that loves to hear weird stories.

I told her it wasn't so different from her university years, spent in libraries and internet cafés, except hers were at the beginning of the twenty-first century. That was her youth, both her sweetest and most rotten years. For me, the sweetness and rot were back in the '90s. It is joyous to experience a fruit's fresh fragrance and its decay, that moment when everything is so vivid.

I could style the opening of this story after *The Lover* by Marguerite Duras: "By the time I was eighteen years old, it was already too late . . ." Or I could imitate Gabriel García Márquez in *One Hundred Years of Solitude*: "Many years later, as he sat by the side of the road, Lu Xiaolu thought about the day he started working at the factory . . ."

I thought about the tone I'd use to tell her this story. I wanted it to feel like coming face-to-face with a lover who'd been absent for many years. I was also thinking that if I didn't pour out these stories now, in my thirties, it would be like a door in the darkness silently closing. My experiences and feelings from that time would quietly rot away.

I told Zhang Xiaoyin that when I was nineteen, my ambition had been to work in a propaganda department. Zhang Xiaoyin found this hilarious.

"The propaganda department? You mean writing blackboard bulletins?"

But the blackboard bulletins didn't need to be written up every day. Working in the propaganda department was pretty laid-back most of the time, with nothing to do at all. When there was a production accident—when someone was careless and died, or careless and sliced off an arm in one of the machines—the propaganda department would issue a blackboard bulletin on safety. If someone had a second child or slipped up and got pregnant out of wedlock, the propaganda department would write up a bit of family planning advice. And that simple job was actually the shared responsibility of more than ten employees.

At that time, my ideal life went like this: each morning I brewed a cup of tea for myself, followed by a cup for the department head; I spread open a copy of the *Daicheng Daily* and sat at my desk waiting for lunchtime. There was a cactus on the windowsill of the propaganda department, and when it was nice outside the sun shone down onto this cactus and cast a shadow, making it look like a sundial. In the mornings, the dial pointed at me; by the afternoons, it pointed to the department head sitting opposite; and at lunchtime, it pointed straight at the office door. If you spent the day gazing patiently at this sundial, you'd find that time slipped away effortlessly.

This was only ever in my imagination—I never actually worked in the propaganda department. People told me I wasn't educated enough, that I was fit only for a worker's job, and an apprentice worker's job at that. Apprentices had a very humble position within the factory hierarchy, and when you were in line for food, you needed to let the old supervisors go in front. Same thing when waiting in line for a shit—always offer them the hole first. It didn't matter if you missed out on a hot meal or ended up crapping your pants. I stayed at the factory for a long time despite all this, although I really can't say why.

"Lu Xiaolu, what's your ambition?" a girl asked me back then.

I told her I wanted to be a poet. Even as my heart was telling me "propaganda department employee," my mouth said "poet." So I wrote a poem and showed it to some girls. They told me it had the charm of Li Qingzhao. I hadn't exactly aspired to her gloomy, feminine style, but the praise made me strangely happy. They told me I had a real way with words and that I should be working in the propaganda department. That struck me right in my Achilles heel. "I'm not educated enough" was my only response. It felt like becoming a poet was a more achievable ambition than getting into the propaganda department.

When I use the word *ambition*, it's mostly not in terms of something you chase after—more like something you'd bargain for if you had the means. Otherwise why, when I was in my twenties, were so many girls so interested in my ambition? At the time, I was an apprentice worker doing physical labor. Generally speaking, people in this profession weren't born with ambition— their brains seem to have been sliced out of their heads. I can't explain where my ambition came from.

"You've really failed in that case, Xiaolu. You're not a poet or a propaganda department employee," Zhang Xiaoyin said gleefully before placing her empty milk tea cup on top of my head.

In middle school I was terrible at math, and analytic geometry problems stumped me completely. The only thing I could see when I looked at the curve of the quadrant was the shape of a girl's breasts and ass. I mentioned this to a classmate who was a bit of a big mouth, and he went and told the math teacher.

"Lu Xiaolu," the teacher said, "your view of life is seriously flawed. Only a pessimist would mistake a curve for a life drawing." From then on every time he drew a curve on the blackboard, he'd turn and give me a pointed look.

The math teacher's words were like a riddle to me. The only terms we learned in our middle-school politics class were *objectivity* and *subjectivity*, *idealism* and *materialism*, *residual value*, and things like that. Marxist-Leninist philosophy didn't generally talk about pessimism and optimism, so I didn't really understand them. At first I thought the math teacher was mocking me. Ours was an average middle school where they taught us from second-rate textbooks. People said trying to get into university while studying from these books was like trying to fly to the moon with a diesel engine—a complete pipe dream. Most of the students from my school went on to become factory workers, while the better among us became shop assistants. Of course, there were also those who stood at the roadside and sold smokes. Can you imagine anything more pompous coming from the mouth of a math teacher at a school like that?

At the time, my choices were: 1) take the college entrance exam and wait to hear that I'd failed; 2) not take the college entrance exam, but instead go straight to becoming a factory apprentice; or 3) not become an apprentice, but instead go straight to the roadside to sell smokes. My pa would often lecture me: "Xiaolu, if you don't study hard, your only option later on will be to sell smokes at the roadside."

To which I'd respond, "What about if I study hard then, Pa?"

"You can go to the factory and become an apprentice," he'd say.

"Pa, do I really have to study hard to become an apprentice?"

"What do you think an apprenticeship is—a walk in the park?"

My father was an engineer at Daicheng's pesticide factory. He spent his whole life there, first in the company of reactors and pipes, and later producing a pesticide known as methamidophos. I heard that a large number of rural women committed suicide by drinking this pesticide. My father used to be an intellectual, and when he was young he had delicate good looks. But more than twenty years in the workshops had turned him into a brawny man with a bristly beard, at a glance no different than anyone else in the factory. Although he'd declined physically somewhat over the past few years, he wasn't over the hill yet. He still had defined muscles, and as his temper got worse he used to beat me quite viciously. I didn't retaliate to spare my mother's feelings and, of course, his pride.

"Pa," I reasoned, "the bottom line is that I really don't want to be a manual laborer. I'd rather be a shop assistant. Being a shop assistant's got to be better than being a worker, surely?"

"If you become a shop assistant, I won't be able to help you," he said. "But if you become a worker, you'll get the chance to go to college later."

That's when he told me about vocational college, or trade school, as we knew it. Because of my shoddy school, I knew next to nothing about colleges and universities. I didn't even know the difference between a degree and a college diploma. I went to ask my high school teacher about all this once, and the prick told me I had no reason to concern myself with such matters. Later my father explained that the Daicheng chemical industry had an affiliated independent vocational college known as Daicheng Chemical Trade School. Employees from the chemical factory all studied there for their diplomas. To get into this college, you didn't need to take any exams. Instead each factory recommended its most outstanding employees as students. Tuition fees and incidentals were covered by the factory, and students received a basic wage. This was known as "escaping one's duty," and it was every worker's dream.

My pa told me that if I did a one-year apprenticeship at the chemical factory, I'd be offered a permanent job. Then we could find someone to get me into trade school. Two years of muddling along there, and I'd have my diploma. I could return to the factory not as a worker, but as a member of a cadre. That's when I'd be assigned to the propaganda department and get to drink tea and read the paper.

Hearing this made me unbelievably happy. After nineteen years of suffering his beatings, all I could feel was gratitude.

"Pa," I said, "is it a done deal? Can you definitely get me into college through the back door?"

He explained that he knew someone in the chemical engineering office. I feasted on his reassurance and did no more schoolwork. Instead I plunged headlong into games at the local arcade, ending up with the second-worst final exam results in my class. Logically speaking, I should have been at the roadside selling smokes, but in the summer of 1992 I received an enrollment form from the chemical factory all the same. I was certain my father had magical powers.

It was only after I started working at the factory that I realized he had deceived me. There were more than three thousand workers, half of them young. They were the ones who did shift work, repaired machinery, and carried sacks, and all of them wanted to try their luck at chemical trade school. Later I found out that among this lot were the factory head's daughter, the party secretary's son, the chairman of the trade union's brother, and the propaganda head's daughter-in-law. They were all workers, and they all wanted to get transferred to the propaganda department. They were all waiting for a chance to go to trade school and muddle along for their diplomas.

"Didn't you say you had someone at the chemical factory office?" I asked my pa.

He placed his hands over his cheeks and said, "He's just retired."

Trade school had become a lottery. At any time it might be possible to win the prize, but no one could say for sure. The price I paid for my lottery tickets was apprenticing at the factory. This was as you'd expect—no one wins a lottery if they don't buy a ticket. According to my father, all I needed to do was work hard, follow orders, and give regular gifts—and I would gain the factory head's favor.

By the time I realized I'd been duped, I was in too deep. To get me into the factory, and a decent trade at that, my family had parted with huge numbers of cigarettes and gift vouchers. Vouchers and smokes were the price my father paid for his lottery ticket. Because it was for his son, he didn't see it as steep. At most I was like Cinderella: even if I didn't have my chance with the glass slipper, I'd still be there to help with the housework. I thought back to my math teacher's comment: Lu Xiaolu sees a curve as an ass, and that makes him a pessimist. I reflected seriously on those words, understanding them to mean that not only did I see an ass when I looked at a curve, but also a curve when I looked at an ass. Someone like this was pessimistic to the point of no return because the world in front of him was nothing more than a blob of glue, and none of his choices were ever going to make the slightest bit of difference.

That year my pa beat me for some minor offense. He'd forgotten that I was already a factory apprentice, a factory apprentice who wasn't going to get into trade school. As my ma shrieked, I threw caution to the wind and fought back. I felt pretty pleased with myself when I was done, and I offered my pa a cigarette. As he smoked it, he told my mother to go out and get us a roast chicken.

I never felt any warmth toward the chemical factory.

We lived in Daicheng, a city with a huge number of factories. It had the pesticide factory, a glue factory, a fertilizer factory, a solvent factory, and a paint factory, which made up the city's chemical industry. Like giant rectums, these factories pumped toxic gas into the air. How could you feel anything but contempt for this bunch of rectums?

Our home was in a new village. These were public housing estates constructed in the early '80s by the various factories and assigned to their employees in exchange for modest rent. They consisted of small apartments of about four or five hundred square feet. Later they were restructured and sold off privately. Housing prices soared, and the retired workers used what they made to pay for their coffins. These new villages were named after the factories they were affiliated with, so the village owned by the textile mill was called Textile Mill New Village and the one owned by the pesticide factory was called Pesticide

New Village. There was also a Meat Packing New Village and a Soap New Village. Although they weren't the most imaginative names in the world, they were pretty easy to remember.

Our home was in Pesticide New Village, very close to the pesticide factory. I don't know which fuckwit chose a plot of land literally 550 yards from the pesticide factory for its construction. In the middle of the night, the factory would pump out sulfur dioxide, which smelled just like rotten eggs, and smoke so thick that magpies dropped from the trees one by one. This sort of place was completely unsuitable for human habitation, but I lived there for a long time all the same.

There were regular explosions at the factory. Sometimes there'd be a bang as if firecrackers were going off in the distance; other times it would be a boom, and the window glass would rattle. From the sound of the explosion, you could figure out how serious it was. When we heard the commotion, we'd call the factory and find out what had happened. There were only public phones back then, and as soon as an explosion sounded, the grocery store doorway would be crammed with people—family members of the factory employees, all waiting for the phone to find out which workshop the explosion had gone off in—who had been injured, who had been killed. The person on the phone would turn around and tell the rest of the people what was going on. Most of the time no one was killed in these explosions, a fact I found quite puzzling. My father told me that before an explosion the meters and valves would show irregularities, and everyone would make a run for it. The explosions with no warning signs didn't tend to happen in the pesticide factory—more at the munitions factory.

That summer, the whole village shone red under the burning clouds at dusk. Our apartment was on the first floor, and we had a small courtyard we used to dry clothes, grow grapes, and make piles of random objects. The floor above would surreptitiously throw cigarette butts and trash out there. My ma was in the kitchen cooking that day while my pa and I sat out in the courtyard playing chess. We suddenly heard a rumble, and a wisp of black smoke started to snake up—another explosion at the pesticide factory. My pa put down his chess piece and began to climb the courtyard wall.

"Why do you care, Pa?" I said. "You're not working today."

"Just having a look," he said.

"These explosions happen all the time, what's the big deal?"

"It's downwind today," he replied. "We need to be vigilant."

He used to tell us that in the event of a factory explosion that resulted in a toxic gas leak, we needed to run against the wind. Toxic gas blew downwind.

I climbed up next to him. There was a crowd of people on the balcony leaning over, watching the explosion together. It had happened during the midday shift, so they were all trying to figure out who'd been on duty. I saw a dark red light flickering from deep inside the factory's outer wall.

My father pointed to it and said, "That's the workshop area, not the warehouse—it's a workshop explosion." Furrowing his brow, he turned to me and said, "If something happens, you must be sure to run against the wind."

I told him I knew. He'd given me this same advice so many times but I'd never had to run, not once. Later we saw Ah San from upstairs running like crazy in our direction.

"Old Lu," he shouted when he saw my pa (Old Lu was Pa's nickname). "This is terrible! It's going to blow!"

"What's going to blow?" my father asked.

"It's a chlorine canister! There's going to be an explosion any minute."

My pa jumped from the wall without a word, dragging me down with him. He grabbed me and dashed to the kitchen, reaching out to turn off the gas cooker. He took hold of my ma and ran like mad toward the bike shed, undoing the lock of his twenty-eight-inch Phoenix bike. Carrying my mother, he jumped on the Phoenix and sped like a hurricane toward the southeast. I didn't have my bike key on me, so I ran after them wearing a pair of plastic sandals.

Ah San caused a complete furor in Pesticide New Village with his frenzied crying, and everyone went running from their apartments. It was the kind of spectacle you usually saw only during an earthquake. Everyone was yelling that there had been a chlorine leak and to run for your fucking life.

My father slammed his feet against the bike pedals and shouted, "Run against the wind! Everyone run against the wind!"

I was following them when I saw Li Xiaoyan's grandma dash out of the apartment block across the street, covered head to toe in soap bubbles. The old lady must have been bathing and just pulled on her underpants because her top half was completely bare. Her breasts looked like two pieces of burlap swinging precariously in front of everyone's eyes. The burlap breasts, together with their owner's panic-stricken face, looked like a teenage dream gone very wrong. The crowds, running for their lives, didn't have the time to marvel at her. But it was the first time I could remember ever seeing a pair of breasts, and even though it was totally warped and inappropriate, I couldn't help looking back a couple of times.

"Xiaolu!" my ma scolded from the back of my pa's bike. "You shouldn't stare at people like that—stop behaving like a delinquent!"

How dumb is she? I thought to myself. Worrying about my morality at a time like this. If the chlorine blew our way I was going to die, and if I died never having seen a woman's breasts, my life really would have been in vain. At any rate, those weren't breasts—all I could see were bits of burlap.

By dusk the three of us had slipped through the huge crowd of people and fled along the motorway toward the suburbs. My father peddled the bike, still carrying my mother, while I trotted along behind them wearing my plastic flip-flops, blisters forming as they rubbed against my feet. My parents showed no signs of stopping. A dozen or so fire engines drove past us, wailing as they went. They were followed by police cars and ambulances. These vehicles disappeared, and the road fell strangely silent; the only sounds were the creaking of the bicycle chain and the slapping of my shoes against the tarmac. The sky went dark suddenly, and to the west all we could see was a wisp of the blood-red sunset clouds. The streetlights started to come on one after another. I could no longer hear the flapping of my shoes. I took the flip-flops in one hand and continued to run barefoot.

My father stopped his bike. "We've come far enough," he said. "The chlorine won't blow this far. Even the mayor must have been poisoned by the fumes by now."

We stopped at a small restaurant in the suburbs where we had egg fried rice. My ma called the factory and was told there hadn't been a chlorine explosion. Ah San from upstairs had been spreading rumors and causing trouble, apparently. The bastard was known for doing nasty things like that. My ma agreed that Ah San really was a piece of work, she said, forever throwing cigarette butts into our courtyard. My pa said we couldn't blame Ah San—it was chlorine we were talking about here, for fuck's sake, and had there not been leaks in the past?

My father was a former supervisor at the factory, and he knew about things like chlorine leaks. Apparently it was always better to err on the side of caution. But my father's tolerance of Ah San didn't mean the guy escaped punishment. Because Li Xiaoyan's grandma died. She exposed her burlap breasts to the entire new village, and Li Xiaoyan's mother told her she'd never be able to hold her head up high again. So the old lady jumped from the building's sixth floor.

Because they couldn't find anyone else to blame, Ah San became the scapegoat. Li Xiaoyan's entire family went down to the police station to report his crime. Li Xiaoyan's mother was drowning in tears as she spoke about Ah San's rumor-mongering and how it had led to the old woman's death. Tugging at the police officer's shirt, she said, "A thug like Ah San must pay with his life! She can't have died in vain." People who overheard her just assumed they were listening to an account of rape. The policemen found her really irritating, but they went to the pesticide factory to investigate further. The factory head told them that Ah San was a destructive individual and should have been arrested a long time ago. Ah San wasn't bothered when the factory recommended jail time—he was happy living off state grain, not considering it different from a business trip. Later he was transferred to a labor education camp under the crime of "harming social stability."

My ma said that Li Xiaoyan's grandma's death was a great injustice, but what Ah San suffered was an even greater injustice. I thought that I'd suffered an injustice too. The first time I got to see breasts, not only did they look like pieces of a burlap sack, but the mere fact of my seeing them caused their owner to kill herself. It was all very odd, and it filled me with dread. It was the same sense of dread I had about the factory, although I had no idea why.

The summer of 1992, after taking final exams, I went to collect my results and received a slap across the face from my father. He told me that with results like these, even cigarette peddling was beyond me. Shielding my neck, I took his slaps, thinking to myself, *Pa, this is the last time you're going to beat me. Next time I'm going to fight back.* He gave me a proper beating and left me with half my face swollen.

"Just you wait till you're a factory apprentice," he said when he'd finished.

That was my last summer vacation. I did nothing but loaf around. Even the weather was against me, and the constant drizzle meant there was no chance of swimming in the lake. All I did was go to the arcade on my own to play *Street Fighter*. One day I exchanged all my loose change for tokens and played for broke, and still that long and boring afternoon dragged on. So I cornered a younger kid and took some yuan off him. The kid tore away from me, and once he had a hundred yards between us he turned back and shouted, "I'm going to sic my brother on you. Your ma's a whore!"

It was like a time bomb having so many bored teenagers together on summer break. They either wandered around on their own or hung out in groups. The combination of scorching weather and boredom sent hormone production into overdrive. I didn't want to get caught up in any brawls, so I used the money I'd grabbed from that kid to buy some ice cream, then headed home.

My father was sitting in the kitchen when I got back. "Where have you been?" he asked.

"Revising," was my automatic response.

My father rapped his knuckles against the table. "Think carefully before answering."

I remembered that I'd finished my exams and sold all my textbooks and revision notes as scrap paper. I changed my excuse to, "Watching movies at a friend's place." I was lying for no reason other than pure habit. Even though I was brought up in a worker's family, there were as many freaking rules as if we'd been nobility. I wasn't allowed to smoke or play video games, to have girlfriends or cut classes. I was forbidden from playing pool or reading books that weren't textbooks, or even just hanging around in the street. I was the only one I knew who had so little freedom.

My pa knew how much I liked video games, and the local arcade was on his regular patrol beat. Lucky for me the guy who ran the arcade was a buddy, and if he saw my pa in the distance he'd whistle and say, "Xiaolu, your pa's on his way." I'd throw down the console and run out the back where I always left my bike. I'd race it back home, whip open my textbooks, and pretend to be studying. My father was never the wiser.

On that particular day, my father wasn't in the mood for my bullshit. He took a form from his briefcase. "Fill this in," he said.

It was a job application from the factory. I filled it in item by item. He found my graduation photo in a drawer and stuck it to the corner using a couple of grains of cooked rice.

"Pa," I said, "where exactly am I applying to?"

"The saccharin factory."

"You're at the pesticide factory." I said. "How come you're sending me to the saccharin factory?"

My father shook his head and told me it was a long story. When I was in lower middle school, my father had gotten my cousin an apprenticeship at the pesticide factory. Unfortunately, my cousin got mixed up with a mafia gang. He beat up the workshop director and swaggered off. The injured workshop director came running to our house to have it out with my pa, his head wrapped in gauze, his left arm in a cast, bite marks on his ear. My pa was indifferent to the poor man's plight. All he said was, "That's just the way it is. If you're a workshop director, you should expect to take some flack."

The workshop director turned to my father in tears and said, "I'll tell you something, Lu Daquan. If your son ever wants to come work at the pesticide factory, I'll make sure he's assigned to scooping up the shit from the latrines."

My father was an engineer and had the same status as the workshop director, so he was not bothered by this threat. Later this man was promoted to deputy head of the factory, responsible for personnel and discipline. So, my father told me, if I really did want a job at the pesticide factory, it would most likely be shoveling up shit. And even if I were still willing, he couldn't take the shame.

My cousin and my father had basically conspired to end my career at the pesticide factory before it had even begun. This wasn't necessarily a bad thing— having my father as a colleague would have been a nightmare.

I hated the pesticide factory anyway because of all those explosions, and because of its sulfur dioxide emissions. If you didn't want to smell its rotten-egg stench anymore, all you needed to do was wait for an explosion and production would halt. If you didn't fancy getting blasted to bits, you just learned to put up with the stench. This really was the ultimate fucking tragedy of life.

So I was destined for the saccharin factory. At least it was quite a charming product. When I was a kid, I used to make popcorn and sprinkle a little saccharin over it. Pesticide, on the other hand, is not the slightest bit charming. If you eat it, you die, and there would be no point whatsoever in smuggling it home.

"Saccharin is pretty much the same as popcorn, isn't it?" I asked my father.

He told me I was talking crap. Saccharin was an important component that went by the chemical name of benzoic sulfilimine, he explained. As well as popcorn it could be added to cakes, toffee apples, and ice cream; its use was widespread. He told me the saccharin factory was very efficient. If what they produced was used only in popcorn, half the workers would already be out of a job and starving on the streets. Later he said, "You don't even need to know any of this, you're not getting involved in product development. All you need to do is to work hard and be a good apprentice."

Hearing this made me really depressed. Not because of the apprenticeship, but because I'd be working with saccharin. There was nothing romantic about a worker who produced saccharin, no mystique whatsoever—it wasn't going to attract any girls. When I used to go out with my cousin, I'd see this group of young guys chatting up girls. The guys would roll up their sleeves to show off the tattoos on their arms, impressing the girls by telling them they traveled for a living. Would my future just be going around telling girls, "I work with saccharin"?

"I don't want to work at the saccharin factory. It's boring," I told my pa.

"Well, what do you want to do then?"

"I still want to be a shop assistant."

"Would you find that interesting?"

"No, it would be boring too."

"See what a hopeless case you are."

My father set me thinking straighter. The factory wasn't a labor education camp, and it didn't recruit based on grades. If it did consider grades, I wouldn't have been offered an apprenticeship or found work as a shop assistant. He only managed to get me this crappy application form in exchange for a carton of expensive Zhonghua smokes. My father told me that shop assistants spend their whole working lives on their feet—as opposed to workers, who got to sit down when they'd worked hard and were tired, or squat down, or even lie down. This was the worker's perk.

My father had missed my point. Although shop assistant work wouldn't be fascinating, I'd still get to stand behind the counter and look around at all the different customers. That had to be better than spending every day with machines. Since I was quite young, I've had this weird habit: I love looking at people through narrowed, scrunched-up eyes. It gives me a bit of a buzz. But if people saw me squinting at machines like that, they'd just think I was strange.

Back then I had an aunt working as an accountant at the People's Department Store, and she'd really wanted to get me a job there. But the People's Department Store announced that after two years of inflation they were having problems moving stock. Customers didn't just go there to shop, apparently—they also wanted to look at pretty girls. That meant that the only recent graduates being taken on by the store that year were pretty female ones. The dream I'd had about life after school, my ambition to be a shop assistant, was ripped apart at the seams. But the customer was God, and if God only wanted to look at pretty girls, the matter was out of my hands.

For the chance to study for free at chemical trade school, I eventually decided to accept the apprenticeship at the saccharin factory. My former classmates had scattered to all four corners of society by then—some to the soap factory, some to the match factory, some to department stores. A kaleidoscopic assortment of careers, the only common thread being that all our jobs required physical labor—the consumption of our calories, not our brain cells.

Before I started at the factory, my father gave me a detailed explanation of the different trades. "Don't expect starting salaries to be equal for all factory apprentices," he told me.

The most important thing in the chemical factory was to get assigned to a good trade. For this you needed to get someone on your side, through cigarettes and other gifts. I asked him what a good trade would be. He said that working as an operator in the chemical factory's production workshop was a bad trade. People had to work three different shifts—early morning, day, or night. It was like having your biological clock turned upside down and made you feel like you were going crazy. That was a bad trade, but there were worse ones still. Like haulers and cleaners. But I had a high school diploma, and the state was unlikely to be so wasteful of human resources and have me moving bricks and scrubbing the can.

Then there were the good trades: maintenance electricians, for example, or maintenance bench workers, maintenance plumbers, factory guards, on-call electricians, pump room administrators, and so on. These people generally worked day shifts, and most of the time they carried out maintenance, patrolled the place, or sat staring into space. They had no production targets and no strict shift changes. They were the nobility among the workers.

My pa explained the importance of having a good trade, like as a bench worker. Most of the time you'd be repairing the factory's pumps, and after work you could go to the street and run a bicycle stand—carrying out repairs and pumping up tires, making back the day's food money. If you were an electrician, you could also do a bit of fixture work on the side, make some extra cash that way. Those trained in these trades were collectively known as "skilled workers."

To me, "skilled workers" didn't sound too different than "sex workers."

My pa told me that on the off chance I didn't get into chemical trade school, being a skilled worker wasn't a bad alternative. A grade eight bench worker's salary was on a par with that of a senior engineer or an associate professor. When he put it like that, I understood the distinction between a skilled worker and a sex worker—a skilled worker got labor insurance, and a sex worker didn't, but neither would enjoy the respect given to an associate professor.

"How do you get to be a grade eight bench worker?" I asked my pa.

"You need at least thirty years of experience and the ability to repair any kind of machinery, and you need to understand English."

"How about something different then, Pa? How about an electrician? A grade eight electrician."

My father thought about it and said, "I don't think I've ever met a grade eight electrician."

After this I never discussed the question of trades with him again.

Summer was almost over. I can't remember exactly what day it was, but a typhoon was passing through Daicheng, scattering raindrops as it went. The battered leaves of the sycamore tree stuck limply to the road's surface. I peddled for half an hour on my bike, following the road through the east of the city. I turned down a cobblestone road, following it along the river until I reached the saccharin factory. The streets were completely deserted, and I felt like I was the only one in the world with somewhere to be. The wind whooshed in my ears. Later I could hear a great roaring howl that completely obliterated the sound of the wind. It was steam being released from the factory's boiler room. I saw two woven mesh doors, and next to them a smaller entrance for bicycles. A pale wooden board was placed on the top of a cement pillar. It said: Daicheng Saccharin Factory.

Many years later, I took Zhang Xiaoyin to show her the factory. We were in a taxi, riding along the freeway in the eastern part of the city. When we reached the river there was a turn in the road, and I asked the driver to stop.

"Come on, let's walk over," I said to her.

I often dreamed about this wide river, and all the cargo ships traveling along it, carrying raw materials to the factories. The chug of their motors sounded like the beginning of a rock concert, but when you listened for a long time, it started to sound dull. I never heard the motors in my dreams; I just saw the cargo ships glide past silently.

To reach the factory, all you needed to do was walk straight, following the river. The road was only the width of two trucks. You'd reach a T-fork in the river where a fifty-year-old bridge straddled it awkwardly. Crossing this bridge, you'd see an enormous smokestack in the distance—an unnamed monument to the chemical factory. Sometimes it belched out thick smoke that marred the sky. Other times it was extremely calm, solemnly pointing up at the passing clouds.

It was a weekend when Zhang Xiaoyin and I visited, so the factory was closed. Otherwise we'd have seen workers scurrying back and forth in their uniforms.

"What's there to see here?" asked Zhang Xiaoyin. "It's just an old factory."

It wasn't just any old factory, I told her. It was part of Daicheng's celebrated state-owned enterprise. There were a couple of thousand workers in there, producing saccharin, formaldehyde, fertilizer, and glue. If it were to close, it would mean another few thousand laid-off workers dumped into society. If they all went and set up roadside cigarette stalls, they'd block up all the streets. If they went to sell fish, they'd mess up the city's seafood market. If there was nothing for them to do, you'd have to set up five or six hundred mah-jongg tables for them, and that wasn't even counting all the retired workers who'd already be sitting there playing mah-jongg.

I told Zhang Xiaoyin that the chemical factory used to be very efficient, and they'd give out an array of different gifts at the Spring Festival. Sometimes they gave us fish, huge fish, more than two feet long. The workers would hang the fish from their bike baskets, and as they raced out of the factory the rush-hour traffic would absorb two thousand bikes with fish dangling from them. It was a pretty spectacular sight. When people from other factories saw this they'd say, "Well, I never. Look how well the saccharin factory's doing—they're giving away such big fish."

Daicheng was a small city, so news about the fish spread quickly. The factory employees would carry their fish back home feeling extremely proud of themselves, and among those proud people was me. My mother would cut up the fish and boil, stir fry, or deep fry it until a pungent aroma wafted out of the kitchen. That's when the neighbors would all start praising me.

"Xiaolu's factory has been giving out fish," they'd say. "They are really efficient. Xiaolu has a very promising future."

Hearing this, my ma would feel proud too.

Zhang Xiaoyin and I stood on the bridge and chatted.

"Do you want to go and look inside the factory?" she asked.

I told her I couldn't go in. The old man who used to work the door was dead, and his replacement didn't know me. So I didn't go in. The road outside hadn't changed, although the old teahouse was no more; it had been turned into a supply and marketing department. There were no other real changes, only that the roadside camphor trees were more profuse than before. With the arrival of fall this area would be full of wild yellow flowers, too common to have a name. At a glance their beauty could be quite frightening. I looked up and saw the layers of overhead pipelines. The pump room extended across the road and all the way out to the river, exactly as before. I stood on the road and tried to look over into the factory, but all I could see was the huge boiler room towering by the outer wall. All the other workshops were hidden deep inside.

I told Zhang Xiaoyin that this was the place that had been the sweetest and the most rotten to me. It was like a piece of overripe fruit dangling alone on its branch. There was a story about a piece of fruit dangling from a branch, waiting for a bird to come and peck at it, but Zhang Xiaoyin didn't find the story particularly interesting. She stood on the bridge and looked out at the T-fork in the river, at the boats coming and going beneath us. We saw a couple of towboats dragging ten barges, trying to pass through. It was more hazardous than a twenty-ton truck trying to go down this road. It reminded me of a little old lady crossing the street. The boatman in charge of the tugboat was yelling, directing the ship very slowly through the fork in the river.

Sometimes boats would get too close and the crews would yell, "Watch out, we're going to crash! We're going to crash! Don't come any closer. We're seriously going to crash." Then there would be a muffled thud, the sound of the boats crashing. The sides of the ships always had thick rubber tires fastened to them so they didn't get damaged when they collided, but the boatmen would swear at each other anyway, with swaggering displays of bravado. If you were lucky you might even see a fight, poles being poked back and forth. Whenever this happened, all the factory workers would stop work and come out to the bridge to watch, shouting encouragement and throwing their cigarette butts down onto the decks. This was a pretty shitty thing to do, because the boatmen all walked around with bare feet.

I told Zhang Xiaoyin that I used to like standing on the bridge watching the ships, a smoke stuck between my lips, enjoying the breeze, but that I'd never just chuck a cigarette butt down like that. These ships transported raw chemical materials—if your cigarette butt were still lit and happened to land in the mouth of the storage tank, and if that storage tank happened to contain methanol or something like it, it would blow that ship into the sky. You'd be blown into the sky along with it. That was a classic act of sabotaging production, and if it killed you in the process, you'd leave behind nothing, not even your good name.

Zhang Xiaoyin told me that the probability of that kind of thing happening was unbelievably low.

I told her that everything in the world had its probability—pregnancy, taking the wrong medicine, slipping on a banana peel. But the fact that people died was absolute. It was how they died that was still open to probability. Imagine me standing there on that bridge, smoking my cigarette, when suddenly I get blown up. The probability might be very slim, but that doesn't mean it won't happen. Take the fact that I met Zhang Xiaoyin. The probability of that happening was very low too. Because I fell in love with her, I loved this probability all the more. But I didn't love the probability of getting blown up into the sky. I've never cared for that idea.

There were always confusing times in life. Generally, the more important the moment, the more likely you were to screw up. The next day you'd wake up and feel as if you'd dreamed it.

In 1992, I stood at the factory entrance in that confused state, feeling as if I were still dreaming, being stared at by the gateman who is dead now. He was diagnosed with cancer before I gave my notice. He'd coughed up a pool of blood at the factory entrance and was taken to the hospital, never to return. But in 1992, he was still alive and well.

"Studying the trade?" he asked me, a cigarette hanging from his mouth.

I didn't understand what "studying the trade" meant, so he explained it—workers "did the trade" and apprentices "studied the trade."

"How do you know I'm studying the trade?" I asked him.

He told me he'd been on duty there for thirty years—if he hadn't picked up enough to work out these things, his life might as well have been for nothing. At the time I thought, *You're a poor old bastard who's spent the last thirty years watching a doorway. Isn't that a waste of a life in itself?*

I stood at the factory entrance and watched the workers coming and going. They were all wearing the same strange-colored uniform; it looked blue but also green, a shade I supposed might be described as blue-green. When I first saw it, I worried I'd turned color-blind or color-deficient. If I were actually color-blind I wouldn't be able to work at the factory. My only option would be to sell smokes on the roadside. I thought about the fact that it wouldn't be long before I'd be wearing that same uniform, walking through the factory corridors, eating there, working there, shitting there, and the dread started to mount in my chest.

When I was halfway through high school, I used to take part in gang fights, usually trailing behind. We'd stir up trouble and get into punch-ups, sometimes armed with bricks. I was driven by this reckless abandon, absolute zero respect for authority. But as I jogged over to the factory entrance, I felt fearful and couldn't work out why. My only thought was that I would no longer have the energy to devote myself to girls and to the people I should be beating up—I'd have to put it all into making saccharin instead. I experienced a *Thelma & Louise*-type sorrow.

I asked the old man at the gate where the labor department was—that's where I needed to report. He pointed me in the direction of an office building opposite the factory entrance. In front of it was a flowerbed with a wizened cedar tree, its branches bare and exposed, like a half-eaten fish. The old man told me I needed to go up to the third floor.

I wheeled my bike into the bike shed and walked up to the third floor. The dimly lit hallway was pasted with banners adorned with slogans like *Carry out safe production, Strive for advancement*. The labor department was quiet, with only one female employee sitting inside. She saw me in the doorway, craning my head to peer in, and said, "Are you an apprentice worker? Come in and fill out your paperwork." As I walked in I saw that she was a young girl with pouty lips. The rest of her appearance was fairly proper, a sharp nose and faint eyebrows, but for some reason her lips were in a permanent pout. Later I realized this was just the way she looked, and I actually started to find her quite cute.

"What's your name?" Little Pouty Lips asked.

"Lu Xiaolu," I said.

Little Pouty Lips found my registration form in a stack of papers and said, "Lu Xiaolu—ha, that's a funny name."

"You can call me Xiaolu if you prefer," I said.

Little Pouty Lips waited until I'd filled in an official registration form, then said in a very serious voice, "Lu Xiaolu, you need to go to the meeting room next door for your safety training."

"What safety thing?"

"It's a safety instruction class you need to attend. Safety is paramount when you work in the chemical factory. Is that understood?"

"Understood," I said.

There were already ten or so people sitting in the meeting room. Later a few more dribbled in, all of them apprentices. I was surprised to see one of my high school classmates among them. He'd been our chemistry class representative. The fact that the chemistry class representative had ended up at the chemical factory seemed fitting. Before I had time to joke with him about it, a middle-aged man with thick-lensed glasses walked in through the doorway, his hair as messy as a chicken coop. He told us he was a safety department cadre.

Before I started at the factory, my pa had given me some basic safety instructions, such as not to smoke in the production zone and not to wander around under piping. If you hear an explosion, take to your heels and run like crazy; and if you come across someone who's had an electric shock, don't assist them with your hand (use a wooden stick instead). His favorite line, of course, was "Run against the wind!" He must have badgered me about this more than a hundred times. When the pesticide factory exploded that time, we finally got our chance to put this into practice.

The information this safety cadre gave us wasn't that different than my pa's pearls of wisdom. Lots of rules: this is forbidden, that is forbidden. I couldn't listen without wanting to drop off. Later he told us he was going to take us on a tour of the safety instruction exhibition. So we shuffled to our feet, me and the dozen or so other apprentices, and walked up to the fourth floor and into a darkened room. He switched on the light, and the sight in front of me jolted me straight out of my drowsiness. He had my full attention.

The room was full of photos of every type of accident you could possibly imagine. They showed minced and half-cooked human bodies—some who'd burned to death, some who'd fallen and broken their necks, some who'd been electrocuted, and some who'd had half an arm lopped off or all the skin stripped off their legs. There was a face that had been soaked in sulfuric acid and looked like a braised pork ball. This didn't look like an exhibition of safety instruction—it looked like an exhibition of torture. The most bizarre photograph was one of nothing at all.

"What's this?" I asked the safety cadre.

"It's someone who was killed by a blast," he said gravely.

"Yes, but where is he?"

"He was blasted into thin air."

I looked at the picture, unsure about its educational value. All it showed was a pile of broken bricks and rubble—it did nothing to spark the imagination. Looking at me, the safety cadre said, "You seem to like looking at this one."

"It's alright," I said. "It's a bit like one of those abstract paintings."

The safety cadre folded his arms and we admired the photo together.

"So which kind of death do you think would be the best?" he asked.

I was so shocked that I couldn't get my words out. He explained that dying in a blast was considered very lucky—those people would be gone as soon as they heard the boom and would experience no pain. Being electrocuted was considered very unlucky, especially by 380-volt industrial electricity. When a person got an electric shock they remained lucid, but they weren't able to throw down the electric cable. They were well aware that they were going to die, but when it happened, it did so very, very slowly. The electric current sent the body's nerves into spasms, which meant that the corpses adopted an array of different positions—some looked like acrobats with their bodies in reverse bows, their heads sticking out from their crotches. No death could be more painful. There were also those who'd had their hands crushed. That sort of pain would remain deep inside the brain forever—and whenever you glanced down and saw your maimed hand, you'd find yourself covered in goose bumps. Then there were those whose faces had been splashed with sulfuric acid—that kind of pain left people wishing they'd died instead.

When I heard this, a shiver ran through my body.

He comforted me by saying, "As long as you always follow the rules, you won't have an accident. Seventy or eighty percent of accidents are caused by people violating the work regulations."

We'd been listening all this time, but this was the first bit of information that had any educational value. "It's never as cut and dried as all that," he explained. "You know the saying: a chain is no stronger than its weakest link. Those few people violating work regulations might not die, but other people might die in the explosions they cause."

This safety instruction session had a huge impact on me, and when I started my apprenticeship my supervisor called me a "sniveling, backboneless wimp." I told him about the accidents in this exhibition, but all he did was mock me and ask why I was paying attention to that guy from the safety department anyway—he was nothing but a pervert, and his nickname was Pu Nani. I asked him what Pu Nani meant and was told that it meant pathetic twat, and if I carried on like that I'd earn myself the nickname Little Pu Nani. On hearing this, I forced myself to forget everything from that room. But I just couldn't shake those images. They became dark shadows in my mind until I actually saw a person die, actually saw a hand being lopped off, a leg, and gradually became more reckless, more like the supervisors.

At the time I asked Pu Nani where the photos in the exhibit room came from. He said they'd been compiled by some high-authority office, he wasn't sure which, and distributed to various industrial and mining companies in what was known as "wise men learn from the mistakes of others." (Pu Nani was exceptionally capable at speaking in proverbs, especially the more pompous ones you usually only see written in books.) But I didn't want to be a mistake that other men could learn from. I didn't want to become a two-dimensional photograph hanging in a dingy room for apprentices to gawk at.

"Do you have the right of reproduction for these images?" I asked.

"I'm in charge of safety instruction, not legal instruction," Pu Nani replied.

Later Pu Nani came over to reassure me. He told me all about probabilities. He told me there was nothing to get too worried about. The accident rate had been pretty low in this factory since it opened, lower even than in American enterprises. Just two electricians had lost their lives, and that was more than ten years ago. But high school graduates like me, with no special skills or electrical training, were fit only for operator work, and with operator work there was no way to get electrocuted—only blown up. No one had been blown up in our factory recently—there was just someone who'd had an ear blasted off. This demonstrated the relatively low death rate for operator work.

Pu Nani told me that out of all the workers in this factory, three had been killed by cars on the road and more than a hundred by cancer, which in terms of probability meant that the chemical factory wasn't as dangerous as a traffic accident, and it couldn't even compete with the incidence of cancer.

When he'd finished telling me these things, he patted me on the shoulder and asked, "Do you know what probability means?"

"Sure," I said, "it's division."

"That's right," Pu Nani said, "You need to figure out the common denominator. Just don't go and end up being that numerator and you'll be alright."

Our safety instruction ended there. Pu Nani gave each of us something resembling a certificate and pressed a blue stamp down onto its surface. I didn't know what the point of it was. It was as if having them meant we could prevent accidents from happening. It felt a bit like the infamous *Little Red Book*. Pu Nani told us we were incorrect. This certificate proved that we'd received our safety instruction. If we had an accident, died, or got injured, it would show that we only had ourselves to blame and that it had nothing to do with Pu Nani. He handed the certificates to each of us with a sly smile and disappeared, looking pleased with himself.

After he'd gone, Little Pouty Lips came by to tell us we were to report for duty at the labor department the next morning at 8:30 sharp. That's when we'd be assigned our different trades. We were released after that, allowed to go back home. When I left the factory, the working day hadn't ended yet. Outside the typhoon winds were still raging, but it had stopped raining. As we walked out through the gates, my high school classmate who'd been the chemistry class representative came over and said, "Lu Xiaolu, I think I'm going to find work as a shop assistant instead."

Many years later, standing on the bridge next to the factory, I thought back to my first time standing there, just after saying goodbye to the chemistry class representative. I never saw him again, although I heard he didn't get to be a shop assistant after all, but joined the agricultural machinery factory to work in supply and marketing.

Back then, standing on that bridge, I'd felt really cut up by the fact that the chemistry class representative was taking up my unfulfilled dream as a shop assistant. Of course, there's no such thing as an "unfulfilled dream" until you're dead. But at that point I felt as if I might as well be dead. I didn't believe I had anywhere else to go—all I could do was go to the factory and make saccharin, or follow the plan my pa had set in place for me and become a bench worker or an electrician. I stopped my bike on the bridge and walked over to the railing. I stretched myself out at a ninety-degree angle, my face turned toward the turbid water. For that moment, the river water filled the whole of my vision.

CHAPTER TWO
KING OF THE WATER PUMPS

My father said that in the factory, you had to learn to "bear and forebear" (they used proverbs like this tongue in cheek), and you had to learn to protect yourself. If there was an explosion, you shouldn't worry about any state property, just take to your heels and run against the wind, run until your legs cramped. Aside from all this, I was to work hard—like an ox—or my dream of going to trade school would go up in a puff of smoke.

"Pa, you've worked as an engineer all your life and had a pretty rough time of it. What right do you have to ask me to do the same?" I asked.

"You don't know the half of it," my pa said. "I worked as a hauler during the Cultural Revolution. I hauled barrels of raw material for three whole years."

"Why didn't you ever tell me?"

"Your father had a period of extreme misfortune," my mother chimed in. "He was too afraid to talk about it. If he had, the factory would have sent him off for labor education."

"You can talk about it now, though," I said. "I'll kill your factory head if he dares send you off for labor education."

My father did actually haul all those barrels of raw material. In 1971, before I was born, he'd been a technician. He'd taken my mother to the movie theater where he happened across his factory head with a female department employee, sitting two rows away. I'd heard that guys and girls conducted their relationships in movie theaters back then, the pitch-black places facilitating surreptitious fumbles with the opposite sex. Others jerked off to showings of *The Red Detachment of Women*. Unfortunately for my father, the factory head turned around and saw him. My father didn't say a word, just took my mother's hand and slipped out. There was no follow-up to this incident: my father and the factory head entered into an unspoken agreement to act as if nothing had happened. Two weeks later, my father went to collect some material from the warehouse. The pesticide factory had an enormous warehouse, and my father was walking around it when he heard something moving. Thinking it was a rat, he went over to take a look. First he saw two pairs of shoes, then a skirt, then a bra dangling from a stack of rebar. Then he saw the factory head with the same female department employee. My father stood between them and their heap of clothing, thinking he was in a dream. If your aim isn't to catch an adulterous couple in the act, but you nevertheless manage to catch them at it twice, you might have a similarly surreal sensation—perhaps you were having an erotic dream. But this erotic dream turned quickly into a nightmare. My father was transferred to the workshop to haul barrels of raw material, each weighing 130 pounds. He had to roll them from one end of the workshop to the other, day in and day out, more than a hundred barrels a day, nearly breaking his back.

"Don't try to stop me," I told them. "I'm going to find that factory head right now. I'm going to break his back!"

"That happened a lifetime ago," my mother said. "The factory head was arrested some time after that."

My father explained that if he hadn't kept quiet, he'd have been labeled a criminal and sent for labor education. Back then it was easy as anything for a factory head to mess with the life of an unskilled technician. He just needed to place a few pieces of steel ingot in the technician's drawer, and the guy would be reported for theft. In severe cases, they could be tried for sabotaging production and get labor education if they were lucky, but could be sent straight to labor reform camp instead. For three years, my father was a closed book. Whenever people asked what he'd done to offend the factory head he'd just act dumb, saying he couldn't remember. Only because of this did he manage to remain unscathed. He kept quiet until the factory head finally got his comeuppance; he was informed on and sentenced to prison. My father gave a long sigh of relief after that. He could go back to normal again.

"You're quite something, Pa," I said, "moving all those barrels of raw material around and somehow, in the middle of all that, making me too. You really were hard at work!"

My mother batted me lightly on the back of my neck.

My father turned to my mother and said, "If it hadn't been for your whining that you wanted to go to the movie theater, we wouldn't have bumped into the factory head in the first place."

"It was your own stupid fault," my mother replied. "You saw a skirt and bra in the warehouse. Did you really have to go over to investigate? Couldn't you have had the good sense to walk away?"

"It wasn't as if their names were written on the bra," my father said. "How was I to know it was the factory head again?"

When my parents started to bicker it was never-ending, so I used this time to do some simple arithmetic. If I had to haul raw material barrels my whole life, it would be from 1993 through 2033. Say I managed to shift a hundred barrels a day over this forty-year period, and say each barrel weighed 130 pounds. Lopping off Sundays, which I'd have off, I'd still have to shift more than seventy thousand tons of the stuff in my lifetime. They wouldn't have to be moved too far, only a couple of dozen feet. It would be like spending your entire life moving a building across the street. An undeniably depressing state of affairs.

The reason I'd been given those safety instructions wasn't because they were afraid I might be killed in an explosion. Pu Nani had explained that this was a matter of probability. Seeing the photos of the dead people might lead you to one of two misconceptions. The first would be thinking that tomorrow you might meet with a similar fate. This was the thinking of people like my chemistry class representative. The other was thinking that this sort of thing would never happen to you. I was of the second variety. I resolutely believed that I would never be blasted up into the sky and fall back down to Earth in pieces. I was certain that I'd die at a ripe old age in my sickbed, surrounded by children, grandchildren, and great-grandchildren. I couldn't see myself as a martyr or a case study. There was no way my photograph was going to be shown in chemical industry bureaus all over China. Then another thought gripped me like a nightmare: what if I was assigned as a hauler? It wouldn't be a case of probability then. Those seventy thousand tons would be my destiny.

My father told me that hauling barrels was done only by migrant workers these days; it wouldn't be given to someone with a genuine high school diploma. That was known as wasting human resources, and it was a matter of great concern to the state.

"Don't worry," my pa said, patting the back of my head, "the lowest position you'll get is as a bench worker."

My father didn't understand my pessimism. I was clear about my destiny, and I knew that even if I got a job as a bench worker, all it would mean was a lifetime resurrecting thousands and thousands of water pipes. If I got a job as a shop assistant, it would be a lifetime of counting renminbi. As a clerk, I would spend a lifetime looking at the sundial. An engineer would mean a lifetime of drawing on graph paper. None of it was interesting. I couldn't say things like this out loud; it was just too pointless and depressing.

I need to explain a bit more about trades: the factory was divided up into two sorts of people, cadres and workers. The way the workers saw it, the cadres never had to do any work. This was not actually the case. The propaganda department had to write their blackboard bulletins; the trade union had to organize their cultural activities; the finance division had to do the accounts, count the money, and pay out wages. All of this was actual work. But the way the workers saw it, this kind of work didn't burn calories, which meant it was bullshit. The workers were jealous of the cadres in their department offices for the simple reason that no one liked physical labor.

Workers were given different grades. The lowest of the low, who were all fuckwits, worked the three different shifts. Those who worked the day shift kicked ass. All the chemical factory bench workers worked day shifts, which meant they could look down on cadres (for doing no work) and on operators who worked the three shifts (and were therefore fuckwits).

I hadn't started at the factory at this point, but I wasn't thrilled by the idea of becoming a bench worker. On paper it sounded boring, running here and there all day with a pair of pliers in your hand. I imagined bench workers as short men with thick necks, unshaven and covered in oil. This was clearly a working-class stereotype; the pity being that by the '90s, the worker-hero image carried little weight. My father, fast becoming irritated with me, told me that bench worker jobs had career potential—when you retired, you could run a bike repair stand. He said it a hundred times: bike repair, bike repair, bike repair.

"Pa," I'd say. "When I'm retired I plan to just play mah-jongg all day. Why would I want to be mending bikes?"

"Learn a craft, and you'll never go hungry—do you understand?" he'd say.

Before I started as a bench worker, my father decided that, to try to rid me of my laziness and bad habits, he'd take me to visit my uncle. He explained that this uncle had been learning the ropes since he was sixteen. He was a bench worker for thirty years, and his hands had become so twisted they looked like pliers, ready to strangle you at any moment. I found his description pretty terrifying. Maybe my father hadn't thought this through. If I grew pliers in place of hands, would he still be able to box my ears so effectively? As the saying goes, desperate diseases must have desperate remedies—to reassure me about becoming a worker, he was ready to pull out all the stops.

This uncle lived in the west of Daicheng, which had been a slum since the Qianlong Emperor's time. Two hundred years later, that hadn't changed much: it was all bamboo shacks and linoleum as far as the eye could see. These shacks would catch fire from a spark, and a slight breeze would burn down a twenty-mile area. That was where my uncle lived. I followed my father through the destitute neighborhood, down the roads, skirting a couple of alleys, passing a public restroom dripping with yellow liquid before entering a pitch-black room where we found my uncle. Their house was pretty much a bench worker shack. The chairs, made of welded iron, were filched from the bench worker team, as were the table and a great sturdy work surface. The electric fan was an old factory desk model with propellers and no cover, liable to lop off your hand at any moment. It was only the bed, made from carved mahogany, simple and unadorned, that looked as if it might have been passed down from our family's Qing dynasty ancestors. My father told me that my uncle had stolen it from someone's house in 1966, during the Cultural Revolution.

Before we were even inside, we heard a woman yelling. This was my aunt. The uncle who could strangle you at any moment was being throttled by his wife and driven from the house. It was my first time meeting him and my aunt. He was built like a brick shithouse, with arms thicker than my calves. When his hands were curled into fists, they looked like tree stumps. My aunt was half his size, but with her hands around his neck, she managed to push him along for five yards and slam the door shut.

My uncle rubbed his neck with his plierlike hands and turned to look at us. It was slightly awkward, but my uncle didn't seem to care. He just patted the dirt from his trousers and took us to eat at the local noodle joint.

Seated there, my uncle started to display his true bench worker colors: the undersides of his fingernails were black with oil, his teeth were stained the color of rust from smoking, and the smell of oil wafted off his body. If I were my aunt, I would have throttled the bastard too.

My father explained why we'd come, and my uncle looked pleased.

"How old are you now, Xiaolu?" he asked, patting my shoulder.

"Nineteen," my father replied for me. "The main reason we're here today is to learn from your experiences, so he's mentally prepared."

"Do you know the most important part of bench work?" my uncle asked, a cigarette between his lips.

I hadn't expected him to ask in such a philosophical way. I just shook my head.

"Skill!" he said. "Skill is the most important part."

He told me that there was a lot of knack to bench work. Turning screws was one example; it shouldn't be just brute force. Even the most brutish of forces wouldn't undo a rusty screw—it would only break off the head, and you'd never unscrew it then. Repairing machine tools was another example. It was very technical, and there wasn't a single person in China with the know-how to use certain foreign tools. If I developed that ability, I'd become a warehouse of foreign exchange, and how much money would I save the country? Another example: equipment maintenance. You needed a good memory for that, because mechanical equipment was like women—if you were fucking twenty different women, there was no guarantee you wouldn't call out the wrong name in bed.

My uncle said that the biggest advantage to bench work was that you could make a bit of extra cash on the side. After work, you could sit in an alley and run a bike repair stand, earning about five hundred yuan a month. To repair bikes, you needed excellent technical skills. You also needed a set of tools, your turf, and, from time to time, to sprinkle some broken glass across the road. According to my uncle, bench workers with exceptional skills held a certain amount of clout with their factory head. Bench workers were also given apprentices, and apprentices had to revere their supervisors, give them cigarettes and rice spirits, or they wouldn't be taught anything and would be stuck forever at grade two, tasked with turning screws. In short, working as a bench worker was more respected than working as a chemical factory operator. Operator work meant all three shifts: day shift one day, sunset to sunrise the next, your body clock turned inside-out and upside-down as you breathed in all sorts of toxic gases and gave birth to deformed babies.

My father listened to my uncle spout these increasingly absurd comments before interrupting to say, "The main reason Xiaolu is going to the factory is so he can take his trade school exam and transfer to a department later on."

"Which department?" my uncle asked.

"He likes drawing. At school he did the blackboard bulletins a few times. So he might go into the propaganda department."

"The propaganda department is a good choice," my uncle said, patting my shoulders. "Xiaolu, you've got drive! The department girls have much better complexions than the workshop girls."

"Why is that?" I asked.

"Isn't it obvious? Chemical factory workshops are filled with toxic gases, and the fumes wrinkle women's faces."

"Enough," my father said. "Enough, Old Six. (Old Six was my uncle's nickname.) You should get back home. Your wife is going to give you hell."

"She fights with me and threatens to kill herself, but she's not actually going to do it. It's fucking annoying."

After we took my uncle home, I began laughing so much I couldn't stand up straight. My father looked displeased. My uncle hadn't had an easy life, he explained. He'd worked as a bench worker at a toothpaste factory. This toothpaste was very bad quality. It was either impossible to squeeze out or it would all spurt out at once. This factory was inefficient, which meant my uncle's salary was low, as was his level of education.

"I don't think he did much work most of the time," I said. "All he did was wander around thinking about women's complexions."

"He has pretty good bike repair skills," my father said. "Xiaolu, if you learn a skill, then even if the factory is not doing well you'll have something to scrape by with. Does that make sense?"

"Would I really be able to scrape by with that?"

"You'd be pretty hard up," my father admitted with a sigh.

My father regretted taking me to see my uncle. All it had done was blacken the bench worker trade and make me anxious about my future. I smelled the cloying scent of the working class on my uncle, which that summer was not yet a resounding smell to my nostrils. He had a full set of bench worker's furniture and slept in a mahogany bed that he'd stolen when he was in his prime. He had a great, strong pair of hands, but was always being throttled this way and that by his wife. You could call him a thief on a dead-end road, or just a devil down on his luck. My father pointed out that my uncle didn't represent all bench workers, and the saccharin factory was not the same as a toothpaste factory— saccharin was a hot-selling product the world over. In 1992, we liked to use the word *efficient*, and the saccharin factory was certainly efficient, which made it very respectable to be a bench worker there.

I gave my father a smoke. "Pa, whatever you do, don't mention the propaganda department again."

"Why?"

"Don't ask me why. If I get to be a bench worker, I'll be happy enough."

The next time I saw my uncle, it was winter five years later. I was cycling through his district when I rode over a heap of crushed beer bottles, and my tire deflated instantly. I found my uncle's bike repair stand and went over to say hi while getting the tire patched. He'd aged a lot; his back was starting to hunch and half his hair was gray. He told me he'd been laid off and was supporting his family entirely through this bike repair stand. My aunt no longer throttled him because she'd been laid off too, and if she throttled him to death the whole family would starve. He fixed the tire and I went to pay him, but he wouldn't take my money. He stooped down to my ear and said, "I sprinkled those shards of glass."

I never cycled through that district again.

I'll never forget going to report at the factory the day after our safety instruction. I stood under the ceiling fan in the labor department. The fan shunted hot air onto my forehead, blowing at it until I started to feel light-headed, as if I were floating off the ground, becoming immortal. Because this memory feels so dreamlike, it often appears in my dreams, where it's been scoured over and over in my mind, smoothed into a shiny lump.

It was the official reporting day. Little Pouty Lips sat behind the desk while I stood. There were six guys standing next to me, and it reminded me of an image from the legend of the Eight Immortals crossing the sea.

Little Pouty Lips looked unimpressed. "Why are there only seven of you here?" she asked. "Where are the others?"

I was tempted to tell her that the safety instruction session had scared away the others, and that the seven of us still here had nerves of steel. We were the death squad; fuck, with our fierce determination, we were Zarathustra. At the time I'd thought their safety instruction was completely messed up. It was only later that I realized Pu Nani actually knew what he was doing. That first lecture had been intended to test our nerves. Those without nerves of steel, those who were not hell-bent on putting down roots in the chemical factory, would sooner or later cause a production accident, resulting in either their own death or somebody else's. They might push the wrong switch, add the wrong raw material, or simply take the wrong lunchbox. When people like this made mistakes, they didn't even feel bad about it. For all the people who died at their hands, it would just be tough luck.

Little Pouty Lips was in her early twenties, and her hair was always tied up in a ponytail that she kept wrapped in a hairnet. This meant it looked nothing like a sleek, sharp pony's tail—more a big, wide sausage hanging behind her head. I couldn't figure out how anyone would think this looked nice, but if this was how she wanted to wear her hair, who was I to care. Little Pouty Lips wore the factory uniform, the neither-blue-nor-green type. I noticed that her uniform had the letter *S* emblazoned across the left breast. Why was there an *S*? Then I realized it stood for *Saccharin*. My father's uniform had a *P* on the left breast for *Pesticide*. The glue factory had a *G*, the latex factory an *L*, and the sulfuric acid factory a *Sul*. They were standardized.

Little Pouty Lips took a stack of pages from a drawer. "It's time for me to read you the factory regulations," she said.

She gave a monotonous read-through of the whole set of regulations. This labor regulation manual was strange, full of punitive regulations: for arriving late, leaving early, truancy, fighting, smoking, drinking, and operating machinery in violation of the work regulations. As she read the part about premarital sexual relations, she had a slightly strained look on her face. Engaging in premarital sexual relations would also result in disciplinary measures.

"This labor regulation manual was compiled in 1985 and hasn't been revised since," she explained.

There were regulations for breaching the birth policy too, and if you did exceed the birth quota, she explained, you would be given a forced abortion. I wondered what the hell any of this had to do with me. If someone tried to force me to have an abortion, I'd kill the bastard.

My line of vision extended past her and out the window. I realized that the labor department was actually a fortress. Up ahead in the distance, you could see the factory gate and the road leading up to it. On the left was the entrance to the production zone, and on the right, the canteen and the bathhouses. If you fitted a machine gun from here, we could be in a watchtower in Auschwitz or Omaha Beach. It was a superb position, the most strategic in the whole factory. Many years later, I met the man who'd designed this building and he told me about prison architecture, the most classic being the panopticon prison, with the sentry in the central position and the prisoners around the circumference. It was an ingenious design with no blind spots, leaving the inmates wondering constantly whether the wardens were watching them. As soon as we started talking about this, I thought about the chemical factory's labor department. Although I'd never seen a panopticon prison, I'd seen the labor department, and it was something else. Nothing escaped their eyes.

My mind had started to wander, and I was brought back into the room by Little Pouty Lips saying, "Lu Xiaolu—bench worker team."

"What's that?" I asked.

"Having a little daydream, were we? You're being assigned your trade," she said impatiently. "Go to the bench worker team and report!"

Pa, I thought to myself, *those smokes and gift vouchers weren't given in vain. I really hope you can get me into trade school.*

Little Pouty Lips dismissed the others but asked me to stay behind. "Lu Xiaolu, why weren't you listening properly when I read the labor regulations? Novice apprentices like you are the ones who make the most mistakes. Don't make yourself too at home in the factory. Oh, of course, you should love the factory like you love your home—that's expected. But don't be lazy and sloppy like you'd be at home. You finished high school, but your exam results were terrible; you should by all rights be doing operations. You've been assigned as a bench worker for some reason, which means you won't have to juggle the three shifts. This is very lucky, and you need to value this opportunity."

"Yes, Chief, I will," I said.

"Chief? I'm not the department head," Little Pouty Lips said. "Chief Hu is at a meeting and has left me in charge of tasks such as reading the labor regulations."

"The labor regulations handbook will be handed out so I can read through it myself, won't it?" I asked.

"It's the personnel department's duty to distribute the labor regulations handbook," she said. "The duty of the labor department is to read it out to you. This is factory policy."

I heard what she said, but I didn't understand the logic. I pretended I did, though, nodding my head repeatedly. She didn't look very old, and the way she was lecturing me seemed over the top. I'm not averse to being lectured by girls, but it's better if they're a bit gentler about it. You might call this masochistic, but now that I was a bench worker apprentice, it was the only fun I was going to get.

Later I asked Pa the difference between the personnel and labor departments. He told me that the personnel department dealt with cadres, while the labor department dealt with workers. An apprentice like me reported to the labor department, and college students belonged to the cadre system and reported to the personnel department. Literally speaking, the *personnel* department related to *persons* and the *labor* department was concerned with *labor*. According to my pa, cadres were fairly well educated and able to read and digest the labor regulations, while workers had to have each clause read out loud to them in order to understand. It was pretty simple logic.

"Isn't that discrimination?"

"Wait until you muddle your way into the cadre system. You won't think of it as discrimination then."

The chemical factory was divided into two parts: the east part was the production zone, made up entirely of workshops; while the west was the nonproduction zone and included the huge office building, the tiny trade union building, the bathhouses, the canteen, the dormitory, and the machine repair workshop, as well as the greenhouse and a huge bike shed. The difference between the production zone and the nonproduction zone was that you could smoke in the latter, and in the former it was prohibited. Smoking in the production zone was subject to heavy fines. Repeat offenders were disciplined in line with the warnings they'd been given—anything up to expulsion.

The bench worker team was on the outer edge of the production zone, where you could smoke—one of the factors that imbued the bench workers with such a sense of pride.

The bench worker team was stationed in a building made from galvanized iron sheeting that had been soldered together, and it was approximately thirty-two hundred square feet. Inside this building were a few sturdy workbenches with a couple of bench vices fitted to the edges, plus a lathe, a planer, and a drill. Planks of plywood had been arranged together in the northeast corner of the room to create a lounge. This was where the workers got changed, smoked, and played cards.

I went to report to the bench worker team, carrying all the items I'd just been issued: safety equipment, two sets of the work uniform, a pair of work shoes, and four pairs of cotton gloves. I went through the door and heard a loud clatter—a section of the tin roof had just blown off. It looked like a kite broken loose as it headed far, far away, turning happy somersaults in the sky, flying higher and higher.

An old worker saw the big piece of tin and said, "Wonder which poor devil's going to have that smash down on him?"

"Supervisor, is this the bench worker team?" I asked him.

"Are you the new one?" he said. "Go inside to report."

I carried my safety equipment inside. A group of workers were sitting outside. Their faces were as grubby as clay monkeys, and they were all smoking. They examined me closely. I saw the bench worker team leader, a buff, red-faced, incoherent fellow who introduced himself as Zhao Chongde.

In a loud voice, the worker next to him said, "Kid, you can call him Good Balls."

I bowed toward the team leader and said, "Supervisor Zhao."

"We all use the suffix Balls for our names here," he said quietly. "Just do as everyone else does and call me Good Balls."

He introduced the team to me: Big Balls, Small Balls, Stone Balls, Horse Balls, Splendid Balls . . . finally there was Wonky Balls, so named because of the shape of his head, slightly off-kilter. The workers propped up his wonky head and said, "Supervisor Wonky Balls works the planer, and all the things he planes are crooked. Even he couldn't tell you how many of the things he produces have to be discarded each year." Wonky Balls looked up when he heard this (strictly speaking, he looked up and to the left), rolled his eyes, and uttered a stream of curse words. The workers all laughed and said, "Don't look down on Supervisor Wonky Balls. He may look like a mere planer, but he's actually in our art troupe."

I was thinking about my surname, Lu, and whether I'd find it funny or tragic to have the nickname Lu Balls. I needn't have worried; the workers were quick to inform me that novice apprentices did not get the Balls nickname right away. I breathed a sigh of relief.

"Which of these is my supervisor?" I asked Wonky Balls.

"Your supervisor's out sick, he'll be back next week. I'll give you something to do in the meantime."

"What shall I do?"

"Fetch some water and sprinkle it on the ground."

I once read the play *Cat on a Hot Tin Roof.* To be honest, our tin roof was too much even for that cat. The material meant that the building was cold in winter and hot in summer. During the summer months, it was like the Sahara desert—you wished you could take off all your clothes and just wear a loincloth. But then winter arrived and it became an icehouse, the cold seeping in. The factory's stray cats never came near the place, because cats weren't that stupid.

This was where all members of the bench worker team were stationed. There was no air conditioning in the summer, only two rusty electric fans wafting warm wind toward your head, blowing at you until you felt drowsy. This was why you needed to get water. You'd carry in bucket after bucket, pouring it onto the floor, where it sizzled. Two minutes later, it would be dry again. The only thing you could do to counter the heat was to keep sprinkling water.

Winter was slightly more bearable because you could light the stove to stay warm. The stove was made from a restructured diesel barrel with a tin chimney that went straight up through the ceiling. Keeping the stove lit required a huge amount of fuel: kerosene, firewood, and old tires were all fine. If we didn't have those materials on hand, we'd burn newspapers and magazines. If none of those were available, we'd have to go out and forage for our fuel.

The apprentice's job was very simple: sprinkle water in the summer and collect fuel sources in the winter.

So I didn't meet my supervisor that first day. The other workers and supervisors made me go fetch water all morning instead, and in the afternoon I had to go around the factory zone with a small bamboo basket tied to my back, looking for things to burn. The supervisors told me I needed to sprinkle water because it was hot, but I also needed to plan ahead and start gathering provisions for winter. These fuel sources became very sought after when it got cold, and by the end of summer and beginning of fall, you should have already started hoarding. "After all, you have nothing else to do," the supervisors said.

Carrying the bamboo basket on my back, I roamed aimlessly about the factory grounds like a rural kid picking up manure. It was my first assignment, so I didn't feel particularly distraught at first; in fact, I found it quite interesting. I discovered that waste rubber and lumps of coal were first-class fuel sources; firewood was second class; newspaper third class; and scraping the bottom of the barrel, you had rags and scraps of paper. The factory aunties would call out to me as I picked up this trash. "Over here, little apprentice! Come over here!" I'd trot over obediently, and the aunties would pull pieces of candy from their pockets, unwrap them, and throw the candy wrappers into the basket on my back. That was how I became the roaming trash basket. Whenever someone called out to me, I'd have to run over to them. Once an auntie called out to me from the doorway of the women's bathrooms. I glanced in her direction but didn't dare go over, scared she might throw her used toilet paper into my basket.

A factory cleaner came looking for me. "Listen here, buddy," he said. "You can't take away all my wastepaper. If you keep going at this rate, you're going to put the entire factory's cleaning staff out of work."

These words caused my self-esteem to shatter like a pane of glass. I thought about my father's words: whatever happened, I still had my senior middle-school education, which put me a cut above the rest. How had I become a trash picker? When I got back home on those first few days and my pa asked me what I'd been up to at work, I told him I'd been doing really well. I'd been learning how to fix water pumps, I told him.

"Seriously?" he asked, looking dubious. "You've only been there two days, and they're already teaching you to fix water pumps?"

"What should I be doing?" I asked.

"You should be sweeping the floor and wiping the table, going to the water room to boil water, washing the master's bike."

Pa, I thought to myself, *it's not even in the realm of possibility for you that my job is collecting trash, is it? This was the fucking job you found me. If I actually manage to make my way into that chemical trade school of yours by picking trash, I'll eat my hat.*

I didn't tell a soul about all that trash I was collecting; I found it too shameful. Wandering around the factory, I'd often see apprentice workers from my intake grinning as they left the water room carrying six thermoses of boiling water, walking stridently toward their teams. The nearby aunties would look at them and say, "Oh, look at the new apprentices, aren't they handsome!" Then they'd see me and shout, "Over here, little trash picker! I have some wastepaper for you!"

I was nineteen that year, and it was the bleakest time of my life. When I was a young boy, I found a rubber ball on the ground, and it felt like finding buried treasure. I was wiping it clean with water from the gutter when I saw a kid my age standing in front of me. He was wearing cream shorts and a matching shirt, and even at that young age, he had his hair combed into a part. With his parted bangs shading his face, he told me that the rubber ball was his, and he reached out a hand to grab it from me. I tripped him up and ran for it, followed by the sounds of his wailing. Later Parted Hair recognized me and would follow me around whining, "My rubber ball, my rubber ball, my rubber ball." I turned to grab him, but he ran away. This continued until one day I gave up and returned his rubber ball. It was pretty much destroyed by then.

I said, "Here's your rubber ball. Don't you dare fucking follow me again."

Parted Hair took the ball and there was more wailing, so I walked over and slapped him hard. All at once he stopped bawling and stared at me with puppy dog eyes, as if I were some kind of monster. Now that I was nineteen and picking up trash, I started to suspect that this was retribution for my years of picking up other people's rubber balls and general bad deeds.

I collected trash for a whole week before my supervisor, Old Bad-Ass, materialized in front of me, leaning against a lathe. He was an angel lighting up the greasy black workbench. "Why is my apprentice collecting trash?" he asked Good Balls. He chucked my back basket in front of Good Balls' apprentice, and without another word took me off to repair water pumps. Good Balls' apprentice was called Wei Yixin, a name with fifty-three character strokes to the twenty-nine in mine. 魏懿歆: the name completely freaked out all the workers and supervisors who couldn't read or write it. There were too many strokes to even count them clearly. No one could work out what his parents had been thinking. Had they deliberately made things hard for workers and supervisors? Good Balls got a headache every time he wrote up the work report. The workers and supervisors teased him, saying, "I could have gone to the can, completely emptied my bowels, and come back in the time you've taken to write his name." Wei Yixin had graduated from college, where he'd studied electronics and mechanics, and now he had a workshop internship with the bench worker team. He had a bit of a stutter, and every time he came across Old Bad-Ass he got so scared he couldn't speak. From that moment, electrics and mechanics college graduate Wei Yixin became in charge of collecting fuel, while high school graduate Lu Xiaolu fixed water pumps. I couldn't figure out if this was wasting human resources, but at least I never had to pick up trash again. Wei Yixin was a very hardworking apprentice and would collect fuel almost obsessively, carrying basket after basket of it back to the bench worker team. Well before winter, we already had a room's worth of firewood and newspapers hoarded, as well as five hundred kilos of poor-quality coal, all stolen from the boiler room. This continued until one day Wei Yixin was discovered by the boiler room supervisor, who punched out two of his molars, putting an end to this crazy behavior.

Old Bad-Ass, my supervisor, was renowned throughout the factory. People told me that being Old Bad-Ass's apprentice would be my life's great fortune. All the members of the bench worker team had Balls as part of their nicknames—only he had the word Bad. That's how extremely formidable he was. From his position of superiority, he looked down disdainfully upon the group of Balls. Now that I'm thirty and a bit fed up with life, I've come across more and more false reasoning. I've begun to realize that you don't get many lucky breaks. Having a good mother-in-law is an example of a lucky break, as is having good neighbors. Bosses and wives don't count. (That's because you don't pick your mother-in-law or your neighbors, and being unlucky can lead to long-term torment.) Having a good supervisor is a lucky break. The logic is the same: you don't choose your own supervisor; they're assigned by the state.

The first time I met Old Bad-Ass, he was leaning against a lathe, talking to an auntie and crunching on sunflower seeds. "Did you know that gold bars should be big and gold ingots small?" he asked the auntie. She blushed and gave him a feeble thump. Old Bad-Ass gave a creepy laugh.

Gold bar and *gold ingots* were dirty words in our factory, but I didn't know what they meant.

"Supervisor," I asked quietly when we went to fix a water pump. "What's all this about gold bars and gold ingots?"

Old Bad-Ass cracked up. He extended the middle finger of his right hand in front of my face and said, "This is the gold bar, see." He formed a ring with the forefinger and thumb of his left hand and held it out in front of me, saying, "Have you seen a gold ingot before? This is a gold ingot." Then he took the gold bar and slid it inside the gold ingot, in and out, in and out.

I smacked myself on the forehead, feigning sudden realization. All I could have said was that my knowledge of gold bars far exceeded my knowledge of gold ingots. Gold ingots existed only in my imagination. This pretense of realization was just to make Old Bad-Ass think I was a savvy kid, and that he'd made the right choice in teaching me to repair water pumps.

It was customary in the factory for apprentices to show reverence toward their supervisors by presenting them with cigarettes. I slipped Old Bad-Ass a box of Hongtashan smokes, which he accepted kindly, and from that point on he started to look after me pretty well, explaining all the factory lingo and slang. Only by understanding these words could you advance from an apprentice to a well-oiled worker.

Old Bad-Ass was over fifty, his hair was graying, and he had a very noticeable pug nose. While he was working, the sides of this nose flared out so much you could have easily fit two big red dates up his nostrils. Of course I never actually tried this, only thought about it.

During one trip to fix water pumps, a workshop auntie standing at the roadside shouted, "Old Bad-Ass! You have a new apprentice, do you?"

"He's a little virgin," Old Bad-Ass shouted back. "Shall I lend him to you to have some fun with?"

"Why don't you lend him to your wife to have some fun with instead!" she yelled.

I muttered something to myself. Old Bad-Ass asked me what I was saying.

"Fuck, who'd want an old auntie?" I said.

Old Bad-Ass told me very sternly not to look down on old aunties. You'd find yourself in deep shit at the factory if you offended them. I told him I understood. At school, we'd had an auntie in the general office who suffered from severe menopause. Her face was always flushed, and her lips were dazzlingly colorful, as if she were wearing lipstick. Her thing was to wear white gloves when checking the bathrooms, and if there was a speck of dirt on the gloves after she touched the window frame, she'd make us wipe it again. We were extremely annoyed by her way of doing things. She'd say that the window-sill had to be scrubbed so clean, she could lick it. This was completely unreasonable. Why didn't she just lick the windowsill clean and save us all the hassle? It's not like we were gigolos—giving our tongues such good training would have been a waste.

I had a natural fear of aunties over forty, in the same way that I had a natural sense of goodwill toward girls in their early twenties. I didn't understand old aunties. Confucius said, "If you don't understand life, how can you understand death?" Well, I didn't even understand young girls, so old aunties were an even greater mystery.

Old Bad-Ass gave me a definitive explanation of the word *auntie*. In the factory, women who were thirty-five or older and married with children were known as old aunties, while women who were thirty-five or younger and married were known as young aunties. Collectively, these two groups were referred to as aunties. They were in a completely different category from the aunties who were your parents' sisters. Of course, not all married women could be included in the auntie category—they had to have some femininity, be it residual, slight, or put on. Women with mustaches and waists like water barrels weren't called aunties but tigers. The general office auntie I mentioned was really a tiger. The difference between the two was that aunties would only roll their eyes, bicker, and give limp-wristed punches, whereas tigers would charge at you, spit in your face, cry and yell, yank women's hair and grab men's balls. Old Bad-Ass told me that being able to distinguish between aunties and tigers was a life lesson.

He divided our factory's women into three categories—young girls, young aunties, and old aunties, while tigers remained beyond categorization, an inferior product. He also explained how all young girls would become young aunties and young aunties would become old aunties; this was the law of nature.

According to Old Bad-Ass, aunties needed to be pandered to. That way they'd form a long-lasting attachment to you. I couldn't understand why someone my age would want a close relationship with an auntie. I might not want a close relationship with them now, Old Bad-Ass explained, but wait until I'd been working in the factory for years and years and had become a middle-aged bench worker. All the young girls would have graduated to the auntie rank, and the new young aunties wouldn't want anything to do with me. My only amusement would come from hanging out with the aunties my age, telling them dirty jokes, and waiting for them to come over and hit me.

Hearing this made me feel glum and listless, like a chicken with the plague. Old Bad-Ass had foreseen my drab middle-aged existence, with aunties as the only rays of light. This picture filled me with despair. Old Bad-Ass explained that I needed to start interacting regularly with all the young girls at the factory, getting to know them, tapping them on the shoulder and patting them on the arm, telling them a few dirty words (but not so dirty that they'd spit in my face). That way I'd enter a shameless middle age alongside them and enjoy these simple pleasures. His lack of shame reminded me of the proverb "A dead pig isn't scared of scalding water." It might not be a very exciting future, but neither would it be completely miserable.

The reason Old Bad-Ass was so notorious at the factory was not due to his penchant for chatting up old aunties, but because he'd once beaten up the workshop director.

My cousin had also beaten up a workshop director. He'd beaten this scrawny monkey of a workshop director so badly that the guy looked like he'd grown a pig's face. He'd bitten the guy's ear too. The head of safety at the pesticide factory had summoned my cousin for a talk. My cousin strode into the office and stripped off his uniform, revealing a tattoo on his chest of Nezha stirring up the sea. Nezha had superhuman powers; he had wheels of fire beneath his feet and a flaming spear in his hand. The tattoo was a complete rip-off of a Shanghai Animation Film Studio cartoon character. The safety department head saw it and said nothing more. They just sent my cousin home and fired him a couple of days later.

Old Bad-Ass was said to have beaten up his workshop director in the early '80s. I'm not sure what the guy had done to offend him, but Old Bad-Ass walked into his office, picked up an ashtray, and smashed it down on his head three times, giving the workshop director a concussion. After he came back to work, the guy got someone to offer Old Bad-Ass a carton of expensive Peony smokes. And that was how the matter was resolved.

Everyone hated that workshop director, but no one else had dared hit him. Old Bad-Ass became the factory hero. He was in his forties at the time, a good age to beat up someone in the factory—his seniority and fists were both sufficiently strong. He was nearly sixty when I became his apprentice, and approaching retirement. His muscles were starting to shrivel and his vision was deteriorating. He wouldn't have been able to beat up anyone anymore. I was still an apprentice, very low in the factory hierarchy, and even if my arms had been a bit brawnier, beating up someone would have been futile. It would have resulted in my immediate dismissal. If Old Bad-Ass and I put our weaknesses together, we wouldn't be able to swat a fly to death; but if we combined strengths, we could have taken on anyone in the whole factory. Of course, this was only ever in my mind. When you're nineteen years old and meet a supervisor who's had the guts to beat up a workshop director, it revs you up a little. Sadly, in the end all I did was follow him around, dismantle lots of faulty water pumps, and meet lots of attractive aunties.

"Supervisor," I said to him once, full of admiration. "You're so bad-ass, you even dared to beat up the workshop director."

"It was nothing special," he said. "The most bad-ass guy shut down the electricity supply."

"Why?" I asked.

"The factory deducted his bonus, and he retaliated by shutting down the electricity supply, halting production in all the workshops. That's the ultimate bad-ass act."

"Have you ever shut down the electricity?"

My mind drifted to Ah San, the bastard who started that rumor at the pesticide factory, got arrested, and was sent for labor education. No doubt the punishment for cutting the factory's electricity supply would be prison.

"I've never cut the electricity," Old Bad-Ass said. "It was someone else."

"Was he arrested?"

"No. If anyone had dared to try, he'd have blown up the factory head's office. There are lots of bad-asses in this factory, not just me."

Later I found out that Old Bad-Ass's most bad-ass quality wasn't beating up people. Neither was it flirting with the old aunties. His real capital was his technical skills. There were more than five hundred water pumps in the factory, and without him, they couldn't be fixed. He could also repair bikes, scooters, and all machine tools—even the noodle machines in the cafeteria. In 1979, he became the chemical bureau's model service technician for repairing an imported Japanese vacuum pump. After he beat up the workshop director, he seemed to turn into a dimwit overnight, no longer willing to fix machine tools. Every faulty water pump he handled had to be scrapped and replaced. The factory knew he was skilled, but also that he had a mind of his own and would be impossible to take on. Technical skills were a worker's capital. The iron blocks planed by supervisor Wonky Balls all sloped to the left, leaving him unable to hold his head up high. He'd never risk throwing caution to the wind and blowing up the factory head's office. He'd never have the chance to play hard and fast. The only role he could manage was as a member of the bench worker team art troupe, being mocked relentlessly until the day he retired.

Most of the water pumps we fixed were in the pump room, which was guarded by aunties. The pump room had a few buttons; pressing the green one would usually get the pump working, while the red one would stop it. The aunties' daily job was to press the red button, then the green one, and then start over. It was very relaxed. Had it been a developed capitalist country, the pump room would be computer-programmed and wouldn't need aunties to operate it. After labor became mechanized, these aunties were "liberated" back home to become full-time housewives, like in the West. But in our chemical factory in 1992 we only had two computers, both of them in the finance department, and most of us didn't know the difference between a computer and a calculator.

Guarding the pump room was similar to the job of a hospital nurse—it was done only by women. This was an unwritten factory rule. If a man were found doing this job, everyone would assume there was something wrong with him.

The pump room was in an obscure corner of the production zone and consisted of a small workshop, less than forty-five square feet. Inside there was a chair and table, and on the table a dial-less telephone. It was impossible to dial an outside line on it; all you could get was a factory extension via the switchboard. On the table were a couple of report forms, documenting each water pump's operating status. The water pumps were outside the workshop. If one were to break, the aunties would place a call to the mechanics workshop, and the mechanics workshop would place a call to the bench worker team, and that's when my work would start.

The first time Old Bad-Ass took me to fix a water pump, he was carrying a wrench. "Come with me," he said. The two of us entered the production zone, bypassing two workshops and going through a small doorway. After lots of twists and turns, we arrived at the back of a storage tank. There we found a workshop with its door open, and an auntie leaning against the door frame, beckoning us in. The place was very eerie. You couldn't hear anything above the roar of the machinery, and no one else came this way. The whole experience felt more like visiting a brothel than going to fix a water pump.

"Oh, hello, Old Bad-Ass," the auntie said. "It's the water pump on the east side that's broken."

"Why are you stuck in here all the time like the white-haired girl?" Old Bad-Ass asked.

This was more obscenity, and I understood it this time. White-haired girl referred to the girl who'd hidden away in a cave and been raped.

When the auntie heard this, she rushed up to Old Bad-Ass and grabbed hold of his lips. Twisting them, she said, "Hey, is that a new apprentice you've got there?"

"Go and take out the screws," Old Bad-Ass instructed me. With the wrench in my hand I went in search of the broken pump, leaving Old Bad-Ass chatting with the water-pump auntie.

Water pumps generally had four bolts the thickness of thumbs that screwed them into the base. My job was to remove the nuts from these four bolts. Because the workshop floor was damp, over the years the nuts had rusted into iron lumps. I put the wrench in place and started to turn it forcefully, using the exact same arm motion as rowing. Later I met a man from England who'd been on the Cambridge University rowing team and had nearly competed in the Olympics. He'd talked about this noble sport, proudly rolling up his sleeves and giving me a look at his biceps, round and smooth, like half-globes. I pulled up my sleeves too and showed him my biceps, which were in the same league as his. The English man was overjoyed and asked me what sport I played. I told him I played Rusty Screws.

I used up all my strength in that godforsaken place unscrewing three of the bolts, but the nut of that last one was fitted so tight, it was like trying to separate two dogs fucking. I sucked about two cubic liters of air down into my lungs, making my neck veins pop out, and my upper and lower molars ground together so much I could hear the crunching. From my facial expression, you'd probably think I was about to shoot my load. I gave it one last tug, and tumbled over as the bolt snapped.

I did a backward somersault onto the ground, crawled back up, then went to find Old Bad-Ass, carrying the snapped-off bolt. He was in the workshop crunching on sunflower seeds with the auntie. I chucked the bolt onto the table, and Old Bad-Ass frowned.

"What's going on, has the bolt snapped?" he asked.

"It wasn't my fault, it just happened," I said.

He told me that I was no better than a beast of burden, and that if I relied solely on brute force and didn't hone my technique, I'd snap those bolts every time. I was reminded of my uncle's words: bench work was skilled work, and unskilled people wouldn't even be able to undo a screw. It turned out he'd been speaking the truth.

Snapping a bolt caused a lot of hassle. You had to use a gas-cutting gun to remove the remainder of the bolt from the base, then fit in a new bolt. This wasn't a job I could do. I was only in charge of unscrewing the screws. Incidents like this happened very occasionally. I dismantled two or three hundred water pumps in my time, and it only happened that once. But the water-pump auntie remembered me and blathered about it to everyone: "Old Bad-Ass's new apprentice is a beast of burden—he only has to touch a bolt and it snaps." After they heard, the other water-pump aunties remembered me too. When I went to dismantle water pumps they'd keep their eyes on me, saying, "Oh, Xiaolu, be careful when undoing the bolts, please don't snap them." They'd gather around to watch as I unscrewed them; the scent of their face creams filling my nostrils and making me want to sneeze.

Once a water pump had been dismantled, migrant workers would carry a new one over on a shoulder pole and a bench worker would install it. Then the migrant workers would take the busted water pump to the bench worker team. There were lots of different types of water pumps, and the heaviest needed eight migrant workers to lift it.

These migrant workers were known in the factory as riggers. Before my time, only farmers from the outskirts of the city were prepared to do this kind of heavy labor; official workers wouldn't go near it. Later the farmers from the outskirts weren't up for it either, and the factory was forced to look for laborers further afield. When no laborers in the county were prepared to do it, the rigging work was assigned to migrants.

I've heard that when people get old, they always dream about their past. This is because they think they no longer have a future—aren't even able to picture one in their dreams. Now that I'm thirty, I often dream about roaming those corridors, carrying my wrench, moving along all those twists and turns toward the factory's remote pump room, where an auntie and a broken water pump are waiting for me. I always feel calm in the dream, with no resentment.

I can no longer remember how I used to feel ten years before making my way to remove those rusty screws. And I've forgotten what all those aunties looked like; all women over forty looked the same to me. There was only one time that sticks out. I'd gone to dismantle a water pump in the saccharin workshop, and as I walked in I started to get a strange feeling. The auntie in there had fashioned the 45-square-foot workshop into an intimate boudoir: there was an orange lamp, light blue curtains, and a Mickey Mouse cushion on the chair. Most terrifying of all was the futon she'd brought in from God knows where. She glanced up at me from her reclined position and said, "Water pump number two is broken. I'll leave you to fix it on your own."

I removed the screws and went back to the workshop. I turned away from the auntie to use the phone and call for a rigger to haul over a new pump.

"How old are you?" the auntie asked while I was waiting.

"Hello! Hello!" I shouted into the phone. "Is this the rigger? Why the hell aren't you guys here yet?"

There was a small mirror on the wall, and I saw the reflection of the auntie's mouth twitching. She turned around lazily and proceeded to ignore me.

I told Old Bad-Ass what had happened.

"What did she look like?" he asked.

"Shapely eyebrows, wavy hair, and blood-red lips," I explained, "and she was reclining."

"That's not reclining," Old Bad-Ass said. "You don't call it reclining if the woman has her legs open."

I rolled back my eyes, trying to remember. "Her legs were closed, actually," I said.

"That woman's name is Ah Sao," Old Bad-Ass explained. "You want to keep your distance from her. When her legs are together, you're safe; but when they're apart, all the men in the factory are at risk. From now on we'll get Wei Yixin to deal with the water pumps in the saccharin workshop."

"Won't that mean Wei Yixin gets in trouble?"

"Don't worry—Ah Sao doesn't like men with stutters. Their tongues are too short. They can't reach."

I have a couple of things to add on the subject of water pumps.

All the broken water pumps were carried into the bench workers' room and heaped in a corner. There they would gather until it was their lucky day to be dismantled, examined, and repaired. As far as I was aware, not many were repaired properly. The bench workers were too lazy to bother. Instead, every couple of months the people from waste storage would come over to take an inventory, then haul them away.

"Hey, Xiaolu, how are your water pump repairs?" my pa would ask from time to time.

I'd brush him off by saying things like, "Oh, I've been learning to repair vacuum pumps for the last few days."

Then he'd inundate me with information about how vacuum pumps worked, always ending with these words: "If you can learn how to fix water pumps, you'll be able to find work at any chemical factory."

"Supervisor, when are you going to teach me to fix water pumps?" I once asked Old Bad-Ass, pointing at all the water pumps in the bench workers' room.

"What's the point of your learning that?" Old Bad-Ass asked. "You'd be better off helping me run the bike repair stand."

"Supervisor, shouldn't you be teaching me something? Otherwise I'll finish my apprenticeship and be out in the world without any skills, and that probably wouldn't be good for your reputation either."

"And if you did learn to mend water pumps, what then?" Old Bad-Ass asked. "Will they give you a bonus?"

"No, they won't," I said.

Old Bad-Ass patted my shoulder and said, "So you'd be better off helping me at the bike stand."

Several years later, I thought of Old Bad-Ass and his sagging flesh, squinting as he assessed the state of the water pumps, the way he walked sideways down the road. He always seemed like a philosopher. Later I thought it through: when a guy's worked forty years as a bench worker, beaten up a workshop director, fixed countless numbers of water pumps, and respects neither women nor knowledge, he'd naturally become a philosopher.

That year the factory sent two cadres to the bench worker team. They said they were there to test my skills and give me a professional appraisal. The lowest bench worker level was grade two, a step up from that was grade four, and the highest was grade eight.

"What grade shall we test your apprentice for?" the cadres asked Old Bad-Ass.

"Oh, grade four, easily," Old Bad-Ass said.

I was so afraid, I was dripping with cold sweat. If they were to throw a water pump at me I wouldn't know what to do with it, save from undoing all the screws. Instead the cadres threw a lump of iron at me and told me to file it into a cube. If I did it correctly, they'd give me a grade four. I held the lump of iron in one hand, took hold of the file in the other, and worked on it for six hours, sweating profusely the whole time. I filed that fist-size lump of raw metal into an object the size of a mah-jongg tile that was neither square nor round. The cadres both held this object between thumb and forefinger.

"This isn't up to standard, is it?" they asked Old Bad-Ass.

"If you think that's bad, you should see the iron sheets Wonky Balls planes. How many of them do you think he gets straight?"

"Forget it," the cadres said when they heard this. "The bench workers in this factory are only here to unscrew screws anyway. Pass!"

"Motherfuckers," I cursed under my breath. They knew all along that all I did was turn screws. What was the point of making me file a lump of iron for six fucking hours?

I passed my grade-four exam, which led to a pay raise. I once boasted to Zhang Xiaoyin that she wasn't the only one who'd passed her grade four; I had too, only mine wasn't in English but in bench work. I was just goofing around with her. I still have my grade-four bench worker certificate in my drawer, with my photo on it, taken by the amateur factory photographer. The backdrop was a sheet of red material, and I was wearing that neither-blue-nor-green uniform. My hair was disheveled, my face pale, and my eyes dazed, and one of my front teeth was embedded into my lower lip. I looked as if I thought I might be pulled out at any minute and shot by a firing squad. You can't blame me for my foolish appearance—the bastard photographer was a complete amateur. He pressed the shutter before my butt was even on the stool.

CHAPTER THREE

A WHITE DRESS FLUTTERING

IN THE BREEZE

Old Bad-Ass had his bike repair stand set up in the entrance to the alley where his house was, not too far from the chemical factory. After work he'd lay out a full set of bike repair tools, then fix and pump tires, check gears, and wipe down bikes. I heard that when he was younger, he used to beat up customers. Now he was old and no longer had the strength to beat anyone up; he'd just squint at them, a cigarette stuck between his lips. The only reason people visited his bike stand was because there was no one within a mile radius who'd dare steal business from him. He told me this was known as a trust racket. If his bad-ass radius had been ten miles instead of one, he could have employed a couple of hundred people, established a bike repair company. I think this might have been his dream, but now that he was old, his dreams held no weight.

His bike repair business used to open at four thirty, but now that I was on board, it could open at two. I'd sit in front of the bike stand while he went to the pump room to find an auntie to cavort with. Operating a bike stand during working hours was classed as truancy, and if you were caught, you'd be fined. Novice apprentices like me didn't have the kind of salary a fine could be deducted from, so we'd just be fired instead.

The bike stand was a simple set-up. If someone needed their tires pumped or repaired, I dealt with it. But if it was a broken axle or a bent wheel, I'd leg it back to the factory and get Old Bad-Ass to fix it. I'd been there a couple of days, and business was dismal. I had a knack for smiling stupidly at passersby, an expression they mistook for bad intent, and even those who really needed their bikes fixed were too scared to come over. This left me happy and idle, but later I started to feel bored, squatting there by the side of the road with nothing to do but inspect the alley. It was a very long alley. The houses on one side were built along the river, and one of these belonged to Old Bad-Ass, although I hadn't been there at that point. This alley had a strange name: Donkey Alley. An old lady who was hanging her clothes out to dry told me that during the Qing dynasty, a kindly man called Dong Qi had lived here. He'd done a lot of good deeds, and to commemorate him this street had been renamed Dong Qi Alley. But over the next couple hundred years, people had started to read it as "Donkey." I thought to myself, *This Dong gentleman was pretty unfortunate— he'd been a philanthropist all his life, and he ended up having his name misread as "donkey."* It went to show that even if you were a good person, it wasn't guaranteed to make you immortal.

Two weeks later, a girl came cycling past. She saw me crouching by the roadside, staring into space like a fuckwit, looking like I was doped up or something. She didn't seem offended by my moronic appearance and jumped off her bike to ask, "Is this your bike stand?"

I was snapped back from my daydream. "Yep," I said.

"How much to have my bike wiped down?"

"A small wipe is two yuan, and a big wipe is five."

The small wipe consisted of wiping the oil and dust off the bike's surface, which was easy. But the big wipe involved removing the wheels, taking out the ball bearings and cleaning them one by one until they shone like mirrors, coating the axles in butter, pouring oil onto the bike chains, screwing all the screws and nuts up tight, and adjusting the brakes. The small wipe was like a back rub at the public baths, while the big wipe was like a full-body massage at a massage parlor. I could give a small wipe, but I'd never given a big one. It was the same as with the water pumps—I could take the thing apart but couldn't fit it back together.

"I'll go for the big wipe," she said.

She was wearing a white dress (which she obviously didn't want to get dirty—hence wanting the bike cleaned). With her eyes shining, she shot me a condescending glare. I'd never had the pleasure of being shot by a girl's eyes before, except in senior middle school, but that was the headmistress, an old woman. She hadn't just glared at me at the parent-teacher meetings—she'd glared at my pa too, scaring us both half to death. Had she been a girl in her twenties in a white dress, with a pair of almond eyes, it wouldn't have mattered if she'd fired one shot or gone at me with a machine gun, I'd have been utterly willing to have her kill me dead.

"Are you from the saccharin factory?" she asked as I looked for a wrench.

"How do you know?"

"Are you kidding? You're wearing your work uniform."

I looked down at myself. She was right. I had on my neither-blue-nor-green work uniform with the *S* on the left breast.

Then she asked, "Are you on the bench work team?"

"How do you know that? Are you from the saccharin factory?"

"That's none of your business."

For some strange reason, I decided not to run back to the factory to get Old Bad-Ass. Instead I pulled a wrench out of the toolbox and started to give her the big wipe. Correction: I started to give her bike the big wipe! It was a mauve woman's Flying Pigeon, with a crooked handlebar that looked like a sexy pair of legs sticking up in the air. The seat cover, still warm, allowed me to cop a vicarious feel of her ass. My heart felt like a frisky monkey and my mind a cantering horse as I picked up the wrench. She sat on my wooden stool, watching as I took off the wheels, polished the ball bearings, then fitted them back into place. She didn't say a word the whole time. She was very pretty, with dark chestnut hair, and I snuck a couple of glances at her as I wiped the bike. When our eyes met, she didn't seem to mind at all; she just continued to shoot me with that impassive gaze. She waited until I'd completed my task before standing up and walking around the bike, asking, "Have you cleaned it properly?"

"It's all clean."

"Give it a ride around for me," she demanded shrewdly.

I jumped onto the bike and pedaled, but I hadn't ridden more than fifty or sixty feet before the front wheel rolled off. It reminded me of how horses are described as falling in stories, with their front legs buckling. Suddenly I saw the blue-gray paving stones tilting up toward me, and then my chin became the landing gear. I stood back up, checking myself over with my hand, but it didn't seem too serious. I'd grazed a patch of skin on my chin, but my teeth were intact. I lifted up the bike, picked up the wheel that had fallen off, and walked back over to her.

"Ouch, bad fall?" she asked.

"Not too bad," I told her. "Close shave."

"You fall over like that and still call it a close shave?"

"If you hadn't asked me to ride it around, you'd have been the one on the ground."

"Cut the crap," she said dryly. "What shall we do first, put the wheel back on or get you to the hospital?"

"Let's get the wheel back on."

I often returned to this scene in my mind: a young worker who has just fallen and scraped his chin fits a bike wheel in the entrance of an alley, as a slightly older girl in a white dress watches from the side, the corner of her mouth twisted with a hint of ridicule. There was no one else around. Things like this shouldn't make you happy, but if they didn't it would all seem fairly miserable. And misery shouldn't be the main theme of your life when you're young. So I'll say that I felt happy and that it felt cool. The fact that a bike repair worker can have an experience like this is pretty fucking romantic.

When I'd fitted the wheel, the girl in the white dress walked around the bike again. "How about you ride it around once more for me?" she said.

I stared at the bike for ages before saying, "Why don't I find a pedicab to take you home instead?"

After she left, I touched my chin. It stung. I took a bandage out of my toolbox and stuck it over the wound, but it didn't do much for the pain—in fact, it made it worse. I sat on the wooden bench and thought about the girl in the white dress. She must have been a saccharin factory employee. What if she reported me for manning a bike stand during office hours? It would be treated as truancy, and I'd be fired on the spot.

I sat on my own in the alley, thinking, *What if she did report me?* Part of me was hoping I would be fired. I'd been an apprentice for one month now. During this time I'd collected trash, sprinkled water, filed a lump of metal, and wiped bikes. I was no different from the generations of apprentices who had come before me, just repeating the same way of life. It wasn't an utterly tragic way to live, but neither was it in any way remarkable. Your whole life could go by without your realizing you were even living it, which made for a fairly pointless existence.

I'd manned the bike stand for two weeks; business had been dismal, and now I'd smashed up my chin. Old Bad-Ass settled up with me. During that time I'd pumped tires for sixteen people and patched tires for four. Pumping tires cost 5 fen and patching tires cost 1.2 yuan, which meant I'd earned a total of 5.6 yuan for his pocket. Two weeks and I'd only earned him a measly 5.6 yuan, Old Bad-Ass said—didn't that make me a fuckwit? It wasn't my fault, I'd been unlucky, I said, which had made me act like a fuckwit. He patted my shoulder and said I should forget it, he'd teach me to mend water pumps instead.

Later Old Bad-Ass and I discussed the matter of mechanical genius. The way I saw it, different people had different talents. Some were suited to becoming writers, others to becoming murderers. Writers and murderers were in the minority, though. Most of the people around me dealt with machinery. Unfortunately, throughout history there haven't been many humans who have been real mechanical geniuses. James Watt was one, Thomas Edison another, and those brothers who invented the airplane. This shows that mechanical genius isn't at all common, possibly as rare as a talent for writing or murder. There were, however, lots more people relying on machines to survive than those who relied on the work of novelists or murderers, which meant that even someone like Wonky Balls could get a job as a planer.

Old Bad-Ass took out a structural diagram of a water pump, then found a broken water pump and got me to dismantle and reassemble it while looking at the diagram. I deftly dismantled the pump, but I couldn't put it back together. It was exactly the same as with the bikes. This proved my lack of mechanical genius. I thought it must have been a problem stemming from my early education. My family wasn't well off when I was young, and our only electric appliance was a palm-size semiconductor radio, which emitted a low sound like a buzzing mosquito. My father would glue his ear to the side to listen, but all it did was give off a constant crackle. Our neighbors gathered around, thinking he was listening in on an enemy radio station, but all it turned out to be was the local weather report. The other mechanical object we owned was also palm-size: a rusty little alarm clock. At six on the dot each morning, it would ring with a noise like the prelude to a rock concert, waking us all in a second.

A couple of my junior school classmates had real mechanical genius. Li Zhi wanted to be a child inventor. In our manual labor class, we used to copy the teacher's origami folding. The paper airplane and the frog may have looked pretty, but Li Zhi's model glider could soar into the sky. The teacher marveled at his talent and got us all to study from him. This child prodigy explained that when he was six, he had taken apart his family alarm clock—and when he put it back together, its hands still moved and its alarm still rang. Inspired, I went back home, planning to do the same with our family alarm clock. As soon as my father realized what I was doing, he swiftly snatched it away. Upon rescuing our noble and loyal clock, he slapped me around a little. The alarm clock was the only thing in our house that kept the time, he explained. If I broke it, he'd be late for work and have his bonus deducted. Slapping me wasn't punishment for the alarm clock as much as for the bonus, which made it more fitting. At this point I decided to cut ties with machinery. Later the child prodigy assembled a radio, and although it crackled, it did still make a noise. I looked at his radio, thinking if I'd taken our household radio apart and we could no longer listen to the weather forecast, the clothes on my mother's washing line would get soaked and I'd definitely be in line for another slap. By the time I was sixteen, my family had a television and a large desk clock. One day that little alarm clock gave up the ghost. It was as rusty as a discus. Recalling that slap from those years before, my pa said, "Hey, Xiaolu, weren't you interested in alarm clocks when you were younger? Ours is broken now, why don't you take it apart and have a play?" I rolled my eyes at him. *Father, I'm sixteen*, I wanted to say. *I've taken anatomy classes—my interest is in the structure of the human body now. I'll leave the alarm clock for you to play with.*

When I was older, I became keenly aware of the importance of early education. If you wanted to be a musician, you should have been bent over in front of a piano since you were knee-high to a grasshopper. If you wanted to be a calligrapher, you should have been cultivating the correct wrist position since childhood. If you wanted to be a mechanic, you should have been dismantling alarm clocks and what-have-you from an early age. I hadn't come across a piano or a calligraphy brush in my youth. At that age, all I knew how to do was sit on a bench and stare into space. So this was the expertise my early education brought me.

Instead of cursing me when I couldn't reassemble that water pump, Old Bad-Ass consoled me by saying that half the mechanics in our metal shed couldn't mend one. All they could do was twist screws, so there was no need for me to be too concerned. There weren't many people with mechanical genius. If every bench worker needed a brain that size, bench workers the world over would be paid as much as surgeons. He took the spare parts from my hand as he said this and threw them on the scrap heap.

Being a bench worker was easy, Old Bad-Ass explained. All the old pump-room aunties needed was for you to change the pump for one that worked, and they'd be happy. Who cared if you could mend the broken pump or not?

Old Bad-Ass was turning sixty that year. He was already past his prime for this line of work. A machine repair bench worker needed to be fairly robust to unscrew all those rusty screws, but you couldn't see a hint of muscle on Old Bad-Ass's arms, only loose flesh. Machine repair bench workers needed excellent eyesight too, but these days Old Bad-Ass relied on his reading glasses. Even more problematic was his failing memory, and sometimes even he was unable to assemble the more complex water pumps.

Old Bad-Ass told me a story about an apprentice he'd taken on three years before. This boy had been a complete idiot when it came to mechanics. Not only was he unable to repair a water pump, he couldn't even dismantle one, couldn't even undo the screws. He'd pick up a wrench with his delicate fingers and turn the screws in this namby-pamby way, as if he were giving the pump a massage. Old Bad-Ass couldn't stand it and smacked him to the ground, beating him until the boy was crying like a baby. Nothing infuriated Old Bad-Ass more than the pathetic sight of people crying, and he shouted at the boy again, slapped him around more. The attractive aunties in the pump room couldn't bear it any longer. They scolded Old Bad-Ass, telling him his behavior was tantamount to child abuse. These old aunties had a decided effect on Old Bad-Ass, who wasn't actually a sadist.

"I promise I won't beat you again," he told his apprentice. "But in return, you must promise never to turn those screws in that namby-pamby way, is that clear?" Those delicate fingers had cost Old Bad-Ass his street cred.

A few days later, something miraculous happened. The apprentice came to say goodbye to Old Bad-Ass, carrying a guitar on his back. He even strummed a tune. Then he gave a little wave to everyone with those fingers so delicate they couldn't hurt a fly. He journeyed south from there to Shenzhen, where he became a busker.

Old Bad-Ass told me that once upon a time he had also played an instrument, the erhu. But when forced to choose between bench work and that two-stringed wonder, he'd chosen bench work. If he'd kept on playing the erhu, he'd be a low-level administrator in the trade union by now, or even cutting around in the cultural center. The line that mending water pumps makes you kick ass was just a lie told to deceive workshop directors and attractive aunties. Actually learning to mend water pumps so that you could beat up a workshop director would be putting the cart before the horse. You'd be better off joining the mafia.

To be honest, I felt a bit jealous of the boy with the namby-pamby hands. He may not have had mechanical genius, but he'd had musical genius—and most important, he'd discovered his talent. What about me? Squatting under that tin roof with the bench worker team, the only thing I had proof of was my lack of mechanical genius. I didn't know where my actual talent lay. I was seriously depressed. What if my talent was for murder, I wondered, what then? Should I kill someone right now to find out? The thought that I might have a talent for writing was even more terrifying. Being a writer was more complicated than being a murderer. No wonder so many writers committed suicide.

I would often lie back on the bench worker team recliner and just let my thoughts drift. What we called a recliner was actually a chair padded with a few leatherette cushions that you could lie across comfortably. The weather seemed to be getting colder, and the temperature in the tin-roofed room had dropped, but I felt very comfortable lying back in this drafty place. My dream to go to trade school felt like it was drifting farther away from me, like clouds dissipating in the sky. I thought of the girl in the white dress and how much I wanted to find her. Girls and college were different. My weakness for girls wouldn't dissipate; it was always there, giving off an unsettling odor.

Zhang Xiaoyin showed me a newspaper article once reporting that Chinese beer contained formaldehyde. She asked me what formaldehyde was. I told her I was very familiar with the stuff: it was used to make paint, textiles, and paper. That strange smell when you renovated your house was formaldehyde, but it could also be used to asphyxiate cockroaches. It was actually the same as formalin, used in medical institutes to pickle corpses. But how had this substance managed to creep into our beer? To my knowledge, excessive formaldehyde gave you rashes, liver necrosis, and kidney failure, caused impotence in men and early menopause in women. It was scary stuff.

"They're a load of sharks," Zhang Xiaoyin said. "Don't drink so much beer from now on. I don't want you becoming impotent."

I told her I'd been exaggerating. I'd come into close contact with formaldehyde and my body was proof that it didn't cause impotence, not unless you poured it directly on my dick.

I explained that the saccharin factory didn't just manufacture saccharin. It also produced formaldehyde, fertilizer, and glue, as well as a lot of chemical raw materials, such as hydrochloric acid, sulfuric acid, methanol, and sodium nitrate, all of which I'd come into contact with, and none of which were any good for you. When I was young I used to say that these chemicals were all dog shit, but formaldehyde was king of the dog shit.

My father once told me that a world where saccharin didn't exist was unimaginable. I was sick and tired of saccharin, but still he tried to convince me: "Saccharin is a food additive. You loved eating popsicles when you were younger. They didn't contain white sugar but saccharin. You can't love popsicles but hate saccharin." He went on to explain, "Formaldehyde is an important industrial raw material. You can't make furniture or material without it. How can you call formaldehyde dog shit?"

The entire formaldehyde workshop was permeated with the strong smell of formalin, the same smell that seeps out of contaminated furniture, lengthy exposure to which could lead to nasopharyngeal cancer and leukemia. But the smell of furniture formaldehyde was nothing compared to the torture of being inside the formaldehyde workshop. You couldn't find a single fly within a quarter-mile radius of that workshop. Within fifty yards, your nose would start to run as if you'd been thrown into a heap of white pepper. After three minutes, your lungs felt like they were going into spasm, and there would be so much pain between your throat and your trachea that you felt like they were being ripped apart.

I often wondered how the operators of these fucking workshops managed not to get asphyxiated. It was only later I discovered that they worked in a sealed-off operating room from which they guarded all that expensive equipment. They had air conditioning, a direct phone line, and beautiful female college-student interns. The bench workers were never this lucky. When we changed water pumps, it was on the workshop floor. The concentration of formaldehyde in the air was in the realm of chemical weaponry. You had to go out every two minutes to take a deep breath of air, then rush back in; otherwise you'd go into shock. Chicken Head, the leader of the electrician team, once gave me a cicada inside a small box that sang joyously. I had it in my pocket as I went to the formaldehyde workshop to dismantle a water pump, and when I left I discovered that the singing cicada's legs were all clumped together. It had been asphyxiated. My lung capacity back then allowed me to dive underwater for two minutes, but when I was waving a wrench around and doing rowing movements, I could only last eighty seconds, and in that time you could remove only one screw. Old Bad-Ass would watch me from fifty yards away. He'd wait until I had four screws in my hand and was sitting on the floor convulsing. Then he'd call for the riggers to come and collect the pump.

I couldn't say if he was abusing his position by making me do this. Old Bad-Ass suffered from asthma, and when he inhaled the fumes he'd fall over clutching his neck. If he were to die, I wouldn't last long. The fact that he was prepared to watch me work from fifty yards away was already pretty big of him. One time the fumes hit me so badly, I passed out. Luckily Old-Bass was nearby and managed to find a couple of passing riggers. They tied me up with rope, strapped me to a shoulder pole, and carried me to the infirmary for emergency treatment. Old Bad-Ass actually saved my life.

If you got formaldehyde on your hands, the skin would wrinkle up within minutes. It would look like you'd been soaking in the tub for a long time. It would become numb as the human proteins were destroyed. When formalin is used to preserve human specimens, that's basically what goes on. It destroys the organic compounds, which prevents the body from rotting. I still remember what that pain felt like, the area crinkling up like an inanimate patch of decaying flesh. It felt like it was about to drop from my body, even though it was still hanging there.

Saccharin was a darling compared to formaldehyde. Saccharin could be eaten. The workers in that workshop were all extraordinarily sweet, sweet from head to toe. How sweet, exactly? Well, if you were eating a salted duck's egg and a saccharin factory worker was fifty yards away, your salted duck's egg would become a sweet duck's egg. Apparently you never needed to add sugar when cooking in a saccharin worker's home, you just called them over and got them to shake their head over the wok. The dish would be plenty sweet. A few times when I've kissed girls they've said, "Wow! Why are your lips so sweet?" They thought I had a special gift, like the legendary Fragrant Concubine. She had a naturally aromatic body, while I had a naturally aromatic mouth. I silently cursed these saccharin workers, wandering around and wafting saccharin all over the place.

The people who worked in the fertilizer workshop had a completely different sort of life than those in the saccharin workshop. Years later I searched online for a chemical product called methenamine. I remembered it being used as a chemical fertilizer, but later it was discovered to have medical uses: "After oral administration, the decomposition of acidic urine produces methenamine, which functions as a disinfectant and can be used to treat mild urinary tract infections. It can also be used for intravenous injections. It can be used topically to cure ringworm, as an antiperspirant, and to cure body odor."

Methenamine stunk to high heaven, so I really don't know how it could have cured body odor. The workers in that workshop were the antithesis of saccharin workers: their bodies always stank, and stank like nothing else. It was a stench that embedded itself in your nostrils and couldn't be washed away. More worrying was the fact that these workers had completely lost their sense of smell. They were totally oblivious to the stink emanating from their own bodies. That meant that they'd be swaggering all over the place, perfectly happy, while everyone else fled the fumes.

Only women worked at the fertilizer workshop. If a male worker went home stinking like that, his wife would rant at him, deny him sex, and possibly start having affairs until divorce became inevitable. But if a female worker stank a bit, she could usually cover it up with perfume. If she stank, she stank. For most men, having a wife who stank from head to toe was better than having no wife at all.

The factory also produced animal feed and glue. Women weren't allowed to work in the animal feed workshop because the animal feed additives they produced were used to get dairy cows to lactate. After working there awhile, women would start to express milk. A woman producing milk for no reason was scary stuff. It wasn't just the young girls and old aunties who found it unbearable—even the tigers couldn't take the indignity. If these women went home leaking milk all over the place and couldn't explain themselves properly, their husbands might beat them to death. The animal feed workshop was therefore the opposite of the fertilizer workshop: it had only male workers. Those workers were also prone to lactating, which was an even more worrying phenomenon, but at least they found it easier to explain the situation at home. In the summer, we'd often see the men from the animal feed workshop with two wet patches on their chests. We advised them to start wearing absorbent bras, or they might turn people on.

The factory had a secret cure for arc eye (this was when your eye was exposed to strong welding rays—its scientific name was electric ophthalmia). This secret cure was human breast milk, which, if dropped into the eye, would help it to heal naturally. At the time I thought this was bullshit, but later I discovered that this cure was in the *Encyclopedia of China*. When you got arc eye, you needed to go to the nursery to find a lactating mother. At least, that was the norm in other factories. You'd get to check out the breast-feeding mothers too. In our factory, this didn't fly. The men lactated also, which meant breast-feeding women weren't needed. Instead we'd just make a dash for the animal feed workshop, pull up a male worker's uniform, press his nipple as if it were a coffee machine switch, and wait for the milk to flow out. I didn't know whether male breast milk was as effective because I hadn't had female breast milk to compare it with. These men produced milk, but not in large quantities, and you could only squeeze out a couple of drops at a time. Sometimes you had to lift up their work uniform and press alternately at each nipple. We were all pretty naive back then, and no one ever accused me of delinquency. You couldn't see much when you had arc eye, so they'd direct their nipples to your fingers and say, "Squeeze here, squeeze here."

Both men and women worked in the glue workshop. The only ones not tolerated there were petty thieves. One worker carried a thermos to work each day. It looked like he was using it for tea, but someone lent it to me once and I poured out a mug of glue. The safety department asked him in for questioning, and he confessed that he'd been taking a thermos of glue home every single day. What did he do with that much glue? The answer: sold it to the hardware store, where it was used for laying wooden floorboards, which were popular at the time.

The factory was the site of rampant theft, and the safety department worked hard to catch perpetrators. They did this via end-of-day bag searches at the factory entrance. There was no mention of our human rights. Pulling someone's pants down counted as a rights violation—what was searching a bag? This initiative resulted in the arrest of a couple dozen thieves. Some had stolen lumps of iron, others gloves. There was one guy who'd been stealing cement from the site for years, filling his lunchbox with it each day and taking it home. He'd been hiding bricks in his bag too, and over three years he'd collected enough building material to renovate his house completely. The most extraordinary case was Supervisor Wonky Balls. When his bag was searched, they pulled out a bunch of manufactured parts, all planed and all defective, slanting to the left. It transpired that before leaving work each day, Wonky Balls would hide all his defective handiwork in his bag and take it home with him. That's why the factory didn't know how much crap he produced each year. He'd sell these defective items to the scrapyard and take home a little extra cash.

Then the initiative to catch thieves and protect production finally scored a big player. The bastard was the factory gardener, of all people. He was involved in greening the place, but he would fiddle with the books: adding ten yuan to the purchase price of each sapling; recording living trees as dead trees, while each dead tree had the potential to die another couple of times. When it was all added up, the auditor realized that the chemical factory and its mopey vegetation actually should have been a botanical garden, with more than a thousand trees and hundreds of high-quality bonsai, as well as banana trees, bush lilies, stargazer lilies, Holland tulips, Japanese cherry blossoms, Mexican cacti, and so on. We all yearned for this green paradise that existed only in the account books.

Back to the girl in the white dress. I'd been looking for her. I was convinced that she was a chemical factory employee, perhaps a laboratory technician or a department cadre. These girls all hid deep inside the office building, like a rare species not often glimpsed. As a lowly water pump fixer, I didn't get to chase girls in those sorts of places; I'd have been kicked out. But I missed her. I had a real thing for the girl in the white dress, and it wouldn't go away. My chin still hurt, but the pain made me miss her all the more.

I went to the bike shed to see if I could find the mauve Flying Pigeon among the sea of bikes, with its crooked handlebars like two legs in the air. The factory bike shed was as big as a movie theater, and navigating around the whole place was more tiring than fixing water pumps. I located more than fifty mauve Flying Pigeons and felt completely lost. I crouched in the entrance to the canteen, crouched in the entrance to the office building, crouched in the entrance to the factory, thinking I might come across her. But she didn't show.

That feeling of being lost was always there between me and her. It was also the only road that would lead me to her. It may well have been fate: if I hadn't been lost, I'd never have found her.

That fall I was dismantling a water pump in the formaldehyde workshop when I fainted. I'd come across an amazingly rusty screw, and by the time my eighty seconds were up I was still in the workshop trying to turn it. Unable to hold on a second longer, I sucked in a large mouthful of formaldehyde air. Inhaling after holding your breath for so long was like ejaculating: you shot your first load and couldn't wait to shoot your second. I inhaled my second and third breaths of formaldehyde air in quick succession. In front of my eyes, there was darkness. My head bumped hard against the pump, and I passed out.

Old Bad-Ass was watching me work from fifty yards away and noticed me slumped to one side. He looked around calmly and spotted four burly riggers passing, carrying a pole and some rope. Old Bad-Ass called them over. The four of them surrounded him, saying, "Which water pump do you want us to take, Supervisor Bad?" ("Bad" obviously wasn't Old Bad-Ass's surname—the migrants just called him this to be polite.)

Old Bad-Ass pointed to the water pump in the formaldehyde workshop, and me next to it, flat on my back. "You're here to carry a person, not a water pump," he told them. "Hurry, pick him up."

A special explanation is needed here: migrant workers weren't scared of formaldehyde. When they breathed it in, it had no effect whatsoever. I, on the other hand, was a feeble city-dweller. Migrant workers could cope with any work the world threw at them—street sweeping, foundry work, construction, coal mining. They worked quickly and efficiently while having insults hurled at them, and they worked for the lowest salaries. If they were blown up in an explosion, not much payout was needed either. Migrant workers were made of special stuff, and having them work the land was a complete waste of their talent. I'd discovered this secret a long time ago, but I didn't tell anyone in case it meant I got shafted. Later other people discovered this too, and they moved all the migrant workers to the cities so the city folk could stay at home playing mah-jongg.

I hereby acknowledge that a migrant worker saved my life. I'll remember this forever. Even when I've become an official and I'm rich, I'll say, "I'll always be a migrant's son." It's best to admit things like this—it means you'll never get blackmailed.

This migrant worker carried me out, and I started puking violently. My puke was pure miso soup, which spilled down his neck. The migrant worker couldn't take it, so he placed me down on the ground. Two of them were planning to carry me. How could they think of lifting me face up, Old Bad-Ass asked them. The filth I puked up would flow down my windpipe and choke me to death. The four migrants flipped me over so I was facing the ground, and each one took hold of a hand or foot. That didn't work either—it would have dislocated all my vertebrae and popped my arms out of the sockets, leaving me too broken to crawl. So they troubled Old Bad-Ass again, asking him if he could support me with one hand under my waist.

Old Bad-Ass was fuming. "Fuck the lot of you," he said. "There's only one of him. Why do we need five people to carry him? You don't even need this many to carry a coffin."

The four migrant workers discussed it awhile, then said, "Please don't worry, Supervisor Bad, we've thought of a way."

Their way was for each of them to carry one of my limbs, while two shoulder poles were laid across my length and the rope tied around my stomach. It must have been a horrible sight, like they were carrying a bound pig or conducting some hideous form of torture that would tear my body in five directions. I was still down for the count, spraying puke along the road. It was a revolting scene, but it amused the onlookers. One of them smirked as he turned to Old Bad-Ass and said, "Hey, is your apprentice dead?"

"Fucking hell, where are your eyes, in your crotch?" Old Bad-Ass said. "Have you ever seen a corpse puke yellow water?"

Old Bad-Ass must have looked pretty damn commanding that day, swearing like a trooper as he made his way from the workshop to the infirmary with vigorous strides, his face flushed. Behind him, the four migrant workers carried the unconscious and vomiting young worker, chanting as they went, shuffling forward with small but rapid steps. The migrant workers were quite excited, telling everyone that they'd been so bored carrying water pumps around the factory all the time, and wasn't it good that today they were finally carrying something different. It reminded them of being back at home in the countryside, the merriment of carrying pigs during Spring Festival.

After I'd been delivered to the infirmary and laid down on the examination table, a female doctor appeared in her white gown. The doorway was still blocked by jeering onlookers.

"Doctor, give him mouth-to-mouth, then insert a catheter!" someone shouted.

"Shhhh, don't distract the doctor," someone else shouted. "She might get it wrong, stick the catheter in his mouth, and do mouth-to-mouth on his dick!"

This made the doctor furious. She took off her surgical mask. "All of you piss off right now!" she bellowed.

"Me as well?" Old Bad-Ass asked with a grin.

"Yes, you as well, you masochist! What do you think this is, a pump room? Now piss off."

Now I'll reveal that this was the girl in the white dress I'd been looking for all this time. Her name was Bai Lan. The first time I saw her I acted like a fuckwit, the second time I was unconscious. I hadn't given an impression she was likely to fall for, but it had been enough to make me fall for her.

Later Bai Lan regaled me with everything that had happened while I'd been unconscious, including the workers' jeering and troublemaking. I was mortified—still am to this day. Fuck, if I'd been given a blow job while having a catheter stuck down my throat, I'd never have lived down the shame.

The workers headed off, laughing and joking, and Bai Lan dealt with me briefly. First she took off my shirt and got me breathing again, then she gave me an injection. She opened my eyelids and looked into my eyes, used a metal stick to poke at my feet while I kicked my legs in enthusiastic response. I was stable, and there was no indication I was going to end up a vegetable. Bai Lan applied some ointment to my forehead. There was a lump the size of a pigeon egg there, tinged purple. After a while, I stopped puking and started to groan. Bai Lan went back to her office and phoned the safety department.

I had a dream that a huge water pump dropped down from the sky and smashed my head. It didn't kill me, which I felt very lucky about. In fact, I'd passed out and smacked my head on the water pump. Everything in the dream was the wrong way around.

I had a couple of other dreams that are a bit embarrassing to recall. After being hit by the water pump, I lay sprawled out on the ground. A girl with perky breasts and a pert bottom came over. I reached out and touched her, fully absorbed. In fact, I'd been taken to the infirmary, where the female doctor was opening my shirt—the person being touched was me. Everything in the dream was the wrong way around.

For some strange reason, I was taken to a classroom next, where the teacher said, "Welcome, class, this is the chemical factory vocational college." Unable to contain my joy, I rushed to shake hands with this teacher as if we were long-lost friends. I looked carefully and saw that he was in fact my senior middle-school form teacher. The reality was that I was alone in the infirmary, which was quiet as a morgue, stripped of my clothes and lying on an examination table like a corpse awaiting dissection. There was no vocational college and no form teacher. Everything in the dream was the wrong way around.

I woke up from this series of strange dreams with a splitting headache, feeling like my brain had been dug out of my head. It was a lovely afternoon, and the sun shone in through the window, lighting up the room. Through the window I could see the canopy of a camphor tree and behind it the factory smokestack, silently belching out its black smoke. Hadn't I been in the form-aldehyde workshop undoing screws? I tried to remember the chain of events. Where was I now? There was an office desk, a set of white drapes, and a painting on the wall of two figures: the one on the left had his stomach cut open and all his internal organs on display, while the one on the right had been skinned completely, revealing muscles that resembled bales of hay. These two mutilated people looked like they were staring at me, their arms open wide like Europeans expressing regret. Only then did I realize I was in a hospital, because only in a hospital did they display pictures like this one. Since the chemical factory smokestack was outside the window, I deduced that I was in the factory infirmary.

I noticed that my work uniform had been stripped off. I had on only an undershirt and my underwear. I crawled down from the examination bed and walked barefoot across the room. I noticed my crotch was bulging. It must have been my erotic dream. If I'd kept dreaming, I would have come. It would have been terrible. I pressed tentatively at the bulge, hoping to calm it down. The bulge didn't calm—it did the opposite, raising its head with even more gusto. I couldn't press at it again or people might think I was openly jerking off in the factory.

I walked around the room. I pulled open the drapes and peered around to discover another small room, with brilliant white walls and a reclining chair in the middle. This reclining chair was quite strange. It was similar to the chairs you'd find at the barber, but with two brackets at the front of the armrests. I couldn't understand what it was, so I walked over to it and sat down.

It was at this moment that Bai Lan, the factory doctor, walked in. "Does your head still hurt?" she asked when she saw I was awake.

"Yep," I said, taking my hand up to my forehead and giving it a rub. It hurt so much when I touched it that I leaped up, then fell back down on the recliner, which gave an odd creak.

"Oh! Do you have to sit there? Quickly, stand up!"

She spoke with so much authority that I felt I had no option but to stand up and expose the agitated central region of my body. At first she looked taken aback, then gave me a mocking look and said, "You're clearly young and healthy; the accident hasn't had too much impact."

I'd been on the wrong end of that mocking look once before—the time I'd hit my chin on the road.

"Oh, it's you," I said.

"So, the knock hasn't given you amnesia. That's good."

"So you're the factory doctor?"

"Yes, do you have a problem with that?"

I thought about it and said, "Why didn't you treat me the day I fell and hurt my chin?"

"I'd taken half a day off. I was finishing work early when I passed your stand. I'm only in charge of factory matters, and only when I'm actually at work. You fell in the alley, and you didn't pass out or anything." She paused and said, "Do I need to give you such a thorough explanation? Sit down on the examination bed."

I sat down obediently and she listened to my heartbeat through a stethoscope, asking me to breathe deeply.

"What's your name?" I asked.

"Bai Lan," she said. Her eyes fixed on a point on the floor as she moved the ice-cold stethoscope around my chest.

"My name's Lu Xiaolu," I said.

"I know. Don't speak, just breathe deeply."

After she'd finished the examination she said, "Everything's normal. But I'll have to keep you here awhile for observation. If you have any more vomiting and dizziness, you'll need to go to the hospital. And for the next few days, you should rest at home."

"Doctor Bai. Why didn't you let me sit on that chair just now?"

She threw me a glance and said, "Why do you talk so much crap?"

Later I got to know her better, but I had to ask again and again before she told me that the chair in question was called a gynecological examination chair, used for family planning checks. I hadn't seen anything like it at the time. If I'm being honest, I haven't seen anything like it since. I cleverly deduced that the two brackets were used to hold the woman's legs, which would mean that her most private organ would be tilted up to the sky. No, not the sky, the ceiling. Bai Lan used to tell me tons of confidential stories from the factory, like about women who had IUDs inserted. I was still young, and hearing stories like this used to turn me on a little. Bai Lan thought of me as a big menace, and a big, boring menace at that. Were matters such as IUDs worthy of such curiosity? She told me that the factory had only the one gynecological examination chair, and someone stupid enough to smack his head on a water pump could easily break it, which would leave all those women with no means to have their examinations, unless we found someone to hold their legs apart. Then she gave me a dirty look, as if I'd actually broken that chair and was now standing there holding women's legs open. I found what she said terrifying, but I was impressed by her imagination.

The gynecological examination room wasn't easy to get access to. That drape sectioned off any potential stimuli. I'd been pretty lucky to see the chair. Bai Lan told me that if I'd pulled open the drapes when the factory was performing gynecological examinations, I'd have been beaten to death. During gynecological examination season, men didn't dare go near the infirmary. If you had an accident during this time, you'd have to go to the clinic a mile down the road to get bandaged.

While she was examining me, I looked up at her face—I felt uninhibited, watching her closely, unflinchingly, thinking the opportunity was too good to waste. The contours of her face were symmetrical, and her big white coat made her look clean and neat, like a hospital doctor. It was hard to think of her as just a factory doctor. I saw something I hadn't noticed in her eyes before: a seriousness, but not in that fucking pretentious way of my senior middle-school teacher. Her eyes were clear too, but not in that frivolous schoolgirl way. She was very intent in her examination of me, her eyes resting on a certain spot on the floor. I wished that I was lying on that floor so her eyes would fall on me.

That would have made me feel very calm. It would have made me forget that I fixed water pumps for a living.

A little later, someone else joined us in the infirmary. He had hair like a chicken coop and thick-lensed glasses. I recognized him as Pu Nani from the safety department. He'd come over to assess the situation. He walked around me, then stared. I hated being the object of high-intensity, close-range staring. I felt like bacteria under a microscope.

"He's okay?" Pu Nani asked Bai Lan.

"Everything looks normal at the moment," she replied.

Pu Nani released a solemn breath of air from his nose, saying, "Do you know what, Lu Xiaolu? You've been violating work regulations, and you almost compromised everyone's safety bonus."

I was an apprentice at that point, with a lowly apprentice salary. I was aware that all official chemical factory staff received a safety bonus of about twenty yuan each month, unless someone had an accident, died, or was maimed, or if there was a fire or explosion in the factory. In any of those circumstances, all factory workers would have their safety bonus deducted. Which was to say that having an accident at work did not earn you much sympathy, just people trailing after you saying, "That's twenty yuan I'm down." You wouldn't get this sort of hassle if you died. At worst, you'd have people praying for you to be reincarnated as a pig. Twenty yuan would be the amount they'd pool toward your coffin anyway.

"How have I been violating the work regulations?" I asked Pu Nani.

"Weren't you violating the work regulations?" he asked.

"I inhaled formaldehyde and passed out—is that in violation of any regulations?"

Pu Nani thought about it and popped out a proverb, "A stitch in time saves nine."

"Have I violated any work regulations? Like hell I have."

If Bai Lan hadn't been there that day, Pu Nani and I would have come to blows. Pu Nani was scrawny and wore thick-lensed glasses, and beating up guys like that was my specialty. You whirled your fists at their glasses and smashed them, and then you could do what you liked. Pu Nani was so arrogant, he didn't even seem to realize he was shortsighted. When he pulled up his sleeves, squaring up to me, I was actually a little surprised. At school, I'd never come across such a brazen guy with glasses.

"If you are going to fight, do it outside the factory, not in my infirmary and not on factory premises," Bai Lan snapped.

"Alright then, let's take it outside," I said. "If the two of us fighting doesn't press your buttons, we could always call other people over for a brawl."

Pu Nani's hand shrunk back when he heard this. "Lu Xiaolu, you'll regret today," he said.

"Lu Xiaolu, are you aware of your status?" Bai Lan asked after he'd left.

"I know, I'm an apprentice bench worker."

"If an apprentice has a fight in the factory, they are dismissed immediately. Are you aware of that?"

I shook my head.

Bai Lan looked at me with that mocking expression. "He was inciting you to punch him. You're such an idiot, you naturally took the bait."

"I get it now. If we were fighting outside the factory, I wouldn't get fired, right?"

"It would be a social brawl then, nothing to do with the factory—unless you crippled the guy."

"You're really smart," I told her.

"Telling you things like this is only going to teach you bad ways," said Bai Lan. "You're still just an apprentice—how are you already such a menace?"

I told her I didn't understand why Pu Nani was so much more concerned about the safety bonus than the state of my head. What were his priorities? My head was only important to me, Bai Lan explained. For others, the safety bonus was the only visible, tangible thing.

"Is that the way you feel too?" I asked.

"Hell is other people," Bai Lan said. "Have you heard that saying?"

I told her I hadn't, but it sounded right on the mark. Not necessarily, Bai Lan said. She also suggested that I shouldn't think too badly of people. I considered it and said it was fair enough if everyone thought their own head was important, and other people's weren't worth twenty yuan. There were more than a billion people in China. If I had an accident and every single one of them had their twenty-yuan bonus deducted, that would be more than two fucking billion yuan, which was too much. They wouldn't get this money back even if they ran me over and killed me.

She looked at me very calmly as I said all this, as if I were talking crap. Then she said, "So you need to look after your own head."

As I was about to leave the infirmary, I realized I was only wearing my undershirt. I started looking around for my uniform. Bai Lan fished it out of a dirty tin bucket. I was dumbfounded to see it was covered in puke.

"People sometimes pee and shit themselves when they've been through what you went through," she said.

"Well, at least I didn't do that," I said with a sigh.

I asked Bai Lan if she could stick a piece of gauze on my forehead, because it hurt a lot. I didn't have a mirror to see exactly what the bump looked like, but seeing as I couldn't touch the area, it was obviously pretty bad.

"There's no need," Bai Lan said. "All you have is a big bump. As long as you don't touch it, you won't need gauze."

"Stick some on anyway," I said. "It'll make me feel better."

So she cut a section of gauze and taped it to my forehead, saying, "Now when you walk out into the factory, everyone will know you have a work injury."

"Yep, that's my intention."

I had an odd thought as I walked back into the factory. I wanted to have my work injury on display. First I'd grazed my chin, now I'd bashed my head and had a big bump on it and was walking around the factory with a patch of gauze stuck to me. I did this first because it made me feel cool, and second in the hope that I might get noticed by the cadres. Since I couldn't mend water pumps or lug around 130-pound barrels of raw material, all I had were my work injuries to prove I was a qualified worker. I hoped they'd feel so sorry for me that they'd send me off to vocational college.

Later I realized that this hope was misguided. Originally there was no concept of hope; it came into existence only because people hoped that it would. I'd seen people who'd had their fingers cut off by machines and had sulfuric acid sprayed in their face, and I realized that all a strip of gauze on the forehead did was incite mockery. It wouldn't bring me a glimmer of hope. Of course, I looked pretty damn cool, so you could say I achieved half my aim. As soon as my ma saw my head, the tears started to fall. Even then, I was unwilling to peel off the gauze. I kept it on until it was dirty and greasy and had caused a rash to spread over my bump. Then I had no choice but to go back to my former look.

After leaving Bai Lan's infirmary, I went straight to the tap and gargled with water, washing the acid taste from my mouth. Then I went back to the bench worker team. I wanted to smash that fucking water pump to pieces. Old

Bad-Ass cheerfully told me that the defunct water pump had started up again after I'd hit my head on it. So it was still where it had been, back in working order.

CHAPTER FOUR

LOVERS ON A

THREE-WHEELED ARK

Being Old Bad-Ass's apprentice naturally won me the approval of the attractive aunties. Old Bad-Ass took me to each pump room to show off my banged-up head, pointing to the gauze on my forehead and saying to the aunties, "Look, he really banged it up. He nearly died in the formaldehyde workshop." He told them that I had a magic head that had bashed the water pump back into working order. He'd been a bench worker for forty years, and it was the first time he'd seen anything like it. The aunties called me over lovingly. I was worried that, gushing with maternal instinct, they might be about to cradle my forehead to their bosoms. If word of this got out, I'd be seen as no different from Old Bad-Ass, another stinking shameless lowlife. I was lucky; all the aunties did was peel back the gauze, and when they saw my big bump they'd say, "Oh, it's purple," in an admiring way. Then they rubbed vegetable oil onto it, with the explanation that vegetable oil cured head bumps. The anointed area was pungent and greasy, and when I went to take a leak the flies buzzed nonstop around my head. I wondered where they'd gotten this vegetable oil. Over the next few days, the bump got smaller. They peeled away the gauze once more, saying, "It's much better and not purple anymore. Let's put a bit more vegetable oil on it."

One time I asked Old Bad-Ass why the pump-room aunties were all so pretty. The pump room was a high-ranking job, he explained. It didn't require manual labor. You spent all day pressing the red button and the green button. You went to work feeling relaxed, and you left feeling content. It was not a job for tigers. Tigers worked only as operators in the workshops. Pump rooms were always manned by those middle-aged women workers, fading beauties with residual charm.

When I was young, I used to feel very anxious around the attractive pump-room aunties. I hadn't yet identified this as a psychological blockage. Old Bad-Ass figured that by middle age I'd be like him, strutting amid a gaggle of pump-room aunties. For a bench worker, it was the best outcome you could expect. But I didn't like it. Maybe it was masochistic, but I preferred the company of the young department girls, those like Bai Lan, who were a bit cleaner, spoke about matters of substance, and had those clear eyes.

Many years later, I met a psychoanalyst. I asked her why I often dreamed that I was on my way to the pump room. I'd left the factory years before, and I no longer missed the young department girls. But I still had this fucking dream that I was carrying a wrench and silently following those winding corridors toward the pump room, where those attractive aunties would be awaiting me. Once I fixed the water pump, they'd take some sunflower seeds out of a drawer and give them to me. The psychoanalyst asked what the pump room looked like. Dark, I said, and humid, the hardest place in the factory to find. She told me that the pump room symbolized a vagina, that my dreams were sexual. My going to repair the water pumps was actually my longing to give these aunties sexual pleasure. Fucking hell, I thought, could that really be it?

Bai Lan told me that pump-room work wasn't as relaxing as I assumed. Being in such a damp, gloomy, cold place for so long gave you arthritis. This condition wouldn't affect you when you were young, but by the time you were old and sitting at home, you'd discover that your knees could forecast the weather. I'd seen pump rooms in winter, when there was only two hours of sunlight. In the cold corners, the ground was covered with a thin layer of shining white ice and the attractive aunties huddled together, shivering. Open flames were prohibited in the production zone, and steam pipes couldn't route through the pump room, so all winter long they had to hug hot water bottles to keep warm. This so-called feather-bed job really wasn't as relaxing as I'd thought. The aunties were like food items past their sell-by date, abandoned in the corner while allowed to enjoy a meager slice of freedom.

It was around that time that I bumped into a senior middle-school class-mate. He was working as a mechanic at the textile factory. We talked about factory aunties, and I told him the ones at the chemical factory were all pretty scary with their lipstick-coated lips, spitting out sunflower-seed shells all over the place, too lazy to pick off the ones hanging from their mouths. Then there was Ah Sao. *When Ah Sao's legs are splayed, all men should be afraid.* That was nothing, this classmate said—had I never met a textile-factory auntie? I told him I hadn't. According to him, the textile-factory aunties got their kicks by pinning their machine repair men to the floor. A big group of female workers would grab hold of his hands and feet and pull down his trousers. Then they'd get a scrap gearwheel and attach it to his dick. When the aunties turned the gearwheel, his dick would start to stand up. Then they'd sit back and watch how he managed to untangle himself from it. I stared at my classmate.

"Have they ever attached a gearwheel to you?" I asked.

He shook his head and sucked in a mouthful of cigarette smoke. "Not yet," he said bleakly. "But it won't be long."

After my infirmary altercation with Pu Nani, he'd taken to coming by the bench worker team regularly to look in on me. I was technically still an apprentice, but I'd passed my grade-four bench worker exam by then and was receiving a grade-four salary, plus half bonus. I'd cultivated a fervent interest in filing lumps of iron. It was an activity that didn't require any brainpower. You just took the different-size iron lumps and filed them into mah-jongg tiles and that was it, task done. This item had no practical use; I filed them solely for my own amuse-ment, wasting state property and my own energy. The one real benefit was that it improved my patience.

If Pu Nani came into the bench worker team and found no one else around, he'd stand behind me, watching for ages as I filed my iron lumps. I have this problem that I can't bear people standing behind me watching as I'm doing something; it makes my skin crawl.

So I banged my file down onto the workbench and said, "Like watching me, do you?"

"You shouldn't learn from your supervisor's roguish ways," Pu Nani said gravely.

"If you think he's a thug, just arrest him."

Pu Nani was speechless. As a safety department cadre, he wielded a lot of power and could arrest any worker who violated the safety regulations, deducting their bonus. But the bench worker team was notorious throughout the factory for being a team of hard-asses. They'd had experience with Japanese invaders and American imperialists. How could a man with the nickname Pu Nani be any kind of threat? We could let the air out of his bike tires in the bike shed, wait for him at the factory entrance, crack a stick down over his head, grab and throw him into the can. As long as we didn't actually kill him we could do what we wanted.

Pu Nani always told me that I'd fall into his hands one day. And what would happen when I did? I'd ask. But he had no answer. Sometimes he got tired of watching me and turned his attention to Wei Yixin instead. Wei Yixin was the college student who'd been sent to the workshops on an internship, and whenever he saw a cadre he reacted like it was a mafia member. All he could do was nod his head and say, "Officer L-L-Liu" (Pu Nani's surname was actually Liu, not Pu).

Pu Nani circled him with satisfaction. "Young Wei," he said, "living in murky waters without becoming muddied, that's laudable."

"You're such a dickhead," I told Pu Nani. "Always coming out with these pompous proverbs."

Wei Yixin's face went white from fright. "Officer L-L-Liu," he said. "W-w-what L-L-Lu Xiaolu is saying has n-n-nothing to do with me."

Pu Nani gave me a pat on the shoulders and strolled out of the shed.

"L-L-Lu Xiaolu, y-y-you shouldn't l-l-land me in the shit like that," Wei Yixin said.

"Oh, are y-y-you, are you still swimming in the sh-sh-shit now?"

We were just about to finish work one day when Pu Nani strolled into the bench worker area. All the workers were present. At the end of the workday when there was nothing to do, sometimes we'd wheel all our bikes in and line them up for a wipe-down. Old Bad-Ass was the most obsessed with his bike. He had a twenty-eight-inch Phoenix that he kept shiny, his bench worker's pride and joy. Whenever Old Bad-Ass wiped his bike, he'd tilt his head sideways and squint his eyes, as if he were giving the bike a massage. After he finished wiping it, he'd pick up his cup of tea, pop a cigarette in his mouth, and gaze over at his bike with an expression of weary satisfaction that looked uncannily postcoital.

We were in the middle of wiping our bikes when Pu Nani burst in. "Who said you could wipe your bikes during work hours?" he roared.

He realized no one was paying the slightest bit of attention. Supervisor Wonky Balls was the only one who seemed to be looking at him, but Wonky Balls' wonky head meant you couldn't tell for sure if he was looking at you or not. Besides, Wonky Balls was someone whose mind regularly wandered. If you wanted him to notice you, you had to readjust his wonky head so he was looking your way. Pu Nani was furious, but the target of his anger that day wasn't me.

"Wei Yixin, stand up!" he said.

Wei Yixin got to his feet feebly, saying, "Cadre L-L-Liu, I was wr-wr-wr-wrong."

"Control your girlfriend, Wonky Balls," one of the workers said loudly.

"Who are you saying is my girlfriend?" Wonky Balls asked, confused.

"Pu Nani, of course. You fuck Pu Nani, don't you, Wonky Balls?"

Wonky Balls started shouting and cursing when he heard this. Pu Nani was even more furious: "Who has the cheek to insult me with nicknames?"

No one paid him the blindest bit of attention; we were too busy laughing our heads off.

Pu Nani went along the row of bikes until he found Good Balls, the bench worker team leader, a burly, red-faced, incoherent man. Pu Nani grabbed him, saying, "I'm going to call the factory head and reinforce your team's discipline, particularly for novice apprentices."

Good Balls went red in the face and said, "Forget it, Liu, let's not make mountains out of molehills."

"Cleaning your bikes during work hours is unacceptable!" Pu Nani said. "It's a serious violation of work regulations."

Good Balls had no choice but to tell us to put away our bikes. I have to say that while the bench workers were a team of hard asses, our leader Good Balls was a complete lowlife, and putting a low-life in charge of a bunch of troublemakers was either a smart move or an incredibly dumb one.

Eventually we managed to curb our laughter and wheeled our bikes to the side. There was only one person left in the middle of that tin building, and that was Old Bad-Ass, sitting on a little folding stool, a smoke between his lips, looking at his bike and talking to himself as if no one else were around: "I've wiped you clean, and now I'll let you dry awhile."

"What's up with you, Old Bad-Ass?" Pu Nani asked.

"What do think of my bike-wiping technique?" Old Bad-Ass asked.

"Don't get glib with me."

"Why don't you call home and ask your wife to come over," Old Bad-Ass said. "I guarantee I'll give her as good a spit and polish as I've just given this bike."

Hell, did we laugh. We laughed ourselves silly. Pu Nani completely forgot he was a cadre and an intellectual.

"I'll fuck your wife, I'll fuck your wife, I'll fuck your wife," he screamed at Old Bad-Ass. We laughed so loudly that his weak little voice was completely obliterated. Old Bad-Ass was pure genius. He completely defeated Pu Nani the intellectual, reducing him to the level of a swearing match with a bench worker while niftily avoiding using any of those dull and commonplace verbal abuses himself.

Good Balls came to smooth things over and got Pu Nani to go back to his office. Pu Nani left and Good Balls was about to say something, but then the end-of-day work bell rang. Everybody jumped onto their bikes and disappeared in a cloud of dust. That was a glorious afternoon for us bench workers. We'd actually gotten one over on Pu Nani from the safety department. He may have been a low-rank cadre, unable to even make it to middle rank, but the experience still gave us a sense of honor and esteem. The bench workers were the most powerful trade team. *Power to the bench workers!* I felt dizzy with euphoria. I never even considered that Pu Nani might run to the labor department to complain about me and my appalling behavior.

Early that fall, I developed a crush on Little Pouty Lips. It wasn't a crush so much—I just liked her a little. She was slender, had a sharp nose and her naturally pouty lips, and when I was at the canteen getting food, I'd often see that sausagelike tail swaying at the back of her head. I plucked up the courage to go chat with her once, but when I walked over and looked at her, she didn't look back. It was as if I were made out of air. When a guy like me checked out a girl and she didn't take notice, there were only two explanations: 1) she was pretending she didn't notice, or 2) she was dumb.

When Pu Nani went to the labor department and made his complaint, he didn't tell them that Old Bad-Ass had shamed him in front of the whole bench worker team. There would be no point. So many people in the factory had been humiliated by Old Bad-Ass. What Pu Nani said instead was that I'd threatened him with a file in an extremely aggressive manner. The labor department considered it dangerous to have such an aggressive apprentice. They could just about tolerate having Old Bad-Ass around, but they didn't want to give him a chance to replicate. This matter was placed in Little Pouty Lips' hands. She called me into her office and made me stand in the window of the gun turret building as she gave me a tongue-lashing.

I've completely forgotten what Little Pouty Lips actually said when she was taking me to task. It's not just that I can't recall it now—I forgot it on the spot. All I can remember is her asking why I'd threatened Officer Liu with a weapon. I told her I hadn't threatened him with any weapon. Apparently he'd told her that I'd pointed a file at him. The silly office girl had obviously never even seen a file, as there was no way one of those things could ever be classified as a weapon. Next time I'd raise my sandal to Pu Nani instead: whipping that at his face would hurt more than any file, and it could never be called a weapon. Plus, my shoes stank.

That was when I had my crush on Little Pouty Lips, but it didn't last long. Her tongue-lashing wasn't a big deal. I wouldn't bear a grudge against a girl for that, but she frightened the hell out of me by saying she'd send me for labor education. I thought back to Ah San. The fact that the factory could recommend a person for labor education was pretty scary. Even my cousin was scared of labor education. Labor education and labor reform were not the same thing. For labor reform, you got a sentence. You could get twenty years, but once you'd done your time you were free to start over. With labor education they also locked you up, but it wasn't a sentence—they just didn't let you back out. There was no way of knowing how much longer you'd be inside. Hope and despair would blend together, and you'd go crazy. I couldn't have a crush on a girl who wanted to send me for labor education, even if she was only saying it for effect. If she'd said she wanted me killed by firing squad, that could have been seen as flirting. But labor education wasn't flirting. Labor education didn't have the slightest hint of romance; it was butt-naked realism. By threatening me with labor education, she was making two clear points: 1) she knew how to fuck me up, and 2) she could actually fuck me up.

There was a middle-aged man with graying hair sitting behind the next desk as I received this tongue-lashing. He said nothing, just looked at me with a blank face. It was only later when a cadre came in and greeted him as Manager Hu that I realized he was Hu Deli, head of the labor department. I'd heard him spoken about a lot. There was a factory saying: *Hu Deli and Old Bad-Ass, both just as fearful as the other. One will get you with the rule book; the other will fuck your mother.* Neither was to be messed with, basically. I felt like the main character in a video game. If I got rid of the minor baddies like Pu Nani and Little Pouty Lips, the big bosses would jump out from behind them. But my life bar was almost running out—any minute I was going to see the words *Game Over.*

Supervisor Old Bad-Ass had a daughter called Ah Ying. She was in her thirties and unmarried. She was strange-looking, with a thick neck and a narrow face that made her look like a hyperthyroid sufferer. Because of our link through Old Bad-Ass, we should have been like brother and sister, but the two of us were never close. To use Old Bad-Ass's own aesthetic terminology, his daughter was a tiger with the *T* crossed and *I* dotted.

Ah Ying also worked at the chemical factory, where she had a neat job overseeing the wastewater treatment. Her daily work consisted of sprinkling powders and potions into the polluted water in a couple of swimming-pool-size ponds of wastewater in order to break down the toxic components. This wastewater was then released into the river. It was a relaxing job—no one checked up on the quality of her work. If she'd wanted to, she could have discharged that wastewater directly into the river, which already smelled so funky you couldn't find a single mosquito there.

Old Bad-Ass had a twenty-eight-inch Phoenix bike. Later, scooters became popular, but they were quite primitive at first. Fitting a motor onto the back wheel of a bicycle would get it running at motorbike speeds. This vehicle was very dangerous: if it went too fast, the wheels could fly off in a similar style to when I fell in front of Bai Lan. Only it wouldn't just be a grazed chin—your entire jaw could fly off in the crash. Old Bad-Ass was the factory's number-one bench worker, and with his extraordinary skills, he was also ahead of the game with his bike-to-scooter conversion, giving his already sizable prestige an even bigger boost. His bike would belt out black smoke and shriek like a bomb carrier. Old Bad-Ass had become a Hells Angel, screaming along in a fog of black smoke. Ah Ying initially rode to work on her own bike, but later started to feel that Old Bad-Ass's bike was flashy and had the celebrity factor fitting for a flamboyant older girl like herself, so she got her pa to take her to work on it. We'd often see Old Bad-Ass, nearing sixty, racing along the road and whooping as he went, carrying a girl behind him. It would have made a pretty romantic scene had the girl not been his daughter. She wore sunglasses just for show, and she had a synthetic leather satchel slung across her body, which made her look like the bad girl in a road movie. I'd ridden his bike, but it went too fast and the seat was too high; all you were resting on was a steel wire and triangular frame (it was just a bicycle, after all). I rode halfway around the factory before feeling that my nerves couldn't take it. I was too scared to squeeze the brakes in case I flew off.

Each morning, the bridge by the entrance to the factory would transform into a vegetable market. All the vegetable growers from the suburbs brought along their produce and set up stalls, packing the place. As soon as these vendors heard the shriek of Old Bad-Ass coming full throttle on this makeshift motorbike, they'd pick up their carrying poles and run like crazy, shouting, "Oh, shit, the bandit bike's back again!" Scenes like this gave Old Bad-Ass even more street cred. Unfortunately, the prestige didn't last long. The bike's motor soon malfunctioned, and after that it broke down regularly. You'd often see Old Bad-Ass peddling his heavy bike, motor attached, on his way to work. This was extremely grueling, especially with his brat of a daughter on the back seat shouting abuse at him.

Old Bad-Ass told me that after he retired, he planned to ride this bike around the whole country.

"Supervisor, at your speed that will take less than a week," I said. I knew that this was his dream, that everyone had dreams. I wanted to travel around the whole country too, maybe even the whole world. Not riding a makeshift scooter, of course. You'd only need to hit a pebble and you'd be catapulted all the way to America.

After its inception, Old Bad-Ass's bike underwent a number of transformations. The final version had gears and five speeds and, apart from the fact it wouldn't reverse, was fairly similar to a Santana. He also fitted it with a clear acrylic sheet to act as a windshield and gave it an electric horn. The horn wasn't strictly necessary, since he never did resolve the bike's noise problem. But the whole thing looked impressive. He'd planned to fit two bikes together to make a three-wheeled motorbike. But he never worked out what to do about the axles on the back wheels, which would need to be lengthened to fit the bikes together. After some thought, he decided that the renovation costs were too high and that two wheels were a better value. He promoted his motorbike technology throughout the factory, and lots of people came to him to get their bikes converted. He'd take a three-hundred-yuan installation fee, and the client provided the parts.

Factory workers began having accidents left, right, and center from these bikes. First, Old Xu from the plumbing team broke his clavicle. Then Fatty Zhang from the saccharin workshop flew off into the river. Next, Stone Balls from the bench worker team crashed headlong into a house. Finally, the local police station called in Old Bad-Ass and ordered him to stop his accident-inducing behavior, fining him two thousand yuan for vending without a license and wiping out his bike repair stand.

I had a good relationship with Old Bad-Ass, but it wasn't the typical bond between supervisor and apprentice—more like between working-class thugs. I didn't learn a thing from him; I couldn't mend a water pump or assemble a bike. But I knew the basics about being a worker, which were pretty vital. According to Old Bad-Ass, people who couldn't even get by in the factory starved to death in the real world. He was upset after his bike stand was confiscated and he'd had to pay out all his money in compensation; his once-mighty ego deflated almost overnight. He grabbed me and, without a hint of shame, said, "Xiaolu, for just two thousand yuan, I'll share my scooter technology with you. You'll make back the capital in two weeks."

"Supervisor," I said sadly, "you forget that I can't even fix a bike."

I'd been to Old Bad-Ass's riverside bungalow in Donkey Alley. There were a lot of rivers in Daicheng, but these so-called riverside houses weren't houses built along the river bank so much as houses built *in* the river, their foundation stones sitting on the riverbed floor. You went in and out through the front door, and the back door opened straight out onto the river. If you lowered a pail, you could scoop up water. These were known as "houses snuggled to the river," with *snuggled* being the operative word. There was a spate of unfortunate incidents at that time. One household was broken into. Luckily the owner came back in time and blocked the front door, yelling: "Catch that thief!" The thief, who wasn't from Daicheng, was unaware of the quirk these houses shared. He pulled open the back door and ran headlong into the river. Someone on the other side of the river said that all he saw was the thief's outline as he soared downward, drawing a majestic arc through the air. A cargo ship happened to be passing, and the thief smacked down onto its deck. He cried out loudly, holding his leg—a fractured tibia, probably. A couple of the crew came over, tied him up, and shoved him in the cabin. All these cargo ships headed far away to north Jiangsu and Anhui, and their crews were known for being avid fighters. Falling into their hands was extremely bad luck.

Old Bad-Ass's house had a low-roofed kitchen on the outside and two bedrooms on the inside, one for him and his wife, the other for Ah Ying. The river water stunk of rot and diesel oil. This smell wafted into the house, along with the roaring of cargo ship engines. Living in these conditions for years on end would turn you into a cantankerous bastard, prone to starting fights for no good reason and suffering from severe hormone imbalance. Their whole family lived there. Old Bad-Ass had nowhere else to go, and Ah Ying had no one to marry.

Old Bad-Ass was fast asleep one night when he was knocked out of bed by a big boat. He opened his eyes to see that his house had a big gaping hole in it, and penetrating that hole was the front end of a huge fucking boat. It was the stuff of nightmares, the kind of experience a tough bastard like Bad-Ass shouldn't have had. The most fucked-up part was that the drunken skipper didn't just refuse to apologize; he actually poked his head through the hole and laughed at Old Bad-Ass, his breath reeking of alcohol. Ah Ying ran through wearing a T-shirt and shorts and gave a high-pitched shriek when she saw what was happening. The boatman saw a semi-naked girl, and because it was dark and he was drunk, he didn't notice how ugly she was—all he cared about was having bare arms and thighs to leer at. Old Bad-Ass jumped to his feet, picked up a stool, and smashed it down on the boatman's laughing head, knocking him into the water. Three or four big guys proceeded to jump from the boat, all of them drunk and holding bamboo boat poles. The front ends of these poles were encased in metal and could double as lances. Old Bad-Ass was poked in the mouth by one—it knocked out his four front teeth. He was lucky, really. If they'd run it into his body, he would have had a hole bored right through him. He turned to run for his life, but he tripped over the doorstep and fell flat on his face.

A couple of the boatmen reached the shore (actually Old Bad-Ass's bedroom). They went berserk, smashing up all the furniture left in the room, then accosting Ah Ying. Ah Ying was a notorious tiger, unable to bag a husband, but not so desperate as to let these boatmen get their wicked way. She gave a flying kick at one man, busting his balls, and bit savagely at another one's shoulder, clamping down so forcefully that she actually ripped off a chunk of his bicep. The boatmen were enraged. They punched her in the eye and were about to lance her with a pole, but the room was too small and the roof too low, which made turning a long bamboo pole around a tricky maneuver. Ah Ying took her chance. She wriggled out of their clutches and screamed for help, summoning all the surrounding neighbors. The neighborhood detested these boatmen, but could usually never do anything about it. Finally they had several in their grasp, thugs and rapists among them. The neighbors descended on the men en masse, feeling safe in the darkness where no one could see their faces, punching away at them, punching and punching until a police car finally arrived.

Old Bad-Ass's house was totally flattened during the brawl. The few household appliances they'd owned had fallen into the river, which was a serious loss. Old Bad-Ass was taken to the hospital, but his four front teeth couldn't be saved. He'd broken a couple of ribs too. Ah Ying was rumored to have been raped by one of the boatmen. It was also said that she'd busted one of the guy's balls and bitten another's arm very badly. The usual chemical factory lies. Next they were saying she'd bitten off one man's testicle, chewed it for a bit, then swallowed it down.

Old Bad-Ass's wife never materialized during this invasion. When the ship crashed into their house, she'd been so scared she'd passed out. When she finally came to, she discovered that the place had been reduced to a pile of rubble, and she fainted again.

I went to the hospital to visit Old Bad-Ass, taking a bag of apples with me. I saw Ah Ying fighting with a nurse in the entrance to the ward. Her left eye was bruised from being punched by the boatman, but this didn't stop her from hitting the nurse. She grabbed the young nurse by the hair, then took her sandals off and whacked them furiously against the girl's head. While the nurse was screeching and crying, there was actually a round of applause from the surrounding patients. I lunged forward and threw my arms around Ah Ying, lifting her clean off the ground. Eventually she let go of the nurse, who ran away as fast as she could, wailing like an ambulance. Ah Ying was left behind making threatening clawlike gestures and waving her slippers around. The crowd of patients who'd been watching started praising me, telling me that I really knew what I was doing. What the fuck did they know? What I'd done was take a huge risk. When Ah Ying went crazy, it didn't matter who you were. Anyone who tried to mediate could potentially get caught in the crossfire. No one dared intervene when she got into fights in the factory; they just waited until she'd worn herself out, then took her by the waist and dragged her off. By grabbing hold of her at the height of her frenzy, I could have met with a similar fate to that boatman—she could have kicked me into eunuch-hood.

I carried her into the ward, where she started to calm down. Old Bad-Ass was horizontal on his bed. He opened his toothless mouth and gave a chuckle. He didn't answer any of my questions, just pointed at his mouth and smiled like a dimwit.

"He's not stupid," Ah Ying said. "He doesn't want to speak because he's got a lisp."

I asked her why she'd been fighting with the nurse.

"The little bitch was threatening to move him to a bigger ward, one with eight people. Did I have any choice?"

Old Bad-Ass didn't want to speak; he just listened as Ah Ying recounted that night's battle. She made herself out to be incomparably brave, biting down on one man's shoulder when landing a flying kick to another guy's balls. If she only knew the rumors about her that were flying around, she probably wouldn't have been looking so pleased with herself. Suddenly I remembered my apples—I'd put the bag down in the corridor to intervene in the fight. I went back out to the corridor to get them, only to discover a couple of patients, their arms in slings and plaster, each with an apple in hand, crunching away. They looked at me with these fucking grins on their faces. *What kind of people were these?* I asked myself.

And that nurse. On my way out of the ward, I passed the duty office and noticed her in there crying, a group of nurses gathered around to comfort her. I liked nurses—their clean white coats were so different from my work uniform that was neither-blue-nor-green, grubby as a clay monkey. I approached her and explained that I was the one who freed her from those tiger claws. I didn't expect her to start sobbing in gratitude and throw herself at my chest or anything, but she might have thanked me at least. Instead the whole group of nurses pointed at me and said, "Get out! Get the hell out! You're a bunch of saccharin factory scum."

I fled. This wasn't an orthopedic hospital after all, but a fucking mental hospital.

While Old Bad-Ass was in the hospital, I had to go dismantle the water pipes on my own. I'd now done this hundreds of times, and I no longer needed him there. One day when I was working, that big asshole Xu from the trade union came looking for me.

"We're going to the hospital this afternoon," he said.

"What for?" I asked.

"To give your supervisor a sendoff."

"Is he dead?" I asked.

"Don't talk shit. Sending him off to an honorable retirement," Big Asshole Xu said.

That afternoon I found myself sitting in the back of a van with a dozen or so young workers banging away at their drums and gongs as we drove to the hospital. That's what retirement was like in those days: pretty intense, with gongs and drums clamoring to high heaven. The sound of the percussion was supposed to signify that all your life's great achievements were over. Old Bad-Ass had beaten up a workshop director and been inappropriate with attractive aunties—truths that all were just accepted. From now on, he'd be an old man who played mah-jongg all day, every day, until he could play no more.

I didn't beat any drums that day. The trade union cadre got me to hold a framed certificate for Old Bad-Ass's honorable retirement, which looked like an award. I carried this into the hospital as if it were Old Bad-Ass's funeral portrait. The rest of the entourage seemed jubilant—only I wore a mournful expression. If my inner life was a world, Old Bad-Ass had just died there. It was sunny that day, no clouds as far as the eye could see. It was his sixtieth birthday.

A lot of things happened in the fall of 1992, but I can't remember any of them. Everything in my mind was murky, like a silent movie with ghostly figures appearing on the screen. Time actually had a fairly decent quality. Through time, those you loved and those you hated all turned into ghostlike shadows, flitting in and out of your memory without rhyme or reason.

Spring was always very wet, but that fall there were twelve days of solid rainfall. This caused the river to rise and was the reason why Old Bad-Ass's house got rammed by a cargo ship. Before that happened, the factory had flooded. The saccharin factory was fairly low-lying, and once the river rose over a certain level, there was a backflow of gutter water that would spray up like a fountain. This water was dirty and rancid. If you'd actually dared to take a sip, you would have found it tasted both sweet and spicy—the sweetness was from the saccharin, and the spice from who knows what. The formaldehyde, perhaps, or the fertilizer. The reason for this backflow was the saccharin factory discharging its wastewater into the river. Each year when this happened, we went on mandatory leave.

During the flood season, the streets were also submerged with river water, and as it receded, a layer of black sludge was left behind on the road. River fish would occasionally swim into the factory, and I once caught a silver carp a foot long in there. Old Bad-Ass told me it wasn't a river fish, but one that had escaped from a countryside pond. There weren't any fish near the factory—just rats, rats, and more rats. Old Bad-Ass warned me not to eat this fish because it was contaminated by all the pollution and chemicals. I decided not to listen to him for once and took home the fish to make a stir-fry. While I was frying it, the smell of kerosene wafted up from the wok. Not even the stray cats would touch it.

Each time these floods happened, factory production would halt and the workers were sent back home while a handful of cadres were kept on duty. Straw bags and laundry bags were placed around the workshops, and a couple of water pumps inside worked around the clock to pump out the flood water.

While all the other workers enjoyed their time off, the bench worker team took turns on duty. Those pumps needed to be monitored constantly when in action, so any problems could be dealt with right away. Good Balls and Old Bad-Ass were on duty that day, and as their apprentices, Wei Yixin and I were naturally there with them. We all sat at the bench worker team table playing cards, rainwater dripping onto our heads and stinking water covering our feet. Wei Yixin was the best at cards. He may have had a stammer, but his memory was amazing and he could memorize all the cards. When Old Bad-Ass suggested making it interesting, Wei Yixin didn't object, and I didn't want to look like a wimp. As soon as we started gambling, Wei Yixin started to lose; he lost so badly that his face went pale. The factory rules were that the person who won at gambling had to treat the others to a meal. All three of us won, so we put our money together to get Wei Yixin a popsicle, which Good Balls offered to go and buy. Good Balls was hard-working and typically took on all the dirty, tiring jobs, which was how he managed to make it to team leader. He went out wearing his sandals.

"Watch you don't step on any electric cables," Old Bad-Ass warned. "You could get electrocuted."

Good Balls reassured him that the electricity supply had been shut down; he'd be fine.

Good Balls returned carrying a couple of popsicles. His face was pale and his legs were shaking. We discovered that he'd sliced open one of his legs on a sharp object, and blood was gushing from a foot-long gash. Old Bad-Ass said he needed to go straight to the infirmary to have it bandaged, but we weren't sure if Doctor Bai was on duty or not. The three of us carried Good Balls, wading through the fetid water all the way to the infirmary building. I saw that the window was open.

"Doctor Bai! Doctor Bai!" I shouted up.

Bai Lan stuck her head out of the window, saw it was me, and said, "What have you done this time?"

I cheerfully told her that there was nothing wrong with me this time—it was Good Balls who'd been injured.

We carried Good Balls up the stairs. Bai Lan took one look at him and said he needed to go to the hospital. It was at this critical moment that Wei Yixin suddenly fell to the floor. His face was pale and he was sweating profusely. Just before he fell he said, "Lu Xiaolu, I faint at the sight of blood."

Blood phobia is a strange phenomenon. Perfectly robust people will fall down as if having an epileptic fit. It makes no difference whether it's a refined lady or a brawny guy; they're both equally likely to be affected. I'd seen Monkey Wang from the plumbing team in a fight. He'd grabbed a red-hot lump of coal and pressed it against his opponent's face (while wearing leather gloves himself). This wasn't just a scuffle—it was like a fight between lawless bandits of old. He'd also bragged about smacking a pregnant woman over the head with a brick. He scared us all to death, and no one dared to mess with him. Then we had our factory medical examination, and everyone lined up to have their blood taken. As soon as Monkey Wang saw those blood-filled syringes he crumpled to the floor, the people around him dying of laughter. That taught us that there was no correlation between whether someone fainted at the sight of blood and their level of brutality. Or, to put it another way: just because someone faints at the sight of blood doesn't mean they won't grab a hot coal and press it against your face.

Old Bad-Ass was furious with Wei Yixin for falling over in the infirmary, and he trampled on his face in his sandals. Wei Yixin didn't give any response, not even a grunt. We had to lay him out on the gynecological examination chair—Good Balls was occupying the examination bed, so there was nowhere else for him to go.

"This no-good piece of shit, playing dead at the moment it matters. No wonder he got accepted into college!" Old Bad-Ass said.

Bai Lan looked extremely unimpressed with Old Bad-Ass's savagery. She explained that Wei Yixin's problem wasn't serious but that Good Balls' was, and we needed to get him to the hospital for emergency treatment. She tied a whole roll of gauze around Good Balls' calf, but it soaked through red in no time.

"Lu Xiaolu, what's wrong with you?" Bai Lan said, pointing at me.

"Me?"

"Why are you just standing there like a rabbit in the headlights? Quick, lift him up!"

I looked at Old Bad-Ass. "Don't look at me," he said. "Production's halted today, the riggers are all at home."

I phoned the driving team and asked for a car. A driver told me not to count on it—water had gone up all the factory vehicles' exhaust pipes, and none of them were starting. The only one that hadn't been drenched was a ten-ton truck. "If you want to have a go at it, you can drive it yourself," he said dryly.

I called him a motherfucker, then raced down the stairs and found a pedicab. Bai Lan got in with Good Balls and covered him with her raincoat. Old Bad-Ass was about to get in the pedicab too, but I said, "Supervisor, if you get in, the thing will topple over."

"You stay here and look after Wei Yixin," Bai Lan told him. "Take his work clothes off and let him get some fresh air, and he'll be fine. There's no point in your coming to the hospital as well."

So we left Old Bad-Ass in the infirmary looking after Wei Yixin. Afterward Wei Yixin told us that Old Bad-Ass had been a complete sicko. It was clearly the first time he'd seen the gynecological examination chair, and he thought it would be funny to pull off Wei Yixin's shirt and place his legs in the brackets. Then Old Bad-Ass just sat there, smoking and getting off on the situation. The on-duty cadres in the factory heard there had been an incident and ran to the infirmary to find out what had happened. There they found Wei Yixin, chest bare and legs akimbo. They were telling people it was the most disturbing thing they'd ever seen.

Meanwhile I was speeding our pedicab through the streets. The water was so deep, it felt like being in a speedboat.

"You sit tight," I told Bai Lan, "I can't see the road ahead clearly, and I don't want to flip you out."

"Stop talking crap," Bai Lan retorted. "You dare slow down and it'll be me flipping you out." Then she said, "Actually, take care of yourself—you don't want to bash up your chin again."

I was focused on driving the pedicab when she said that, so I didn't see if she was smiling or not.

I sometimes think back over this scene: the rain pelting down, no people on the streets, no boats in the river, just us zooming along in that pedicab. Whenever I think about it I have to remind myself that it happened in 1992. That confuses me, because it feels like something that happened a long, long time ago. Say it had happened in prehistoric times, and we were in Noah's Ark—then my falling in love with Bai Lan would have been destiny because there was no one else to love, only her. She hadn't been thinking things like that. All she'd been thinking about was saving Good Balls' life. I wanted to tell her that there actually were no other girls in my life to love, and that's why I loved her. Did that diminish my love for her? Or make it more genuine?

I was in a real state by the time we reached the hospital. My legs were shaking, and my waist felt as if it had been snapped in half. I haven't mentioned yet that this pedicab was a piece of shit. The seat cushion felt like it was made of metal, and my crotch was in agony as I drove. I must have looked like a woman on her period with my shorts covered in blood.

The hospital was quiet. A couple of figures lingered at the emergency room entrance. The hospital was close to the chemical factory, but it was very run-down. There was no ramp to the emergency room, so we couldn't access it in the pedicab. I had to help Good Balls down. He was suffering from shock, his lips were pale, and he had drool dangling from his chin. Bai Lan helped him onto my back, and I carried him up to the emergency room.

"Why does Good Balls feel so heavy?" I asked Bai Lan. "My grandma once told me that dead people become heavier. Is Good Balls dying? I really don't want him to die on my back."

"If you don't want to him to die, move faster," she roared.

I carried Good Balls into the emergency room, and Bai Lan went in with him. I sat alone on the steps outside the waiting room, gasping for breath— Good Balls was a fat bastard weighing about two hundred pounds, and I felt like my heart was about to explode. A little later, Bai Lan came out and sat beside me. I was wearing my work uniform, and Bai Lan had on a cream-colored shirt. We were both soaked through from the rain, the only difference being that I looked like a sewer rat and Bai Lan looked like a girl out of an erotic magazine, her shirt clinging to her body and her white bra visible underneath. The size of her breasts was nothing to write home about. But the overall picture was stunning.

I took a smoke out my pocket, but the pack was soaked. Bai Lan ran over to the little shop by the entrance, braving the rain, and bought me a pack of smokes and a plastic lighter. Then she ran back. I sat on the steps like an old pervert, unable to take my eyes off the way her clothes clung to her body. She tapped a smoke out from the pack and stuck it in her mouth like a natural. The rest of the pack she gave to me. She stayed there by my side.

"So you smoke too?" I asked.

"Not regularly, just when I'm bored."

"How's Good Balls?"

"Being treated, he should be okay." Gesturing at my lighter with her chin, she said, "Don't you know to light a cigarette for a girl?"

Obediently, I lit the cigarette. She inhaled deeply and exhaled a thin wisp of smoke from the gap between her lips.

"I'm so sorry," I said. "I'm an apprentice bench worker. I don't even know 'ladies first.' All I know is that on the road, you should give a *lady* the right of way, but boy, are there a lot of *ladies* on the road. If you gave them all the right of way, you'd never get anywhere."

Bai Lan tilted her head and looked at me. "Lu Xiaolu, you're really something," she said.

"What does *really something* mean?" I asked.

"It just means that being a bench worker who knows about *ladies first* is pretty impressive." She patted the back of my head and said, "That was a close one, Xiaolu. Good Balls nearly died."

I asked her how Good Balls could be so feeble that a simple cut on the leg had nearly finished him off.

"He lost too much blood," Bai Lan said. "How can you be so medically unaware? Oh, I forgot—you're a bench worker."

We talked a little about people dying. I told her that my cousin had a friend who'd gone out looking for a fight, and he ended up being stabbed in the thigh with a knife. They'd stabbed through into his artery, and he very nearly died. This was probably what she'd been saying about losing too much blood. While taking the safety instruction class, I'd seen a wall of photographs of dead people, all of whom had died too easily. Pu Nani told me it was a case of probability, but the way I saw it, it came down to luck. Even a murderer couldn't catch a lucky person, while those who had bad luck would die from a simple cut on the leg.

"You're one of the lucky ones," Bai Lan said, giggling. "You hit your head on a water pump and were just fine. In fact, you actually managed to fix the water pipe that way."

The way she was patting my head felt lovely, and I thought to myself, doctors are just doctors—when they pat you, it's neither too light nor too heavy. It feels damn near perfect. If only I could be patted by her like this forever.

In a while a doctor came out and asked Bai Lan to sign a form. She turned around and went off to deal with the doctor without another word to me. I sat outside on my own, feeling deathly cold. I took off my work uniform and my shirt and wrung out the water, then sat there bare-chested, chain-smoking.

About an hour later, a minivan arrived from the factory and two cadres jumped out. When I saw the van being driven by Supervisor Cao from the driving team, I started seething.

"Who the fuck answered the phone, Old Cao?" I shouted through the car window. "Wasn't it only a ten-ton truck you had?"

With a cigarette between his lips, Supervisor Cao grinned at me and said, "It's got shit-all to do with me."

I stared at him, wanting to lunge and beat him. But I was too exhausted. I couldn't have beaten up anyone. All I could do was express my anger through my eyes. I wouldn't actually have dared to hit Supervisor Cao. He was the big boss of the driving team and a senior working-class thug, just like Old Bad-Ass. He'd had as many apprentices and apprentice descendants as a cow has hairs on its back, and you'd be a dimwit to offend someone like that. Normally he chauffeured the factory head, and the factory head wouldn't have let me get away with beating him up. Seeing Supervisor Cao made me realize that bench work really was worthless. The drivers were the real nobility among the workers.

The two cadres went toward the emergency room. I thought they might ask me about the situation, even tell me what a good job I'd done, but they seemed not to even see me. I jumped into the minivan, offered Supervisor Cao a smoke, curled up on the back seat, and fell asleep. I slept really deeply, and had lots of vivid dreams. Then I felt someone prodding me.

"Ma," I shouted, thinking it was her. From beyond the horizon of my drowsy world, I heard a snigger. I opened my eyes and saw Bai Lan.

I sat up and looked at her stupidly. The sky was gloomy, the rain still falling. I'd slept for an entire afternoon, and when I woke up everything seemed topsy-turvy. From inside that upside-down space, inside my broken consciousness, I saw her. Her face was flushed not from shyness, but from heat.

The van's engine shuddered. The two cadres were sitting in the front, but all I could see was the back of their heads.

"Are we leaving?" I asked Bai Lan.

She nodded. "We're heading back now. Zhao Chongde is stable."

"Well, that's good," I said.

"Lu Xiaolu," Bai Lan said in a very, very gentle voice. "The pedicab's still at the hospital entrance. You need to drive it back to the factory."

CHAPTER FIVE

BAI LAN

Bai Lan's infirmary was in a redbrick two-story building two hundred yards from the labor department office building. The infirmary was at the end of the second-floor corridor, past the union, the youth league branch, the library, and the family planning office. Bai Lan was in the end room all on her own.

The workers referred to this as the "little red building." It had been built in the 1950s and originally used as the factory office, but later, when it was no longer big enough for that purpose, they built a five-story office tower. This little building with its forty-year history had been constructed without frills. It had cement flooring and poorly lit corridors. But it was sturdy, one of the features shared by all the buildings from that era: earthquake-proof, water-proof, and explosion-proof. You could see the faint outline of early slogans on the walls, limestone brushed with large boldface characters: *The working class lead* . . . The rest of the characters could not be read clearly. I'd seen the same slogan in my father's factory, so I knew the rest: . . . *everything. Everything* was an empty reference, really. What it actually meant was that they lead nothing. I'd pondered this question before. I'd looked at the workers around me—Old Bad-Ass, Wonky Balls, and all the attractive aunties—and they were a ragtag bunch. Asking them to lead everything was a complete joke. I was a worker too, but I knew I couldn't lead everything—not even a fraction of everything, not a chance. I was nineteen at the time, and I followed all the orders I was given. The rest of the time, I'd stand at the bottom of the small red building, staring up at the infirmary window in a daze.

I inquired about Bai Lan and gathered a few snippets of information about her through the workers' network. I'd found out that she'd studied at Beijing Medical College. No one knew why, but she'd been expelled from there and forced to return to Daicheng to work as the saccharin factory doctor. There weren't many rumors about her in the factory because she tended to keep to herself and didn't cavort with boys. She was twenty-three and very pretty— logically speaking, she should have had a boyfriend, or at least a swarm of boys around her. It wasn't like this didn't happen in the factory: Little Pouty Lips was constantly surrounded by young men from different departments. They'd bring her food, chat with her—she was never allowed to be on her own. If she wanted to be alone, the only way would be to go to the restroom. She was like a damsel surrounded by her white knights. But Bai Lan didn't have anyone. She was isolated, cheerless, and haughty, and normally she spent her time hidden away in the infirmary reading a book. When it was time to get lunch, she'd ask Hai Yan from the library to bring her back something. She didn't use the factory bathhouse to wash. As soon as she finished work, she rode her Flying Pigeon home. That was just the way she was, hanging alone at the end of that dark little corridor like a grafted fruit in a season where there were no flowers or fruit. It was as if she'd been forgotten by the factory. An apprentice like me, who wasn't on any medication and didn't need any injections or gynecological examinations, shouldn't really have gotten the chance to meet her, but fate had insisted on dirtying her bike and bashing my head, and so meet her I did.

She had very little to do in the infirmary. The family planning office brought in another doctor for the annual gynecological examinations, so she didn't need to lift a finger for that. Most of the time she was just in charge of the more commonly used medicines: cold tablets, isatis root, berberine, and so on. Everyone knew these medicines weren't very effective but wouldn't kill you. Of course, she did have one responsibility, which was to give the factory workers emergency treatment—unfortunate wretches like me and Good Balls. But this kind of work was completely random, half-dead people passing into her hands. If she accidentally killed them, it wouldn't be her fault. She hadn't actually graduated from college, so I'm not sure how she'd managed to sneak her way into the factory.

Factory doctors weren't to be trusted, in my father's opinion. They were extremely hard to please. When you needed them as a doctor, they'd say they were workers; but if you ordered them around like workers, they'd tell you they were doctors. Having two sides to her identity, both of which could serve her, made Bai Lan, in my experience, pretty difficult to date. The doctor my pa dealt with at the pesticide factory was an old man who'd been a barefoot doctor during the Great Leap Forward, and he had no real medical skills. He also lacked courage. There was a female worker who'd had sulfuric acid splashed on her chest and was brought to the infirmary. She should have had her clothes cut off and been doused in water. The old man clearly knew the first aid procedures, but he was unwilling to strip off her clothes. All he did was look at her chest while desperately wringing his hands. At that moment he didn't feel he was a doctor, he felt he was just a fucking man, and a morally upright man at that. Everyone in Pesticide New Village knew about this, and even the most uneducated old ladies said he wasn't really a doctor—only a man no one could respect.

I met Bai Lan completely by chance. She hadn't just stripped me in the infirmary. She'd also moved around a stethoscope over my chest. When we became closer, she started to give me dietary advice, predicting that I'd have a beer belly by my thirties, and advising me to eat less pig offal and drink less cola. If you think this is what a doctor should be doing, you're very, very wrong. She was only a factory doctor, and a factory doctor should be like the old man at the pesticide factory, displaying nothing but moral decency. Whoever died as a result was not their concern.

Once the flood water receded from the factory, I went back to work. I saw that the infirmary window was closed and knew she wasn't there. I didn't give up, though. I went to take a look. The infirmary door was closed. Hai Yan from the library next door told me Bai Lan had a fever and was resting at home. I walked back down the dark corridor wistfully and lit a smoke. I thought about the way she looked with her cigarette, that thin wisp of smoke trailing out from the gap between her lips; nothing like how I looked, puffing smoke brazenly out of my nostrils like a jet plane. I found her smoking demeanor extremely attractive. She'd also taught me that it was polite to light cigarettes for girls. At a dinner party a number of years later, all the girls had cigarettes ready to light. I passed the flame to all of them at once, impressing everyone. Other aspects of my behavior might have been lacking, like whether to go before or after ladies on the stairs; I never could figure out that one. This proved I was not actually a gentleman. It was just that lighting cigarettes for ladies had become a conditioned reflex.

I was in the pump room by the river one day, dismantling a water pump on my own. It was dirty as hell in there and overrun with rats. No one dared offend the chemical factory rats. They'd all grown up eating pig offal, which made them big and fleshy; they didn't even bother running away when they saw people coming. After I dismantled the water pump, I crossed the street and went back to the factory. At the entrance I bumped into Bai Lan. She was looking well. We could have exchanged a few words, but I was feeling grumpy that day because 1) Old Bad-Ass had just been retired, and 2) the rats.

"Lu Xiaolu, why are you so filthy?" she asked when she saw me.

"Would bench work be bench work if it weren't dirty?" was all I said in response before carrying off the broken water pump in the direction of the bench work team, feeling dejected and depressed.

"Lu Xiaolu, I have something to tell you," Bai Lan said. "Come to the infirmary at lunch."

I finished lunch early that day and changed my uniform. I had two sets of the uniform. You were meant to change into one pair when you washed the other, but I never changed or washed mine. One set was as dirty as a dishcloth, and the other set was straight off the shelf. I put on these new work clothes and made my way to the infirmary, my mood slightly improved.

Bai Lan was alone in the infirmary, sitting cross-legged on the examination bed reading a book. She saw me come in and slipped her feet back into her shoes.

"Why did you want me?" I asked.

"That's what I was going to ask you," she said. "I heard you came looking for me."

"It was nothing, really," I said. "I just came to say hi. How is Good Balls?"

"He's out of the hospital," she said, frowning. "You don't always call him by that nickname, do you? It's not very nice."

"Even the factory head has a nickname. It's protocol," I said.

"So do you have a nickname?"

"Yeah, I'm Magic Head."

She laughed. I didn't understand what was funny.

"Lu Xiaolu, stop talking crap," she said. "I want you to help me with something."

I asked her with what. She told me it was nothing in particular, I just needed to sit there, and that was it. I wasn't to move regardless of who came in, and I shouldn't say anything.

"I can't do that," I said. "What if Hu Deli from the labor department comes in and sees me here? He'll deduct my bonus."

Bai Lan sighed and gave a faint smile. "Okay, it's not going to be Hu Deli," she said. "It's Auntie Qin from the canteen."

As soon as she mentioned Auntie Qin, I knew what the deal was. Our factory canteen had a very fat auntie who was in charge of selling the meat dishes, and her surname was Qin. She had a bright red face, even more vibrant than the cheeks of young girls, and from a distance she looked like a pantomime character. She stood at the canteen's meat service window day in and day out, not just keeping an eye on the pork meatballs and braised fish but observing every face in the factory as well. And like all bored middle-aged women, she tried to be a matchmaker for all the single people. I'd heard that matchmaking was an addiction; one day without it, and they'd start to feel uncomfortable in their own skin. Auntie Qin was dedicated to the work of improving the lives of single men and women. First she'd ask if you had a girlfriend or boyfriend. If you didn't, she'd start rubbing her fingers together, looking up at the clouds, muttering something—a spell, perhaps, for the heavens to throw a suitable partner down from the sky. "Ah ha!" she'd suddenly say. "Do you know such-and-such person from such-and-such workshop? You relax and leave it to me." This was the unsolicited match. There was also the agent match, when you saw someone you liked in the factory and asked Auntie Qin to set it up for you. Auntie Qin didn't charge a penny for this service—in fact, she operated at a loss. If you accepted her matchmaking or entrusted her to find you a match, she'd put an enormous spare rib or a huge meatball into your rice bowl.

She was supposedly very conscientious about these matches. She never set up random ones. She'd set up young office guys with young lab girls; day-shift guys with above-average-attractive three-shift girls; young three-shift guys with below-average three-shift girls; old bachelors with widows; wonky necks with squinted eyes—that was her matchmaking style. It was actually quite scientific, using the same rationale as a man with a doctoral degree marrying a woman with a master's degree and a man with a master's degree marrying a woman with an undergraduate degree. Auntie Qin had a sophisticated way of looking at the world. She maintained especially good rapport with attractive young girls and guys, treating them like high-quality products. She wouldn't match up these people with each other—instead she introduced them to average-looking partners from well-off families. She explained it as the law of mixing meat and vegetables. Auntie Qin was extremely against my type, a bench worker apprentice who coveted young department women. This was seen as wishful thinking. If I'd asked her to match me with Little Pouty Lips, she'd end up offering me an ugly young girl with lots of money, and the amount of money would be directly proportional to how ugly the girl was.

Auntie Qin did have an unquestionable ability for bringing people together. If you rejected her match, however, you were done for. The smallest spare ribs and meatballs that had been left out overnight would appear in your rice bowl. When I heard that Auntie Qin was paying Bai Lan a visit, I congratulated her.

"Who's she matching you with?" I asked.

"Xiao Bi from the propaganda department, I think," she said.

I didn't know Xiao Bi from the propaganda department, so I said, "Oh, he must be the one who writes the blackboard reports."

"Don't talk crap," Bai Lan said. "The propaganda department isn't all about blackboard reports."

"All I've seen is their blackboard reports." I paused, then said very intentionally, "Well, I should leave you to it. You don't need me here as a third wheel."

"She's been bugging me for ages and I'm fed up with her, but it's so awkward getting rid of her. If you just sit here for a while, she'll get annoyed and leave."

"Dealing with Auntie Qin isn't that easy. She'll come back again and again until she's matched you."

"That's what annoys me the most. It never ends."

"Oh, by the way—was this an unsolicited match from Auntie Qin, or does Xiao Bi have a crush on you?"

Bai Lan's face flushed red. "Xiao Bi arranged it," she said quietly.

I sat cross-legged on the examination table, my smelly feet open to the air. Bai Lan told me my shoes were a problem, that they caused athlete's foot. I was wearing a pair of leather sneakers at the time. I say leather, but it was actually synthetic leather. I bought them from a roadside vendor, and they didn't let my feet breathe at all. I didn't really have a choice; I couldn't afford good-quality shoes, not that they would be suitable for dismantling water pumps anyway. Didn't the factory issue us leather sneakers? Bai Lan asked. Please, I told her, you worked in those sneakers for one day and your socks were so worn that your toes poked out of the front and your heels at the back. I'd already wasted dozens of pairs of socks. Other workers and supervisors wore their sneakers without socks, but I couldn't do that. My feet were too sensitive.

Bai Lan frowned. "Your feet might be handy now, actually," she said. "Hopefully you'll be able to fumigate out Auntie Qin!"

Auntie Qin did turn up, those rosy red girlish circles on her cheeks. She was followed by a tall boy with a pale, clear complexion and glasses who I assumed correctly to be Xiao Bi. I hadn't expected Auntie Qin to bring him with her. Because I was there, Auntie Qin kept her voice deep and low, like a secret agent. Bai Lan kept her voice low too, so I couldn't hear what they were saying. Xiao Bi wandered around the room, sizing up the decor; he ran his eyes over me, the corners of his mouth turning up slightly. He seemed to be smiling, though the rest of his face remained expressionless.

The conversation between him and Bai Lan went like this:

"Hi, I'm Xiao Bi. My full name is Bi Guoqiang."

"Hi, I'm Bai Lan."

"This is my first time at the infirmary."

"Really?"

"I often see you around."

"But I don't often see you around."

"Because I don't often need to see a doctor. Hee hee hee."

"Hee hee hee."

"I haven't been at the factory long. I graduated from the chemical factory vocational college. And you?"

"Hee hee hee."

"It's quite nice in here."

"Hee hee hee."

While this was taking place, Auntie Qin strolled over to me, and the way she looked at me gave me goose bumps. Generally when Auntie Qin looked at you that way, it meant your wedding day was around the corner—and if that didn't give you goose bumps, there was something wrong with you. But I'd promised Bai Lan, so I had to stay.

"What are you doing in here, Lu Xiaolu?" Auntie Qin asked.

"Being reexamined," I said.

"Being reexamined for what?"

"My head. I knocked it on a water pump a while ago, and I still get dizzy spells."

"Oh." Auntie Qin nodded pensively. "Are those your feet making that stench? It's too much."

"I can't really smell anything these days because of the bump to my head."

Auntie Qin looked at me sympathetically. "When you're better, I'll introduce you to a girl. You'll have to do something about those smelly feet first: bathe them in ginger water, otherwise the only girlfriend I'll be able to match you to will be one with bad breath."

Fuck, I couldn't stop myself—I burst out laughing when I heard this. This woman was too cute for words: matching smelly feet with bad breath. I took my hat off to her. That pairing method was just like rice hybridization experiments. The child I sired might be a double champion with bad breath and smelly feet. When that child was old enough, we'd put in a request with Auntie Qin to find him a partner with body odor. By the time my grandchildren came along, they'd be biological and chemical weapons.

I was laughing so hard, I interrupted the conversation Bai Lan was having with Xiao Bi. Bai Lan walked over and made a big show of saying, "Oh, Auntie Qin, you mustn't excite Lu Xiaolu. He must have damaged his brain stem, because he often overreacts nowadays."

I almost laughed myself off the examination table after that.

When Auntie Qin and Xiao Bi were leaving, Xiao Bi shook hands with Bai Lan. His mouth had stayed upturned throughout. He didn't even look at me, which proved he had a lot of self-discipline. After they'd gone, Bai Lan and I discussed him. I said that I liked the corners of his mouth, always upturned, and when he laughed it reverberated from his chest. But he was very restrained with it, only giving three or four syllables of laughter. *Hee hee hee* showed it was funny, while *hee hee hee hee* showed it was extremely funny. That first *hee* was generally quite loud, and each subsequent *hee* was quieter. I thought Xiao Bi might eventually become a department head or factory head.

Bai Lan said, "You've been observing him closely. If you learned to laugh like that, who's to say you wouldn't make it to department head too?"

I never would, I told her. I was a bench worker. If a smile like that appeared on my face, it was because my brain stem really had been severed. My mouth naturally curved downward, giving me the look of a hired killer. As for the way my laugh sounded, I couldn't learn to *hee hee hee*. When I laughed, it started out quiet and got louder, and the longer it went on the more powerful it became—also just like a hired killer.

"Lu Xiaolu, I do believe you're jealous," Bai Lan said.

I sighed. Xiao Bi embodied all my ideals at that time. He'd graduated from the chemical factory vocational college, he worked in the propaganda department writing blackboard bulletins, he was neat and tidy and sophisticated. Even his taste in women was spot on, for fuck's sake. While I was just a lowly water pump fixer who didn't look like he'd amount to much more than that.

I told her about all these things: the chemical factory vocational college and the propaganda department. She listened quietly without a smile or an interruption. It was only once that she told me I was jealous of Xiao Bi. After that, she said it wasn't jealousy but admiration. I didn't really get what she meant by admiration; I thought it must have meant very, very jealous.

"What's the difference between admiration and jealousy?" I asked.

She thought about it and said, "Jealousy means you'd be willing to cause the person damage. You wouldn't be able to cause Xiao Bi damage, so you can only admire him."

I found this comment pretty tasteless but couldn't work out why.

Not long after, Bai Lan and I bumped into each other again. "Thanks for your help the other day," she said. "Auntie Qin hasn't come looking for me again since."

"Fuck," I said. "That probably means I've been eating old meatballs all week!"

By running fast and driving that pedicab like my life depended on it, I saved Good Balls' life. The factory said it would reward me with a thirty-yuan bonus. I'd done a lot of good things at the factory, none of which had been rewarded before. I'd also done a lot of bad things, none of which had been punished. It was only this one time I was given thirty yuan. My ma was ecstatic when I told her. She said that her Xiaolu had finally grown up. If she ever got sick, I could drive her to the hospital in a pedicab too.

This meant that Good Balls' life was only worth thirty yuan, I told Bai Lan.

"Don't be so arrogant," she said. "When the migrant workers saved your life, they weren't given a cent."

"That's not what I meant," I said. "When I saved Good Balls' life, I was basically following your instructions. You're the one who should be rewarded."

"I'm a doctor," she said. "It's my job to save lives. If I mess up, I'll be punished. You wouldn't have been punished for moving too slowly, would you?"

When she put it like that, I realized I was actually pretty great. "Yes, yes, you're right. You were just carrying out your duties, while I was helping someone on my own volition. It's completely different."

She just rolled her eyes and said, "You really sound educated with your long words, like *volition*. I've never met a bench worker quite like you."

"Fuck, it's nice of you to notice," I said. "How about we go spend this thirty yuan on something to eat. I'll treat you to KFC."

Daicheng's KFC opened in 1992, and overnight it became the most popular place in town. Before, Daicheng had been a dirty city; the streets lined with open-air food stalls glistened with filthy rainbow water. The majority of Daicheng's restaurants were noodle joints where flies buzzed around everywhere, and when people finished their bowls, the waiters would empty out the soup dregs, sluice the bowls around in a plastic basin, then use them to serve the next person. Even the more upmarket restaurants lacked air-conditioning and had only electric fans, and don't even get me started about the central heating in winter. As for the waiters, each one looked grumpier than the last. You'd often see them getting into fights with customers in the street, sometimes a bunch of customers beating up a waiter and other times a group of waiters beating up a customer.

Before you ate your noodles, you'd have to play a game of musical chairs. This meant running into the noodle joint, looking past the crowd of people, and aiming for the empty stool. You'd pick it up and take it to the counter to get a ticket, then you'd carry the stool along to the stove counter to pick up your noodles. Only then could you finally put down your stool, sit on it, and eat your meal. If you didn't manage to bag a stool, you'd just have to eat standing up. Daicheng folk saw eating standing up as tantamount to begging, and they thought it would bring shame on their ancestors. The craftier noodle joints used benches instead of stools; these couldn't be lifted and carried when you ordered your noodles. People often got into brawls trying to get a space on a bench, and the bench became a violent weapon.

It was a time of enlightenment when Daicheng got its first KFC, and everyone started to understand what eating out was all about. It should be somewhere bright and clean, with background music, not buzzing with flies, and the wait-staff should not beat up the customers. Human beings were not pigs. They couldn't put up with grumpy faces all their lives—this was why human beings evolved. Human beings are said to evolve generation by generation, but in the '90s it seemed to happen year by year. The '90s were just strange like that.

As I sat with Bai Lan in the fast-food joint, I told her that my senior middle-school dream had been to be a shop assistant. She found it funny and asked if it wasn't slightly unusual for your dream job to be as a shop assistant. I told her my dream job in elementary school had been even more extraordinary—go out with my cousin and collect protection fees. What about when you were in elementary school, she asked. I told her I couldn't remember, but probably kid's stuff: join the People's Liberation Army or the police. I'd wanted to be an artist for a time too. I'd been pretty good at drawing, women's faces in particular.

I brought the conversation back to Xiao Bi. "Xiao Bi writes up the blackboard bulletins at the factory entrance, I've seen him doing it," I said.

"You should study, Lu Xiaolu," she said thoughtfully.

"My pa wanted me to get into chemical trade school," I said.

"Chemical trade school's stopped running, it's no longer admitting students. Didn't you know?" she said. "Do you still remember that plump girl in the laboratory? She's the factory head's daughter. She went to study at trade school this year but was sent back."

"What's she going to do instead?"

"We're talking about you!" Bai Lan snapped. "What are you going to do?"

"I don't know."

"You should go study at a self-taught college or evening college. It would be good for you. Do you really want to be a bench worker all your life?"

"But you need to pay your own way at those kinds of colleges."

"Are you the one being stupid, or is it me?" Bai Lan asked.

She was furious and sucked down her cola, staring out the window to show she was ignoring me. I honestly didn't know what to do. If I hadn't gone to the factory for my apprenticeship but had become a roadside cigarette vendor instead, by now I'd have been doing trade. I'd have been importing goods, I'd have been counting money, and I wouldn't have had time to consider taking classes as an adult. I could have been thinking of nothing at all, just building my cigarette enterprise from a roadside stall into a grocery store, then a restaurant, by which time I'd be old and could just go off and die. I'd never thought that being a bench worker would end up so complicated and give me such a headache.

"Bai Lan, what does a slipped uterus mean?" I asked, trying to cheer her up. Her eyes widened. "What the hell?"

It was like this: I'd gone to the factory to mend a water pump one day and heard a few three-shift aunties talking. One of them had said that her uterus had slipped, and another said that would make things easier. I wasn't sure exactly what a slipped uterus meant, but I figured it had to be some sort of illness. Even though I didn't know how it slipped or where it slipped to, it couldn't be a good thing. How, then, could it make things easier? I took this question to Old Bad-Ass, who told me that if your uterus slipped, you were allowed to transfer out of the workshop and get a more menial job, such as guarding the storeroom or looking after the water pumps.

There were lots of female workers in the factory back then, all of whom had the same problems on all their medical records. If it wasn't fibroids, it was uterine prolapse, but they were all gynecological problems. If you put a woman on the three shift, her uterus was liable to fall out at any point. The factory head could dismiss workers, he could make workers do the hardest and dirtiest jobs around, but he couldn't be responsible for wombs falling out of middle-aged female workers. Their relatives would stab him to death. This was the factory's principle of survival. Because you were treated so well if your uterus slipped, I'd heard that once they'd had a child, a lot of our factory's female workers would go and get a certificate saying that theirs had slipped. Slip, incomplete and complete uterine prolapse, they gave their workshop directors headaches. So many women had a slipped uterus. How could he look after them all? I felt sorry for workshop directors in this situation, because if he looked after one woman, the other women would all say he'd slept with her. You wouldn't need everybody to stir up trouble then, you'd just wait for the workshop director's wife to charge into the factory with murder in her eyes.

"You're a novice apprentice," Bai Lan said. "How the hell do you come up with such degenerate questions?"

This was a question about physiological well-being, I explained. It wasn't sordid, only slightly gross subject matter. Besides, Auntie Qin wanted to introduce me to a girlfriend. What if she found me someone with a slipped uterus? Wouldn't it be terrible if I said the wrong thing?

"Okay, then I'll explain it," Bai Lan said, picking up a piece of fried chicken. "Look, this is a bit like a womb."

I started feeling dizzy when I heard this, and the fried chicken I'd been chewing slipped from my mouth to my plate.

"A woman's uterus sometimes prolapses after she gives birth, and in serious cases it will actually slip out. Someone who has this condition will never again be able to engage in heavy labor—she needs to take it easy. Does that make sense?"

"Does it really slip out, or do they just say it does?" I asked.

"Lu Xiaolu, you're so boring."

Bai Lan got so annoyed with me, she started choking. If we ever got married, I'd probably make her so angry she'd choke to death. We left KFC and walked the streets. She walked very slowly, saying nothing. It was dusk. It was getting dark earlier, which meant that fall would soon be over. A decade ago, when I was at the factory, I finished work at 4 p.m., when it was still very light. You could have a snack, then head home or whittle away some time in the streets. These days it's the opposite. My office is brightly lit, but when I finish work and go out to the streets, I find that it's already dark. Crowds of shadowy people push onto buses under the neon lights. It feels like you've been on an international flight and are dealing with jet lag. This is Shanghai I'm talking about.

I told Bai Lan I'd been messing with her by talking about the slipped uterus. I thought it was funny, but she didn't seem to, so I didn't bring it up again. Bai Lan told me she didn't like the factory, didn't like the people there or the conversations they had. I told her I didn't like it either, especially when people called me "little apprentice" or "little bench worker." I didn't think these quibbles were worth getting angry over because it was the truth, not rumors or wishful thinking. Wishful thinking and rumormongering were different ways of doing the same thing, and both made you feel angry and resentful. The factory was reality, and slipped uteruses were reality too; there was nothing absurd about them. I was willing to discuss the issue head-on, call a spade a spade.

We pushed our bikes along a narrow street bracketed by high walls. A sycamore tree grew in the street, and some dead leaves had fallen to the ground. Bai Lan stepped on these leaves with her shoes, and each leaf crunched. She said that in summer, the tree branches were blown by the wind and the leaves rustled. In the fall, they fell to the ground and stepping on them made them crunch. Each leaf had its own unique sound. Their rustling was beautiful, and their crunching was beautiful. But if you stepped on those same leaves a second time, they would be silent.

This conversation had no basis in reality, and it made me long to kiss her. But I was pushing my bike along, and anyone who's ever done this knows that pushing a bike along is not advantageous to kissing, especially if it's a first kiss. When you're on a date and want to kiss, you aren't allowed to talk either; you have to be quiet for a certain time. You can't be talking and kissing at the same time—that was just looking for a slap. I was slightly scared of Bai Lan. She wasn't very easygoing—to use a cliché, her moods were as unpredictable as the weather. I thought of her magazine-model look when she'd gone to buy me cigarettes at the hospital. It was an image I couldn't forget. All I had to do was picture it, and I'd get dizzy from wanting to kiss her and who knows what else. But there was a bike between us, quite a hindrance. I was still young; I could have said, "Be my girlfriend," waited for her to agree, then found somewhere to stop and kiss her tenderly. But I didn't think of that, only about how I wanted to kiss her but couldn't reach. I didn't speak. I kept thinking about it while she continued to sing to herself on the road. I abandoned the idea of the roadside kiss—the infirmary was cleaner anyway. She thought I was listening to her singing, when actually I was completely stressed and overwhelmed by terrible ideas.

I walked her home to New Knowledge New Village. It was the residential area where Daicheng College's faculty members lived, a place with quite a dense population of intellectuals, the complete opposite of Pesticide New Village. Pesticide New Village was full of chickens and ducks, basically a big farm, while New Knowledge New Village was very quiet, with rows and rows of windows shining with orange lights, shrubs all around, and the only sound the chirruping of cicada. We walked along gently, the insects all pausing when we passed, waiting until we were far enough away before starting up again with their singing. Their pausing felt like some sort of salute to us both. In Pesticide New Village, this would be prime time for home karaoke. Countless numbers of microphones simultaneously emit their eerie shrieks and howls into the night air, making it feel like some Romanian Gothic castle.

"Here we are," she said, stopping.

"Shall I leave you here?" I asked.

She nodded and said, "Go home and think about what we talked about this evening."

"I will," I said. "Adult college. Seeing as I won't be able to go to chemical trade school now, I'll just have to try adult college."

I watched her walk up the stairs. A window on the third floor lit up, and I thought, *That's Bai Lan's room.*

It was the first time I'd been to New Knowledge New Village. It was a very quiet place with a nice atmosphere. On my way back to Pesticide New Village, I thought, *Hell, now I'm going to have to put up with their incessant karaoke.* But there wasn't any karaoke that night. Instead there were two people having an argument through their microphones, cursing at a hundred decibels with reverberating effects, which circled around Pesticide New Village. I wished they would pick up butcher knives and start stabbing people, kill them all so we could just have some quiet. But there was no stabbing, only these two people swearing enduringly into their microphones. "Motherfuck-ker-ker-ker!" Their creativity was enough to make those around them want to commit suicide. That was where I lived.

There was a serious incident at the factory that fall. I remember it clearly because it was two days after I'd taken Bai Lan out to eat. When people get old, a lot of their memories come back only with the help of other memories. It's as if a letter sent from the past has returned many years later, and it still feels quite fresh when you read it. I'd been planning to visit the infirmary to kiss Bai Lan. I'd planned it all out, how I should move things forward in an orderly way. Back in senior middle school, I'd kissed a girl who was at the same school, but it hadn't gone well. She wasn't bad-looking; she'd twisted away from me a couple of times, then given in. I'd often go kiss her after that, and she no longer resisted or bothered to twist away. I assumed kissing was just a thing you did with your chest forward and your butt back.

I was thinking about the act of kissing as I dismantled that day's water pumps and it made me clumsy, a lot slower than I should have been. I suddenly heard a female worker shouting, "Shit! Come quickly, Ah Fang from the control room has climbed up the smokestack!" All the workers in the chemical factory stopped working immediately. They abandoned their stations and ran toward the boiler room.

Our factory's boiler room had a big smokestack. What a waste of a sentence—what factory's boiler room doesn't have a big smokestack? The smokestack in our boiler room was a hundred feet high, thick and solid, built in the '50s. Factory smokestacks generally had ladder-style steel rungs that repairmen climbed up. The steel rungs on ours were odd—they were all very close together, which made it look like a jungle gym at a playground. Any child could have climbed up. This was pretty dangerous. I have no idea why the factory hadn't locked up this tower. But instead they just hung up a sign that read: "Danger: unauthorized people should not enter." Would people who wished to commit suicide pay this any mind? They'd probably climb up first and think about it later.

That was how Ah Fang got up there. No one noticed her climbing until she reached sixty-five feet and her feet went limp, and she just hung there. She was discovered like that, and everyone in the factory ran over and crowded around. I need to explain the Ah Fang situation briefly. She'd been having an affair with a man from the administrative department, which had become public knowledge. This man had a wife who was one of the factory's most notorious tigers. This tiger said she was going to scratch out Ah Fang's cunt. Most people took things like this as a vague threat, but those familiar with tigers knew better. She'd do exactly what she said. She wouldn't have a problem with scratching out anyone's cunt, as long as it wasn't her own. If I were Ah Fang, I'd have climbed up the smokestack too. When you see a tiger, the best thing to do is climb a tree. When I was young I was taught this by a junior school teacher who specialized in telling us how to deal with tigers, bears, and crocodiles. I still have no idea why.

Ah Fang hadn't only climbed up the smokestack—she wanted to jump off it. It had become a big deal. There were only three people in the history of the factory who had attempted this. The first was in 1961, and he'd had his food coupons stolen. Losing your food coupons back then was like being sentenced to death. He climbed up about thirty feet but was so famished he couldn't get any higher—plus, if he had climbed any higher it wouldn't have been easy to communicate with the people down below. The factory head pleaded with him. The chemical factory wasn't a government body, and it still had some heart. The head didn't want someone to die like that. The guy up the smokestack wasn't prepared to climb down for the life of him, but neither was he prepared to jump. There was no real difference between thirty and ninety feet—it was only a matter of how many pieces you broke into.

. "I want to eat buns!" this man shouted down to the factory head. "I want to eat meat buns!"

"I'll give you buns," the head replied, "I'll give you all the buns. Just come down, and you'll have buns."

The man on the smokestack didn't believe it. He was scared that the factory would punish him if he came down. This stalemate went on and on until they were all at their wits' end. They called the canteen's head chef, who pounded a spoon against a rice bowl, shouting, "It's meal time—lard, vegetables, rice, and cured meat!" The onlookers turned green with envy. The man on the smoke-stack realized he was in the wrong place. If he stayed dangling up there, he'd get nothing to eat. So he came right down. As soon as his feet touched the ground, he was hustled away by the safety department.

The second time was in 1971 and involved a factory vandal, although I'm not sure exactly what he vandalized. He climbed up the smokestack in the early morning mist, up to the very top. No one was around. At the top, he smoked a cigarette. He must have sat there for a while, then jumped. When the police came to inspect the scene, they found a recently smoked cigarette butt at the top of the smokestack and deduced that he must have jumped from a hundred feet. Sixty-five or even thirty feet were high enough to kill you—there was no real need to climb so high, but he'd done it anyway. It must have been so he could look at the surrounding scenery. I'd heard that the mist was pretty heavy that day, so he can't have seen much. Still, standing on the smokestack, jumping into the mist, must have been an intoxicating feeling. That's just my guess—I've never actually been up there.

Ah Fang was the third. She was dangling from the sixty-five-foot mark, displaying the power of love. For buns, you'd climb to thirty feet. For love, you would climb to sixty-five. But if you climbed to a hundred feet, to the top, it was for no reason other than wanting to die. This showed that love ranked higher than hunger, but not as high as death.

I ran to the scene. All I could see was a crowd of people in their neither-blue-nor-green uniforms interspersed with a few in olive-green police uniforms. These weren't actual policemen, only chemical factory police. Everyone had their heads tilted up, as if they all had nosebleeds. All the attention was cen-tered on Ah Fang, a control room maintenance worker who was dangling from the wall of the smokestack. The weather was good that day. A plume of white smoke was rising from the smokestack, and the clouds in the sky looked like fish scales. I was a long way away. All I could see was a figure the size of a match-stick. I couldn't see her face. The person next to me seemed to have extrasensory abilities, however, and was chatting animatedly to everyone: "She's crying! She's trembling! She's about to jump!" If she were about to jump, she wouldn't fall onto concrete but a big sea of heads. A couple of the aunties couldn't hold themselves back; they started to cry, saying, "Oh, the poor child, seduced by that lecherous cadre. No choice now but to climb the smokestack and jump to her death."

I clawed my way through into the middle of the crowd, where I saw Bai Lan. Where she was standing, she wasn't going to be of any use whatsoever. If Ah Fang really were to jump, all Bai Lan would be able to do was confirm death. Those around her thought that since she was a doctor, she should be taking responsibility, so she stood there shouting, "Ah Fang! Ah Fang!"

I prodded her and said, "I'll climb up and carry her down."

"It has nothing to do with you," she said. "If you go up there, she could kick you down."

I told her not to worry—I'd wear a safety harness.

At this point Ah Fang shouted, "None of you come up here. If anyone comes up, I'll jump!"

"Someone go get Wang Taofu," Bai Lan said.

Wang Taofu was the lecherous cadre.

"He's been beaten up and injured by his wife, so he didn't come to work today," the factory police told us cheerfully.

"What shall we do?" Bai Lan asked me.

I shook my head, unable to think of a plan. This wasn't a case of driving a pedicab and risking my own life—this was climbing a smokestack. If I climbed up and she jumped down, I'd be even more to blame for her death than the lecherous cadre.

The main factory leaders were all out at a meeting that day, and the deputy head, who was in charge of sales, was the only one present. When told to take charge of the situation, he scratched his head and said, "Romantic problems . . . that's not really one for the head of sales."

So I went to the propaganda department. The propaganda department usually just did the blackboard bulletins and lacked experience in face-to-face encounters. The head of propaganda was very hesitant, so a worker called them a group of fucking Pu Nanis. On hearing this, the head of propaganda went to fetch an electric bullhorn and chose twelve members of the propaganda department to go to the scene, including Xiao Bi. Their group took over the area where Bai Lan and I had been standing. The workers saw the way they were standing and said, "The only thing these propaganda workers are good for is guzzling and boozing."

The head of propaganda didn't pay them any attention. He just lifted his bullhorn and tested the sound. Then he shouted, "Ah Fang, your behavior today is classed as sabotaging production. Come down right away! I repeat, come down immediately!"

Ah Fang burst into tears on the smokestack.

"Ah Fang, Wang Taofu has already been beaten up," the propaganda head shouted. "The factory will sort out this thing."

When they heard this, the aunties behind him started throwing sunflower seeds at the back of his head and said, "You might as well just push her down, you prick!"

The propaganda head ignored them and shouted loudly, "Creating a disturbance is not permitted. You will all return to work!"

"Kiss my ass, you swine," a worker behind him said.

Xiao Bi suddenly grabbed the bullhorn from the head of propaganda. With calm dignity, he turned to the workers behind him and said, "Quiet, everybody. Stop making trouble. The important thing is to save her." The workers went quiet. Xiao Bi pointed the bullhorn back up. "Ah Fang, I'm Xiao Bi from the propaganda department. Can we please talk? How old are you?"

Some words came from Ah Fang's mouth up there that I couldn't hear, but oddly Xiao Bi seemed to hear them clearly.

"How is a twenty-four-year-old still looking for drama? You must trust that there are people in the factory who will protect you and speak for you. The factory won't endanger your future after such a small incident, and we will not allow anyone else to harm you."

There was a thunder of applause from the gathered workers.

"If anyone in this factory causes you trouble, they'll have me, Xiao Bi, to deal with. I'll be the first to stand up and speak for you!"

Auntie Wang from the propaganda department grabbed the bullhorn and said, "Xiao Bi is the son of the chemical bureau's deputy chief. You believe what he's saying, don't you, Ah Fang?"

"Oh! Oh!" the onlookers murmured with astonishment.

Ah Fang eventually came down, and Xiao Bi became the man of the hour. Before now, people had thought of him as a neat and clean young man from the propaganda department who didn't have much to say for himself. Now they all knew he was the son of Mr. Bi, the deputy bureau chief. He'd become an overnight heartthrob for all the young girls in the factory's departments. Who could blame them? Xiao Bi's calm resourcefulness had won over Ah Fang and won over the aunties. He'd been right on the mark regarding Ah Fang's state of mind: she hadn't actually wanted to kill herself, only to escape the tiger. When Ah Fang came down, Xiao Bi noticed that her legs and elbows were covered in scrapes, so he told Bai Lan to take her straight to the infirmary. While she was doing this, I dispersed the crowd of onlookers, telling everyone that the drama was over. It was time to get back to work. Bai Lan took Ah Fang's hand and led her to the infirmary. Ah Fang was crying, her head resting on Bai Lan's shoulders. I was caught among the stragglers moving in the general direction of the infirmary.

Back at the infirmary, Bai Lan applied iodine to Ah Fang's scratches. As usual, there were onlookers clogging the doorway. We suddenly heard a disturbance on the landing.

"Shit, the tiger's coming," someone yelled.

I felt a tornado-like gust whoosh past my face as Wang Taofu's wife bolted her way into the infirmary. She extended a fingernail toward Ah Fang and shouted, "I'm going to scratch out your cunt!"

The bitch was well over 170 pounds and had a dark complexion, a crooked mouth, and hair like steel wire. She wasn't so much a tiger, more a wild boar. All the cadres had gone back to their offices, leaving Bai Lan in the infirmary with a handful of idlers there to watch the excitement. No one had expected Wang Taofu's wife to arrive so quickly and in such a fury.

"What was that play of death for?" she growled. "Go on, jump off the building! I'll jump with you!"

If I could rewind certain scenes from my life and watch them in slow motion, this scene from the infirmary would certainly be in the top five. Bai Lan rushed over like a rugby player and grabbed hold of the tiger's waist—to be precise, she used all her strength to restrain the tiger. The tiger went crazy, grabbing Bai Lan by the hair and shaking her with all her might. Bai Lan didn't let out a sound, just opened her mouth and clamped down ferociously on the tiger's waist.

With a startled scream, Ah Fang leaped up from the examination table and jumped onto the window ledge. I saw her figure flash past the slightly yellowing tree canopy.

Freeze frame.

It was about ten years ago that I realized what a shitty thing violence was. It didn't only cause harm—you got punished for it too. People aren't born violent. Sometimes violence is just God casting his die, and it can land on anyone. Take me, for example. I'd been twitchy and aggressive since the day I started at the factory, and I was always looking for someone to take on. But in all that time, I'd only ever come to blows with that water pump. I'd go around covered in grease, my face pale, and I would stagger rather than walk, like a natural-born killer. But strangely, I didn't end up getting into many fights. This showed that fate hadn't cast its die my way, but my adrenaline still surged in vain. Instead fate had his eyes on Bai Lan the pacifist, getting her to bite the tiger so hard that the woman cried.

We crawled to the window ledge and looked down to where we saw Ah Fang sprawled out beneath the tree. She was crying too. The fact that she was still able to cry was a good sign. The factory got a car to take her to the hospital to be checked out, where they discovered she'd fractured her tibia. But I digress. After the workers had dispersed, the tiger was taken to the safety department for questioning, blubbering the whole way there. She knew she was up shit creek. That afternoon, the bench worker team sent me to the formaldehyde workshop to dismantle a water pump. I was wondering what would happen if I got intoxicated and passed out again. Doctor Bai might not be in the best frame of mind to save my life. In the end, I got Wei Yixin to dismantle the pump instead, while I changed into my clean work uniform and made my way to the infirmary.

I pushed open the infirmary door but found no one inside. Hai Yan from the library walked over and told me that Xiao Bi had come looking for Bai Lan and the two of them had gone out together. She blinked at me. I said nothing, just sat down on the examination table, lit up a smoke, and waited for Bai Lan to return.

I sat on my own like that for a long time. I always felt that I needed to think things over, to reflect on them. Now that I'm thirty and thinking back on the first half of my life, I realize there weren't many moments that required reflection. What was the point? The first half of my life was characterized mainly by sudden realizations; like tires punctured by nails, awakenings like this didn't require reflection. Each time I felt the need to reflect, I'd find a quiet place and sit down. I wasn't hoping to come up with a perfect solution. Sometimes I'd fall into a confused slumber; at other times, I'd smoke half a pack, stand up, pat the dust from my butt, and head back home.

The infirmary was silent. If everything in the world could be this silent, it would be a good thing as far as I was concerned. Had I been a thug, you could say that sitting there I felt tired of all the fighting and drama. But I wasn't a thug, just a water-pump-fixing apprentice. And the fighting and drama hadn't had anything to do with me. So all I could think was how good silence was. For no particular reason, I just yearned for silence.

About two hours later, Bai Lan came back; she gave a small start when she saw me. I was sitting on the examination table, swinging my legs, with four or five cigarette butts on the floor. I smiled at her. Later she told me my smile that day had been quite menacing, and the hand I was holding the cigarette with had been shaking, and she didn't know why. I told her I'd been worried that Xiao Bi might be standing behind her. I didn't see Xiao Bi there after all, but damn, was I agitated. I was only nineteen, after all. No wonder I'd looked like I was having a heart attack, she'd said.

Bai Lan told me not to smoke in the infirmary again. I nodded and flicked my cigarette butt out the window. I asked if she was feeling any better.

She looked at me, and with sudden rage said, "Like hell I'm feeling better. Look at my hair. She pulled out clumps of it."

She lowered her head to show me. The tiger had pulled out bits from all over Bai Lan's head, so there was no actual bald spot. In the past they used to torture prisoners by pulling out hair a clump at a time. It left ugly bald spots, like soya beans all over the scalp. But that wouldn't happen in a fight.

"The bitch actually yanked my hair," Bai Lan said.

"Lucky you bit her," I said. "It reminded me of that proverb 'A rabbit will bite a human if it's scared enough.'"

"Oh, is that right? You're usually yapping around like a savage little wolf dog. When it came to the crunch, where were you when I needed you? You could have tried to throttle her."

I laughed when I heard this. "What reason would I have had to throttle her?"

Bai Lan said I was athletic but clumsy. Driving a pedicab hadn't posed a problem for me, and neither had bashing my head against that water pump. But my reactions were slow, and I lacked any sense of urgency. The only purpose someone like me could serve was as a human shield, a hard laborer, or a boorish servant. All problems requiring use of the cerebrum and cerebellum would render me incompetent, because I was sheer brawn. I asked her what a human shield was. A kind of bodyguard, she explained, employed just to block bullets.

"Actually, Lu Xiaolu," she said, "you're not even up to a human shield. You're basically just a human stump."

Hearing her assessment was disheartening.

"If that's how you feel, I'll go hit Wang Taofu's wife for you," I said.

"Hit her with what?"

"With a brick!"

There was no need to hit Wang Taofu's wife, Bai Lan told me. The woman had already been bitten quite badly and was still being held in the safety department, crying over making Ah Fang jump off the building. The safety department didn't like this tiger, but they hadn't had the opportunity to deal with her before. This time they'd caught her fair and square and threatened to detain her. This tiger was extremely crafty and said she hadn't gone to threaten Ah Fang, just to visit her. If Bai Lan hadn't grabbed her in the way that she had, Ah Fang never would have jumped. She rejiggered the story so that Ah Fang had lost her footing and fallen off the building while Bai Lan and the tiger were having their skirmish.

"I'll act as witness," I said. "The tiger said she wanted to scrape out Ah Fang's . . . you know."

"Don't bother," Bai Lan said, going on to explain that someone else had volunteered to testify before me. That noble act was not to be mine.

"In that case, I wouldn't hit the tiger," I told Bai Lan. "I've never hit a woman, not even one with a dark face and a twisted mouth. But I'd hit her for you."

"Hit who?" she asked.

"Whoever dares mess with you."

She gave a laugh that was halfway between amused and mocking.

I hadn't asked about Xiao Bi this whole time. But then I remembered and brought it up. Bai Lan told me Xiao Bi had wanted to comfort her and explain about being the deputy chief's son. But apart from that, it was nothing.

"Where did you go?" I asked.

"We just walked by the river," Bai Lan said.

I said nothing. My image of that river was black and smelly, and walking along it wasn't romantic in the slightest. Even so, workers liked to squat by the side of the river because there were boats moving through it, and when people were bored they liked to watch moving objects. The factory machines appeared motionless—if they started to move, they were about to explode. Clouds moved, but too slowly, so watching boats was generally regarded as the best option. The workers who'd been watching these boats saw Bai Lan and Xiao Bi together. If you took the dirt and the stench of the river water out of the picture, it was actually pretty romantic. The workers came back saying that Prince Bi and Doctor Bai were in love—the two of them had been spotted strolling along the river together. This rumor spread to the departments, where someone declared them a very good match. Someone else said that Doctor Bai was a quick mover, gliding in and catching the deputy chief's son in her pocket.

When the gossip and lies reached my ears, I remained very calm and didn't get the least bit jealous. Jealously has a sense of hierarchy—namely that you can only feel jealous of people who are roughly in your league. When I was in senior middle school, I was jealous of the class monitor because he was liked by the teacher, but I wouldn't feel jealousy toward a student from a top high school because he'd be a league above me. Just like I wouldn't get jealous of a champion long-distance runner; we simply weren't birds in the same cage. By the same rationale, I couldn't feel jealous of Xiao Bi, because he was the deputy chief's son.

As Bai Lan had said, I should feel admiration rather than jealousy toward Xiao Bi. Later I managed to override this admiration—to admire a guy over a girl was pathetic, bordering on obscene.

"It should be Xiao Bi who feels jealousy and admiration for me," I declared to Bai Lan.

The fact that he didn't seem to feel this way put me in a bad mood. Fuck it, I was a bench worker—why was I so sensitive? Had I actually cracked?

For a while I thought Doctor Bai and Xiao Bi might be an item, but a month later someone told me that Xiao Bi had a new girlfriend, the daughter of some leader from the municipal party committee. Doctor Bai was completely out of the picture. The workers were very excited. They thought Bai Lan had been rejected, and they waited for her to climb the smokestack. Unfortunately for them, Doctor Bai couldn't care less. She disappointed everyone. Everyone but me.

That fall, everything turned chaotic. Sometimes there was too much happening, and other times it just felt lonely. I got pimples on my face for the first time since high school. I had regular sore throats too, and because my body was burning up, I felt that the world around me was burning up too. My mother saw a doctor of traditional medicine, and when she next had an appointment, she took me along. She got this doctor to feel my pulse, and he told me that my lungs and stomach were overheated. I thought that my respiratory and digestive systems might be in bad shape, but he didn't think so. He told me to spray my mouth with watermelon frost and I'd be fine. I've never understood traditional Chinese medicine.

Early that winter, the family planning office put up a notice that read: *Female workers who do not yet have an IUD should report immediately to the infirmary to have one fitted.* This notice was written on a piece of window-size pink propaganda paper and stuck up in the entrance to the canteen where everyone would see it. The female workers knew the implications right away. They lowered their heads and walked out. It was the gang of male workers who didn't get it and crowded around the notice, chewing over the words. It said "female workers who do not yet have an IUD." Did that mean virgins who didn't have one would have to go get one too? An employee from the family planning office happened to be walking past, a steamed bun in his mouth, and he was grabbed by the male workers and asked to explain the matter of the virgin IUD. This man thought that while the workers were being pretty crass, they did have a point, so he tore down the poster. The next day there was a piece of green propaganda paper in the canteen entrance with these words: *Married women who do not already have an IUD should make their way to the infirmary as soon as possible to have one fitted.* Again the workers crowded around and stopped this family planning department employee. "So does this mean that all unmarried women in the factory already have an IUD, and it's now time for the married women workers to have them fitted?" The family planning office employee looked bewildered; being responsible for family planning was starting to feel like postgraduate studies in logic.

He should have been laughing in those workers' faces and saying, "Go home and ask your mothers." This was the only proper factory logic.

Once the work of fitting IUDs began, I was no longer allowed in the little red building. I couldn't even stand outside the building. It was only old aunties going in and out. Old aunties were usually fairly relaxed, but they were deadly serious when it came to this. You were allowed neither to witness it nor ask about it. Male workers were pretty intuitive. Folklore had it that this part of a woman's body represented doom. Working-class people were very conscious of this, and only a pervert would try to get a glimpse.

During the IUD fitting period, Bai Lan was not to be seen. I was still going to work, battling with rusty screws day in and day out. When I was at school, one teacher told us to be like a screw that never grew rusty. It was only after I started at the factory that I found out all screws grew rusty. The only advantage to this kind of work was that my muscles were getting bigger and bigger. Before starting at the factory I'd been quite puny, but as a bench worker I could eat six buns in a row for lunch—and when I finished, I'd go to the pump room and give all those calories to the screws. Who wouldn't turn into a stud doing a job like that?

There are a couple of other things worth mentioning on the subject of my quest to beat up someone for Bai Lan.

The two of us had been walking down the street late one night when we happened upon Wonky Balls in the doorway to one of Daicheng's movie theaters. He was wearing a woolen peaked cap, a black overcoat, and a pair of black-rimmed spectacles. He had the collar of his coat turned up, which made his wonky head look a little less wonky. If it hadn't been for the fact that he was being beaten up by a gang, I wouldn't have recognized him. I had no idea why he was dressed like that. I could imagine Wonky Balls as a transvestite or an exhibitionist—the only thing I couldn't imagine was him looking ultracool in a movie theater doorway late at night.

These old thugs were beating him pretty badly. When young thugs beat up people, they like to aim for the face; but an old thug kicks the body, leaving not a spot of blood on the face. Four of them surrounded Wonky Balls with their hands in their pants pockets, kicking him back and forth as if he were a soccer ball. They seemed to be doing it solely for amusement, rather than to cause him real harm. But completely undermining your opponent's strength in this way would naturally injure his self-esteem. This was Wonky Balls through and through. Had this happened to Old Bad-Ass, he'd have bitten off all their dicks by now.

Bai Lan and I went to help him out. Using all my strength, I managed to drag one of the thugs off Wonky Balls. This guy's hand was still in his pants pocket, and he stumbled. Supervisor Wonky Balls took his chance and zoomed off. I had no idea Wonky Balls the planer could run so fast. In the blink of an eye, he disappeared into the night. The four thugs were taken aback too. One moment they'd been bullying a short-ass with a wonky head, and the next they had a strapping lad on their hands. Not even the Monkey King could shape-shift that fast. The next day I found Wonky Balls, wanting to ask him about this incident. He was crouched over his planer, wearing his shabby old uniform. But he refused to acknowledge what had happened. All the other supervisors backed him up, saying there was no way it had happened. Wonky Balls in a trench coat, wearing spectacles—it sounded like an alternate universe! The more I spoke about it, the more I started to disbelieve it myself. I was tempted to pull down his trousers to check whether his butt was covered in bruises. But Wonky Balls jumped up and zoomed off, just like the night before. That was when I realized that sprinting was his stunt in the bench worker art troupe, allowing him to flee danger in the nick of time.

I really got myself in it that night. I'd intervened as a courageous gesture, but the victim ran away. If there was going to be a fight, it would be a thuggish one. I wasn't sure whether to race away, dragging Bai Lan with me, or let her get a head start while I stayed behind to play dice with death. I felt something being pressed into my hand. I looked around to see a brick made of dark sticky mud. Bai Lan had handed it to me. While I was in this state of helpless agitation, she winked at me.

One of the thugs was tall and stocky with long hair. "Hey, you're Lu Ba's younger cousin, aren't you?" he asked. Lu Ba was my cousin's nickname, and when he was my age, he was always lurking around outside the movie theater. I admitted that I was indeed Lu Ba's cousin. "Hey, when you were little, I took you to collect protection money, do you remember?" Long Hair asked. I told him I couldn't remember. It was a long time ago. "I haven't seen you in forever," Long Hair said. "You've really changed." I found this strange: if I'd changed that much, how had he even recognized me? Long Hair went on to say, "Now you look exactly like Lu Ba."

I still had that brick in my hand, but I didn't end up hitting anyone with it. Again, Bai Lan got to have a good laugh.

"Was that your cousin they were talking about? Well, they say the apple never falls far from the tree."

I asked her why she was talking shit. Was my family a thug family? Thugs weren't born thugs. Einstein and Newton were born the way they were, but I didn't believe that thugism was innate.

"I didn't say you were born a thug. All I said was that you have a family that shares certain characteristics. If it's too close to the bone, just pretend I never said it."

"How about that brick?" she asked later. "I handed it to you just in the nick of time, didn't I?"

I told her it hadn't been a brilliant plan. It hadn't been a red brick she passed me, but a black brick. After being baked in the sun and soaked in the rain for so long, it was so soft it crumbled in my hand. You wouldn't even be able to beat a chicken to death with a brick like that. Bai Lan told me that there hadn't been anything else. She'd performed a mean feat finding a brick in the cinema doorway in the first place. I told her that in situations like that, she just needed to run for it—handing me a brick was more trouble than it was worth.

She giggled and said, "You could run and hurl a brick at the same time."

I couldn't continue this discussion with her. I told her she was getting carried away and being impulsive—she didn't want to kill anyone.

In the spring of 1993, I spent my life looking around for bricks. I wanted to beat up Director Wu from the canteen. At lunch the canteen food had been bad, and everyone who ate it got diarrhea. The rule at the factory canteen was that cadres ate lunch at 11:30 a.m. and workers ate at noon. The cadres got some choice of food, but by the time it got to the workers, it was all leftovers and cold dishes. This pissed off the workers, and at the workers' congress they'd pound the table and criticize the system. The logistics department would go to the canteen and ask if there was any way that everyone could eat lunch together to avoid a worker revolt. Director Wu explained that this was absolutely impossible. There weren't enough hands on deck in the canteen to feed the workers and cadres at the same time. For a while, it was changed so that the workers ate before the cadres, but this resulted in their serving us half-cooked rice and meatballs that were pink and raw in the middle. The workers were agitated and brought the matter up at the workers' congress again. Director Wu said that nothing could be done—there were ten times as many workers as cadres, and the canteen staff couldn't cook the food in time if the workers ate first.

We'd all hated Director Wu for quite a while. I couldn't even figure out how the head of the canteen had been made a director. Common sense told me that alongside the factory head, team heads, and chief physicians, people with the title "director" should probably not be beaten up. I suppressed the urge for a long time.

The food-poisoning outbreak that spring affected only the workers, while the majority of cadres were fit as fiddles. I call it food poisoning, but it actually wasn't very serious. There was no real vomiting, fainting, or convulsions—everyone just had diarrhea. But the workers were all furious: first because the cadres were completely unaffected while the poor workers suffered, and second because a lot of workers hadn't made it to the can in time and wound up shitting themselves.

Everyone thought of Doctor Bai when this happened. I'd often sung her praises. She wasn't Bai Lan, she was Mother Teresa. I ran to the infirmary, which was packed with people who'd come to get medicine. I waited for the crowd to subside before going in to say hi. She slipped me a packet of berberine and said, "We received this medicine as an emergency delivery from the clinic. Remember to drink lots of water, and if you start vomiting, come back and see me right away."

"There's nothing wrong with me," I said.

"Didn't you eat at the canteen?"

"I did," I said. "I ate at midday. I had a big portion of noodles."

"Oh, there was nothing wrong with the noodles. The problem was with the meat," she said. "Do me a favor and move these cases of medicines outside."

As I was doing that for her, another seven or eight people leaped into the infirmary looking for medicine, disappearing as soon as she dispensed it, moving as quickly as ghosts.

"That guy looked like he had cholera," I said.

"Have you ever seen a case of cholera?" Bai Lan asked. "Please don't add to the chaos."

After she kicked me out, I went wandering around the factory. Production had pretty much ground to a halt. People were running around in all directions, hectically hoisting up their trousers. Some would be running, only to squat down suddenly and say, "Oh shit! It's come out." I needed to pee but found the restrooms full of grimacing, anguished people. There were only a couple of restroom blocks in the chemical factory, which wasn't really enough to deal with a case of mass diarrhea. I turned around and headed back. I ran to the doorway of the office block washrooms, but inside it was the same story, packed to bursting with workers and supervisors. I had no choice, so I ran to the narrow lane behind the building to take a whiz there. I lifted my head and saw Pu Nani, also pissing. When he was done and about to leave, he said, "Lu Xiaolu, you're not permitted to shit here."

"Fuck you," I said, "I'm just taking a piss."

"All the workers have the runs, and you're just taking a piss?" Pu Nani asked skeptically.

So I unzipped my pants in front of his face, and as I pissed I said, "Get away from me or I'll piss on your fucking foot."

No one was held accountable for the factory food-poisoning incident. Bai Lan ran to the factory office to shout at them, but the factory office employees were reluctant to help. They didn't really understand why this matter would make a factory doctor so agitated. It wasn't as if she were working at a United Nations refugee camp. Bai Lan asked why Wu hadn't been punished for such a large-scale food-poisoning outbreak. The factory office employee considered the question, then said that they didn't have a procedure for this. They'd never had a case of mass diarrhea before. They just handed out the berberine, and that was that. Bai Lan corrected him, saying it wasn't mass diarrhea but mass food poisoning. The factory office employee explained that they all referred to it as mass diarrhea—unsurprisingly, "mass food poisoning" sounded too serious, not great for their image.

The factory office employee explained to Bai Lan that Director Wu wasn't very educated and didn't know much about food hygiene. You figured that out as soon as you entered his house and saw that his kids' faces were all covered in roundworm bites. But Director Wu was the factory head's brother-in-law, and taking him to task was not easy. Director Wu had been a victim of this incident himself—he'd also gotten diarrhea from the food, which proved he hadn't contaminated it on purpose. Since it wasn't deliberate, there was no need to punish him. It had only been a kilo or two of pork, after all. When Bai Lan heard this, she smashed the factory office thermoses, one, two, three in total. The factory office employee watched quietly until she'd finished, then he said, "Miss Bai, you've expressed your anger and voiced your complaint. Now go back to work." She was stuck. All she could do was head back to the infirmary, pale-faced and defeated.

"Bai Lan, you really are something else!" I told her. "You actually smashed the factory office thermos."

"I smashed three of them."

"Even if you gave me three thermoses of my own, I still wouldn't be brave enough to go to the factory office to smash them."

"We're not the same, you and me," she retorted. "You're an apprentice worker. What do I have to be scared of? I'm Mother Teresa, aren't I?"

Even though she'd smashed the factory office thermoses, Director Wu continued to go around as happy as could be. It was only the supervisor in charge of procurement at the canteen who was transferred, sent to the saccharin workshop to be an operator. Our factory was strange like that. If you got into trouble, you were transferred over to produce saccharin. It served the same function that being exiled did in the old days.

"Leave it at that now," I advised Bai Lan. "If you continue, it'll get back to the factory head."

Talking like this was probably enough to get me transferred.

"It's an institutional problem through and through," Bai Lan said. "It can't be solved."

At the time, I didn't understand the term *institutional problem*—still don't, if I'm being honest. I often hear economists on television discussing institutional problems. They debate it back and forth. They ponder whether factories should be private or collectives and I think, *For God's sake, whoever wants them should just fucking have them.* If a factory is forever making its workers go to work with diarrhea, the institution is not a good one; if, on the other hand, it gives them time off to recuperate, it might retain some credibility.

"You should go see Xiao Bi," I told Bai Lan. "Ask him to have a word with his father. That would be more effective than smashing a hundred thermoses."

"Do you have a condition that makes you feel unwell if you don't mention Xiao Bi at least once a day?" she asked.

"There's an alternative. I'll go punch Director Wu."

"Punching him won't do one bit of good," she said.

I explained to her that workers didn't actually care about food poisoning. As long as it didn't kill them, it wasn't a big deal. What the workers cared about was the diarrhea itself. The chemical factory's workers had been poisoned by toxic gas until they were more dead than alive. It didn't matter if you were in the middle of working or fucking, you needed to breathe, and if there was a toxic leak, you were dead. I was a bench worker and perfectly aware that I was no Sylvester Stallone—merely an ant holding up a biscuit, an extremely small and frail creature displaying extraordinary strength. Who was heartless enough to give the workers diarrhea? Who would have been heartless enough to pull the plugs out of their rectums, deflate them until they were pretty much waste products? People who did shitty things like that were basically scabs, saboteurs, and counterrevolutionaries. If you couldn't punch them, who could you punch?

"You're just sticking random labels on people," Bai Lan said. "Do you even know what *scab* and *counterrevolutionary* mean?" She warned me not to get involved. Punching Director Wu would be a mistake, and it wasn't even my grudge to avenge.

"We've been talking about this forever," I told her, "but you still don't get it, do you? What's the difference between public revenge and personal revenge?"

I thought of the saying "to avenge a personal wrong in the name of public interest." *If I punched Director Wu on Bai Lan's behalf, it would be the other way around*, I thought: to avenge a public wrong in the name of personal interest.

My cousin's girlfriend used to say there was nothing that special about people's backs, but my back was so fine it was sure to get me recognized. These were her actual words. This isn't me blowing my own horn and saying that my back was fine.

So when I decided to get revenge on Bai Lan's behalf, I needed to be careful not to be recognized from the front or back. I observed Director Wu's daily routine for a few days. I was a novice worker, which meant I couldn't punch a director in public; that would anger all the factory directors. However, matters were taken out of my hands. One day when the factory was particularly quiet, Director Wu was walking through the dormitory area, where a number of boiler room supervisors happened to be sitting. During the food-poisoning period, the boiler room supervisors had suffered from diarrhea. They hadn't all managed to fit in the restroom, and some had been forced to crap on the coal pile. The coal pile had been handy, but no one in the world actually enjoyed shitting on coal. Afterward they'd had to shovel their own shit into the boiler. When the boiler room supervisor saw Director Wu, his anger came to a head. Without a word or a threat, he picked up a brick and clumped the man heavily over the head. Director Wu crumpled to the ground, the blood pouring down his head.

The whole place was quiet. Afraid that he might die if they left him there on the ground, the supervisors helped him up and took him to the infirmary to be bandaged. There's no way I could have been so tolerant.

Bai Lan saw those big brawny beefcakes coming in, holding up a bleeding man, and when she saw the man was Director Wu, she shouted, "Where's Lu Xiaolu? Where's he hiding?"

Those boiler room supervisors all knew me and they said, "Haven't seen him."

"Did he beat the crap out of this man and just run off?"

"Lu Xiaolu didn't beat him up, we did," the supervisors said.

"It wasn't that I was too slow," I regretfully explained to Bai Lan. "It's just that the boiler room supervisors are utterly bad-ass. What do they have to lose? If they say they're going to punch someone, they follow through and actually punch them, no damn foreplay. It's not the same for me, I'm an apprentice. I can't hit people in public."

"Lu Xiaolu, you really act like a mobster. Who knows what you're going to be like when you're middle-aged," Bai Lan said.

I learned a lot of new words from her, and *mobster* was one. I didn't care, I told her—besides, I was only nineteen. I'd turn over a new leaf later. For the time being, all I thought about was going around grabbing bricks and hitting people. People with hard heads were allowed to think like this, while people like Bai Lan ran to the factory office swearing like a trooper and smashing thermoses.

"You really are a mobster, you've admitted it yourself," she said.

"Save it—it's six of one, half a dozen of the other," I said. "You've bitten someone and smashed thermoses. I grab one brick, and that makes me a mobster?"

"Are you going to rely on bricks your whole life?" Bai Lan asked. "Go to college, get married—all with bricks in your pockets?"

I'd joked with her before, saying she'd seen nothing of the big bad world. Hitting someone with a brick was nothing. I'd seen tons of gang fights.

"What have you seen?" Bai Lan asked seriously. "You've seen nothing. Have you seen tanks and machine guns? I've seen both."

I shuddered with fear when I heard this. I asked her to elaborate, but she wouldn't.

Bai Lan and I were always bickering. My workplace was constantly noisy, while Bai Lan's infirmary was quiet as a morgue. Both places were bad for the temper. The first caused mania, the other depression. Sometimes I felt it might be the other way around—that I was depressed and she was manic. She wasn't very happy with my mobster tendencies, and she said she'd never hand me another brick again. She also said that I wasn't a little wolf dog but a little rabid dog. I disagreed: rabid dogs bit whoever they saw. I still had some principles.

The canteen food improved dramatically after Director Wu's beating. The workers' food caught up with the quality of the cadres' meals. The meatballs doubled in size, and there were no more pebbles in the rice or insects on the greens. *Thank God you got beaten up, Director Wu*, I thought. The fact that the quality of the lunches improved overnight after his beating showed it really had been his doing. Wasn't that just tempting us to act like mobsters? Naturally I didn't share these thoughts with Bai Lan. Inside, I knew that acting like a mobster was no good. My problem was that if I didn't behave like a mobster, how would I behave? How should I have behaved? If I turned over a new leaf, what kind of person would I become? These were questions I couldn't answer.

CHAPTER SIX
THE DON QUIXOTE OF LIGHT
BULB CHANGING

When Zhang Xiaoyin and I told each other stories from the past, I'd often say proudly how I used to be an electrician. She couldn't understand why this would make me so proud. Her uncle used to be an electrician, and now he was a factory head. I felt a twinge of inadequacy when she told me this. Becoming an electrician had been an impossible feat in my mind.

In that dead-end chemical factory in the early '90s, everyone had wanted to be an electrician. Electrical work was laid-back and skilled, which made it the most respectable trade in the saccharin factory. If you had a grasp of the factory's circuit distribution map, even the workshop director had to bow down to you. The technical requirements for an electrician were pretty high; it wasn't like bench work and plumbing, which you could make up as you went along. If an electrician's skills weren't up to scratch, he could electrocute himself. It was survival of the fittest.

When I started at the factory and received that safety instruction lecture from Pu Nani, he explained that people who violated the work regulations were at risk of killing themselves and others. These words were prophetic. Sure enough, in 1993, it was proved that a chain was indeed no stronger than its weakest link. A couple of supervisors on the electrician team were carrying out major maintenance and repair work. One was up a ladder doing the wiring, while the other went outside to shut off the electricity. By some terrible twist of fate, he pushed the wrong switch. The cable that shouldn't have been live was now running with a 380-volt current. The supervisor inside was totally oblivious and reached out to start working on it. He had enough time to scream out before tumbling backward off his ladder. He hit the back of his head on the ground and fell into a coma. He was taken to the hospital and died not long thereafter. As a result of the accident, a police car full of public safety officers drove to the factory and arrested the supervisor who'd pushed the wrong switch.

"Do you think they'll view this as me turning myself in?" the supervisor asked one of the safety department employees.

"Just go," the safety department employee said. "You'll get a maximum of ten years."

There was another supervisor at the scene who saw the whole thing, and he was so deeply traumatized that his brain malfunctioned. He remained dumb for two weeks, during which time he was unable to eat, shit, or piss unassisted. The factory had to transfer him to the technical department, where he looked after supplies and poured the tea. People couldn't work out if he was actually dumb or just acting. His family said that his mental trauma should be treated as a work injury, and the bill should be footed by the perpetrator. Dealing with the supervisor who died was relatively simple: they issued the standard work injury compensation and paid for his funeral. It was much harder to deal with the guy in custody. If he were sentenced, his family would be up in arms, storming the factory with twenty or thirty people in tow and smashing every thermos in the department building.

Whenever there was a production accident, it affected the entire factory—six months of safety bonuses up in smoke. For a time, the factory had slogan posters pasted all over the place: *Ensure safety in production, Safety first,* and *Safety alarm bells ring forever.* The safety department convened a one-off training session, gathering up all the workers who tended to be slapdash with safety. They were given a lecture followed by an exam, and if they didn't pass, their bonuses were deducted. Pu Nani said that the bench workers were the most lacking in safety awareness, and he called me in to be retrained. If I failed the exam twice, I'd lose half my monthly bonus. In the end, I didn't have time to take the exam because I had water pumps to fix.

Since this weak link had left the chain broken, more links had to be fitted. The electrician team found themselves down three men in one fell swoop, and they were no longer able to perform their duties effectively. When my father learned this, he ran to the chemical factory office with lightning speed, offering up gift vouchers and a carton of Zhonghua cigarettes to both the machine repair workshop director and the leader of the electrician team. The following week there I was, carrying a bag of labor safety supplies, on my way to join the electrician team.

My trade school dream had been dashed, but that wasn't my father's fault. Thinking about it like that made it easier for my mind to handle. And electrical work wasn't a bad option. I'd made it to the pinnacle of the working class at least. Graduating from a bench worker to an electrician was an astonishing feat, and I was filled with admiration for my father.

You had to have an electrician's certificate, or you couldn't get a post. You had to take an exam to get an electrician's certificate, and a bureau curriculum exam at that. And even if you did obtain your electrician's certificate, it didn't guarantee you a job as one. It was completely up to the factory who became an electrician and who didn't. There were plenty of electricians on the team who'd done the work for years without certificates, while there was a supervisor in the boiler room who'd passed his electrician exam and had a certificate, but never managed to break into the electrician team. I started at a grade-four electrician's salary. This was due to filing that lump of iron on the bench worker team, which earned me a grade four that transferred to the electrician team. The whole process was pretty strange, and I couldn't get it quite straight in my mind. Bai Lan said it was a management issue, that our factory was far too disorganized. I said that disorganized management wasn't always a bad thing; it had worked out to my advantage this time. You couldn't always draw the short straw—you had to get a lucky break sometimes.

When I was on my way to work one day, a young worker called Jiao Tou from the saccharin workshop stopped me. Jiao Tou was hugely ambitious, always taking part in training sessions to try and escape the saccharin workshop. The more ambitious he became, the less inclined the factory was to transfer him. I'd heard that this was also the way of dialectics, as the saying goes: *Divine will is hard to predict.* Jiao Tou pointed at me and said, "Do you have an electrician's certificate, Lu Xiaolu?"

"Nah, I don't," I said, like a dimwit.

"If you don't have an electrician's certificate, how are you qualified to be on the electrician team?"

Naturally I wasn't going to mention my father's gifts and cigarettes, so I just said, "I don't fucking know. How are you qualified to interrogate me? Do you have an electrician's certificate?"

Jiao Tou immediately pulled a small hardbound book from his bag and waved it in my face, saying, "This is my electrician's certificate, have a look!"

"Turn it over for me. This could just be your one-child certificate. Trying to pull my leg, are you?"

Jiao Tou pushed the book into my hands confidently. It wasn't an electrician's certificate after all, but an accountancy certificate. Jiao Tou was very apologetic. "Sorry, that's the wrong one." Then he took the actual electrician's certificate from his bag and gave it to me to look over. It was another small book affixed with his photograph, a seal stamped across his face. "You've gone through the back door, Lu Xiaolu," he said. "That's very bad practice. I've taken exams and gotten lots of certificates, and here I am still producing saccharin. It's so unfair."

"Holy crap! Which other certificates do you have? Let's have a look."

He took out a grade-one computing certificate, an office automation certificate, a national-level dance-training certificate, a grade-three chef certificate. He showed me so many, I started to feel dizzy.

"These are all from exams I genuinely took," Jiao Tou said. "You don't have a single certificate, Xiaolu. Exactly how are you qualified to be an electrician?"

I looked at him as if he were insane and said, "Jiao Tou, if you keep bothering me, I'm going to batter you and all your certificates."

He made a quick retreat when he heard this.

Later I had a chance to self-reflect and started to feel bad. I'd been too harsh with the guy, undermined his self-esteem. But I had no plans to find him and apologize—neurotic types like him scared me. I couldn't figure out why a worker would take exams for so many different certificates, and none of them higher than a grade one. What was he trying to do? Later I heard he'd taken his legal certificate exam. If he passed and was awarded that, beating him up would become problematic, so I decided to keep my distance.

It was Little Pouty Lips who took me to report to the electrician team. She'd called me into the labor department on my way back from the pump room, and I was wearing the uniform I hadn't washed for close to six months. It was no longer neither-blue-nor-green, but a deathly black. Getting a space on the bus couldn't be easier, but I risked being beaten to death. I had a work belt the width of a brick around my waist, hung with a multicolored array of wrenches. On the left were two adjustable wrenches, and on the right four sets of cylindrical ones. My back pocket was stuffed with a pair of pliers and a screwdriver, and I had a Hongtashan tucked behind my ear. My body gave off the strong stench of the working class. I was no longer a timid, flustered apprentice.

Little Pouty Lips looked me up and down, frowning in disgust, and asked why I was dressed like a gangster. I told her that the factory was undergoing major maintenance and repairs, and I needed tools. I may have looked a bit boorish, but at least it proved I was hard-working. This answer didn't seem to satisfy her.

"Didn't we issue you with labor safety supplies?" she asked. "Where's your toolkit?"

I told her it had rotted through ages ago.

"Lu Xiaolu, I presume you know you're being transferred to the electrician team today," she said. "Your pa's really something. When is he going to get you transferred to the departments?"

"Don't poke fun at me," I said, sniggering. "Anyway, sitting in department offices gives you piles."

As she was taking me to the electrician team, she said, "Lu Xiaolu, your conduct in this factory has been terrible. Chief Hu actually wanted you transferred to the saccharin workshop to work the three shifts."

"You shouldn't believe what Pu Nani said about me. My conduct's been pretty good, actually. I saved Good Balls' life and was awarded a thirty-yuan bonus."

"People can't just rest on their laurels," Little Pouty Lips said. "And it's not as if you saved the factory head's life. It's not worth being that proud."

"Fair enough," I said. "I'll be sure to reform myself thoroughly."

"You really do talk crap," she said. "Don't you remember that I was the one who did your application for that thirty-yuan reward?"

"You gave me such a severe disciplining, it's only right that you also should give me the odd reward when it's earned. You can't always show me the stick and never the carrot."

"Oh, for God's sake, are you still bearing a grudge? You threatened him with a file! If it weren't for your father's help, you'd have been transferred to the saccharin workshop a long time ago."

I sighed and gave her a detailed explanation of the function of files. Files didn't have blades—they had two functional sides and a blunt end. What did she think I'd do, file Pu Nani to death? That would be pretty novel—I'd never heard of it before. I felt just like that harmless file being waved wantonly about, then forced to face a lump of metal.

"So that's what a file looks like," Little Pouty Lips said. "I guess you're right—you couldn't brandish one of them like a weapon."

What a fool, I thought to myself. I wondered if she could even tell her ass from her elbow.

Little Pouty Lips took me to the electrician team, which I felt pretty grateful about. I knew the team members—we played cards and smoked together—but having Little Pouty Lips take me there gave me more cred. Later I found out the real reason she'd brought me had been to see someone else.

Ten years later, if you asked me to describe the appearance of the electrician team station, I'd have to say: 1) it looked like an opium den; and 2) it looked an awful lot like an opium den. It was worlds away from the leaky, drafty station for the bench worker team. The electrician team was stationed in a cement building built like a bunker. You went in through a small door and followed a corridor. Further inside was an arched doorway, like the entrance to an Arabian palace. There wasn't a single window in this building—it was pitch black, with the only light cast by a couple of small lamps. There were a couple of office desks blackened with age, but behind them were recliners rather than chairs. The electricians were sprawled out on these recliners, smoking. No windows meant no ventilation, meaning none of the smoke in the room could disperse; hence the comparison to an opium den. I never really liked it there because if you spent too long inside, you were likely to get cancer. But as an electrician, you had no choice but to put up with these crappy conditions.

The only job I ever did on the electrician team was running around changing light bulbs for people. Electricians had to be able to repair motors and circuit breakers, install wiring for low-voltage circuits, climb telephone poles, and so on, all of which were very complicated. I was not involved with any of the technical work—it was all completely incomprehensible to me. "Don't worry, you'll learn it all in time," the supervisors told me. "In the meantime, why not just go and change the light bulbs."

Old Bad-Ass had already come to the conclusion that I had no mechanical talent. I couldn't repair water pumps, so he figured it was best just to write them off. Putting a bunch of water pumps into waste storage for no good reason was pretty reprehensible. If I'd been a doctor rather than a bench worker, I'd have been working the people in the crematorium to death. As I regarded other people's lives as having a similar value to my own, I should have placed a similar value on the existence of water pumps. The fact that I couldn't didn't sit well. Now that I was an electrician, I no longer needed to feel that way. When a light bulb went out, there wasn't a person in the world who could fix it. If you found someone who could repair a light bulb, he'd be even more of a genius than Edison, because when Edison invented the light bulb his intention wasn't to let people fix them. He just wanted the used ones to be unscrewed and thrown in the trash and replaced with new light bulbs. From a calorie perspective, this job was a hundred times easier than bench work. The only drawback was that water pumps didn't break that easily, whereas there were often problems with light bulbs, and there were a couple of thousand light bulbs in the factory. Changing twenty or thirty light bulbs per day therefore became my bowl of rice.

Changing a light bulb was easy. All you needed were a flashlight and ladder. According to Bai Lan, running around the factory with my ladder day in and day out made me look like a chimney sweep, and she thought I should be carrying a broom too. I'd read a story about a chimney sweep who dropped down a chimney, where he met the daughter of a wealthy family and their friendship blossomed into love. This was an English story, and it was pretty romantic. Unfortunately, I'd also read *Oliver Twist* and knew that chimney sweeps often got stuck in chimneys. The people down below would light the fire, totally unaware that he was up there, and the lad would become roast duck. Roast duck was delicious, but not romantic. Because of my brawn, I'd be sure to get stuck in the chimney and meet with a similar fate. All I can say is that Bai Lan had a wild imagination. But she was happy about my becoming an electrician, that's for sure.

Electricians didn't need to wear work uniforms because electrical work was very clean. The level of cleanliness was proportionate to the electrician's technical skills. The supremely bad-ass superiors spent eight hours in the workshop without getting a speck of dust on their clothing. That was skill. It was only during the major maintenance and repairs, when the big bosses were around, that we put on our work uniform. Normally we were kitted out in trim-cut lapel collar jackets. Lapel collar jackets were very popular in the early '90s—double-breasted with gold buttons, preferably, as it looked more impressive. It was also popular to wear harem pants at the time, loose-fitting, with anything between eight and sixteen creases along the waist. Harem pants worn with the lapel collar jacket with its gold buttons, plus a pair of white leather sneakers, made us look like a bunch of complete dickheads. Strutting around the factory in that outfit scared the shit out of people. Those who knew us would just think, *Oh, it's the electrician team off their rockers*, but others thought we were a group of foreign investors coming to inspect the place. These outfits had another special feature: the lapel collar jacket was very long and the harem pants made your legs seem very short, so we looked like a group of real odd-bods: long, trim torsos and legs like pegs. I still felt pretty cool.

I didn't have a lapel collar jacket at the time. At the beginning I had to go out in my work uniform, which meant putting up with people mocking me. Even the workshop aunties didn't trust me dressed like this, and it was having a big impact on my work. Dressing like them was important for my factory image. I begged my ma to take me to the tailor to get a lapel collar jacket with vertical stripes. Up close it looked like prison garb, and from a distance like the uniform worn by the doormen of old-school Shanghai clubs. My mother was pleased when she saw me, and she told me I looked dignified. I swaggered around everywhere in that suit. Later I stopped wearing it because only migrant workers wore lapel collar jackets—city dwellers had moved on to wearing single-breasted jackets with small collars. Lapel collar jackets came to symbolize migrant workers. This was amusing, as they wore them to lay bricks, pick up trash, and drive pedicabs—not that different than what we'd worn them for.

During the summer months, we could no longer wear the suits. We still wore the harem pants, but with nothing on our upper bodies. Our eight-crease harem pants along with our bare chests made us look like a group of Arabian dancers. Summer mornings, we rode bikes to the electrician team station, took off our shirts, and stood around smoking like that in the electrical team doorway. We loosened our belts a notch so the pants were baggy. They hung at our hips, revealing a small tuft of pubic hair three inches below our navels. The supervisors cheered us when we passed, while the young girls went bright red and ran away quickly.

Bai Lan was shocked when she saw my dance attire. She stood there, mouth agape, while I hurriedly yanked up my pants to hide my pubes. Later she told me that wearing big, loose-fitting pants like that was a good thing—it meant if I ever got an erection, I could hide it. I immediately remembered the time I'd passed out in the infirmary—fuck, talk about hitting a person where it hurt. She teased me again, saying, "I'm worried your appearance might give all the old aunties nosebleeds."

Not long after joining the electrician team, I was sent out on my first assignment. The electrician team leader wanted me to go to the refrigeration workshop to change a light bulb. The electrician team leader was about thirty years old, and his nickname was Chicken Head. This wasn't a particularly great nickname, but he'd previously been known as Chicken Dick, which was decidedly worse, so as team leader he was upgraded to Chicken Head. Chicken Head gave me a 380-volt light bulb, telling me there were two types of light bulbs—220-volt and 380-volt. Putting a 220-volt light bulb into a 380-volt socket would create a miniature bomb. Shards of glass would fly in your eyes, blinding you. I gingerly took hold of the light bulb, and Chicken Head repeated that I was to go to the refrigeration workshop to find Huang Chunmei.

"Who's Huang Chunmei?" I asked.

"An extremely fat girl. About twice your width. You won't have a problem recognizing her. If you can't find her, ask anyone. They all know Huang Chunmei in the refrigeration workshop."

His description made me feel uneasy. Chicken Head saw this and frowned. "What are you afraid of? A fat girl really scares you that much? What would you do if you met a thin girl?" He spoke in a slangy dialect that made him difficult to understand.

Chicken Head called another young worker over and told him to go with me. His name was Xiao Li and I hadn't met him before. Xiao Li told me he'd just been transferred over from the rubber factory.

"I've seen Huang Chunmei before," he said. "She's very fat."

"Yup, that's her," Chicken Head said. "A fat tiger."

The two of us set off for the refrigeration workshop. Xiao Li was a year older than I was and had been to technical college, where he'd trained as an electrician. We were both new, and together we felt more confident. So, carrying a light bulb, shouldering the ladder, and whistling a tune, we went in search of the fat tiger.

"So these women are known as tigers, are they?" Xiao Li asked me along the way.

"What did you call them at the rubber factory?"

"We called them *locusts*, *vegetable skins*, or sometimes just *dirty rotten women*."

I asked Xiao Li why Chicken Head had said fat women were easier to deal with than thin women. Xiao Li scratched his head and said, "I'm not sure. My supervisor at the rubber factory used to tell me thin women were very potent. That they could bleed a man dry."

A note about thin women: this concept was beyond my understanding of sex at the time. I always thought that fat girls would be harder to deal with because they had bigger bodies. Thin women being scary seemed to defy logic. Later a friend who studied biology told me that from a biological perspective, the factory folklore was true: organisms with larger bodies tended to have weaker reproductive systems—elephants, whales, and pandas, for example—while small organisms had more robust reproductive systems; rats were a classic case. I remembered the aunties in the factory: their sallow faces, scrawny bodies, and powerful libidos. This biologist told me that sex was a war of shapes, but the outcome of this war wouldn't necessarily be divined by body size. All my confusion when I was young was due to my mixing love, sex, and fighting into one topic.

Xiao Li and I got to the refrigeration workshop and peered through into the control room. It was a ghost town without a person in sight, and there was certainly no Huang Chunmei. It was actually pretty scary. We could have gone straight to the safety department to report them because an unsupervised workshop could have an explosion at any time.

"Huang Chunmei!" Xiao Li cried out brightly. "Huang Chunmei!"

But the boom of machinery, a noise like a jet roaring overhead, stopped his voice from carrying. We split up to search, and in a little while Xiao Li dashed over saying he'd found Huang Chunmei. I followed him to the far corner of the room, where some women's underwear had been hung out to dry in front of the ventilator. It looked mostly like odd little bits of cloth, but in the middle hung an enormous white cloth bag.

"So, where's Huang Chunmei?" I asked Xiao Li.

Xiao Li pointed toward the big cloth bag and cried, "This must be Huang Chunmei's bra!"

The biggest bra I've ever seen was fluttering away in that dingy corner, white and poorly stitched, its straps in a tangle from the ventilator blasts.

"This has to be hers," Xiao Li said. "Unless there's more than one fat girl working in the refrigeration workshop."

We couldn't help ourselves. Xiao Li and I felt compelled to go up to the bra and touch it. Even though we knew it was a fairly disgusting thing to do, we just had to prove to ourselves that we weren't hallucinating.

"So we've found her fucking bra," I said. "What good does that do us?"

"Are you dumb?" Xiao Li said. "All we have to do is stay near the bra and keep watch, wait for Huang Chunmei to appear. She must have worn her bra to work."

"Who says it's a goddamn bra, anyway?" I said. "It's clearly a parachute."

That's when a great shadow appeared, hovering in the doorway of the refrigeration workshop, swaying softly. She shifted into our field of vision, and I knew for certain that it was her: owner of the parachute, Huang Chunmei. What I wasn't expecting was that instead of shooing us over to change the light bulb, Huang Chunmei put her hand in her pocket and fished out a handful of sunflower seeds. She squeezed them from her basin-size fist into our palms.

"Come on, have some seeds," she said.

I grasped a heap of them, still warm from her hand. Huang Chunmei wasn't actually a tiger—she was just a bit fat. She had a nice personality. She stood by as we changed the light bulb, watching and chuckling, helping us keep the ladder steady. Later she showed us the sweater she was knitting, an item the size of a mosquito net. She was still unmarried and nearing her thirties. Had she been a bit thinner, she'd no doubt have made an excellent wife. She even asked us if we knew any suitable men to introduce her to. Xiao Li and I exchanged awkward glances, unsure how to respond.

Back at the electrician team station, I told Chicken Head that Huang Chunmei wasn't a tiger. Chicken Head didn't care. He just assumed all fat women were tigers, regardless of whether they had nice personalities. I told him this way of thinking was unfair.

"Is your job really this laid-back?" Chicken Head asked. "Had time for a chat with her, did you? Offered you a snack, did she?"

Xiao Li and I nodded earnestly. Then we told him about the parachute episode. Chicken Head laughed his head off and told us we were sickos. A week later, workers from the plumbing and bench worker teams were all racing over to take the piss out of us. They were calling us perverts, saying we liked to look at bras. That we'd gone up to the bras to sniff them. Later the story evolved, so now we were thieves specializing in bra theft. Up against a crowd of our supervisors in their work uniforms, Xiao Li and I couldn't have found the words to explain ourselves, not if we'd had a hundred mouths.

I was nineteen back then, and my only wish was for those light bulbs to keep on shining. I wasn't a rapist or a pervert—I just had a healthy interest in women's bras. I hadn't gone as far as actually stealing a bra or sniffing one—this was just the workers' rumormongering. But in this world, you had to battle for your right not to be labeled a pervert, which was all pretty boring, really. Once you'd been branded, you were stuck with it. People were never going to forget that I was a *pervert*. Sometime after, a peeping tom was reported in the women's showers. The first thing the safety department did was interrogate me and Xiao Li. They asked about our habits and told us we were prime suspects, or at the very least believed to be accomplices or conspirators.

In a year, I'd gone from being a young and naive boy to a morally degenerate, bra-stealing pervert. It had started with a bunch of workers teasing us, but the whole thing had escalated. And we were never going to find out who'd been badmouthing us. Back on the bench worker team, I'd been Old Bad-Ass's apprentice and no one had dared mess with me. But on the electrician team, I had no one. Overnight, I'd become one of the dispossessed. Maybe it was Chicken Head who started the rumors. He was the electrician team leader, so I couldn't start a fight with him—and even if I could have, I'd have been unlikely to win. It was common knowledge that Chicken Head had two brothers and four brothers-in-law all working at the factory. If this army came at me, they'd squash me flat. If I were looking for a quick way to die, insulting Chicken Head was the way to do it.

I didn't have a supervisor for my work on the electrician team. I had to learn the skills by myself. But I had big problems picking any of it up. Xiao Li came from technical college and had solid skills. He taught me how to install wiring for a circuit breaker and fix a motor. But these jobs were very complicated, and his instructions went in one ear and out the other. It was obvious I didn't have any talent for electrical work, either. Xiao Li never got angry with me. All he said was, "You'll have to stick with me, then. You can be in charge of changing the light bulbs."

I rode my bike to work each morning, following the public highway through the suburbs. It was a vast road with a huge flow of people on their way to work, a muddle of bikes and trucks. The cyclists were all bleary-eyed, while the truck drivers had come from far away and missed out on a whole night's sleep, so all of them were drowsy behind the wheel. The combination of these two types of road warriors often resulted in accidents. I saw someone scrape against a truck and fall to the ground, never to rise again. One morning I saw an old lady crossing the road to buy groceries when a truck hurtled over her and zoomed off. These were like scenes from a movie, and they feel very strange to look back on.

Before I left for work each morning, my ma would warn me to be careful. Daicheng was developing its industrial zone at this time. All the farms and fields were being flattened, and factories built in their place. Everywhere you looked were huge dump trucks filled with earth, trundling along the roads like tanks. It seemed as if these dump trucks were fitted only with gas pedals, because I never once saw their drivers brake. I thought only kamikaze pilots drove with such zeal. Before boarding the plane, Japanese kamikaze pilots would gaze in the direction of Mount Fuji, tie a strip of cloth around their heads, then shout *Kimiyago!* very loudly before nose-diving to their death. The dump truck drivers didn't shout or tie strips around their foreheads—they were happily and safely tucked up in their trucks. It was the people outside whose lives were in danger.

Each morning on my way to work, I shared the road with dump trucks, transport trucks carrying chemical raw materials, and trucks loaded with excrement. These different trucks refused to give way to each other. The dump trucks were powerful, and the excrement trucks stank to high heaven, but the chemical material trucks were the worst: either highly toxic or highly flammable. I once saw a dump truck and an excrement truck having a race along the road. Their Schumacher-style thrill-seeking was a nightmare for pedestrians, who had yellow earth and shit spraying out at them from the backs of the trucks. Like rain water but sticky, like snow but brown, like volcanic ash but putrid. The trucks zoomed past, leaving the pedestrians screaming in disgust.

My mother kept up her habit of telling me to watch out for trucks until the day she died. She loved me dearly, and she was petrified about my being knocked down by a truck. Not everyone who is loved will die under a truck—that would be far too cruel of fate, and people's nerves wouldn't cope. My mother's subtext was: don't get squashed to death between an excrement truck and a dump truck. She was quite right. Being squashed between those types of trucks would be utterly degrading. What an idiot, everyone would say, seeing such a big truck heading toward him—couldn't he have just gotten out of the way?

There were the chemical raw material trucks too, of course, but I wasn't scared of them. They were all from my factory, and the drivers knew me well. They were aware that if they knocked me down and killed me, I'd run to the driver's office and punch in their faces.

Now that I was an electrician, my mother began to worry that I'd get electrocuted. I explained that there were four different types of electric shock, categorized as follows:

1) Shock from a 220-volt current: this was a household electric circuit, and generally speaking it wouldn't kill you.

2) Shock from a 380-volt current: this was an industrial-use circuit that could immobilize you. If this current passed through your heart for fifteen seconds, you were extremely likely to fall down dead.

3) High-voltage shock, meaning anything over 10,000 volts: if you came into contact with this kind of current, it would mean instant death. We're talking barbecued chicken; we're talking burned so badly, even your own mother wouldn't recognize you.

4) Split down the middle by a bolt of lightning. This is the most powerful type of shock, so strong it could blast a house off the planet.

Actually there was one more type of electric shock: the shock from an electric baton. If you wanted to try that one out, you could go to the defense team and ask them to show you. When my mother heard all this, she was petrified.

"Don't you even think about going near the high-voltage electricity. I don't ever want to not recognize you."

My father looked at me. "Come on, do you really think he's stupid enough to mess around with high-voltage electricity? He probably couldn't even reach that high."

I took my mother's concerns to heart. Each morning I fretted about being knocked down by a truck; and once I was inside the factory, I'd start to worry about being electrocuted. This state of mind did nothing whatsoever for my ability to pick up electrical skills. I carried out my duties with extreme caution, or in supervisor terms, I was "as timid as a dick in winter."

"You can't be a sparky without getting belted," Chicken Head told me. "The guys who do live-line work are the real hard-core ones."

I asked him what live-line work was. Xiao Li, standing nearby, explained it meant carrying out electrical maintenance work while the main switch was on—i.e., when the electric current was running. If your skills weren't up to it, you were in trouble; it would either short circuit or you'd be electrocuted.

Chicken Head was already rolling up his sleeves at this point. He found a distribution board, reached a hand in, and touched it briefly, saying, "Yup, that's live."

He turned to me, looking very pleased with himself. "So how's that?" he asked. "Aren't I something?" I looked at him, stupefied, nodding like mad. "Go on, you try," he said.

Feeling pressured, I reached my hand across to the distribution board and, discovering once and for all that I was not an insulator, let out a piercing shriek. My whole body pulsed as if it had been fired at with a machine gun. The current surged up through my fingers and toward my elbow. This section of my arm felt like it was being consumed by flames. I pulled back my hand, and everything went calm once more. The electricity was still in the distribution board, I was still on the planet, Chicken Head was still a member of the human race. I looked at Chicken Head, working hard to control my rage, resisting the urge to thrust my clenched fist into his face.

"If you touch it every day, you'll get used to it," he told me blandly. "And if you get used to it, you won't be scared anymore."

Not long after, Chicken Head was given his own apprentice. Yuan Xiaowei was timid when it came to his work, lacking even more confidence than I did. Chicken Head did his same trick, reaching a hand into the distribution board and touching it before turning to Yuan Xiaowei and saying, "How was that?"

"The current's been switched off," his apprentice said, a huge grin across his face.

"If that's what you think, you touch it."

Without needing further encouragement, Yuan Xiaowei leaned over and reached in. He let out a shriek as bloodcurdling as mine had been. But that wasn't the end of it.

"You'll do this once a day now," Chicken Head stated coldly.

From this point on, every day at noon, Yuan Xiaowei would let out that same howl of pain. We'd all race over to the doorway, smoking cigarettes as we watched. It was way too cruel, and the sounds of his cries echoed in my nightmares.

Xiao Li was far from impressed. He explained that there was a knack to how Chicken Head touched the distribution board. But the way Yuan Xiaowei was going about it would kill him sooner or later. I wasn't really bothered by this. As long as Chicken Head wasn't making me touch the distribution board anymore, I couldn't care less who died. I continued to heft my ladder around, changing those light bulbs. Any time there were jobs involving live lines, I'd shrug my shoulders like an Italian and say, "I don't know how. You'll have to get someone else."

I live in Shanghai now, in a house crawling with cockroaches. It's one of those old-style horseshoe-shaped buildings. The bedroom faces north, and there's a shared bathroom and kitchen. A retired couple live opposite. They never speak to me, and they hardly seem to speak to each other either. Perhaps they're both mute. I wonder whether I'll be that pathetic when I'm their age—I'm a complete motor mouth at the moment.

The horseshoe-shaped building has very poor electric circuits. They're the same as in the factory: a red wooden distribution board fitted with an electric meter, a fuse, and a switch. The electric wire here is pretty worn. When I first pulled it open to take a look, I saw it was made from poor-quality copper wire. The electric wire I'd been using back at the factory had all been copper. I explained to Zhang Xiaoyin that it was a real fire hazard. Zhang Xiaoyin and I live together, and when we have time, we go around the apartment with bug spray, then count the cockroach corpses.

A few days ago, there was an unexpected power outage in our apartment. A second later, the power returned. A second after that, it cut out again. This happened four times. I was watching a soccer match at the time, while Zhang Xiaoyin was in front of her computer writing a story. She didn't save the file in time, and the two thousand characters she'd written were lost. The only thing I lost was watching a mediocre goal.

"What's going on with the power supply?" she asked.

I jumped up from the sofa. As a former electrician, I knew it wasn't a problem with the power supply. All the electricians at the power supply bureau had formal training and were above shoddy work like this. This kind of work could burn up all the household appliances, turn them into a heap of scrap metal.

I rushed out of the apartment door and saw the old man from across the way standing in the corridor in front of the switchboard, taking blind stabs with a screwdriver. I screamed, "Fucking hell! Can't you even fix an electric circuit?"

He glanced at me and said coldly, "There's been a power cut at my place, what does it have to do with you?"

"Fucking hell, you old wuss. Do you think you're going to fix the electric circuit that way? You need to push your house's circuit breaker!"

"Are you cursing me?"

I shook my head. I didn't have to explain myself to an old man like him. I rolled up my sleeves and ran to his place. By the light of the corridor, I located the circuit breaker on top of the door frame. I jumped up and pushed. The fluorescent lighting in the room flickered, jumped a couple of times, and once again began to emit its dim light. Two of the fluorescent tubes had blackened and looked like they'd need to be scrapped soon.

The old man staggered into the room when he saw the fluorescent light. He pushed me out the door, saying, "Behave! Who said you could come into my house?" Then he slammed the door in my face.

"Screw you!" I shouted through the door. "If it weren't for me, you'd have electrocuted your sorry ass."

I went back into my place and shut the door. Zhang Xiaoyin told me I had a bad temper. I explained that I couldn't stand it when people played around with electric switches. Those things really could electrocute you. The horseshoe-shaped building was so small, and if our neighbors across the hall had a funeral, it would be annoying as hell. I lit a smoke, ready to tell her a story about the electrician team. But the old man from across the corridor chose this moment to hammer on our door.

"Take your trash out of the kitchen, Mr. Lu."

"Screw you, old man," I shouted. "Don't think I won't hit you just because you're old!"

Back when I was an electrician, my temper was never this bad. I had only the most basic electrician skills, which meant I tended to keep a low profile. The workers still respected me, because if I didn't change their light bulbs they wouldn't be able to work, play cards, or knit sweaters. They might even be unlucky enough to fall into a drain if it weren't for me. In those dingy workshops, the light bulb was the only source of light. When we changed them, it was usually Xiao Li at the bottom supporting the ladder while I scooted up like a monkey. I'd unscrew the old light bulb and screw in the new one. Things really were that simple.

The supervisors were all pretty vulgar. They called light bulbs *bollocks* and fluorescent tubes *dicks*. So when they phoned the electrician team, they'd shout out, "There's a bollock that needs changing!" or "We've got a dick out here!"

Xiao Li said that unscrewing a light bulb from up on a ladder was actually quite dangerous. If you got an electric shock, you'd fall—and falling backward from six-and-a-half feet up meant landing on the back of your head. In martial arts novels, this part of the body was known as the *jade pillow*. If you smashed it, the worst-case scenario was that you died—best case, you'd be a paraplegic and unable to lift your neck. You'd never make love again, and even jerking off would be a task.

So changing a light bulb was a two-person job. This wasn't a waste of manpower. If there was no one supporting the ladder, there was a chance it would slide down the wall, and the person doing the work above would be fucked.

When we changed light bulbs, we took White Rabbit candies along with us as well as the ladder, so if we came across girls we could offer them around. Then we'd sit down at a table with the girls and chat awhile. Doing your rounds like this meant that changing one light bulb took half a day. I'm not saying half a day as a metaphor for a long time—I'm talking literally half a day, four whole working hours. On the bench worker team, the only women I'd come into contact with were the pump-room aunties; and although they had their own charm, I felt awkward being around them too long. Working on the electrician team, I got to go to laboratories and the workshop control rooms, where I discovered all the young, unmarried girls worked. These girls were fragrant like sweet honey, the apples of the young workers' eyes. Spend a little time by their sides, and you didn't want to be anywhere else. If you got bored talking to one girl, you'd just move on and chat with the next. Anytime someone came into the electrician team looking for me and Xiao Li, the answer was always the same: "They're out changing a light bulb—I'm not sure where exactly."

From time to time Chicken Head would lay into us. "Like fuck you've been off changing a light bulb," he'd say. "I come back here after two games of mah-jongg, and you expect me to believe you're still changing that same freaking light bulb?"

"Not our fault," Xiao Li said. "We change the light bulb, and then we're asked to help the girls mend their electric fan and their hairdryer."

"Oh, and I expect you offered to wash their underwear for them as well," Chicken Head said.

"Of course not," Xiao Li said.

"The girls said they'd like you to go there too next time," I said. "They've got an electric heater that needs fixing. It's a bit beyond us."

"You must be fucking joking," Chicken Head snorted.

The factory supervisors regularly heckled us because of the bra-stealing rumors. But the aunties were all really understanding. They even went to our supervisors and said, "Dear me, what is the problem? That kind of behavior is completely normal from a couple of adolescent boys. Are you telling us you never stole a bra when you were their age?"

The supervisors would rack their brains and say nothing. Later we defended ourselves to the aunties. We hadn't stolen the bra, we told them. We'd just caught a glimpse of Huang Chunmei's parachute and felt the need to study it further. "Oh, her bra, yes," the aunties said. "Even the Americans want to carry out studies on that."

The pervert incident gradually faded from the aunties' chatter. The supervisors listened to the aunties, and if the aunties said we were normal, we were normal. From then on, whenever they wanted a light bulb changed, they'd call up the electrician team, and say, "Hey, Chicken Head, we have a light bulb that needs changing—put your guys Xiaolu and Xiao Li on it, please."

Chicken Head would roar with laughter and say, "Do you think I'm running a brothel here, that you can just call up and order your woman of the night?"

Whenever a call came through, Xiao Li and I would pack up our tools and get ready to strut our stuff. If some other supervisor turned up in our place, the aunties would be disgruntled. The following day, they'd deliberately damage a couple more light bulbs, asking for us by name again. We really were like a couple of escorts. This went on for a while until the labor department found out and got angry, calling it "veiled pornography." That was the end of our escort career.

That year, I changed light bulbs in every corner of the factory.

I'd been to every big workshop; I'd been to the boiler room, the canteen; I'd been to the men's washrooms and the women's washrooms, the men's bathhouse and the women's bathhouse, the men's changing rooms and the women's changing rooms; I'd been to the factory head's office, the registry, the driving team, the waste storage. There were light bulbs all over, so my shadow hefting that ladder traveled all over too. Xiao Li and I had inspected a dozen or so bras drying across a rope in the women's changing rooms, all different sizes. The number-one hobby of female workers in this factory seemed to be washing their bras during work hours. Once they'd washed them, they'd dry them in the changing rooms where no one would see them or care. These bras were mostly white or flesh-colored. You'd occasionally see a pink one. The most exhilarating was seeing a black bra, so fucking avant-garde. I'd look at these bras for a long time. I was nineteen and unmarried, with no girlfriend. I lived a monklike existence. When I think back on it, how I'd loiter around underneath a row of bras hung up to dry, I have to admit that I was sexually repressed.

Other places you'd leave as soon as you'd changed the light bulb. The factory head's office, for example. There was nothing interesting about that place, and having the factory head start to recognize your face would be a complete disaster. There was a beautiful girl in the factory head's office. She sat behind a desk wearing a pair of gold-rimmed glasses, her black hair bound up, showing a smooth white forehead, much like a Greek statue. She sat quietly watching as we changed the bulbs, not speaking or moving, looking like a statue set behind the desk. If she hadn't been so beautiful and lifeless, I might have offered her one of my White Rabbits.

As an electrician, you were authorized to visit all the places in the factory that were usually out of bounds. I went to all the sacred places, including the factory head's office, the registry, and the finance department. I also went to the women's restrooms, which weren't that sacred—but when the light bulbs weren't working, the female workers could fall in the latrines, so we had to go there. The women's restrooms weren't particularly interesting, either. If we spent too long changing the bulbs in there, the female workers waiting outside would start shouting, saying we were good-for-nothings and would be just as useful if we fell down the can.

Then there was the women's bathhouse. "Is there anyone in there?" we'd holler three times outside. Only then would we risk heading in to change the light bulb. Bathing during working hours was not permitted, but there were still a number of female workers who would sneak in there. If an electrician team member forgot to shout out, it would be a case of the chimney sweep lad meeting the bathing girl, like the kid's story but with a far more tragic ending.

One day, Six Fingers from the electrician team went to the women's bathhouse to change the light bulb. I was supposed to go but I was playing chess with Chicken Head, so Six Fingers took the ladder and went off by himself. It was midday and the bathhouse was completely quiet; he could hear no water, no voices, only a cuckoo calling from a tree outside. Six Fingers was generally a bit absentminded and forgot to shout out before going in. He carried his ladder in and came face-to-face with a completely naked female worker, her ample breasts and pubic hair lathered in white soapy bubbles. Six Fingers threw down his ladder and ran. A damp head poked out from behind the women's bathhouse door curtain. "Catch the scoundrel, catch Six Fingers!" she shouted.

The safety department apprehended Six Fingers, but they soon released him. During their investigation, the safety department discovered that the girl had been bathing during work hours while Six Fingers had just been carrying out his normal work duties. This made her the one in the wrong. The problem was that this woman was unmarried.

"Six Fingers will have to marry her. Problem solved," Chicken Head said. That scared all of us. It wasn't the olden days, when seeing someone naked meant the two of you had to get married. "Hey, Six Fingers, why not go underground for a couple of days?" Chicken Head suggested.

Before Six Fingers had a chance to respond, four brawny guys charged in, followed closely by the female bather in question. She pointed at Six Fingers. "That's him," she said. The four brawny guys took out butcher knives and said they were going to gouge out Six Fingers' eyes. There were no windows in the electrician team station, giving Six Fingers no escape route. He raced around the room until they caught him and pressed him down onto the table.

"Fucking hell," Six Fingers said, "Surely you don't need four knives to gouge out my eyes."

We were all scared to death. His opponents' knives were long and wide, with blackened metal that gave off the unsettling salty smell of blood. Chicken Head was the only calm one. He dropped the teacup lid to the floor. "Had your song and dance now?" he asked.

"No, we haven't had our song and dance yet," the female worker said. "Stand aside, Chicken Head, or we'll gouge your chicken eyes too!" The female worker waved her hand as she spoke, and suddenly two of the four butcher knives that had been pointing at Six Fingers were pointing at Chicken Head.

Chicken Head became immediately compliant. "If you have something to discuss, let's discuss it properly. So he saw something he shouldn't have. Why don't I act as middleman? We'll settle this according to the old-school rules. Is it fun to dig out eyes? Why don't we get them to consider becoming lovers instead?"

The female worker's face went pale first, then flushed red, as if from shyness. She looked at Six Fingers, who was lying on his back across the table, his shirt in disarray and his eyes filled with panic. Six Fingers was a puny little junior electrician. He had triangular eyes and big buck teeth, and though he wasn't yet thirty, he was already balding. He was from a farming family, and his parents lived with his mentally challenged younger brother in the countryside, where they worked the land. Six Fingers had only a junior-school diploma; he'd stayed in school until third grade before leaving to look for manual work. Six Fingers had a sixth finger on one hand; hence his name. He was the exact opposite of the person you'd want as your romantic partner. He was a dictionary of defects.

"Who'd want to marry him?" the female worker said through clenched teeth.

"Well, what do you think we should do?" asked Chicken Head. "Who do you want to marry?"

The female worker raised her head and looked around sternly at the members of the electrician team. We junior electricians, only there to watch the drama, gave a collective shudder and ducked out one by one to have a smoke. Being chopped to pieces was one thing, but having to stand in for Six Fingers and marry the girl would have been worse than death.

"What would have happened if it had been the two of us who bumped into her naked?" I asked Xiao Li. "Which one would have had to marry her?"

"I think we'd probably have been made to draw straws," Xiao Li said.

"What if it had been an old woman?"

"Then we'd have had our eyes gouged out. If they gouge out your eyes, you don't need to draw straws."

You didn't need four butcher knives to gouge out one pair of eyes—they'd pulled them out for effect. All you needed to gouge out an eye was a section of galvanized pipe three centimeters in diameter; household water piping would do. You set it up in the eye socket, hit a hand against it, and *pop*: the eyeball drops down from the pipe. If you held a wine glass underneath, you could brew the eyeball to make alcohol. Chieftains did this in the olden days using bamboo tubing. Butcher knives were pretty unscientific.

Chicken Head finally sorted it all out. Six Fingers didn't end up having to marry the girl or having his eyes gouged out. However, he was pretty depressed. She was such an ugly, tyrannous girl, and she had caused such an uproar over being seen naked—so the fact that she still hadn't been willing to marry him made Six Fingers worry he'd never find a wife.

"Six Fingers, don't set your eyes on city girls," Chicken Head advised. "By rural standards, you must be quite a catch."

Chicken Head issued us a warning: after this incident, we should be a lot more careful about where we went and what we got up to, especially me and Xiao Li. Changing light bulbs wasn't a game—we needed to learn from Six Fingers' ordeal.

But Six Fingers' bad luck didn't end there.

In the spring of 1993, we went inspecting bras all over the place. I'd become a sexually repressed deviant. I thought it was just me and Xiao Li suffering in this regard, but the factory was actually full of people just like us. My former supervisor Old Bad-Ass's daughter Ah Ying was one. She was thirty-two, and all the men her age were married. She didn't want to be anyone's second wife, so she had her sights set on the unmarried males under thirty at the factory.

When Ah Ying was younger, she'd stated categorically that the three-shift males shouldn't even think about trying to date her. The men who worked three-shift gave a collective sigh of relief, then laughed about it, developing it into a popular factory joke. The day-shift guys took detours when they saw her, scared she might have plans for them. Ten years Ah Ying waited, her boudoir a ghost town (or, in supervisor-speak: until there were cobwebs between her thighs).

Those spring days were extremely long and muggy, and this doziness enveloped you. The air around the wastewater treatment room floated with foam that looked like snow or catkins or falling blossoms. If you didn't object to the fact that it was actually scum from the wastewater treatment, it was really quite beautiful. It reminded me of the scenes depicted in ancient Tang poetry, the boudoir sorrow of a woman awaiting her husband's return. Ah Ying sat in the wastewater room and telephoned Auntie Qin from the canteen to ask for a match with Six Fingers from the electrician team.

"Oh, the peeping tom, the one who saw that girl bathing? Who'd be blind enough to set their eyes on him?"

"I would!" Ah Ying roared in response.

Auntie Qin hurried off to make the match. She was very pragmatic about it: Six Fingers, do you want to marry a city girl? In that case, Ah Ying is your only option.

Six Fingers turned to me and said, "Xiaolu, you were Old Bad-Ass's apprentice. What's his family like, in your opinion?"

I shook my head. It had been a long time since I'd seen Old Bad-Ass. I didn't know if he was traveling far and wide on that cruddy old motorbike or not. All I could say to him was, "Six Fingers, be careful."

Ah Ying and Six Fingers started dating. The whole factory knew about it and compared it to "a toad eating a crow." These workers were all pretty harsh. After they'd met up a few times, Six Fingers explained that Ah Ying was actually quite sensitive and hadn't wanted to bite off his you-know-what. Whenever they went out to eat, Ah Ying picked up the bill. Her eating may not have been an attractive sight—lips smacking together as she chewed her food—but it didn't turn off Six Fingers. He wasn't really all that great himself.

Falling in love changed Ah Ying's whole personality. She started waiting in line at the canteen for food, and when she went to the women's restroom the men in the next cubicle no longer heard her talking.

"Love really can change a person," Chicken Head said.

Six Fingers was in high spirits too. He wore the lapel collar suit jacket with gold buttons and styled his hair like the Hong Kong singer Aaron Kwok. Only his bald patch was at the front, so his hair didn't cover his eyes like Aaron's—in fact, it barely covered his forehead. She was the first girlfriend Six Fingers had ever had. At first we were worried about him, but later we realized that Six Fingers and Ah Ying were very well suited, and we could even see them getting married.

Xiao Li and I were coming back from changing a light bulb one day, and as we arrived at the electrician team entrance, we saw an old woman standing on a stool. She'd hung a belt from the door's ventilation window and fastened it into a noose that her head was inside. We recognized her: Six Fingers' mother. In a state of shock, Xiao Li grabbed hold of her legs while I rushed into the electrician department to let people know. Six Fingers was just lying there smoking.

"Six Fingers, why are you fucking smoking in here when your mother is dangling from the door frame?" I yelled. "Come quick!"

The crowd ran out when they heard this. Six Fingers hurried over to his mother and fell with a thump to his knees. "Ma, why are you so upset?"

"Is that Ah Ying your girlfriend?"

"Yes."

Six Fingers' mother burst into tears. "If you marry that girl, you'll disgrace your father. It would be better if you died. You're going to bring suffering upon our whole family."

We all felt confused at this. How would Six Fingers marrying Ah Ying disgrace his father? Had his father had his leg over with Ah Ying? Everybody knew that Six Fingers' father was a rural man; he raised pigs and planted crops. He was even worse-looking than Six Fingers. Six Fingers quietly explained the story: it happened on the bridge to the factory entrance at dusk, when lots of farmers lugged their vegetables over and set them out for market. Ah Ying had a nasty habit of leaping onto the bridge to buy greens. She'd grab a cabbage, snap off all the outer leaves, and take home the tender leaves in the middle. If she was in a good mood, she might drop a couple of cents, but if she wasn't she'd give them nothing. She scared the shit out of these farmers, who would lie out across their bamboo baskets when they saw her coming to protect their produce, as if performing an aerobics move. Ah Ying would say nothing, just take her shoes off and whack them against the back of the farmers' heads. Six Fingers' father was one of the farmers who had been on the receiving end of her beatings.

"She's beaten up my father at least three times," Six Fingers explained, "and stolen his cabbage hearts more times than he could count."

"Did she know it was your pa at the time?" I asked.

"No, she didn't," Six Fingers said. "But he's never going to forget her face."

We lifted Six Fingers' mother down from the chair. The old lady's crying was loud and resounding, and it had the up-and-down lilt of her regional dialect. The factory idlers all flocked to the scene, and in no time she was hemmed in by a hundred workers who were only there to enjoy the drama. Six Fingers' mother recounted how Ah Ying had used the bottom of her shoe to hit Six Fingers' father. She repeated this detailed description again and again for the revelers. Everyone found Six Fingers' mother's rural accent very amusing. They were laughing as they listened, some translating the bits that others found unfathomable.

Six Fingers started crying. "I'll obey you, Mother. I won't date her anymore."

I thought that when Ah Ying heard about this, she'd come running over brandishing the bottom of her shoes, slap Six Fingers across the face repeatedly, and even hoist this old rural woman back up in the doorway and hang her again, properly this time. She didn't do any of this. She surprised us all by slinking back to the water-treatment room, where she sat in silence. She continued to sit like that: the tiger nobody wanted, no better than a written-off water pump. She sat inside her room, watching the foam float up and fill the air, imagining it as snow or blossoms, still free to imagine. She remained like that for such a long time that her bulky silhouette became etched in my mind.

Xiao Li and I became factory brothers.

I didn't really have any true friends. At school I'd hung out with my classmates, but I hadn't kept in touch with them after starting at the factory. My social circle was limited to people at Pesticide New Village and the saccharin factory, a line between these two dots, and I couldn't think where else I'd go to make friends. The only relationships I was interested in were with the opposite sex. I had no concept of befriending other guys—if I didn't desire a person, I tended to ignore them. Then I met Xiao Li. Together we'd marveled at Huang Chunmei's bra and been bad-mouthed, called perverted youngsters, which had given us a false sense of fellowship.

One day Little Pouty Lips blocked my path. "Lu Xiaolu, did you and Li Guangnan really look at Huang Chunmei's bra?" she asked.

"God, are you really as boring as all the workers?"

"I asked you a question—yes or no," Little Pouty Mouth said.

"We're not in a court of law. I don't need to give you an answer, do I?"

"I bet it was you who took him to see Huang Chunmei," Little Pouty Lips said, her face reddening.

"You're wrong, actually. It was he who took me. The bra was his discovery."

Little Pouty Lips really started to get angry. She turned to walk away, her sausage shaking in front of me.

Later I told Xiao Li about this incident.

"I was just about to ask you if you'd been talking crap in front of Du Jie," Xiao Li said.

"Who's Du Jie?" I asked.

It was Little Pouty Lips' real name, he explained.

"What's she to you?" I asked.

Xiao Li and Little Pouty Lips had been classmates throughout junior and middle school, he explained. They'd sat at the same table for five of those nine years. Little Pouty Lips had been pretty fierce as a student, while Xiao Li had been rather meek. The teacher may have been a bit of a sicko, because he got a kick out of putting them together, mainly to watch Little Pouty Lips bully Xiao Li. Who would have guessed that in the end this bullying would give way to love? After leaving school, Little Pouty Lips went to technical secondary school and studied business management or something, while Xiao Li passed his exam for technical college and studied to be an electrician. You'd think that because Little Pouty Lips was being groomed as a cadre and Xiao Li as a worker, the two of them should have called off the whole thing. But they were childhood sweethearts with feelings for each other that ran deep, and they completely forgot their class differences. Xiao Li had transferred from the rubber factory to the saccharin factory to be with Little Pouty Lips. I couldn't help but give a sigh of regret when I heard this. I'd bullied all the junior-school classmates I'd ever shared tables with, made them snivel and cry. I'd been in it for the instant gratification. I hadn't played the long game, thinking that when I was older I might want one as my girlfriend. None of them would ever want to talk to me again. I was actually pretty lucky that they weren't turning up with their boyfriends to seek revenge.

After that, Little Pouty Lips was always going on about how I was leading Xiao Li astray. By summer, her formerly well-behaved boyfriend was walking around with his chest bare, wearing harem pants that revealed his pubic hair—much to the delight of the old aunties—and had basically become a stinking, shameless lowlife. I explained that it really wasn't me who'd led Xiao Li astray. We'd both started going around with bare chests and our pubes on display at the same time. We'd learned it from the electrician team supervisors. She refused to hear this. It was as if I'd stolen her beloved toy.

When she'd first taken me to the electrician team to report, it hadn't actually been to give me kudos, it had been so she could see Xiao Li. Their dating had been completely on the sly, because like puppy love at school, it would have been misunderstood. Little Pouty Lips was always surrounded by young department employees, but Xiao Li had no one—only me to go and change light bulbs with. Having a factory romance was a pain in the ass, it turned out. It attracted far too much attention. Cadres and workers made irresponsible comments, resulting in pair after pair of them being sent to the saccharin workshop to work the three shifts. They'd even stagger the shift frequency, making one half of the couple work the early shift while the other did nights, so it became a romance between an owl and a chicken. Keeping the romance secret was a clever way around this. If you managed to keep it under wraps until you had your marriage certificate, the leaders would be too embarrassed to deal you a dud hand.

After the Huang Chunmei bra incident, Xiao Li and I had another mishap together. We never spoke about it—not because we were scared of Little Pouty Lips finding out, but because we were scared we might get beaten to death.

One afternoon in May, Xiao Li and I went to the boiler room to change some light bulbs. We knew all the boiler room supervisors; they were the best fighters in the factory. They were all short-asses, but they were so ripped that they looked like inflatable men, and they were all dark-skinned. They were pretty easy to get in with: you just offered them a few smokes, job done. The boiler room supervisors were extremely low maintenance.

The supervisors pointed at the iron ladder and said, "There are seven dud light bulbs up there."

"Fuck, that's weird. All seven blew at once?" Xiao Li said.

"They didn't blow at once, they blew one by one. But we thought you could change them all at once—saves you running here seven times."

Xiao Li and I rushed to the supervisors with our thumbs up. "Buddies, that's really decent of you."

The supervisors laughed and said, "Up you go then, you don't need us to lead the way."

The boiler room was on the edge of the factory. Beyond it was the surrounding wall, and beyond that, residential buildings. It was pitch-black because the lighting was dim, and there was coal ash all over the place. It was very hot too. People who worked in these sorts of places contracted lung disease when they got older, even the brawny ones. If they were unable even to puff out the air in their chests, all the effort that went into achieving their incredible physiques would have been in vain.

Everyone who lived in this neighborhood was aware of our factory's boiler room. There were four types of harmful substances within the chemical factory: toxic gas, polluted water, soot, and female tigers. The soot came from the boiler room. There was soot flying through the air throughout the year, no matter which way the wind blew. When it rained, the water would trickle down from the eaves, black and inky. Residents often came to the factory armed with brooms and sticks. They'd put their clothes out to dry during the day, returning that evening to find they'd all turned black. When the men got home and saw the clothes, they gave their wives lightning-fast slaps across the face. The wives yelped in pain, then rushed to the factory to make a fuss.

This soot made the nearby residents look like they had darker skin than everyone else. The kids looked like members of the Special Forces, and you couldn't even tell that they were Chinese. When it rained, these kids had white lines down their otherwise black faces, making them look like zebras.

Xiao Li and I climbed up sixteen feet on the iron ladder to arrive at the first level, where we came across the first dud bulb. We climbed up further, where we found the second and third bulbs. The boiler room was massive and there were windows everywhere, but they didn't do much to light up the place. Some sections of glass were no longer there, while others had accumulated a thick layer of soot.

I was changing a light bulb on the third level when Xiao Li suddenly kicked me and said, "Look." I looked around blankly. Xiao Li pointed through the window. "Over there."

He was pointing at a two-story house with an inner courtyard. This was the most common type of Daicheng residence. We were positioned slightly above its roof and could see in through a window, where a girl was taking off her clothes slowly. First she took off her undershirt over her head, revealing a flesh-colored bra. Because her bra was almost the same color as her skin, from far away I actually thought I was looking at a woman who had no nipples. Next she took off her bra. Her face was obscured by the eaves this whole time—all we saw were her bra and her breasts.

I immediately thought back to Li Xiaoyan's grandma, her bits of burlap sack, and that awful chaotic scene. Of all the breasts I've seen since, there have never been another pair of burlap sacks; only round, full ones with real nipples. Each time I thought about this, I got a headache so bad it felt like being bashed in the back of the skull with a hammer, and I needed to take an aspirin.

European sailors from the great voyages of old often suffered from sexual frustration. They'd see a manatee up ahead in the ocean but would mistake it for a mythical creature with breasts, which they called a mermaid. In the same way, we bored electricians saw actual human breasts—we had no immunity against this.

Xiao Li and I watched in amazement until the girl finally left the window, and the black eaves obstructed our line of view. If we could have destroyed with our eyes, we'd have blown those eaves to smithereens. I heard Xiao Li swallow loudly. I swallowed too. We both kept completely silent.

After a while, Xiao Li said, "We should never tell a soul that this happened."

"Do you think I'm dumb? Haven't we already suffered enough grief from the Huang Chunmei episode?"

This would be a hundred times more serious than the Huang Chunmei episode, Xiao Li explained. Pretty much everyone who lived there was in some way connected to the factory. Some were even family members, for God's sake. If word of this got out, we'd have people coming after us before we knew it. We'd be killed in this boiler room. They'd bury us in soot, and we'd become a couple of old mummies. Or they'd destroy our bodies to get rid of the evidence. They'd throw us in the boiler, and we'd be burned to a crisp. My heart stopped as I was thinking about this. I wasn't scared of being burned to a crisp, but being mummified was too fucking scary. Bai Lan took me to see the perfectly preserved "Loulan Beauty" at the natural museum once. I was actually pretty unlikely to become mummified—so many people get burned to a crisp in the desert; turning into a mummy was actually very rare.

I spent a lot of that year worrying that I was sexually repressed, although I only had a limited understanding of what that term meant. Sexual repression was thinking about girls when there were no girls around. I didn't know the term for thinking about girls, then suddenly having one conjured up in front of you who starts taking off her clothes. I took the matter very seriously. I thought it was divine retribution for the burlap-sack incident. When I look back on it now, I realize it was nothing. All I'd seen was a semi-naked woman, nothing compared to what Six Fingers had seen. I'd been nineteen at the time. Being alive nearly a fifth of a century before encountering a semi-naked lady didn't make me particularly lucky. But neither did it make me particularly unlucky. If I'd been really down on my luck, I'd have seen Huang Chunmei naked and then been forced to marry her. All these were things that Xiao Li said.

CHAPTER SEVEN
IN THE FIELD OF HOPE

If you were to go to the chemical factory today, you'd see the same entrance as ten years ago: a gatehouse structure made of cement, with a woven mesh door. Many people had spent their whole lives coming in and out of this entrance. Further east are the suburbs, big stretches of fields, and between the fields a highway that leads all the way to Shanghai. This road looks perfectly straight, as if the field had been cleaved with a watermelon knife.

The chemical factory had a very long perimeter wall, about eight feet high. Even in my lapel collar suit I could leap up onto this wall without getting a speck of dirt on me. I'd usually climb up onto the section of wall near the driver team, as it was fairly clean and I was unlikely to land in some ditch. Everyone knew there were lots of ditches in the chemical factory. It wasn't waste water flowing through them, but boiling water and hydrochloric acid. If you fell in, you'd be boiled mutton by the time they pulled you back out.

Climbing walls was my hobby. When I was young I used to watch the cartoon *Laoshan Daoist Priests*, about the art of walking through walls. I was fascinated by this practice, which sadly doesn't exist in modern society. Since I couldn't learn to walk through walls, I had to learn to go over them instead. I happened to have a natural-born talent for this, and I thought I might go on to become a commando. Other people said I was just a natural-born thief. My school office had caught me climbing walls a couple of times. "We have a perfectly good main gate, why can't you just go through that?" the headmaster asked. When I was unable to explain, he called me a natural-born thief and said I was unlikely to amount to anything.

I often cut school, so most of my wall climbing was over the school wall. At work, it was in the other direction; I used to arrive late, so I'd jump over the wall and into the factory. There were lots of trees growing outside the chemical factory wall. With my legs in the splits, I stepped up between the outer wall and the tree trunk until I could leap onto the wall. I'd stand on the top of the wall for a while, too scared to jump down. I'd surveyed this wall. It was sturdy, built from red brick, the lower half and the top coated in concrete. The foot of the wall had grown mossy over the years. The soil on the outside of the wall was black and had lots of grass growing from it, while inside the soil was red, yellow, blue, and green, dyed an eclectic range of colors by all the chemicals. The top of the wall was shiny white from all the bird shit and covered in dead leaves and parasol tree seeds, with the occasional stray cat crouching nearby, but that was it.

Standing on top of the wall and looking over the road outside gave you a strange perspective. You could see pedestrians crossing the road and the cars driving down it, and it felt like watching a movie. I once saw a man rush to the corner of the wall. He failed to notice me crouched just above him on the wall, and he pulled down his zipper, whipped out his dick, and took a forceful piss just below me. The stream of piss tinkled as it hit the base of the wall. I remained there squatting above him, watching quietly with a smoke stuck between my lips. A speck of ash fell down and landed on his dick. He shuddered and lifted his head. When he saw me, he started cursing the hell out of me.

I didn't curse back. He might have the wrong impression seeing me crouched up there on the wall and think I was some kind of supernatural being. I remembered my headmaster's words: a natural-born thief. I'd never even stolen a pair of factory gloves. There were lots of reasons people might climb walls—some were thieves, some voyeurs, others did it just for a sense of otherworldliness. Those in the last group were poets, although poets didn't generally go around ashing cigarettes on other people's dicks.

I walked along the wall after that incident, careful to avoid the dense foliage where caterpillars sometimes lurked, causing painful itching if you brushed up against their bristles. I walked along to the part of the wall near the driver team, jumped onto a truck, and slipped down to the ground. I'd forgotten to put out my cigarette and still had it in my mouth as I made my way toward the production zone. I hadn't walked ten yards when someone suddenly yelled, "Lu Xiaolu! You're doing a stroll-and-smoke!"

A stroll-and-smoke meant having a smoke in your mouth as you wandered around, and it was the most dangerous thing you could do. It could blast all the factory equipment into the sky. I wasn't doing it on purpose. I knew full well that I'd be the first thing to fly into the air if there were an explosion. I'd pay for my destructive behavior with my own life, which wasn't really my style. I hurriedly stamped out the cigarette, only to hear that same voice yelling, "Lu Xiaolu, you're littering with cigarette butts!"

Littering with cigarette butts in the production zone could also lead to explosions and fires. This was common safety knowledge. I was irritated and wanted to curse whoever this meddling person was, but before I had a chance, he appeared like a whirlwind before me. As soon as I saw him, my anger drained away: I was standing face-to-face with Hu Deli, head of labor.

Terrified, I turned to run, but Hu Deli grabbed hold of my suit. I tried to struggle; I didn't like having my clothes grabbed, and besides, it was my only lapel collar suit. I tried other escape tactics, such as pressing forcefully against his wrist. I could have tripped him at that point, but I didn't dare. And kicking the head of labor in the balls would mean waking up tomorrow in prison. I pressed down on Hu Deli's wrist, but it had no effect—I'd obviously been working my biceps in vain. Under his grasp, I was made to perform dramatic twists and turns, like I was dancing the rhumba. He still had me in a plierlike grasp with his right hand while his left hand pinched my wrist, twisting it around behind my back. I gritted my teeth to stop from yelling in pain.

Hu Deli lifted my jacket at the back, then deftly tied the material around my wrist and knotted it. This was taking things too fucking far. This was the job of the police, not the head of labor. He led me toward the labor department. Workers and supervisors laughed as we passed, saying, "Good job, Hu Deli!" Hu Deli looked pretty pleased with himself. If it hadn't been for his labor department status, he'd have been on the receiving end of a kick in the fucking balls, I reminded myself.

He marched me back to the labor department. The first thing I saw was Little Pouty Lips' gloating expression. Hu Deli told Little Pouty Lips to take out the labor regulations handbook.

"Check and see how he should be punished. We should be giving this kid the death penalty."

I started to feel dizzy, thinking this would be my whole year's bonus up in smoke. But when they checked the penalty for a production-zone stroll-and-smoke, it was only twenty yuan. Littering with cigarette butts was another twenty yuan, and there was absolutely no mention of climbing the wall. That made my total fine forty yuan.

"How can the fine be so little?" Hu Deli asked Little Pouty Lips.

"That's always been the fine, Director Hu. The labor regulations haven't changed since 1985."

"It's not enough. He should have two months' bonus deducted at least!"

"That would be illegal," I said. "It would be avenging a personal wrong in the name of public interests!"

"I am the law here!" Hu Deli said. "I'll say how you're punished!"

One more thing about when Hu Deli caught me in the production zone: there had been a bird flying overhead, and it released a splash of shiny white shit. This bird shit should by all rights have landed on my head, but because of the tussle and struggle, it landed on Hu Deli's head instead. He didn't notice it, and seeing it at such close range, I couldn't help but laugh. In laughing I lost my strength, allowing Hu Deli to subdue me.

I couldn't understand the significance of that bird shit, whether it was symbolic or carried some secret message. But it was really fucking funny. The world is made up of infinite coincidences. If I had to choose between being hit by bird shit and being caught by Hu Deli, I'd choose the bird shit, because all you needed to do was shower and it was dealt with. At the same time, I felt that my encounter with Hu Deli wasn't a coincidence, which meant that the bird shit had been destined for Hu Deli. I couldn't be unfortunate enough to be the recipient of both bits of bad luck, could I?

My relationship with Hu Deli deteriorated from there. In Xiao Li's words, I was a dead man. Little Pouty Lips gave us some inside information: apparently the labor regulations were being revised. From now on, jumping over walls would be punished the same as theft, no exceptions, whether you had something in your pocket or not. According to these new regulations, a stroll-and-smoke would be punished with a five-hundred-yuan fine. The fines for late arrival and early departure were also raised accordingly. The workers and superiors all hated my guts. They said I was the one rat dropping that ruins everyone's soup. They hated Hu Deli too, but the things they called him were too obscene to repeat here.

In order to uphold these new regulations, Hu Deli would stand at the factory entrance every morning to catch latecomers. At five minutes to eight, he'd stroll to the front desk, where he'd stand waiting for the work bell to ring. At eight on the dot, the front desk bell would ring. He'd wait for it to stop, at which point you were officially late for work. There was no punch-card machine back then, so catching latecomers was manual work. This brought the concept of lateness into a focused debate. At the factory entrance, there was a straight white line. If a worker had the front wheel of his bike over the line at the moment the bell stopped ringing, but the back wheel was outside the line, did that still count as a late arrival? Sometimes an employee would be obstructed by people outside the white line, possibly intentionally. Did that count as a late arrival? Others claimed they'd already started work and only wandered out to buy a pack of smokes. Did that count as a late arrival?

The rule of thumb to avoid capture was: it was better to be one hour late than one minute. Hu Deli was a cadre, not a gatekeeper—he couldn't spend all day at the front gate. At eight-thirty, he'd stroll back to the labor department and sit in the gun tower, occasionally looking out over the factory entrance. You just needed to come into the factory backward, so all he saw was your ass. Then you'd dive into the nearby bushes, home free.

At the beginning, Hu Deli used to catch me regularly. "Lu Xiaolu, you're late!" he'd shout with glee. I'd tremble and tumble from my bike, caught fair and square. He'd grab my collar and make me fill out a late form. He made a public example of me, forcing me to stand at the entrance holding a sheet of paper that said: *I was late*. This was how you dealt with lazy young workers, Hu Deli explained, particularly ones like me with no prospects. He explained that the most important quality a person could have was a sense of shame.

The factory entrance was completely deserted as I stood there serving as a public example. All the other workers were working. I held up the piece of paper but didn't know for whom I was meant to be holding it up.

Hu Deli stood across from me, assessing my level of shame. "Lu Xiaolu, you have no shame in your eyes," he said.

"Chief Hu, do you want me to stand naked, so I do feel shame?"

"Hold the paper higher," he snapped. "Higher still!"

While I was serving as a public example, some girls poked their heads out of the nearby laboratory building and started throwing sunflower-seed cases at me. I knew these girls; I often went to change light bulbs for them. I'd give them candies and tell them ghost stories. I really liked them because they were all very clean. They wore white, gownlike lab coats with only a bra and panties underneath in the summer months—through the thin white gowns, you could see the vague outlines of their underwear. As soon as I thought of the laboratory girls, I'd enter a fantasy world. Even the sunflower-seed cases falling down on my head made me happy. I was like that ancient scholar in *The Plum in the Golden Vase*, who would walk past a brothel to be hit on the head by seed cases thrown by the girls up above, leaning against the railing. It was a sexual fantasy, really. When Hu Deli wasn't looking, I'd smile up at the girls and even wave at them. This would give them the green light to wantonly scatter handful after handful of sunflower-seed cases down onto my head. I had no idea where they got hold of so many of them. They must have been collecting them just to rain down on lazy young workers. As soon as Hu Deli turned to look at them, they whipped their heads back inside the window, disappearing like a group of frightened mice. I really respected this about them—they were never going to fall into Hu Deli's hands.

I'd describe Hu Deli as a hunter standing at the factory entrance, poised to pounce on his prey. Naturally, those mouse-quick laboratory girls didn't rouse his interest. But I was the big black bear he'd been hunting for so long. He only needed to shoot me, and he'd live up to his glorious title: head of labor. If you caught a black bear, you'd skin him too, hang him on the wall to show off. This would be the black bear's destiny. But you couldn't demand a bear to feel shame, for fuck's sake. That was too tall an order. Could a bear really be held responsible for his own sense of shame?

I wasn't stupid, and after being caught a couple of times, I started to learn from the supervisors. If I was late for work, I'd just dive into the teahouse. That teahouse is gone now. It used to be a dingy bungalow, no shop sign. The first thing you saw when you walked in was a wood-burning stove with a pot of water constantly boiling on it. There were two twenty-watt light bulbs hanging overhead, a couple of tables blackened by age, and a couple of benches that were shiny from all the asses that had sat on them. This was where the old men from the suburbs drank their tea. "Oh, look, another latecomer," they'd tease whenever they saw me.

You'd dawdle in the teahouse for long enough to watch two whole games of chess and drink enough green tea to make you need to piss, and that would take you up to roughly nine o'clock. By this time, Hu Deli would be back in his gun tower. I'd leave my bike at the nearby bike stand and ask the bike repairman to keep an eye on it for me. Then I'd leap nimbly over the wall and into the factory. Sometimes my movements were so lightning-fast that the only thing the old gateman saw was a blur in front of his eyes, which he thought was a stray cat streaking past.

The teahouse wasn't completely failsafe. Who knows what prompted Hu Deli to suddenly stroll in there one day during his watch. As soon as he walked through the door, he clocked me sitting there playing chess. He gave a frosty laugh. "That's your entire monthly bonus gone," he said. My blood ran cold, and I couldn't concentrate. I made a wrong move in the game, and the old man I was playing wiped me out on the spot. I had to cough up my small change.

After our teahouse cover had been exposed, I started going to the games arcade a little farther away to play *Street Fighter*. This was more fun than chess— and safer. The only problem with video games was that I lost all sense of time. When I eventually remembered I needed to be at work and ran out of the dingy games room, the sun was already high in the sky, and it was about time to head to the canteen for lunch.

I would often find myself serving as a public example alongside a very tall dude whose nickname was Long Legs. Long Legs was about my age, and worked as a plumber. Hu Deli also made him hold up a piece of paper that said: I *was late*. Long Legs had more of a sense of shame than I did, and more of a sense of fear. He was scared shitless whenever he saw Hu Deli and would become submissive, holding the sign even higher. He was six-foot-two and held the sign higher than eight feet in the air, which meant no one could read what it said. So Hu Deli assumed that Long Legs was screwing around on purpose, being even more shameless than me.

Long Legs served as a public example for only ten minutes before the head of the plumber team called him back in—there was no one else available to mend pipes. A brief note about plumbers: they were responsible for the installation and maintenance of the chemical pipelines. This was an odd kind of trade,

as it could be either very leisurely or as tiring as hard labor. To be more precise—
if you didn't do the work and just let the pipes leak, you'd find it very leisurely.
But if you went around checking all the pipes in the factory (which, lined up
end-to-end, equaled about 650,000 feet), it would make your job hard labor.
Our factory's plumber team was very lazy. The supervisors were all completely
work-shy and shunted all their responsibilities onto one person: Long Legs.

The way I saw it, going to work but not actually working got pretty boring.
It was better to keep busy. The plumber team supervisors had come up with
another kind of work: playing chess. There were a couple of supervisors there
who'd made it to the second-division amateur league. This gang of supervisors
had disproportionately large hand muscles, so they made chess look like a thug's
game; it must have had something to do with their trade. When plumber team
supervisors played chess, they did so standing up, cigarettes between their lips
and cups of tea in their hands. There were always four or five chessboards laid
out in that small team station, and they played with such complete absorption
that the whole world could have collapsed without their noticing. Seeing as
they were so busy playing chess all day, the supervisors were unable to attend to
their duties. Each time a pipe leaked, they'd point to Long Legs and say, "Go
on, Long Legs, fix the pipe!" And Long Legs would scurry off diligently with his
tool kit to attend to the work. Unfortunately for him, he was the only member
of the plumber team who couldn't play chess.

Xiao Li and I made our way to the boiler room to change a light bulb one
day. The image of that semi-naked woman beneath the eaves was still fresh in
our minds. Clearly we weren't always going to be so lucky. We had climbed up
to the highest platform level, where it was pitch-black, when we heard a rum-
bling above us and felt a sudden heat. I'd just extracted the dud light bulb when,
from a dark corner, a sallow face appeared, watching me from an illuminated
spot. At first glance I thought it was detached—all I could see was this head
floating through the air. I dropped the light bulb all the way down from the
sixty-five-foot platform.

The head looked at us happily and even called out our names, "Xiao Li! Lu
Xiaolu!"

I took a closer look and saw that it was Long Legs. With his height, no
wonder I'd mistaken him for a floating head.

"Fuck, Long Legs, what are you doing up here?" I asked.

"Fixing pipes," he said.

"Come out of there," Xiao Li said. "You nearly gave us a heart attack hiding like that."

Long Legs emerged from the darkness. His work clothes were too wide for his thin frame and too short for his long body; it was an interesting look. The plumber team supervisors had given him all sorts of nicknames: Long Legs, Crane, Bamboo Pole, Fire Poker, Compass, Zombie, Stilts. Chemical factory supervisors were the masters of rhetoric, and the nicknames they came up with were always spot-on. But they were a team of assholes, leaving Long Legs to carry the work of eight men just because he didn't play chess, and teasing him relentlessly on top of that.

Long Legs was lying when he told us he was fixing a pipe. Xiao Li and I weren't born yesterday. In one glance, we saw something was up. The top level of the boiler room was the most secluded place in the factory, and there was almost never anyone up there. People usually went to such places only if they were up to no good. Xiao Li made a circuit of the platform but failed to find anything untoward.

"What are you looking for?" Long Legs said.

"Did you bring a woman up here with you?" Xiao Li asked.

Long Legs went pale with shock. "Don't talk crap," he kept saying. "If something like that got out, it would be the death of me."

"Come clean, Long Legs, what are you doing up here?" I asked.

"Fixing pipes," Long Legs said.

"You don't even have a wrench on you. What kind of pipe are you fixing without a fucking wrench?"

Long Legs looked like he'd just had a shot of Chinese medicine. He was frowning and pursing his lips so furiously that from the side, his usually flat face looked almost C-shaped. This was Long Legs' trademark facial expression.

"Long Legs, you haven't been jerking off up here, have you?" Xiao Li asked.

Long Legs looked like he was about to faint. "You have a seriously dirty mind," he said. "I'm here reviewing my class notes, if you must know."

"What freaking class notes are these? Are you preparing for the eighth-grade plumbing exam?"

"I'm reviewing my language-class notes."

Long Legs was a plumber—why was he studying language? He wasn't even smart enough to learn chess, which might have lightened his load somewhat. Xiao Li explained that Long Legs was taking part in the adult college entrance exams. Long Legs nodded and took his revision materials out of his back pocket. Sure enough, it was a book entitled *Language*. Language had been my favorite subject at school, but by now I'd forgotten most of what I'd learned.

In Xiao Li's opinion, Long Legs was screwed. If the head of his team found out about it, they'd break his long legs. I told them it wouldn't be that bad—he wasn't actually their slave, how could they stop him from taking the adult entrance exam?

"You can't let this get out, Xiaolu," Long Legs said. "If you do, I swear I'll kill myself. I'll do it in the doorway of your house."

I pushed him away in disgust, saying, "Long Legs, you're such a big freak!"

Xiao Li was right. Although adult college entrance exams were open to any young person within the prescribed age range, the factory was very opposed to them. Every young worker who took the exams was seen as overlooking his proper duties, getting above his station, prone to dawdling and fickleness. The best way to deal with young workers like this was to send them to the saccharin workshop to work the three shifts. We both reassured Long Legs that he could relax. If he got transferred, there'd be no one to fix the pipes.

"I'm so sick of fixing pipes," Long Legs moaned.

Long Legs had tried on multiple occasions to transfer to the electrician team. The electrician team was more relaxed, and a tall guy like him wouldn't even need a ladder to screw in light bulbs; the most he'd need would be a small stool. The problem was that the plumbers needed tall people, too—the pipes in the chemical factory were all fixed overhead.

In order to transfer trades, Long Legs went to see the plumber team leader. He invited him out to lunch to request the transfer. The level-two amateur chess player ate his meal quietly and calmly, waiting for Long Legs to make his request, at which point he wiped his mouth and said, "You need to go find Chicken Head. If he agrees, I won't oppose it." So Long Legs went and found Chicken Head and invited him out for lunch. Chicken Head wiped his mouth and said, "You need to go find the workshop director. If he agrees, I won't oppose it." So Long Legs went to find the workshop director and invited him for lunch. The workshop director was hard to pin down, and he had to issue three lunch invitations before the man finally agreed to do him the honor. The workshop director wiped his mouth and said, "You need to go find Hu Deli. If he agrees, I won't oppose it." As soon as Long Legs heard Hu Deli's name, he started to quake. He ran to the office building and stopped in the labor department doorway, pacing up and down, working up the courage to go in. Hu Deli saw him coming, and without giving Long Legs the chance to open his mouth, he said sternly, "Long Legs, I heard your workshop report is out, and it says you aren't happy with your job!" When Long Legs heard this, all his courage dissolved in his stomach.

We urged Long Legs not to lose hope. If he was transferred, the plumber team supervisors would actually have to do some work. Their chess levels would drop, which would drag down the whole factory, possibly even the whole country. Long Legs didn't know whether to laugh or cry. He was utterly depressed. Sometime later, Six Fingers gave Long Legs a terrible suggestion. He taught him Japanese-style motivational techniques. Each morning, he was supposed to get up and say his affirmations to himself in the mirror. He should shout them loudly with his fists clenched, and this would give him hope. Long Legs didn't know what to shout, so Six Fingers said, "You should look in the mirror and shout, 'I am an electrician! I am an electrician!'"

That day in the boiler room, Long Legs pleaded for us to keep his secret. If the plumber team knew he was studying, they'd send him out to do the grimiest and most arduous chores, keeping him dog-tired so he had no energy left to study. He actually started to cry as he was telling us all this, his face turning eggplant-purple. His tears scared us. This crane looked like a woman when he cried, and he made revolting whimpering sounds. We comforted him with a pat on the head, which also wiped the soot from our hands. We promised we wouldn't say anything, but Long Legs was still not convinced.

"Let's swear brotherhood to each other," he suggested suddenly. "That way you two can't rat me out."

"How about you become our sworn sister instead?" I said, mocking him.

Long Legs opened his eyes wide at me and said, "You really don't respect me at all, do you, Lu Xiaolu?"

I didn't want him to take it the wrong way—I was worried he might actually cry himself to death. So I told him we would be sworn brothers, and I meant it too. Long Legs asked for one of our knives, explaining that to swear a sacred oath, we needed to cut our palms and hold them together so our blood would mix, which would make us brothers.

Xiao Li pulled out his utility knife, worn and shiny, and said, "You make the first cut."

Long Legs took the knife and looked at it for a long time before saying, "Cutting ourselves would be too painful, and mixing blood might give us hepatitis or something. Let's just swear an oath."

So we all raised a hand and swore this oath: "Chen Guowei, Lu Xiaolu, and Xiao Li hereby become sworn brothers. If any of us betrays the others, may God and the devil punish us, hacking us into a thousand pieces."

"Are you satisfied now?" we asked Long Legs when we'd taken the oath.

"Let's create a rank order. We'll work it out from age," Long Legs said.

Xiao Li was the oldest, Long Legs second, and I was youngest. I was tempted to make some wisecrack about calling him "Number Two," but I was scared he'd cry again.

Long Legs had already told us his life plan: pass his night college exams and major in mechanical and electrical integration. Once he graduated, he'd give enough gifts to get through the back door to become an engineer. Then he'd transfer to the departments and work his way up to department head. It was a great plan, each step a thrilling adventure.

Long Legs didn't manage to keep his secret after our oath of brotherhood. But we weren't the ones who let the cat out of the bag. The plumber team started its major maintenance and repairs to all the factory's pipelines. The plumber team supervisors had no choice but to put down their chess pieces and do a bit of token work. They were relying on Long Legs for this. He was the backbone of the operation, and they couldn't do without him. The unfortunate thing was that they were completely without him.

The plumber team supervisors couldn't find Long Legs anywhere. They couldn't have been more worried if they had lost their own sons. The factory was filled with their wild screaming: "Long Legs! Come fix the pipes! Long Legs! Fix the pipes!" They screamed like this for ages, but there was still no sign of him. Before he'd always been very obedient, appearing in front of them when called, like a well-trained dog. The supervisors were at their wits' ends, looking all over for him. One of them wanted to call to report him missing. Another suggested going to his house to report him dead, certain he'd drowned in the storage tank. Then one of the boiler room supervisors ran over, pointing to the wisp of black smoke snaking up from the smokestack. Everyone understood what this meant. Ten minutes later, Long Legs was being yanked down from the boiler room, his *Language* book pulled from his back pocket.

Long Legs was close to losing his way. His adult college entrance exam was looming, and if he didn't get in, he'd have another year of working for the plumber team. Less than five minutes after he'd been pulled down from the boiler room, he disappeared again. This time he was caught in the scrap storage room. He was subsequently captured in the canteen, the library, and the men's showers. Long Legs asked me to beg Bai Lan to let him use the women's examination room—it was the quietest place in the factory and there was no way the supervisors would dare burst in. He knew I was on good terms with Bai Lan, but I didn't agree to ask her. A sophisticated new sport was being practiced by the plumber team: fox hunting. A group of supervisors would encircle Long Legs in the factory woodland and seize him. Later it evolved so that all the supervisors in the factory would surround him. Whoever ended up catching Long Legs would be rewarded with a Hongtashan cigarette by the plumber team leader. Everyone was much happier since this incentive had been introduced. In the end, the plumber team started sending two supervisors to escort Long Legs to and from work. They'd have their eyes fixed on him the whole time, whether he was eating or taking a crap, which meant that this six-foot crane had no way of escaping. He had no choice but to get on with his work obediently.

A word about the factory pipelines, which were actually pretty interesting: before I joined the factory, my father warned me to keep my distance from the pipes. These pipes were all different colors, and it was worth knowing what they all meant. The green pipes carried water, the red pipes raw materials, the white pipes steam, and the blue pipes inert gas. Most of these pipes were fixed midair, twisting and turning like intestines. When you didn't have work to do, you were better off not loitering under the pipes. If the water pipe leaked, it was no big deal, but it was pretty scary if the sulfuric acid pipe leaked. I'd seen someone standing under the sulfuric acid pipe when a wisp of white smoke actually started rising from the top of his head. He looked like a celestial being one minute and was rolling on the floor like a panda the next.

The pipes in our factory were designed by an engineer called Baldy Liang. He was extremely innovative, putting the sulfuric acid pipes directly above the water pipes, which ran into the bathhouses. If the sulfuric acid pipes had a leak, it would start dripping onto the water pipe and soak its way in. It would run through the water pipes into the bathhouses, where the bathers would feel themselves in sudden pain. As soon as you felt these low concentrations of sulfuric acid raining down onto your body, you'd crawl to the window and yell to get the attention of the people outside: "Fucking hell! The sulfuric acid pipe's leaking again!"

Baldy Liang wasn't a complete sadist. The shower water wouldn't actually harm the body—in fact, it functioned as an antibiotic, curing vaginitis and posthitis, but it felt hot and stung the skin, and most people didn't tolerate it very well. Baldy Liang was extremely proud of his innovation of having the people in the bathhouse report anytime the pipe leaked, and he wanted to apply for an international patent. All the factory employees hated his guts. Who wanted to be an automatic alarm system while taking a shower?

Some of the anger toward Baldy Liang was directed at Long Legs too. People who'd finished work and were having a shower would suddenly shout out, "Ahhh! The sulfuric acid pipe's leaking again! Where's Long Legs?" Someone else would report that he was soaking in the bathhouse pool. Four or five supervisors would drag Long Legs out of the water, shouting, "Long Legs, you motherfucker, go mend the pipe!" Long Legs would go red and fall silent. Dripping with water, he'd pull on his cotton trousers and run out. As he was running, a dozen or so damp heads would poke out the window of the women's bathhouse, cursing him. "Long Legs, you motherfucker, go mend the pipe!"

A note about Long Legs: in his own words, he was living in a world where life was worse than death. There were lots of crazy people in this world. Most of the time they'd act completely normal, but as soon as they saw Long Legs, they'd go crazy. He was the *key* that turned people crazy. I advised him to go have an operation, get six or seven inches amputated from his legs, and people would stop bullying him. The factory was like that. If you looked different from other people, it triggered the desire to hurt you.

Long Legs lived in hiding. Finally, the plumber team supervisors started to get really anxious. They bashed open Long Legs' toolbox with a hammer and found his stack of notes. They burned them to cinders on a stove. When Long Legs came back, he found his toolbox wide open. "The joke's over, give my notes back," he told the supervisors.

"We burned them," the supervisors said.

"If I promise I won't hide anymore, will you please give me my notes back?" he begged.

"We burned them," the supervisors said.

Long Legs took out a wrench. "Come on, you motherfuckers, give them back to me."

"We burned them," the supervisors repeated.

Long Legs picked up the wrench and held it above his head, as if about to attack. If it had been me pulling that move, the supervisors would have been running for their lives. But sadly for Long Legs, he couldn't look threatening. The supervisors just stared at him. Then they took their hats off and leaned forward so their heads were under his wrench. "Strike me here—strike here, and I'll get six months' work injury leave," they said. Long Legs saw seven or eight heads, but at first he didn't dare to strike them. Then he didn't know which one to strike. Finally he hit his wrench against the supervisors' chessboard. Those chessboards were made of steel plating, the grid scratched out with a scraper. When the wrench struck, all it did was make a loud noise and give off some sparks. The supervisors laughed their heads off. Long Legs burst into tears and ran toward the river.

Xiao Li and I saw the whole thing from the doorway of the plumber team station. We'd even seen the supervisors burning his notes. One old supervisor said that the plumbing team supervisors were as hard as nails. That same year, they'd rebelled against the factory armed with spears (bits of piping with both ends sharpened). They'd attacked the library and burned all the books. Compared to that, what did Long Legs' battered study books matter?

He may have been a complete wimp, but Long Legs was still our sworn brother, so Xiao Li and I followed after him all the way to the bridge. Long Legs climbed up onto the bridge railings, his tears dropping down onto a cargo boat in the river below. A hiccup-y sound emerged from his throat, as if he were choking to death. We grabbed onto his waist, terrified he was about to jump. My grandma once told me you should hold someone by the head if they were planning to smash themselves into a wall; take them by the feet if they were about to hang themselves; and grab them by the waist if they were intent on jumping into a river. These were all suicide prevention techniques. But Long Legs didn't want to die. He gripped onto the railings, his feet pressed against the side of the bridge, like a bow we were pulling taut. Finally he relaxed his grip, and we carried him back to the street, where he sat on the curb and sobbed like a girl. He cried so much that his face was track upon track of tears.

"Lu Xiaolu, Xiao Li, you two aren't bullying Long Legs again," the workers shouted as we passed.

"I'm going to quit," Long Legs told us when he'd stopped crying.

"Where will you go?"

"I don't care where, I'm just going to quit."

"But where will you go?"

Long Legs couldn't say. We couldn't answer this question either. We sat beside the river. The river was very wide, and the water was black. The question of where else to go was unthinkable. If you did think about it, you'd also have to ask yourself, "Where did I come from?" and "Who am I?" These weren't the fucking questions an electrician should be asking. Long Legs couldn't quit. All he knew was plumbing. I was even less adept; all I could do was screw in light bulbs. At that point, a workshop manager ran out of the factory and pointed at Long Legs. "Long Legs, go mend the pipes!" he said. Long Legs was sick of crying. He stood up pliantly and followed the man back inside. I sat on the edge of the road and lit a smoke. I waited until it had burned all the way down before standing up and dusting myself off. Then Xiao Li and I went to change another light bulb.

"You're young, you have good technical skills. Why don't you go try your luck at a foreign enterprise?" I asked Xiao Li.

Xiao Li explained that foreign enterprises were very strict and would fire you for the smallest offense. State-owned enterprises might be screwed up in a lot of ways, but they didn't fire their workers unless they actually beat up a workshop director.

I didn't really have a concept of foreign enterprises back then. I just knew they were factories run by people from Hong Kong and Taiwan. The main difference between them and state-owned enterprises was that the pay was higher. Xiao Li did the math. In the saccharin factory, we worked for two hours each day and idled around the remaining six; but in the foreign enterprises, you had to do nonstop work for eight hours. It didn't mean they paid you four times as much, though, and that was the bottom line. I bumped into an old senior-middle-school classmate some time later. He was working on an assembly line in a Korean factory. He told me he had to put in at least ten hours a day and even ask permission to use the restroom.

In the '90s, Daicheng was developing its own industrial park. There were dump trucks everywhere, rampaging through the streets. These dump trucks carried earth from some fields that they used to level other fields to construct factory buildings. Six Fingers told us that a group of people in suits had come to his village and told the villagers they'd dig them a free fish pond. The villagers were overjoyed—farming fish was far more profitable than working the land. So the excavators drove into the village, working day and night to dig out this fish pond. Six Fingers' father woke to find that their family vegetable patch was now a square pit that went at least ten feet down, so deep that if you fell in, you'd find it hard to climb back out. By the time his pa recovered his senses, it was too late. Their house appeared to be standing on a hill surrounded by deep pits. When it rained, their house became an island, and they had to use a barrel like a canoe to get anywhere. There was nothing Six Fingers' father could do, so he put guppies in the pond and started to farm them. But one day the small chemical factory in the village discharged its wastewater, and all his fish died.

Six Fingers' family vegetable patch eventually became the site for an industrial park. "Six Fingers, your house has a massive swimming pool, but unfortunately it's only got a deep end," we teased.

Daicheng's industrial park was to be a Singaporean investment, we heard. All the cadres in the city were nervous because the Singaporeans involved were going to pay a visit. I hadn't been familiar with Singapore before this. I'd heard it was a country. I'd heard it was a city. Later I learned it was both a city and a country. According to the *Daicheng Daily*: "Singapore is a gardenlike city, clean and safe and, most important, rich."

In 1993, I heard an odd speech. A couple of leaders had gone over to Singapore on a fact-finding mission and had gathered some young people together to report their findings. We sat in a small meeting room watching a lengthy slideshow. The leaders explained that in the future, Daicheng would be a city short of manpower. A large number of foreign companies would develop there, and this would mean plenty of work for us. The young people in the audience found this news heartening. But, this leader explained dramatically, the people of Daicheng needed to be improved. Singapore had very strict laws. Anyone caught spitting on the street was pulled in and given lashes with a whip. This whip wasn't like our fathers' whips. It was a specially crafted leather whip. Like shoes, there were different sizes of whips, and each individual would be assigned his or her own specialized whip and inflicted with individualized pain. The kids got the kids' whip; the women got the women's whip; the retired workers got the retired workers' whip. When these whips cracked down on your skin, they turned you into an invalid, and you'd need to spend the next month in bed. After your injuries healed, you'd be pulled in for a second lashing. This cycle would continue until they'd decided your punishment was over. The most important thing we were to remember was that Singapore operated by Rule of Law. You couldn't use personal connections and go through the backdoor. If you committed an offense, it wouldn't make a difference if your father was the chief of the public safety bureau. The leader finished his speech with this and gave us a sinister smile. I thought to myself, *If that was what Rule of Law meant, how could anyone insist China was governed by Rule of Law?*

I knew nothing about the law back then, and hearing crap like this scared the hell out of me. I kept expecting this South East Asian garden state to send its troops into Daicheng. The troops would stand in the streets wearing red armbands, and anytime they saw any uncivilized behavior, they'd lash their whips. They didn't even have to fine people because they were so very rich, they didn't need our renminbi; they'd prefer to practice their hobby of whipping people. Because they were so civilized, they would find plenty of things to offend them, and most of the people in my factory would probably be shown the whip. I listened to this speech in a confused haze. They were probably standing there with their whips right now, waiting for us. So why was everyone looking so cheerful? Later Bai Lan told me that there was something wrong with my head. I'd gotten the content of the speech completely garbled if that was the impression I came away with.

But I did feel paranoid about the industrial park and these foreign enterprises, and it all stemmed from hearing that speech. A citywide patriotic cleanup was launched on the eve of the Singaporeans' arrival. Even Pesticide New Village implemented a major cleanup and rodent-control initiative.

"Will the Singaporeans be coming in here?" my ma asked the street management employee.

"Your guess is as good as mine," he replied. "But rodent control is essential. Imagine if a rat ran into their hotel."

After the rodent extermination activities there were no fewer rats, but they had poisoned a large section of Pesticide New Village's chicken and duck populations. These birds couldn't be eaten, so they were left out on the grass to rot. By this point, the Singaporean visit had been called off. They'd decided to invest in an industrial park in another city instead, so no one bothered cleaning up the dead chickens and ducks.

A word about foreign enterprises: working for one was one of the objectives Daicheng residents were always striving for. There were two other common objectives—getting into college and opening a grocery store. That was it. Working in a department was a dream rather than an objective, because striving for it was no freaking use. There was something simmering beneath the surface in the saccharin factory at that time. Lots of people wanted to try their luck at a foreign enterprise. I thought Xiao Li would go, or even Long Legs. I never imagined that Six Fingers would be the first to dip his toes in the water.

The day Six Fingers told us that he was going to a Taiwanese enterprise to work as an electrician, we were all very surprised.

"Six Fingers, have you quit?" we asked.

"No, I haven't," he said. "I have lots of vacation time saved up, enough to take three months off. I'm going to transfer to the Taiwanese enterprise and work for three months. If I like it, I'll quit working here. If I don't, I'll just come back."

"Don't you have to transfer your file?" I asked.

"They have a three-month probationary period, so there's no need to transfer files. Do you know what a probationary period is?"

I really didn't have a clue. The saccharin factory had no such thing—when you started, you just signed a contract.

"Xiaolu, you need to see more of the world," Six Fingers said. "Foreign enterprises are cutting-edge, and their management style is very modern."

We complimented him on how smart he was. Six Fingers loved being told that he was smart.

So Six Fingers went off. But a week later he was back, looking like he'd been beaten up: his face was swollen and bruised, and he had a scab on his lip.

Six Fingers told us that the Taiwanese enterprise was in a town a fair distance away. Every morning at five, the factory sent a battered old minibus to collect the workers and take them to the enterprise to start work. Most of the workers lived in the factory. Six Fingers didn't like that the foreign enterprise factory vehicle was a minibus and in pretty bad shape. Another strange thing was that the minibus didn't drive into the factory entrance but parked in the road. The workers had to clock in at the entrance and walk in on foot.

On his first day at work, Six Fingers got out of the minibus, clocked in, and walked confidently into the factory. He discovered that there was something very strange about this Taiwanese enterprise. The workers walking in through the factory gate were all completely silent; no one was chatting, let alone laughing. Eight safety guards stood at the factory entrance wearing armed service uniforms. You could buy uniforms like this at street stalls—they were usually worn by migrant workers and young thugs, so Six Fingers didn't pay them much mind. The thing he couldn't understand was why there were eight safety guards standing at the gate during work hours. At the saccharin factory there was only one—Hu Deli. Moreover, this Taiwanese enterprise had only two hundred workers but somehow needed eight safety guards, while the saccharin factory had just five factory police to deal with a couple of thousand employees. He suddenly worried that this place was a labor camp.

Six Fingers stood hesitantly at the entrance, looking around. A safety guard walked over and said in a strange dialect, "Hey, fuckwit, what are you looking for out here, ghosts?" Six fingers was livid. Six Fingers was an electrician. He may have been ugly, but he was exceptionally skilled, and the saccharin factory police had never dared give him any lip. "What the fuck are you saying?" Six Fingers asked, pointing at the safety guard. He'd barely uttered the words when he felt a boot in his ass, followed by a punch in the head. In no time at all, he had sixteen fists upon him and was being beaten like a dog. The workers continued to walk by in silence. No one turned to look or tried to break it up.

Six Fingers was beaten so badly, he lost consciousness. When he came to, he found that he'd been thrown down at the side of the state road. Stuffed in the pocket of his shredded shirt, he found a dismissal notice. Six Fingers didn't get it. He hadn't even gotten to work, but he had for some unfathomable reason been savagely beaten and given notice. The state road was full of cars driving at breakneck speed. He reached his hand out to stop a car, but they all thundered past—not one slowed down. Six Fingers followed the state road back. He walked very slowly, feeling as if he might have broken his lower back. As the sun set over the hills, he saw a shimmering pool of water. In the center of the water was an island, and on the island were a couple of little country cottages. He knew he had found his way back home.

After Six Fingers' beating, we all lost interest in the idea of working for a foreign enterprise. Having nowhere to go was in itself a kind of joy. As Schopenhauer once said, all happiness is an illusion. When we had free time, a couple of us young workers would go sit on the edge of the flowerbed, watching all walks of factory life. We saw Wang Taofu's wife chasing Wang Taofu. They ran from the production zone to the office buildings and from the bathrooms to the canteen. It was like that American cartoon *Tom and Jerry*. Wang Taofu was in the register department. He was quite lean, and because of the Ah Fang incident, we all called him "the letch." When his wife chased and hit him, she'd always have something in her hand. Sometimes it was a broom, other times a steel pipe. She was fierce, noisy, and unstoppable, while Wang Taofu was completely silent, focusing only on escaping. The workers would always clap and cheer when they saw scenes like this one, telling the pair to keep at it. Whereas when the cadres saw it, they'd frown and mutter, "This kind of behavior is unacceptable."

Later, Wang Taofu's wife added another string to her bow—throwing bricks. When she was unable to catch up with Wang Taofu, she'd simply grab a brick from the wall and lob it at him. This was no longer a domestic squabble: a brick could smash his skull and kill him. But the sweet thing was that the bricks she chucked never hit him. She was sometimes so close, she could have taken the brick and smacked him right on the back of the head with it, but she'd always just miss, the brick sailing past his ear. Chicken Head said she was missing on purpose. Their violent stunts were fast becoming a TV show. She'd throw bricks haphazardly, breaking factory windows, and everyone started putting tape over the glass to stop fragments from flying in their faces.

One day, Wang Taofu's wife chased him down a dead-end alley. He looked desperate. He had a wall in front of him and his wife behind him, and behind her was a group of workers, all there to watch the action. I imagine he was wishing he could grow a pair of wings and fly up into the sky. Wang Taofu gestured that he was stopping. He walked up to his wife and gave her a sudden slap across the face. Then he squatted before her with his head lowered and let her vent her spleen. The old hag really was a formidable woman. She howled when he slapped her, then kicked Wang Taofu over, sat on his chest, and took a wire hairpin from her hair. She used this hairpin to scratch a tic-tac-toe grid into Wang Taofu's cheek.

I had cow pox when I was young, and they'd left a scar like a tic-tac-toe grid on my arm. Seeing someone do the same thing on their own husband's face was pretty spectacular. The markings on Wang Taofu's face scabbed up. A few days later, the scar faded and looked more like a *T*.

T for *Tiger*. Now every time we saw Wang Taofu, we were reminded of how fucking awesome his tiger wife was.

As well as married couples chasing each other around and beating each other up, we'd also see scuffles between cadres and workers. One day, Blind Fang from the scrap storage room pushed the head of safety into the latrine. Blind Fang wasn't really blind, that was just a nickname. The general explanation for this nickname was that he had no eyes and destroyed whoever got in his path. The head of safety had been walking through the production zone. He needed a whiz but didn't have time to go back to the office building. He found a nearby restroom where Blind Fang happened to be taking a shit. Blind Fang was crouched in the urinal, shitting. This was fairly gross, as all the people who came to piss after would be forced to stare at his shit. The head of safety was furious when he saw this and let loose a torrent of abuse. It was completely normal for someone of his ranking to challenge behavior like this, but most workers would just have let it go. The shitter raised his head when he heard the abuse. The head of safety drew in a cold mouthful of air, realizing he'd been shouting at Blind Fang!

"Don't move," Blind Fang told the head of safety. He wiped his ass, hitched up his pants, and walked over to him. He took the sheet of toilet paper he'd just used to wipe his ass and smeared it on the head of safety's face. While the head of safety was freaking out, Blind Fang pushed him into the latrine. This all happened at lightning speed and was over before the head of safety realized what had happened. I heard that Blind Fang was the bad-ass to end all bad-asses. By the time we'd run over to see what all the fuss was about, it was all over. All that remained was a trail of shitty footprints.

We didn't understand it. The head of safety was almost five-foot-eight and well-built, while Blind Fang was only five-two and a bit of a humpback. How the fuck had Blind Fang managed to push the head of safety into the shit pit? You still don't understand Blind Fang, it seems, Chicken Head said. He was the one who shut down the factory's electricity supply. He'd had his bonus deducted for some small misdemeanor. In response, he hadn't said anything or threatened anyone, he'd just made his way to the power distribution room in the production zone and, with one hand, cut the electricity for the entire factory's production—a total of four workshops. There was a big boom, and the saccharin factory fell completely silent. The motors stopped turning, the boilers stopped boiling, and the reactors stopped reacting. In an instant, the thousands of tons of raw materials in the formaldehyde workshop being heated electrically in the oven turned into a heap of waste material.

Before, when Old Bad-Ass had mentioned this guy—the legendary anti-hero who was so fucking kick-ass he'd actually shut off the factory's electricity supply—I'd never in a million years have guessed he was talking about Blind Fang. I told Chicken Head I'd heard he'd carried an explosive package into the factory director's office too. It hadn't been an explosive package, Chicken Head told me, but a detonator. Pulling down the power switch was a criminal offense for which the safety department had wanted to arrest him. For sabotaging production he should have been sent for labor education at the very least. No one expected Blind Fang to react by rushing to the factory head's office with twenty detonators strapped to his body. The factory head had been close to retirement and was scared shitless. No one does a lifetime of revolutionary work only to be blown up days before retirement. So Blind Fang wasn't arrested, and the factory head was not blown to bits. Blind Fang was such a destructive lunatic that they decided the safest thing would be to transfer him to the scrap storage room. It was a sinecure. Plus the place was filled with bits of junk he could smash to his heart's content.

We were all speechless when we heard this. Chicken Head summed up, saying that the head of safety didn't lose on grounds of physical strength—he lost on grounds of spirit.

People, eh, we said to Chicken Head after learning about Blind Fang. You never could tell about them. Dark horses. I'd always known that Old Bad-Ass was someone who shouldn't be messed with at the factory; now I knew he wasn't alone. Chicken Head sneered and said, What the fuck do you know? We didn't have a clue who the real dark horse was. Later Chicken Head showed us that it was the old man who did the sweeping. He was thin and shriveled, with pale skin that made him look slightly European.

"Do you know who that is?" Chicken Head asked.

We shook our heads. The man who did the sweeping was old and lonely. He lived in a nearby bamboo shack, rarely spoke, and never met anyone's gaze directly. According to Chicken Head, he'd been commander of the Kuomintang youth division, becoming a major-general when he was twenty. He was at the army base of the military general, Huang Wei, and was captured by the Communist army during the Huaihai Campaign and locked up for years. When he was released, he started sweeping the floor in our factory. The old man had studied in London and spoke fluent English. He still had a number of sub-ordinates in Hong Kong and Taiwan. I heard that an old subordinate came to visit him, wanting to take him off to live out his days in comfort. The old man grasped his broom and said, "I must obey the words of the Communist Party."

While working as an electrician, I went to the factory bathhouse daily. The bathhouses were across from the workers' dormitory area. The men's bathhouse was on the first floor and the female bathhouse was on the second. The men's bathhouse had a big bathtub and a shower room, but the female bathhouse didn't have a tub. I'd always imagined the women crouching in the bath; later, when I actually went into the women's bathhouse, I discovered they only had showers. I'd gone to the women's bathhouse to change a light bulb, not as a peeping tom.

But in 1993, a peeping tom was caught in the dormitory. He'd been watching the female bathhouse through a telescope. Our factory dormitory was a very shoddy three-story building, constructed from wood and crawling with rats. You wouldn't normally wish to go into such a place, for fear that 1) the building would fall down and crush you to death, 2) it might catch fire and burn you to death, or 3) you'd get bitten by a rat and catch the plague. The peeping tom had been crouching in the third-floor corridor, watching in quiet ecstasy. But when the sunset glare fell onto his telescope, it reflected back through the window of the women's bathhouse, dazzling one of the female workers. She peered in the direction of the light and figured out what was happening. She ran out of the bathhouse, shouting, "Catch the scoundrel!"

The scoundrel in question was Baldy Liang's son, who worked as a manager in the formaldehyde workshop. Baldy Liang had made such vile pipes, and now, finally, the masses had him in their grasp. Father and son should both have been strung up in the factory entrance, stripped, and beaten with a Singaporean whip. But the old fellow was extremely cunning. He told the factory head that his son wasn't a perverted voyeur; he was just fascinated by the human anatomy. His son's aspiration had been to go to medical school, but as it turned out, all he did was produce formalin for the medical institute. This had given him a doctor complex, and he was always hoping to look at human bodies. Baldy Liang held engineer status at the factory (who knows how many boxes of Zhonghua cigarettes that had cost him). Surprisingly, there was no punishment; they simply let his son go.

The day Baldy Liang's son was found out, a few of us dashed into the dormitory building. It was very quiet in there, with the sun just about to set. A couple of rats scuttled across in front of me, squeaking away. Long Legs, Xiao Li, and I were pretty curious. We wanted to know if you really could see from there into the women's bathhouse. We stood in the window, about three hundred yards from the bathhouse, but you couldn't make out a thing with the naked eye.

"Look," Xiao Li said, suddenly yanking my arm and pointing to the wall beneath the window ledge. I looked closely and saw a trail of sticky white goop hanging from it. It was the same fluid that came out when I dreamed about women. I'd never thought to shoot it out all over the dormitory wall though. The fact that men have penises is a good thing. But taking them around and ejaculating wherever you please is unjustifiable. Long Legs' eyesight wasn't very good, and he moved closer to get a proper look.

I freaked him out by saying, "Long Legs, if I were to kick you in the ass, that stuff would stick to your nose."

We explained all this to the safety department. We told them that Baldy Liang's son did not have a doctor complex—it was bona fide voyeurism, and we'd seen the spunk to prove it. Surely doctors didn't get turned on when performing operations? Ejaculating right into the patient's abdominal cavity? This was too much fucking bull. But the safety department employees didn't believe us; they saw us as a couple of inconsequential young workers, jealous of Baldy Liang's son because he'd gotten to see a naked woman and we hadn't. What could you say to a bunch of cadres who thought like that?

One day I went to change a light bulb. I was standing on a ladder when I noticed that under the eaves on the opposite wall, someone had written: *Hu Deli is a dickless wonder.* I examined it for a while, wondering who'd done it.

"Why are you checking that out?" Xiao Li asked. "It was obviously you who wrote it. Who hates him more than you do?"

I wouldn't do such a pointless thing, I told him.

"Then why don't you scrub out the words?" he said.

I told him it wasn't my job to do things like that.

That winter, the factory conducted an evaluation of its exceptional employees. We stood in front of the billboard at the factory entrance, looking at all the photos of that year's exceptional employees, which were stuck in the glass display case. Among them were Bai Lan and Hu Deli. Early the next morning, there was heavy fog. I got to the factory early, and passing the billboard I noticed someone had drawn on the outer glass with a pen. Bai Lan now had a mustache on her face, and Hu Deli a dick in his mouth. It was pretty funny. I smudged out Bai Lan's mustache but wasn't sure I wanted to wipe out Hu Deli's dick. The dick was incredibly lifelike and pretty gross, so I didn't really want to touch it. Someone walked over then, so I quickly turned around and fled into the dense fog.

CHAPTER EIGHT

WILDFLOWERS

I spent many nights after leaving the factory scribbling about it in my notepad. Sometimes my writing would be suffused with sadness, other times filled with joy. I never wrote about Bai Lan, except for this once. By the time I came to write about her I was thirty, and it was only a few disjointed stories. I found I couldn't just sit down and write about her all at once. It just couldn't be done. In my limited life, I've let her go time and time again, but I've always picked her back up again. I was no longer expressing love but nostalgia. But it was a nostalgia that came from the deepest part of my body, inside my blood. And it wasn't all for Bai Lan, but for the others too.

Every fall, you could see the wildflowers outside the factory from Bai Lan's infirmary. Most of them were yellow, but some were orange. This species of flower had no name. These short wildflowers grew along the outer wall of the factory, flowering into the distance on both sides of the freeway. It was extraordinarily beautiful, like the blazing sun illuminated on the ground. This sea of flowers stretched unbroken, save for the shadowy areas where it seemed to stop. But in the open areas, they'd flare up again, offering this sudden brilliance. Their flowering season was fairly long: from October until the landscape frosted over. During this time, they would always appear in my line of sight with their proud indifference. When they were in full bloom, passersby would sometimes pick them, then discard them offhandedly on the road, where they'd be run over by cars, their little yellow petals completely mangled. But even this didn't destroy their beauty.

I loved standing at the infirmary window. Sometimes I'd go up there and find that Bai Lan was out. The door had no lock, so I'd go in without permission and just stand there. At first when she came in and found me, she said nothing. But when it had happened a few times, she said, "Xiaolu, when there's no one in a room, unless it's your own bedroom, you shouldn't just charge in."

"You always speak in such a roundabout way," I said. "No wonder I don't understand a thing you say."

She shook her head. "It's impossible to get you to understand anything. Have you been called in by Hu Deli again lately?"

"No, I haven't," I said. "Recently I've been very well behaved."

Whenever we spoke about Hu Deli, she'd always call me a "little rebel."

I wasn't a little rebel, I told her. All workers were like this, arriving late and leaving early, jumping over walls and insulting people. Bad behavior was universal to workers. Writing poetry would make me a little rebel in the world of workers. I told her about my cousin, the one who collected protection fees. Even he wasn't a rebel—there were actually more rules and regulations in the mafia circle than there were in our factory. And who would dare disobey them? If my cousin were to take college entrance exams, that would make him a little rebel within the mafia world. But there weren't many rebels like that. It wouldn't get you beaten up or mocked mercilessly. I always thought ideals that got you beaten up were worth sticking to, while ideals that got you teased were harder to take.

"You have a point," Bai Lan said, "but you're still a little rebel."

There was nothing I could say to that.

In the spring of 1993, I attended the chemical bureau model deeds presentation with Bai Lan. Each factory sent ten representatives chosen by the union, which still thought quite highly of me.

After choosing a couple of outstanding employees, that big asshole Xu from the union remembered how Bai Lan and I had saved Good Balls' life, which he reluctantly decided to consider a model deed. So big asshole Xu called me over and explained that I didn't need to go to work on Saturday afternoon; I was to attend the presentation at the bureau instead. I had zero interest in the presentation, but naturally I was willing if it meant having time off work, especially if that time were spent with Bai Lan.

Bai Lan and I rode our bikes to the auditorium of the chemical factory bureau. Big red banners were hung up inside and it was brightly lit and thronging with people, which created a banquet-style atmosphere.

Bai Lan wanted to sit in the corner, but I wanted to sit in the front row. She told me I was crazy, it was the managers who sat in the front row. Then how about the second row? I said. We sat behind a balding man, and I lit a cigarette. Bai Lan told me you probably weren't allowed to smoke inside. When I looked around, I saw seventeen or eighteen workers with cigarettes. When we were listening to the presentation, the leaders at the front were smoking too, as were the model deed–doers on the stage. There was no concept of "no smoking" areas at the time. As long as it wasn't a production zone and no one was going to get blown up, cigarettes could be smoked anywhere and everywhere.

I surprised myself by actually enjoying the model deed presentations. One person had fallen into the septic tank and someone else had saved him. The person who'd fallen in had been rescued, but his savior died. Someone else had fought bravely against a group of thugs who'd come into the factory to pilfer steel. This hero used a handheld flashlight to fend off four thugs armed with knives. He was stabbed and seriously wounded, but he managed to use his flashlight to smack one of the thugs on the head. Someone else had been working for the factory year-round for free, cleaning the sewers. His wife wanted to divorce him because it had become his addiction; meanwhile, he'd failed to do anything about their own house's leaking roof. When one worker discovered a toxic gas leak, he didn't run away but toward it and turned off the valve. He saved many lives but was asphyxiated so badly in the process, he became a vegetable.

I told Bai Lan that before hearing these stories, I thought the way I'd rescued Good Balls had been pretty awesome, and that I should be one of those onstage giving a presentation. It was only now that I realized what I'd done wasn't worth shit. These people's model deeds were really something.

"Hey, have you ever seen that Japanese cartoon *Knights of the Zodiac*?" I asked her. "They were kick-ass heroes too."

"Shut your mouth. What's all this 'Zodiac nights'? Stop talking crap," Bai Lan said.

Next an old man went onto the stage. He was an old hero who'd sliced off four fingers and half the palm of his left hand while repairing an imported machine. He extended the hand to show us, and we saw that it had four meaty things projecting from it. This old hero praised his doctor for his regenerative surgery. The operation had been miraculous, he said. The doctor had made an incision in his ribs and buried what remained of his hand in there, sewing it back up and making him look like someone with his hand permanently in his pocket pulling out his wallet. A couple of months later, the damaged hand was removed from his ribs. A clump of flesh had grown there—only it wasn't bifurcated, so the doctor cut this flesh into four strips with a knife, just like cutting carrots into fingers. Then he bandaged it again, and it turned into four fingers. He could have cut it into eight fingers instead. Having eight fingers on one hand would have been very cool, like an octopus.

When I heard this and looked back up at the four fleshy sticks, I started to regret sitting in the second row. It was pretty grim and was making me start to feel queasy. I glanced toward Bai Lan, who was looking attentively at the old man, nodding away, enthralled. I had to remind myself that she was a doctor, not a sicko.

I asked Bai Lan what you should do if someone sliced off their finger. I had a female classmate who operated a planer in a factory. From time to time, people had fingers sliced off there, and in a year you could fill a bowl with all of them, which was fucking scary. Not long before, that classmate had chopped off one of her fingers, fainting on the spot from the pain. The surrounding workers got her to the hospital. A young apprentice had heard that severed fingers could be reattached, so he picked hers up, pickled it in alcohol, and took it to the hospital. The doctor didn't say a word when he saw the finger but had it sent away to be used as a specimen.

Bai Lan rolled her eyes and shook her head. "He pickled it in alcohol?" she asked. "How can people be that dumb?"

"Doesn't alcohol stop things from rotting and disinfect them?" I asked.

"Pickling something in alcohol completely destroys the tissue function. You should find an ice cube, and if you can't find one, a popsicle will do."

By the time the presentations were over and we were back outside, it was after five.

"I never want to go to a presentation like that again," I moaned. "I'd have finished work at four. It's not worth it."

"Let's go out to eat," Bai Lan said. "It's on me."

We walked up the street looking for a restaurant. Bai Lan and I never had a regular haunt. I suggested noodles, but she said they were too humdrum, and why not western food? So we went into a noisy and crammed steak house.

It was the only place in Daicheng where you could use a knife and fork. The tables were made of big wooden blocks, a bit like butchers' chopping blocks. And the seats were fucking benches, only longer and wider than the ones at the noodle joints. The waitresses shuttled through the crowd carrying sizzling steaks on iron plates. Some people weren't eating but singing frenzied karaoke at a twenty-nine-inch television. They were singing Zhang Xueyou's "Kiss Goodbye." This wasn't really a western restaurant. I'd seen western restaurants on TV: they were quiet, with candles and waiters dressed like bridegrooms.

"You're talking about French restaurants," Bai Lan said. "This restaurant is styled on the American Wild West."

We sat down among a crowd of female students, all sharing the same bench. One of the students had extremely large breasts that she rested on the table for convenience. When the iron plate of steak was carried out, it was sizzling so much that the oil splattered on her chest and she jumped up, shrieking. I watched with amusement, but Bai Lan pinched my arm and said, "Don't stare at her, you little delinquent."

As I was laughing, I recalled the incident with Li Xiaoyan's grandma and how my mother had said the same thing to me. Remembering that Li Xiaoyan's grandma was dead made me feel sad, and I didn't laugh any more. I will always wish that I hadn't seen the burlap-sack flaps, and that she hadn't jumped from the building. That way I'd still have a clear conscience.

It was very inconvenient chatting with Bai Lan while sitting the way I was, so I straddled the bench to talk to her. She couldn't have straddled it, as she was wearing a skirt. Even if she hadn't been, she may not have wanted to talk to me while straddling a bench.

"Xiaolu, do you know you're not like the other young workers?" she asked.

"In what way?"

"I can't really say, but in the future, you should probably go on to do something else."

"What else?"

"Can you stop speaking to me in such a feeble-minded way, please?"

I said I'd explain how I was different than other people. I told her my math teacher once told me that I was a pessimist. I thought that people like us were everywhere, but later I found out that this wasn't the case—pessimists are actually in short supply. Some people should be pessimists naturally, but they play mah-jongg or sing karaoke, which really brightens them up. I was surrounded by people like that. I wasn't sure how I should be seeing the world, pessimistically or optimistically. When I was small, I thought that an event was either happy or sad, with no common ground. Now I realized that sadness and happiness could coexist in the same event. Bai Lan biting Wang Taofu's wife, for example. Lots of people thought it was hilarious and laughed their heads off, but it had made me sad. It had made me sad because I wished I could have bitten the tiger for Bai Lan. That was how I was different from other people. It was only a minute difference, not enough to make me think I should be doing something else with my life. But there was a river running between me and the rest of the world, with both sides thinking the other side was delusional.

"Bai Lan, I love you," I said in a quiet voice in that rowdy old steak house. But it was too noisy, and I couldn't even hear my own words clearly. She didn't react at all when I said it. I thought about raising my voice and saying it again, but saying the same thing twice in a row seemed too fucking stupid. The first time had been because I loved her, the second time would be purely so she could hear it. So I pretended I hadn't said anything.

I finished the plate of black pepper steak, feeling like I hadn't eaten anything. This steak wasn't even up to the standard of our factory pork chops. But I didn't want to eat anything else, I wasn't in the mood. I offered her a smoke, but she waved it away, saying it was too noisy and that we should leave. By this point there was a karaoke rendition of Black Panther's "Don't Break My Heart." This time it had the original soundtrack as backing and sounded pretty good.

We stepped outside and started walking intuitively in the direction of New Knowledge New Village, first pushing our bikes and, when we were tired of walking, riding them. I told her a couple of funny stories about my team: Long Legs, Six Fingers, and Yuan Xiaowei. Some of the things I said made her laugh, others made her frown.

At New Knowledge New Village, she stopped her bike. Out of habit, I turned to head home, but she said, "Why don't you come up and sit awhile? I have something to show you."

So I parked my bike and followed her up the stairs of her building and along the dark corridor. I wasn't sure if it was more polite to go in front of a woman when walking up the stairs or whether "ladies first" still applied. All I knew was that as I walked behind her, her pencil skirt looked very sexy. My eyes were level with her skirt, and although the corridor was dark, I could see everything clearly. I couldn't have avoided looking even if I'd tried.

I can still visualize Bai Lan's old-fashioned two-bedroom apartment. The quality of the building was no better or worse than those in Pesticide New Village. There was no living room, and the balcony was very narrow. This apartment had probably never been renovated. The cement flooring made it look half-finished, and the window frames were wooden, dabbed with a layer of green paint that was peeling. She lived on her own in this place. She pulled the light cord and went to the kitchen to boil some water, while I took myself to the south-facing room and sat down. She came in a little later carrying a saucer of sunflower seeds.

"I'm boiling some water, and then I'll make the tea. Care for some seeds?"

I told her I didn't want any seeds but asked if I could smoke.

"Sure," she said. "The ashtray's on the desk."

Her furniture was pretty basic, almost dormitory-style. The only unique piece was the desk next to the wall, arranged with rows of medical books and a random assortment of other books: cooking, language, classical poetry. While she was making the tea, I pulled out *The Illustrated Book of Obstetrics and Gynecological Disease* and flicked through. I didn't see a single photograph in the whole book. All the organs were sketched, and some were even shaded out. When Bai Lan brought in the tea, I happened to have it open to the page about molar pregnancy. I really couldn't work out how a pregnant woman might possibly give birth to a baby with a full set of teeth—even the wisdom teeth, which probably tells you a lot about my mentality at the time.

She snatched the book out of my hands. "What are you looking at this for?" she asked scornfully.

I told her I was just looking. It wasn't like it was porn or anything. I told her I felt sorry for the people who'd had to illustrate this book. One of my relatives studied fine art. There was nothing funny about studying fine art and ending up doing illustrations about gynecological disease. It would be even worse than being an electrician.

"What a load of crap you're talking—this is science!" Bai Lan said.

Later she reached in her drawer and took out a piece of paper, saying, "Look at this." I saw immediately that it was a night college application. I told her I knew what it was because Long Legs had taken his night college entrance exams and had been chased around like a dog by everyone until he'd nearly tried to drown himself in the river.

"Don't be so obnoxious," she said. "I'm telling you this with total sincerity. You must take the night college entrance exam. You're working the day shift, so your evenings are free. There's nothing to stop you from going."

"It will mean I have to take adult college entrance exams. I've completely forgotten all my language and math."

She took out another piece of paper from her drawer. "This is an enrollment application for the adult college review class. There's more than a month left, so if you start going to class now, you'll still be able to catch up."

"I'll think about it," I said.

"Have you thought about other factors, Xiaolu—things like making your ma proud?"

"I make my ma proud by going to work and earning a wage. If I got into college, she'd have to send me a monthly living allowance. Fuck, do you think she could afford that?"

Bai Lan tossed the two sheets of paper back in the drawer and said, "Forget it. It's like talking to a brick wall. You just waste away your life."

I really didn't want to talk about this with her. She was a factory doctor. What did she know about what could happen if I took the night college entrance exam? I was sure to get sent to the saccharin workshop to do the three shifts, and working that shift meant you couldn't go to night college unless you skipped two-thirds of the syllabus or were absent most of the time. These two things conflicted. The factory used it as a method to control young workers who studied at night college.

I paced the room. Her room faced south; the north-facing room was locked. "Do you live in this apartment all alone?" I asked.

"Yes."

"What about your parents?"

"They're both dead."

I didn't dare ask her any more questions. I drank a lot of tea, then went to take a piss. She had an old-fashioned squat toilet, with the water tank fixed above and a string to pull to flush the water. I reached up to pull it but discovered the string had snapped. So I ran out, grabbed a stool, and climbed up to reattach the string.

"Oh, the string to the water tank is broken," Bai Lan said, "It snapped last week."

"Don't you flush it?" I asked.

"I bring over a bucket of water and flush it with that."

"I used to have a classmate whose house was like this," I told her as I was fixing it. "When he took a crap, he flushed it with a bucket of water. But once he tipped the water in too quickly, and his shit floated out all over his feet."

Bai Lan frowned. "Why do you only remember disgusting details like that?"

I told her I couldn't help it, my brain only stored disgusting details. I never remembered nice things. I must have been born that way. A person whose skull is filled with shit has no future. What freaking night college is there for people like us?

Bai Lan waited until I'd fixed the flush, then asked, "Have you washed your hands? Before you eat and after you use the restroom, you should always wash your hands. Did you know that?"

I told her I knew. I'd rinsed them in the water tank as I'd been mending it to save water. "Sometimes I really look down on you," Bai Lan said.

She told me it was getting late, and I should probably be heading home. So I respectfully made my way toward the door. At the door, I told her I'd thought about it: I did want to take those night college review classes, and I did want to go to night college. Anything to make her happy. I told her I thought it would make my ma happy too. Anything to make the two of them happy— even become an outlaw and spend the rest of my life on the run. She hugged me when she heard this, then kissed me on the lips.

Some time later, we both discussed what had happened that day. She told me she had been moved by the way I'd mentioned her and my mother in the same breath. She told me I was very good at sweet talk, and it was a different kind of sweet talk and had made her want to kiss me. She also talked about the time we'd saved Good Balls. I'd been sleeping topless in the minivan, gotten confused, and called her "Ma." At the time she'd had a strong impulse to kiss me, but she restrained herself because of the cadres sitting in front.

I reminded her of the night at her place when she'd told me she looked down on me one minute, then kissed me the next. If I'd been an intellectual, I'd have been very irritated—I'd have seen her as the Carmen of the infirmary. But I screwed in light bulbs for a living, which meant I didn't have too many distracting thoughts, which was probably for the best. All I could do was continue to carry on in my outlaw way. The world looked down on me. People thought I was a shit. But Bai Lan never made me feel that way. I wasn't so dumb as to confuse being looked down on and being liked, was I? If I couldn't tell the difference between the two, I'd be better off going out and getting run over by a car.

She kissed me. Another day when we discussed it, she said she was surprised I hadn't told her that I loved her. I explained to her that I'd said it already. At the steak house, in the infirmary, in the pedicab, even in Donkey Alley that first time we met. She told me those times didn't count—she wanted to hear me tell her I loved her. So I said, "Bai Lan, I love you."

But on the night when she first invited me up to her apartment, she cupped my face in her hand when we kissed, which made me feel like a mouse caught in a trap. My mouth was squeezed into a daffodil shape so long that my tongue couldn't reach out. She didn't seem to care. After she kissed me she said, "Alright, go home. Take care on your journey."

I didn't really want that to be it, so I took hold of her face and kissed her back the same way she'd just kissed me, letting her have a taste of how it felt to be a trapped mouse. Then I released her, stroked her hair, and left. I zipped down the stairs, making her terrified that I was going to fall in the pitch-black and kill myself. I was actually used to running down stairs like this. The staircases in public housing were all the same, seventeen steps to a flight, and there was no chance I'd lose my footing. She'd wanted to call out and stop me, but I was going too fast. Had she shouted out, the people of New Knowledge New Village would all have leaned out their windows and seen me. So she sighed, shut the door, and let me run away.

I can remember her bed. It was a single bed, very neat and decorated plainly with a green pillow. When I saw it, I tried to picture her sleeping. On the weekend, would the early-morning sunshine fall onto her pillow? Did she ever fall out of bed while dreaming? I even saw a couple of twisted strands of hair on her pillow. Every time I thought of these things, an overwhelming sadness filled my heart. Her bed was too small and flimsy, just like the stolen tattered and torn moments we spent together. This was a bed made for sleeping, and sleeping only. If we had enjoyed more and longer times together, the bed might have left a better impression.

It was only later that I figured out the value of being able to curl up on your own, close your eyes, and fall into a deep, dreamless sleep. A bed made for sleeping signified another kind of happiness.

Long Legs was accepted into Daicheng College that year for a night college major in electrics and mechanics. He was over the moon and invited his sworn brothers out for a meal. There weren't many places to eat near the chemical factory. There was a noodle joint swarming with flies, where mice dined alongside people and the waitress, a middle-aged bitch, was always rolling her eyes. The other option was a teahouse that served only tea, no food. Neither of these was suitable for a celebration, so Long Legs took us to a drive-through joint by the side of the freeway. It looked alright. A couple of young girls with bleached hair stood by the side of the road, beckoning to passing cars. These were the waitresses. Long Legs ordered enough dishes to take up half the table, most of them vegetarian. The only dishes that weren't vegetables were fried snails and fried eggs. He'd brought a couple of bottles of beer, and the three of us started to drink. We'd downed half the beers when we heard a bike ringing its bell outside, then Little Pouty Lips ran in.

She'd finally cut off her sausage ponytail, which was all thanks to me. "Your girl looks like she has a sausage hanging from the back of her head," I'd told Xiao Li a good number of times. He hadn't dared say anything to her at first, but later my influence seeped through, and once when his guard was down, he'd let it slip. Little Pouty Lips didn't say anything, just took herself down to the hairdresser's and got her hair cut short—to the ears. This showed that she and Xiao Li were genuine childhood sweethearts, meant to be. The way they were with each other was completely different from how they were with other people. Had I been the one to bring up the thing with the sausage, she'd have really laid into me. Long Legs and I were used to her lip.

With the arrival of Little Pouty Lips, Long Legs ordered a plate of mincemeat vermicelli. We made a customary toast, and after several rounds of drinks, Little Pouty Lips said, "Long Legs, this time you're screwed."

Long Legs' face fell. Little Pouty Lips had brought some inside news from the labor department, and it was very bad. She may have looked sweet, but she was actually the black cat crossing his path.

"What's up?" Long Legs asked.

"Hu Deli knows you've been accepted into night college," Little Pouty Lips said.

"Who let that out?" Long Legs said.

"The entire factory knows," she said. "When you filled out the admissions form, you included your work unit details, didn't you?"

"But if you don't fill in your work unit details, you can't take the exam."

"So all Hu Deli had to do to find out was make a phone call. He heard your results were good," Little Pouty Lips said. "You passed everything."

Long Legs stood up and paced the restaurant, saying, "I'm fucked, I'm fucked. I'm definitely going to be transferred to the saccharin workshop and get the three shifts now." He looked like a wolf in a cage, pacing back and forth so much that his eyes looked dazed.

"Long Legs, sit down and talk to us," Little Pouty Lips said.

Long Legs put both hands on the table for support and stared at her through eyes that had suddenly become very bloodshot.

"Fuck, you're really scaring me!" Little Pouty Lips yelled.

"What did Hu Deli say?" Long Legs asked. "Is he going to put me on three shifts?"

"He didn't say. He just said that there was no point in your studying mechanics and electrics. There are forty or fifty people in the factory who've studied the same major, and they're all doing the three shifts. So, unless you study plumbing . . ."

"Night college doesn't have a plumbing major!" Long Legs shouted. "The reason I'm going to college is because I don't want to mend pipes anymore."

The three of us sat bolt upright, nodding, as his spittle sprayed in our faces.

Little Pouty Lips consoled him, saying, "Don't be too upset. You're not the only one. There's someone else here studying accounting."

"Who's that then?" Long Legs and Xiao Li asked at the same time.

"Me." I lifted my hand and gazed out of the window.

I'd been concealing this information from everyone. Only Bai Lan knew I'd gone to the review classes, taken the adult college entrance exams, and been accepted. I'd never imagined that Hu Deli might phone the night college to ask about it. As Long Legs said, to take the night college exam you had to fill in your work details. I'd written "Daicheng Saccharin Factory" without thinking. Had I known, I'd have just written "freelance."

Long Legs jumped up and grabbed me by the neck. "How did you manage to get into night college?" he asked, "You haven't been reviewing, so how did you do it?"

"You're a technical college graduate, you've never taken college-level exams. I graduated from upper middle school, so I have more of a foundation than you."

"We're fucked," Long Legs said, "we'll both get the three shifts now."

I told him he was crazy—it wasn't like we were a couple. I thought it was much more likely I'd get the three shifts.

"Hu Deli says you'll never become an accountant," Little Pouty Lips said. "You'll become corrupt."

I told her that it was a statement of dubious logic: if I were never going to become an accountant, how would I have the chance to become corrupt? Little Pouty Lips didn't discuss things like this with me; she wasn't really one for logic. Smart talk like this was only worth having with Bai Lan.

Long Legs asked me why I'd chosen accounting. I told him I'd tried for an arts review group because it meant I wouldn't have to take chemistry and physics exams; science was my weakness. It was only when I'd gone to fill in my enrollment form that I discovered the only two majors this made me eligible for at the night college were secretarial and accounting. I was fucking depressed. I'd actually thought I might be able to study at the Chinese literature department or something, but I had only two options. I thought for a long time, but still couldn't figure out what to choose. In the end, the teacher in charge of enrollment got impatient and told me not to dawdle. So I asked him, "Do I look more like a secretary or an accountant to you?"

The teacher looked me up and down a couple of times, shook his head, and said, "You don't look like either."

So I closed my eyes and picked accounting. If I didn't look the part, I didn't look the part—perhaps I would as I got older.

"Chief Hu didn't actually say he'd put you on the three shifts, but you should both be careful," Little Pouty Lips said. "I've heard they're expanding the saccharin workshop and are short on manpower. Next year they're planning to transfer at least a hundred people to the three shifts."

This fact was later substantiated. The day-shift workers became very jittery, while all the workers already on three shifts gloated. Some of the low-level cadres wrapped up presents and requested transfers to other factories. Construction of the new saccharin workshop was in full swing. The bigger the building got, the lower our hearts sank. There was an earthquake during construction, but unfortunately it wasn't large enough—all the tremors did was cause the pump room by the river to collapse and the rats to run out. But the saccharin workshop remained safe and sound. When production started, the movements inside would be equal to an earthquake of Richter scale 7.0, apparently. This building wasn't going to collapse unless someone actually placed a bomb in it.

Having been accepted into night college, I then spent the entire summer in a foul mood waiting for the semester to start. But my parents were both in great moods. My mother almost cried, thinking I was finally getting motivated and making something of myself. My father fought to control his excitement, and in a deep and choked-up voice said that our family hadn't raised any college students before me, only thugs like my cousin. So my achievement brought honor to our family name. Was a Mickey Mouse college really worth his getting so excited, I wondered? I wanted to back out of my studies, but now there was no way. I felt I was being made to walk the plank.

My mother broadcast the news to our entire apartment corridor, shouting, "Our Xiaolu's been accepted into college."

One of our neighbors found it quite confusing. "Huh? Isn't your Xiaolu working as a saccharin factory electrician?" she asked. "Is the college recruiting workers, farmers, and soldiers too?"

"It's not a workers, farmers, and soldiers college. It's a night college," my mother explained.

"Xiaolu really is coming up in the world," this neighbor said. Then she went home and smacked her own son on the head and told him he should take a page out of my book: holding down a job while studying, earning money and working toward a diploma. I seemed to be monopolizing everything good in the world.

There was a high school kid in our building. He was at a top school participating in an advanced youth training program. He had jam-jar spectacles, bandy legs, and a slightly disabled appearance. This disabled boy's mother had also told him, "Learn something from Lu Xiaolu, boy, be all you can be! Work hard and be determined!"

"Night college is a load of crap," the disabled boy told his mother irritably. "I could have passed their entrance exams back in junior three."

His mother gave him a severe talking-to, telling him he was far too arrogant. The disabled boy was 100 percent right, in fact: night college was a load of shit. The diploma wasn't worth the paper it was printed on, and it was also going to land me in the saccharin workshop. Two years later, the disabled boy didn't take entrance exams for Tsinghua or Peking University, but for the Buddhist Institute—instead he shaved his head and went off to become a monk. His mother nearly cried herself to death. She came to our house wailing, "I knew this would happen. Wouldn't it have been better for him to go to night college, like Xiaolu?"

This was when I realized that all mothers in the world had psychic powers. Back when she'd told her son to be more like me, she hadn't actually meant for him to learn from my self-motivation and progress, but from my willingness to get myself out there, make contact with society and other human beings. My mother's way of thinking was just the same. There was no way that night college was going to lead to a factory accounting job, but it might mean I'd end up marrying a girl who'd been to technical college—maybe even a graduate, if I was lucky. This was also in the spirit of getting myself out there. Sadly, neither I nor the disabled kid was in any way able to understand our mothers' painstaking efforts.

That year, Long Legs and I were told we might have to go to the saccharin factory to work the three shifts. First, the two of us had been accepted to night college, and naturally such people deserved such a work assignment and were expected to produce saccharin, get frustrated out of their minds, work their asses off, and start longing for death. Second, I didn't have any skills. All I could do was turn light bulbs, which made me easily replaceable, while Long Legs was the number-one scapegoat on his team. If those at the top wanted to pick people for saccharin production, Long Legs would definitely be the first person they'd sell out.

Six Fingers gave us an awful suggestion. He said that if we wanted to get somewhere, we should chat up the factory head's daughter. This girl worked in the laboratory and looked so much like her father that when you saw her, you'd think about him. People often use the phrase "like father, like daughter," but they didn't usually resemble each other to this extent. If you slept with her, you might blink and think you were fucking her father, which would be too terrifying for words. Like the factory head, this girl was short and fat, with a round face and a pair of thick-rimmed tortoiseshell glasses. There was nothing that could be done about having the same figure and face shape as him. But why, oh why, did she have to wear the same glasses? The factory workers were a pretty cruel bunch, and they used to laugh behind her back, saying that she wore two bras, one for her breasts and the other for her cheeks.

When Six Fingers told us we should be chatting up the girl with two bras, we both shook our heads. Six Fingers warned us not to be complacent—she was pretty arrogant and rebuffed most people. So we both nodded. Yes, we got it, she was the factory head's daughter, she had reason to be arrogant. Of course she was ugly, otherwise everyone would be trying to chat her up, and how would she have time for all of that?

Six Fingers said he'd heard Auntie Qin was looking for a love interest for the girl with two bras. She'd been turning the offices upside-down trying to find eligible young men. There had been a number of hopefuls, and seeing as even the department guys, usually a wimpy bunch, were willing to give it a shot, we electricians and plumbers were even more game. Long Legs and I dithered for a while. Why not let Long Legs get it on with her, I suggested—my reputation was too bad. Everybody agreed.

"I won't be able to compete with the department guys," Long Legs said.

Chicken Head slapped him on the back of the neck and said, "If you manage to chat her up successfully, you'll be a department guy too, won't you?"

"If I manage to chat her up, what will happen to Xiaolu?" Long Legs asked.

We all slapped the back of his neck then and said, "If you damn well manage to get off with her, do you think Xiaolu will be assigned to the three shifts?"

There were various ways of flirting with factory girls; the simplest was to deflate their bike tires. I had an aunt who was a worker and had been incredibly beautiful in her youth. Once she'd discovered her bike valve was missing at work. She was fretting about it when a young worker with strong, handsome features appeared before her. "Is your bike broken?" he asked with concern. "Why don't I fix it for you?" Like a conjurer, he produced a valve. Being young and naive, my aunt fell for this helpful young worker, and later he became my uncle.

Others would come to the team and boast about their talents. That same uncle went to my aunt's team, blowing his own trumpet about how he could sew, knit a sweater, cook. He kept glancing over at my aunt as he made these audacious claims. Overhearing these things, my aunt swelled with admiration, because in the '80s young men who could knit sweaters were a total find. It was only after they were married that she realized he'd been completely bullshitting her—he could do none of those things. But my aunt actually managed to land on her feet. My uncle continued to use his wild boasting stunt until some years later, when he became party secretary for the entire factory.

A word about the saccharin factory's laboratories: they were heavily guarded and most people weren't allowed in; only the electricians were free to come and go. There were more than a hundred fluorescent bulbs in the laboratory building, and one would blow almost every day. Normally we'd save them up and change them all in one go. But when an electrician was in a good mood, he'd nip over there, change the bulbs, and give the electric circuits a service. This meant that flirting with lab girls was the electrician's calling. But the laboratories were out of bounds for Long Legs. Long Legs was a plumber, and while the laboratories had lots of light bulbs, lots of beakers, and lot of meters, there were no fucking pipes. If Long Legs were to go in and out as he pleased, he might run into a female lab technician changing her clothes, which would be very unfortunate. As I explained before, female lab technicians often wore their bras and panties directly under their white lab coats. If the person he ran into wasn't the girl with two bras but an old auntie with one bra, he would have been either sent to the safety department or ravaged.

Six Fingers suggested that I take Long Legs with me next time I went to change bulbs in the lab. It was a terrible suggestion, but it was still an option. Long Legs would trick everyone by dressing up as an electrician, and we would be there to protect him.

Under the guise of checking the electric circuit and changing some bulbs, a group of us electricians went into the laboratory, taking Long Legs with us. But the best-laid plans of mice and men and all that. We'd forgotten to find out if the girl with two bras was at work that day, and she happened to be on vacation. Long Legs was pretty frustrated. He was bored to death in the laboratory, so decided to climb onto a table and change a bulb, but he ended up giving himself an electric shock and tumbling down onto the floor. Two aunties took hold of poor old Long Legs, crying out his name. We all rushed over and found him with his head cradled in the crook of one auntie's arm, looking like a fallen martyr as she gave him a chest massage with her free hand. Finding it hard to watch, we picked up our tools and walked off. As we were leaving the laboratory building, we heard footsteps. It was Long Legs bounding after us.

Long Legs was totally incompetent, according to Chicken Head. "Just look at Xiaolu—he sits with the girls, nibbles seeds with them and tells them jokes, takes four hours to change a light bulb. Hell, you're making me think it should be Xiaolu trying to get it on with the girl with two bras."

"Xiaolu, if you get somewhere with her, it'll be just the same, won't it? If you manage to chat her up, don't forget about getting my office transfer too."

I gave them some halfhearted hemming and hawing, because to be honest, this whole thing was making me anxious. The electrician team were a bunch of big-mouths, and if our plan got out, and the factory head heard we were trying to hook up with his daughter, Long Legs and I would be bound for the boiler room.

We ended up lucky. Just when it was looking like we were destined for the boiler room, our factory head was transferred away and replaced by a new head. The young department guys immediately abandoned Operation Two Bras, with no further plans to proceed. We breathed a sigh of relief and backed off too. This girl was a hot potato nobody wanted to touch. If you did, you'd probably get sent to the boiler room by the new factory head. Political struggle really was cruel.

The new factory head took his post, and we all waited for the saccharin workshop's expansion project to be shelved. Instead he surprised us by planning an even greater expansion, aiming to turn us into the major production site of saccharin for the whole world—to become so productive that all other saccharin factories would be forced to close. The shortfall of three-shifts workers went up from a hundred to a hundred and fifty. All the sinecures were reassigned, even the people carrying the canteen slop. Everybody cursed the new head, hoping he'd die without male heirs. He didn't actually have any children, so the plan to win over the factory head's daughter was well and truly sunk.

Something else happened that year that made my mother happy. I joined the youth league.

At the start of fall, Chen Xiaoyu came looking for me. She was the newly transferred league secretary, a sweet-looking girl. There were a lot of sweet-looking girls at the time. I complimented her by saying that she looked like the sweet-faced singer Yang Yuying, which pleased her a great deal. This was a while ago, of course. I suspect if you used that same compliment on a girl these days, the response would be a slap.

"Aren't you a member of the league yet, Lu Xiaolu?" Chen Xiaoyu asked.

I shook my head. She'd touched a sore spot. In middle school, I'd tried to be like the top-grade students, typing up my youth league enrollment statement in time for the submission deadline. Every spring between junior two and senior three, I'd spend the Tomb-Sweeping Festival vacation sitting at my desk, analyzing the contents of my soul. But I had a problem writing these league statements. I'd always describe myself as a completely tragic figure, aware that saving the people from tragedy was one of the party slogans. The league secretary at my school called me over, saying, "We're recruiting members, not running a soup kitchen! You go back home and think about it a bit more."

A couple of days later, I beat up someone. He was a younger kid at my school, and I beat him senseless. Whenever he saw me after that, he'd start shaking. At night, he didn't dream about naked chicks, he dreamed that I was sitting crossed-legged and giving him a crafty smile, and this actually turned into a wet dream. The only explanation for his weird behavior was that he'd been possessed by a ghost, so he started seeing a psychiatrist. The whole school found out about this, including the league secretary, who called me back in, saying she'd been mistaken when she'd asked me to think about it. I didn't need to think about it any further.

There's something in China called a personal file, which I'd read about in novels. These were intimately connected to your life's happenings, but you weren't allowed to see your own file. Your junior school teacher could write a comment about you such as: *This student is very lewd.* This comment would enter your file, and it would be the same as having your face branded. You wouldn't be able to see this branding yourself, but others could. It was extremely difficult to clear these charges, because a second teacher wouldn't be prepared to testify to clear your name by saying, *This student really isn't lewd.* Instead, the second teacher might say: *This student's lewdness is very deeply hidden.* Words like that could finish you. How could you prove you weren't lewd unless you could show you suffered from erectile dysfunction? Even then you could still have lewd thoughts, but without the accompanying lewd bodily actions: hidden very deeply.

I beat up this guy so badly he went mad, that was an indisputable truth; I wasn't being wrongly accused. However, as to whether his wet dream counted as madness, I couldn't say.

Neither did I know whether this incident had been entered into my personal file. If it was in my file, I was uncertain about what this might mean about my future as a league member. When Chen Xiaoyu asked me to join, it reassured me that the beating and wet dream incident couldn't have been in my file. Even though I'd done some pretty fucked-up things in my time, I'd done some nice things too: helped people, become an electrician, studied at night college, and I'd managed to get myself a fantastic girlfriend. I was at the height of life, and now here I was, being given a chance to turn over a new leaf.

I felt pretty happy about joining the league. All people have an urge toward self-improvement, even when they're at their lowest. Don't people about to be executed still see sunlight and feel joy?

"What should I write on my application form?" I asked Chen Xiaoyu.

"If you don't know many characters, keep it simple and sincere," she replied jokingly. "Just write your thoughts down, and that should do the trick."

Her reply really bummed me out. Did she have me down as someone who didn't know many characters? This encounter dented my confidence. I told Chen Xiaoyu that my conduct in the factory had been pretty poor, that Hu Deli had caught me being late a number of times, and he had deducted so much of my bonus that I was left with only single digits. I felt ashamed even to be considered to join the league.

"Didn't you save Zhao Chongde's life?" Chen Xiaoyu asked. "That's excellent conduct and shows definite promise for the future. You have good things going for you."

"Okay, Xiaoyu," I said, "as long as you're happy, that's what counts."

She looked extremely pleased when I said this.

I went along to the canteen to be sworn into the league alongside another dozen or so workers. That asshole amateur photographer took our picture again. He didn't dare do a shoddy job this time, and my picture came out looking good. Auntie Qin from the canteen was the only one lowering the tone. Watching the fun and frolics from the side, she pointed at me and said, "Lu Xiaolu's had his head bashed silly, how's he being asked to join the league? And his feet smell so bad, you wouldn't want to get near him."

One thing I could never get to grips with was why certain people thought I was kind, worth nurturing and having heart-to-hearts with—while the other half seemed to think I was nothing but a piece of garbage with no possible future other than working the three shifts in the saccharin workshop. This confusion permeated most of my youth, and perhaps it could be thought of philosophically. Later I considered it this way: the first group included those dear people I wanted to write poems for, sing songs and tell dirty jokes to, and write very caringly into my novels; while the latter half were bastards, motherfuckers eight lifetimes over. This dualistic view on life was pretty childish. As Nabokov once said, all novels that aim to settle scores end up being written badly, whether the scores are historical or personal. It can also make you seem like an angry motherfucker, and I really don't like motherfuckers, especially angry ones, so I tend to be very critical of the way I think.

After becoming a league member, I'd often go to Chen Xiaoyu's office at lunch. Her office was also in the little red building next door to the library, just a little further down from the infirmary. I found this place, to use a slightly indiscriminate word, nice.

Chen Xiaoyu was passionate about literature and the arts. Ba Jin's novel *Harvest* was often propped open on her desk. "So, are you interested in literature?" Chen Xiaoyu asked as I was thumbing through it.

"Yes," I said, without hesitation. "Yes, *Harvest* interests me a great deal. But if I read it on my own, I might have a problem with the vocabulary because of all those characters I don't know." Chen Xiaoyu knew I was teasing, but she wasn't angry. She handed me a newspaper and explained it was the factory paper. She told me to feel free to write an article for it and submit it to her if I was interested.

I leafed through the factory paper. It was the size of an exam paper folded in half. The front page was internal factory news and the fourth page commendation of model workers, while the second and third pages were youth literary and artistic works: essays, poems, calligraphy, and seal cutting prints. This newspaper had a great name: *Saccharin Today*.

"It's a new paper, and we welcome your comments," Chen Xiaoyu said.

I had no comments to make. The main reason I'd come this way was to see Bai Lan, but I thought I'd look in on the young department girls on the way. I got to go to the offices a lot as an electrician, but I still didn't know many of the girls there. They were all very pretty, and being in close contact with them felt like committing an offense even more risky than writing poetry. I'd often think of myself as the mud and them the lotus flowers; my sole purpose in life being to make them appear more lustrous and attractive. After I joined the league, I'd see a cluster of department girls in the league office. They were so very near, some even brushing shoulders with me. So many pretty girls, all of them older. I hated the fact that they all saw me as a little brother. It was a shame they were still so pure and untouched, like untarnished crystals, and tended to ignore me. I remember one extremely attractive young department girl. She had an oval face and a fine complexion, and she was always smiling. You wouldn't find a complexion like that on the face of a girl on the three shifts. Everyone told her how pretty she was, and that she had a "professional smile." At the time, I didn't understand what was meant by a professional smile. I thought they must mean a courtesan's smile.

Equally splendid were the department guys. At lunchtime, they'd cluster in there too. They came from the propaganda, labor, safety, finance, supply, and sales and registry departments. They'd often be holding a literary magazine borrowed from the library. They were very refined, and when conversing with the girls, they'd be sure to mention Su Tong's novels and Zhang Yimou's movies. The young guys who worked in production all had their heads in some obscene martial arts novel, like *Possessed Sluts*, also borrowed from the library as it happened. They had cigarettes stuck between their lips and spat indiscriminately, their voices as loud as motors. You could tell the young office boys from the young production boys at a glance. I was the only one who was slightly different. I had a copy of *Harvest* in my hand, even though I was an electrician.

Being the way I was meant I was looked down on by the department youth, who thought I was a pretentious bastard, while also being looked down on by the production youth, who also thought I was a pretentious bastard. It was only Chen Xiaoyu and Hai Yan from the library who said, "Lu Xiaolu is a talented young worker with literary aspirations." Please note—not a talented young *man* with literary aspirations, but a talented young *worker*.

Nineteen-ninety-three was the year when I had nowhere to go. As I worked in the factory, the world outside was changing fast. In the '70s, the factory and the world outside were pretty much the same. In the '80s, dance halls and video rooms appeared on the outside, and the factory's recreational facilities started to lag behind, although some factories added dance halls and video rooms. Later there were video arcades and internet cafes and saunas on the outside, and the factory could no longer keep up. You couldn't really expect them to turn the workshops into leisure centers.

The only recreational site that never changed was the library. It was the wonderland of the state-owned enterprise. At lunchtime, the saccharin factory library would open and *Possessed Sluts* would be laid out alongside *John Christopher*, as well as all sorts of magazines and a chaotic array of cassette tapes. This library had a complete collection of twentieth-century foreign literature; the People's Literature Publishing House's editions of the ancient classics; and, as you would expect, a huge array of counterfeit martial arts and romance novels. When telling Zhang Xiaoyin about my past, I told her there had been so many books in the library that I'd wanted to read. At first it had been *Possessed Sluts*, but I followed it with others, foreign classics and Chinese avant-garde literature. My aim was simple: I wanted to make myself seem like a guy who was studying at college, be it a Mickey Mouse college or not.

Now that I live in Shanghai in a place crawling with cockroaches, I sometimes dream about the chemical factory library. It was very clean there, with no roaches—although in certain seasons, you'd have some gnats flying in through the window. I would sit inside reading, the only ceiling fan in the room turning the book's pages for me. The wind would curl up the pale blue curtains, and time would pass without my noticing. Bai Lan, Chen Xiaoyu, Hai Yan, and other young girls were similar to these books in that they were gathered in my memory and put away in a quiet place. When I was young, I had lots of older-sister figures—but now that I'm in my thirties, where have they all gone? I was browsing a secondhand bookshop in Shanghai one day when I pulled out a book that had been stamped with the words: *Daicheng Saccharin Factory Library*. It was *Tale of Ochikubo*, translated from Japanese by Feng Zikai. I carried this book off in my pocket feeling very sad. It felt like finding a long-lost love letter in a trash can. I remembered that when I handed in my notice, I still had a copy of André Gide's *The Counterfeiters*, which I didn't return to the library. My ma saw it one day and got very worried. She thought now that I was out of work, I was going to start counterfeiting money to make ends meet. I've carefully kept all these factory library books together in a corner of my bookcase. When I die, I will leave them for my son to read.

When I think back to the saccharin factory library, I remember the manager there, Hai Yan. She was a fairly well-known Daicheng poet, and her poems were often printed in the evening paper. Later I came across a couple of other girls called Hai Yan, and they all had creative genes. There were painters, photographers, and those passionate about writing. Why did all the girls called Hai Yan have this unique feature? My theory was that they'd been influenced by reading Maxim Gorky as schoolgirls. Hai Yan is the Chinese for "sea swallow." In literature classes at school, the teacher made me recite the poem "The Song of the Sea Swallow." I stood up and in one breath read: "'The Song of the Sea Swallow' by Maxim Gorky on the vast ocean . . ." The language and literature teacher threw the blackboard eraser at my head and told me I was never going to be like that sea swallow with its noble aspirations. That's my guess on why girls called Hai Yan always have this sparkle to them.

It was pretty fucking awesome that the Daicheng evening paper actually published poetry. I couldn't believe that my writing was going to appear in lead type. The first time I saw my words in print, those lopsided hieroglyphics transformed into square boldface characters, I was so excited I thought I'd faint. The fact that my words had been turned to type made them an irrefutable fact—like a slap on the face, or an exhibitionist caught naked on the street by the police.

A quick note about how I started writing poetry: one day, Hai Yan said to me, "Lu Xiaolu, you're not the same as the other young workers, are you?" I'd already heard this from Bai Lan, and now I was hearing it from someone else. I felt a real fluttering of excitement, thinking I had found my soul mate. I asked Hai Yan in what way she thought I was different. She said it had something to do with the fact that I was reading Les Misérables while the other young workers were reading Possessed Sluts. The reason I'd thought to read Les Misérables was to understand what misery was. It was a good book, Hai Yan said, very inspirational. Fuck, could Les Misérables really be called inspiration?

Hai Yan took a couple of poetry journals out of her drawer and said, "Take these. You might find them interesting." These poetry journals weren't from the library, they were her personal copies. The factory didn't actually have any journals; no poetry journals, at any rate.

"Composing poetry, eh?" I said. "Isn't that just dividing sentences into lines?"

"You've got some nerve!" she said. "Why don't you try your hand at it? Write a couple, and if they're any good we can get Chen Xiaoyu to publish them in the factory paper."

I couldn't imagine writing poetry, let alone getting it published in the factory paper. It was asking for trouble, but it would still be cool. Hai Yan had been the factory's only poet up until then. She was very pretty and very smart, and all the management liked her. I think people in the factory saw her poetry writing like some kind of handicraft, not that different from embroidery. I became the saccharin factory's second poet, but I was an electrician and my reputation wasn't great. Some people thought I was an asshole, but I wasn't sure what I was. When Hu Deli saw my poem, he said it was a typical case of not engaging in one's proper work, and that I should be sent to the saccharin workshop as a form of "poetic justice."

Now I know that people who write poetry have this quirk: they like to try to get other people to write poetry too. Chen Xiaoyu and Hai Yan may have discovered my talent, but by so doing they delivered me to the mouths of lions. When the workers and supervisors saw me coming, they shouted: "Poet! It's the poet!" I was so embarrassed, I wished that the ground would just swallow me up. The cadres tended not to tease me. They just gave me cold looks. When I went to the restroom, I'd hear people squatting inside, reading my poems out loud. Then they'd twist the factory rag up and use it to wipe their asses. I really didn't get why I'd become the literal butt of so many jokes. At first I thought they were jealous of my talent, but later I realized that they saw my poetry as doggerel.

I regretted putting my poetry out there. I'd been doing okay before that. But I'd put in all this effort now, and in so doing left myself wide open. Now that I'm thirty, things like this don't embarrass me. But when I was nineteen, it felt like if trouble didn't find me from this direction, it would find me from another. So what the fuck was the difference? Life was a bitch.

I was changing a light bulb in the laboratory on my own one day when the lab technician girls said, "Oh, it's Lu Xiaolu! He's a poet now." I told them not to mock me; that I was an electrician first and foremost. That's when they told me I wrote really well, and my poetry had a feeling of Li Qingzhao. I thought about it for some time and decided it was sort of a compliment from the heart, which made me happy. To reciprocate, I taught them a game I'd just learned at night college. It was called "pen spirits." The game was pretty popular with college girls, but the factory girls hadn't come across it yet.

I explained the game a bit, pulled open the blind, and laid a sheet of paper on the desk. I wrote a couple of characters on it and recited a spell or two. One girl volunteered to hold the ballpoint pen with me, while the girls around us started getting nervy, their little faces flushing. This was a pretty funny game, and one of the best ways ever to flirt with girls. Some mysterious force made the pen start to spin slowly around the paper. "The pen spirit is here, the pen spirit is here," they marveled in soft tones. "You're amazing, Lu Xiaolu, where did you learn that? You really must teach us."

At that point, the main door of the laboratory was thrown open and in came a group of cadres. The lab girls squealed and scattered like mice, leaving me on my own at the table, the ballpoint pen still in my hand, staring at the cadres in confusion. The first one I saw was Hu Deli, followed by Pu Nani and Xiao Bi. This made me wonder if I might actually be dreaming; you don't expect to see all your adversaries together like that. At that point, a tall, thin, middle-aged man walked up to me. He was wearing the neither-blue-nor-green work uniform, while I was wearing my lapel collar suit. He pointed at me and asked, "What team is he from?"

Hu Deli took a step forward and said, "Electrician team."

This middle-aged man's face remained stoic. "Send him to the saccharin workshop to work the three shifts," he said. Then he pointed at Hu Deli and asked, "Is this what you call management?"

Later I learned that this middle-aged man was the factory's newly appointed head. That day, he'd taken a couple of office cadres out to make a surprise inspection. All I knew about him was that he was a notable entrepreneur, and that under his management our factory had become the only state-owned enterprise in Daicheng not to lay off anyone. He'd caught me fair and square: I was done for, no wriggle room. Presenting him with a hundred cartons of Zhonghua cigarettes wouldn't have made the slightest difference.

All factory heads at that time had "entrepreneur" as their title. Daicheng had a saying, "There may be poor factories, but there are no poor factory heads." That was the year the layoffs started in Daicheng's light-industry enterprises. Workers were given a pay packet of around a hundred yuan before being "liberated" back home. Our factory was another story. While other factories were being sold off with all their equipment, ours was expanding, and huge numbers of the staff were sent to work the three shifts, the front line of saccharin production. Our factory head became known as "the real entrepreneur," as opposed to "the ordinary entrepreneur" or "the bankrupt entrepreneur." I hadn't thought any of this would concern me. I'd heard lots of people say he was formidable and I'd thought, *Then let him get on with being formidable.* Going on the three shifts was shitty, but being laid off was shitty too. It didn't make a difference to me—I'd either do hard labor or become a gigolo. These were my two future paths.

CHAPTER NINE
THE BATHHOUSE

If you asked me to tell you my favorite place in the factory, my answer would depend on how I was feeling. If I were feeling emotional, I'd say the infirmary. If I were feeling proud, I'd say the library. If I were feeling insincere, I'd say the posts from which I fought my battles. If I were feeling rebellious, I'd say the small hut where the driver team raised dogs on the sly. But none of these was my real favorite. Like everyone else, I loved that cursed bathhouse. It was a choice that didn't show me to be any different intellectually or physically from anyone else.

I've described the way the bathhouse looked. Now I want to describe the people inside. And seeing as I was never fortunate enough to see the women without their clothes on, you'll have to make do with my descriptions of naked men. These men could be divided into two types. The first type was the young men, who possessed their young men's "vitality" whether they were in good physical condition or not. The second type included the middle-aged and older men who were either in good working order down there, withered, or defunct. You wouldn't know any of this in normal life, but as soon as they were stripped bare, the cat was out of the bag. Occasionally young children came in, swimming in the water with bare bottoms. They are not on my list, however, because I am not fond of young children. It was pretty awesome seeing the boiler room supervisors bathe. A gang of them would come in, and with a "Hwoar!" they'd strip out of their dirty clothes, revealing toned bodies like twisted towels.

Without a word, they'd jump into the pool. Which was pretty depressing actually: like seeing fallen gangsters. Then there were the posers: Six Fingers, for example, wearing his thick gold chain as he bathed, both arms outstretched and resting on the sides of the pool. He warned me to make sure my nipples were visible when I bathed like this, because when they were submerged people might mistake me for a girl. I didn't think so, but I soon enough observed that his chest was flabby, nothing like my strong, tight pecs.

I've been to a couple of public bathhouses in my time, including the sauna and the large public baths that came later, and they all had a lot of rules. You weren't allowed to soak in the pool when your body was lathered in soap, for example. You weren't allowed to wash your briefs in the pool. You weren't allowed to swim. But in the factory bathhouse, there were no rules. People even pissed in the water. Some years later, a friend and I went to a large public bath. I bounded toward the pool, but my friend had some sort of compulsive cleanliness disorder. "For God's sake," he shrieked, "you're not actually going to bathe in the big pool, are you? It's too dirty."

"It's not dirty, damn it," I said. The water looked fine.

"Do you know how many people have sexually transmitted diseases?" this friend asked.

I climbed out as soon as I heard this. I thought about how naive I'd been during my factory years, assuming that the pool water just happened to have mud in it, rather than realizing it was mixed with dust from the bodies of a thousand men, one or two who could have been suffering from gonorrhea, syphilis, or something else.

As a bench worker I was pretty respectful, making regular trips to the bathhouse with Old Bad-Ass, carrying his towel and his soap. I'd wait by the side while he washed, and when he was done, he'd lie on the edge of the pool and I'd give him a back rub with a twisted towel. I was the most diligent and sycophantic apprentice. After I rubbed him down, I'd sprint across to the shower room and save him a tap, shouting, "Here, supervisor, here!" When other people heard this, they thought I was the fucking Monkey King. These days were behind me now. After Old Bad-Ass retired and I was transferred to the electrician team, I'd come here to bathe with Long Legs, Xiao Li, and Six Fingers, finally with a little status of my own. I'd often see Wei Yixin from the bench worker team still giving Good Balls his back rub. Good Balls had basically found himself a lifetime's supply of free massages.

We used to poke fun at each other in the pool and splash water like happy young maidens. Sometimes two of us would gang up and push the other underwater and make him drink a mouthful of it. I was pushed under once, and I swear, the water was actually sweet. This was because the saccharin workshop operators had already bathed earlier that afternoon. Once we got too rowdy, antagonizing Wang Ming from the safety department, who ran over and grabbed Six Fingers by the chest. Six Fingers was astonished because he was naked, so there wasn't a stitch of clothing to be grabbed by. He realized Wang Ming was actually pinching his pecs, leaving him no means of escape. Six Fingers gave a bloodcurdling scream, and we rushed over and dragged off Wang Ming. A fight ensued in the water. We weren't a match for Wang Ming, but Six Fingers managed to rise up and leave a scratch on Wang Ming's butt, revenge for having his pecs pinched.

After we soaked, we used the showers. We had a ritual of using towels to whip our lower halves. I'm talking about whipping each other's lower halves—if we'd been whipping our own, it would have made us a group of self-flagellation practitioners. Long Legs was the most unfortunate in this regard. Being so tall made him pretty easy to whip. He was very skinny too, and in my experience skinny people always seemed to have bigger dicks. Since he was both tall and well-endowed, it seemed a pity not to whip him. Sometimes he'd wash his hair in the shower room, and when his face was covered in soap bubbles and he couldn't open his eyes, we would launch a sudden towel attack on his butt. When he spun around, we'd unleash a torrent of whips to his front. He wouldn't be able to retaliate while being whipped, and by the time he'd rinsed the soap off his face and started cursing the hell out of us, we'd be long gone. We bullied him without restraint. We were addicted to serving up those lashings. We dreamed about pinning a target on his private parts. Long Legs would leap around frenziedly with his hand over his vital organ while we laughed insanely and whipped his butt with our towels. Long Legs actually burst into tears once. Xiao Li and I pulled back and gave him an apologetic look. "You're complete assholes," he said.

Long Legs had one way to get back at us: when we were washing our hair, he'd sneak over and turn off the cold tap so scalding hot water would flow out. The person under the tap would scream out in pain, but Long Legs would have run away by then. He never did this to me and Xiao Li, because he knew that we whipped him only out of love, not like the others who did it purely as a form of bullying. When I look back, I feel very sorry that we did that to him. Why did I think that whipping his dick was a reasonable expression of my affection?

Washing your hair in the bathhouse back then meant using a factory-issued plastic container filled with shampoo. You poked your forefinger in, dug out a blob, then rubbed it over your head. It had a lardlike consistency and came in strawberry, pineapple, or orange scent. Whichever one you got, your head wound up smelling like fruit.

"Tell me which fruit smell you like best, and I'll use that one from now on," I told Bai Lan.

"Oh, durian flavor," she said.

Seeing as I wasn't from the south and I'd never come across durian, I had no idea about the stink. So I started asking people if they'd come across any durian-scented shampoo, making them laugh their asses off.

I saw a commercial for Head & Shoulders shampoo on TV one day and was the first one in the factory to try it out. Bai Lan recommended it to me because my hair was oily. When the other bathers saw me using it, they were intrigued and raced over to borrow some. They unscrewed the lid and emptied big dollops onto their palms. The ten-yuan bottle was finished in an instant. One guy was so vile he even rubbed it into his pubic hair, making his nether regions both fragrant and dandruff-free.

Bathing was also a time to carry out anatomical observations—or, in layman's terms, to see who had the biggest dick. When you were seeing the same ones again and again, this game got boring. Long Legs was always the champion in this department anyway. One day, Long Legs discovered that Yuan Xiaowei's was staggeringly huge, much bigger than his own, a revelation that shook the entire bathhouse. Yuan Xiaowei was Chicken Head's apprentice. I've mentioned the way Chicken Head forced him to touch the electric gate each day, giving him a 220-volt electric shock. Because of this, all the supervisors started saying, "Damn, who knew that electric shocks could have this effect. It's incredible!" We ran back to the electrician team.

"Fucking hell," we said to Chicken Head. "Xiaowei's schlong is humungous!"

Chicken Head didn't believe it, and so Long Legs used his hands to indicate a pretty unrealistic length. Six Fingers stood next to him, saying, "I can testify— it really is huge."

Chicken Head scratched his head, saying, "That's normal if it was hard at the time."

"No, it was that long when it was limp," we all said.

"It's huge! It's just huge!" Six Fingers kept saying. We'd all seen Six Fingers' dick and had never once whipped him, scared of injuring his pride, because it was pretty hard to see the target.

Chicken Head patted Six Fingers sympathetically, saying, "Six Fingers, no need to be down on yourself. Big schlongs don't mean everything. The most important thing is technique."

Six Fingers sighed and said, "But who am I going to find to practice my technique with?"

Long Legs was pretty hyped when we learned this news about Yuan Xiaowei. "Now you won't need to whip me anymore, you can whip him instead," he said.

We explained that we whipped him either because we were feeling affectionate toward him or because we felt like bullying him, and it gave us a twisted sense of pleasure. If we started whipping Yuan Xiaowei, people would just say we were jealous. It would show that we knew our dicks were inferior to his. Fuck, who would display their insecurities that obviously?

Yuan Xiaowei became famous throughout the factory. The electrician team had discovered a new form of Homo sapiens. There were subtle changes in the attitudes of the workshop aunties. Before, they'd always requested me and Xiao Li from the electrician team. Now they'd say, "Oh, Chicken Head, send Yuan Xiaowei over to change the light bulb." When Yuan Xiaowei went, the aunties would all gaze at his crotch while he went about his work, completely oblivious. A couple of times, Six Fingers went with him. Six Fingers was a fantastic electrician, and changing a light bulb was demeaning for him. Standing next to Yuan Xiaowei in front of the aunties, his sense of self-worth took an even greater hit. When Six Fingers came back, he was furious. He moaned that the aunties hadn't paid him the slightest bit of attention; they'd just surrounded Yuan Xiaowei and talked with him. Xiao Li and I were left happily idle while all this was going on. Our dicks may have been small, but as long as we didn't have to exert ourselves at work, we were fine with that.

The bathhouse was very hot, and the factory workers liked to bathe until their bodies were softened and relaxed. Often they'd have the steam valve opened fully and roaring loudly, and the guys would soak alongside the heat and the noise. After a while you'd start to feel dizzy, seeing stars, and your legs would turn to jelly. A retired old worker died in there once. He had white hair and a bulging stomach. They said it was a heart attack.

You couldn't stay inside for very long after you'd finished washing or you'd end up covered in sweat. When you left the bathhouse, you'd see the aunties and young girls coming down from the women's bathhouse on the floor above, their wet hair loose and their faces flushed, as if in heat. The girls shouldn't have let just anybody see them in this state—it led to sexual fantasies. But all the women in the factory had been seen like this by all the men. There was no law against it. Unfortunately, I never got to see Bai Lan in this state because she didn't bathe at the factory.

Bai Lan was a bit of an eccentric. The whole factory knew this, but they tended to humor her because of her important position at the factory. I humored her too because of her important position in my heart. Plus, I had a better understanding of those eccentricities. No, not an understanding, I'd had more . . . experience with them. Even though I'd made out with her that one time, I'd never been given the preferential treatment I felt I deserved. She didn't like it when people asked questions. She'd either respond with silence or be evasive, but she showed me her temperamental side. When she was in a good mood, she could be quite chatty; but when she was in a bad mood, she'd get very impatient. I once asked her why she didn't bathe at the factory. She happened to be in a pretty good mood and said, "I've never liked washing in public places. I find it embarrassing."

"What's embarrassing about it?" I asked. "Who'd be looking at you? It would only be women there."

"Do you know what the women's bathhouse looks like?" she asked.

I told her I did: the women's bathhouse had no pool, just showers, and the showers no longer had heads, so all they produced were columns of water. I knew all this from going in to change light bulbs.

"Lots of women crowd around a single shower head," Bai Lan said. "Most line up, but some of the more overbearing ones just barge in front. They do this when they're naked, and it all feels slightly shameful. When I was little, my aunt took me to bathe, but she didn't really look after me there, and it left a bad taste in my mouth."

"I can't believe you've never bathed at a public bathhouse. Are you a foreigner or something?"

"Of course I've bathed at one. Back when I was at college. But I wash at home now. How is it any of your business anyway? If you say I'm a foreigner again, I'm going to lose it."

I'd hung out at her place and seen her restroom. She had quite a decent cast-iron bathtub set into cement and laid with random tiles. There were hot and cold taps, but only the cold tap worked; the hot tap was just for show. She had to boil water, then carry the kettle into the bathroom to pour in the bath, then add cold water, until she was finally able to take a bath. This was the opposite of relaxing, and if you were washing your hair, it would be particularly tiresome. In winter you'd turn into an ice pop, and I really don't know how she stuck with it while remaining so smug about it. It was as if she were some sort of transcendent being.

I quickly took care of her blocked bathtub.

First I grabbed the plunger and gave it a bit of suction. Then I took a length of steel cable and passed it through the plug. I did this for so long, I felt worn out and was drenched with sweat. In the end, I took an iron hook and fished out a tangle of horrifying, slime-covered hair. Hair is very romantic when laid out on a pillow, but completely disgusting when it's blocking a drain. She didn't seem at all fazed. She just looked at it and said, "Ah, see what else you can get out of it, will you? Otherwise it will be blocked up again in a day or two."

"Aren't you disgusted by this?" I asked.

"Don't forget that I'm a doctor," she said. "I might have a slight cleanliness complex, but bodily matter doesn't bother me."

"Is it going to be like last year when I fixed your bike, Doctor Bai? I rode it around to test it before you got on. Seeing as I've unclogged your drain, shouldn't I take the first bath to check it out?"

"Piss off!"

I told her she looked so freaking pretty and had this cleanliness complex, but in actual fact she was a slob. My mother washed our bathtub regularly with a scrubbing brush. She'd fish out the hair from the plughole every time she was done having a shower. When the drain wasn't flowing well, she'd get my pa to unblock it. Our house may have been a bit of a wreck, but they kept it at four-star hotel standard.

"Look at you," I told Bai Lan, "you haven't even washed your bowl from breakfast."

She looked a bit ashamed. "I live on my own, which makes everything simpler."

"Wouldn't bathing at the factory bathhouse make things simpler still?"

"You've gone on and on about how I should use the factory bathhouse, what's with that? Do you have a telescope set up or something? Is your plan to watch me washing?"

In the end she got pissed, and turned away, ashamed. Then she walked over and kissed me.

"Stop talking crap and get on with your work. Here's your incentive."

"Isn't that the kind of incentive landowners' wives use to make the hired farmhand do all the hard work?" I ran as soon as I said this, a slipper flying after me.

A few days later, Long Legs was fiddling with a bathhouse pipe. When he came out, he told me that the shower room had been installed with new shower heads that made showering a lovely and relaxing experience. We all went to try it out, and sure enough, it was really refreshing: the column of water that had felt like a whip was now gentle drops of rain sprinkling over your head, sprinkling over your body, sprinkling over your dick. There was another issue—when the water pressure was strong it could make your balls swell, so I'd always been too scared to give them direct exposure. Now the problem was solved.

"There are new shower heads in the bathhouse," I told Bai Lan. "It's very pleasant."

"In what way is it pleasant?"

I wasn't prepared to tell her the thing about my balls, I was too shy. But I could tell her how relaxing it was when the water sprayed down over your head. Describe how pleasurable washing your hair could be, especially for girls with long hair. Now all the girls in the factory could frolic under the new shower heads, and she'd be the only one miserable and missing out.

She was quite moved when I said this and said, "When I'm feeling brighter, I'll give it a try."

Finally the day came when a proud Doctor Bai walked into the women's bathhouse, her wash bucket in hand. I was pretty pleased. She'd twisted my arm about going to night college, and twisting her arm to get her to use the bathhouse was just my pointless revenge. I didn't know why I'd been doing it, only a vague feeling that people should be more open; that they should push against any psychological barriers they might have. Looking my adversaries straight in the eye worked for me, and I figured that for a fierce girl like Doctor Bai, it should work too. I'd never have thought that night college and the bathhouse would end up giving us both so much trouble.

Bai Lan was talking and laughing with Little Pouty Lips as she carried her stuff out from the women's bathhouse. When she lifted her head, it wasn't me she came face-to-face with—I hadn't even been aware this was happening—it was Wang Ming from the safety department.

We had a ranking system for the women in our factory that placed them all in order of attractiveness. This ranking could change at any time: new people came to the factory, and old people aged or left. The number-one pretty girl in the factory was the ice sculpture in the factory head's office, without a doubt; the second prettiest was in the finance department; and the third prettiest specialized in marketing. Bai Lan's ranking was a little controversial: she came in at about twenty. She and Little Pouty Lips ranked about the same, but it was nothing to be proud of—auntie Ah Sao shared that position too. (As for handsome guys, I was number one.) The two of them had finished showering and were walking down the steps in a cloud of steaming mist. Bai Lan's wet hair was draped over her shoulders, where it soaked the top of her shirt, and her cheeks were pink. This was how she was seen by Wang Ming—who liked what he saw. A while later, Auntie Qin from the canteen came out, also shrouded in steam. As she was the matchmaker, she casually called out, "Doctor Bai has a fantastic figure, I saw it with my own eyes." I'd just come out of the male bathhouse and fumed that it was this old lady I'd run into and not Bai Lan. Hearing her words made me jealous and angry, and I had a serious urge to take my bar of soap and ram it into her mouth.

"Don't wash in there again. Auntie Qin was outside shooting off her mouth about your figure," I told Bai Lan.

"What did she say about me?" she asked, clearly agitated.

"Auntie Qin said you had a good figure."

"In what way did she say it was good?"

"She didn't give specifics. I'd probably have to invite her out for a meal before she'd divulge those kinds of details."

"So why don't you invite her out for a meal then?"

"What do I need to invite her out for? I could just invite Little Pouty Lips out and get the same information from her. She might even have told Xiao Li already. In that case, I'd only need to give Xiao Li a smoke and he'd tell me."

"You wouldn't dare," she said, scowling at me. "Anyway, I'm never going to wash in there again."

I felt myself relax. A moment later, I was feeling two-faced and down on myself, uneasy. Human beings really are just too freaking complicated.

Since Bai Lan and I had kissed, I'd been walking around feeling like I was living in a trance; my body was weak, like after a hot bath. Love definitely didn't give you strength—it actually zapped it from you, sunk you into an embarrassingly gentle state. Whether I was standing up or sitting down, I was always thinking of her and would often find myself smiling. I'd forget the time, staring into space as I bathed and ate. Bai Lan had clogged my mind completely, and I'd get mad when anyone interrupted these daydreams. It was such a beautiful feeling, but later I remembered Ah Ying, and how she'd been when she was in love with Six Fingers, and wondered what the big deal was. When I was back home and lying in my bed, I wondered how I could compare what I was feeling to what that clown felt. It completely undervalued the whole thing.

A few days later, Little Pouty Lips pulled me to one side and said, "Wang Ming is pursuing Doctor Bai."

"Wang Ming is a piece of work," I said. "He fights, and he fights nasty."

"That day I went to the women's bathhouse with Bai Lan, we bumped into Wang Ming," she told me. "There was something strange about his facial expression. I wondered then whether he was looking at me or at Doctor Bai. But then yesterday I went to the library after work and I saw him leaving the infirmary."

"This doesn't necessarily mean he's pursuing her," I said.

"Women have excellent intuition," she said. "Wait and see what happens, if that's what you prefer."

I gulped, unable to speak. Xiao Bi from the propaganda department had been transferred to the bureau by now and had married the bureau chief's daughter, cutting off all contact with Bai Lan. Getting along in the factory had toughened me, while Bai Lan had her sharp edges: the two of us had become such hard-asses that we had no rivals in love. But suddenly here was Wang Ming. He wasn't gentle and sophisticated like Xiao Bi—the guy I could never compare to. No, Wang Ming was like me: full of piss and vinegar.

"Let him bring it on!" I shouted.

"I know you like Bai Lan, but who do you think you are?" Little Pouty Lips said. "You should just stick with looking out for Long Legs."

I smiled. She didn't know that I'd kissed Bai Lan, and that for those lips I would punch Wang Ming to the ground. After all those days of feeling sapped of strength, I was back up and running at full capacity.

Wang Ming was a strapping guy, and he was an excellent fighter. I wasn't actually very good at starting fights. He actually dared to start fights in the bathhouse, when his ass was bare. He was nothing like Director Wu or Pu Nani. If he were up for a real fight, I wouldn't have a chance in hell. I weighed it for a while but couldn't think of a better option. Puncturing his tires in the bike shed was way too juvenile.

Little Pouty Lips could see what was going through my mind. "Don't do anything rash," she said. "Wang Ming is a retired veteran—you're no match for him. And you can't punch him. If you do, they'll send you for labor education."

"I have a lot of respect for retired veterans," I said. "There are quite a few in my family, actually. One fought in the Korean War, another in the Vietnam wars. There's a martyr too."

I cycled back home so angry, I was ready to explode. My mind was bubbling with ideas of how to strike down Wang Ming in the bathhouse. How could I tell him that he wasn't allowed to harass Bai Lan? Should I stand in the factory and shout at the top of my lungs that Bai Lan belonged to me? It was a difficult situation; I really couldn't cope with feeling so emotional. I turned into New Knowledge New Village. It was a Sunday. I saw Bai Lan's bike parked in front of the house and her clothes drying out on the balcony. I ran up the stairs and knocked on her door. There was no noise or movement for a long time, but then after a while I heard her walking up the stairs, shuffling along with her feet encased in slippers. She had a bag of pears in one hand and a big pear in the other hand that she was eating.

"Did you wash that first?" I asked. "You shouldn't just bite into it. Aren't you the one with the cleanliness complex?"

"Someone gave them to me, they've been washed," she said. "I love pears. I'll peel you one in a bit."

"Who gave them to you?" I asked.

"Wang Ming from the safety department. He lives just opposite." I followed her into her place, watching in silence as she peeled the pear and handed it to me. I took a bite, but found it too sweet and couldn't bring myself to take a second bite.

"What's been up with you these last few days?" Bai Lan asked. "You need to cheer up."

"Why didn't you let him bring them into your house?" I asked. "Why did you go there to pick them up?"

Bai Lan said nothing. She threw her pear core out the window and calmly said, "Do you think my house is a place people can just come and go to as they please?"

"He could have brought them to the door, or to the bottom of the stairs to your apartment. I never said you'd let him into your bedroom."

"You're so infuriating," Bai Lan said. "Do you have to confuse the hell out of everything before you're happy?"

"Everyone in the factory is aware that Wang Ming is pursuing you, Bai Lan. Including me."

"That's crap," said Bai Lan. "How come I'm not even aware of it?"

She was right, I supposed. The whole thing had been Little Pouty Lips making a stab in the dark, and nobody in the factory was actually aware of it. Then I saw the pears on the table again. No, Little Pouty Lips had damn well guessed right.

"Wang Ming really isn't very educated. He's not at all well-suited to you. He's vicious when he fights. Did you know that not long ago in the bathhouse, he grabbed Six Fingers by the pecs? Six Fingers was in pain for a long time and still hasn't fully recovered. Imagine if he grabbed a girl's chest like that? How would that feel?"

Bai Lan laughed so much when she heard this that she collapsed across the table.

"He isn't the type of person you want to get involved with," I insisted. "You're naive. You think that you can just take a bag of his pears with no repercussions. What are you going to do tomorrow when he tells you these pears are from some tree in his garden that flowers only once every three thousand years and makes you immortal, and if you don't agree to be his girlfriend, you owe him a bag of the elixir of life?"

"How is it any of your business?" Bai Lan asked.

I started to feel kind of bummed out at this point, so I got up awkwardly and said goodbye. She didn't try to stop me. I felt even more bummed out clutching that pear with its one missing bite, and I ate the rest as I walked off. She was an odd girl, I thought to myself—even odder than me. Even odder than I'd thought she was. But I didn't actually believe she'd go out with Wang Ming from the safety department.

A word about Wang Ming: I only knew a limited amount about him. He was twenty-six or twenty-seven. He'd started at the factory as a bench worker, then been drafted into the army as a tank driver. When peacetime resumed, he was awarded second-class honors, which put him in a powerful position. When he returned to the factory, it was no longer as a worker but as a safety-department employee. You didn't see him around very often—he was a low-level cadre who kept a low profile. I hadn't been exaggerating when I'd said those things to Little Pouty Lips: my grandfather really had been in the Korean War, and when he returned he'd been extremely humble, working as a bus driver; and one of my distant cousins died in battle on the front line of Laoshan in the 1980s and had been given a quiet burial in Yunnan. But these things didn't count for much. If we hadn't had a martyr in the family—and my mother found this fact terrifying— I'd probably be in a military barracks now.

Wang Ming and I didn't really know each other. Up until this point, the only impression he'd left was the incident with Six Fingers in the bathhouse. I tended to avoid the safety department, and he didn't come out much, so the only place we really saw each other was at the bathhouse, sitting opposite each other, naked and vulnerable. I'd been working out like crazy around this time. Every day, I'd do about a hundred push-ups, a hundred crunches, run two miles, and work the chest expander with four springs. I felt like a transformer. After finishing work, I strolled into the bathhouse, shed my clothes, and hopped into the pool, making a huge splash while the old workers around me raged in silence. I soaked back into the pool and closed my eyes.

"If Wang Ming shows up, make sure you splash water in his face," I told Six Fingers.

"There's no way I'm doing that. If he comes, you piss in his face. I'll have your back."

"You're such a freaking letdown," I told Six Fingers. "He beat you up, and as your sworn brother, I want to get revenge for that. But you're too chicken to take the lead. You've done nothing to retaliate for that beating."

"I already have my own back," Six Fingers said. "I scratched his butt. If you want to die, fine, but don't drag me with you."

I gave up and sat in the water, regaining my composure. Sometime later, Wang Ming turned up. He crouched at the other end of the pool, separated from me by a thick layer of steam. He closed his eyes, remaining still for some time. I didn't move either, just watched him. Suddenly his eyes flicked open, and he stared at me. I dodged his gaze, thinking that this was all so fucking stupid. I went back to staring at him calmly. He was unwilling to admit defeat. I got tired and lay out on the edge of the pool, calling Long Legs over to give me a back rub.

Another time I was going to the infirmary when I came face-to-face with him as he was leaving.

"Hey, are you Lu Xiaolu?" he asked.

"Yep."

"You're about to be drafted," he said. "They're holding physical examinations in two days."

I ignored him and walked past into the infirmary where I saw Bai Lan sitting beside the table, her head lowered as she wrote.

"I just saw Wang Ming," I said.

"Mm," she replied, tidying away the things on the table. She lifted her head and said, "Wang Ming has asked me to go see a movie with him."

"Go for it," I said as if this was something she needed my permission for.

Bai Lan gave me a very strange look, but said nothing. Silence descended. I paced up and down the infirmary, touching objects and looking around. Bai Lan stared at me. I picked up a crushed cigarette butt from the ground, and said, "Did that shithead smoke in here?"

For a moment she was too shocked to speak, then she said, "Yes, that was his."

I took Bai Lan to see a movie, and ingeniously she suggested an all-night showing, so we both took off the following day of work. We were the only ones in the movie theater that night. The movie was boring. A beam of blue light shone out of the darkness above our heads like a blade. It landed on the screen, where it turned into an image that rushed toward our eyes like a mighty force of soldiers. The two of us started out sitting in the front row thinking it was pretty cool, but we couldn't stand what felt like a visual attack and moved to the back row instead. With her knees up against the back of the seat in front of her, Bai Lan sunk down in her seat, staring intently ahead. Later in the night, she started to fade. She leaned against my shoulder and fell asleep, and later she turned and slept across my elbow. I stroked her soft hair for some time, thinking that I was nineteen and she was twenty-three. What was going on here? I was getting sleepy too, almost drifting off, when suddenly she was wide awake.

She lifted her head and said, "I don't hate Wang Ming, you know. He's really not as bad as you made out."

"Are you still dreaming or something?" I asked.

"Yes, I just dreamed about lots of things from the past. I don't hate him, you know—I'm just a bit scared of him."

On the way home that morning, the air was cool and refreshing, and the road was clear—no traffic, no traffic jams.

"Have you ever thought about leaving Daicheng, going to explore somewhere else?" Bai Lan asked.

"We've had this conversation before," I said. "Why are you still trying to make me go to night college?"

"I was wrong, let's not talk about that." Bai Lan said, "You just pass your night college exams and when you graduate, you can work in one of the departments—that's one route to happiness."

"That way I'll be worthy of you," I said. "Who gives a shit about the safety department!"

Around that time I could have joined the army, but that plan was quietly dashed by the powers that be. It was only later that I realized the factory hadn't wanted its fine young workers, its technical backbone, to be drafted into the army, because that would mean there would be no one to do the work. Neither did they want people like me to become soldiers. I was known for my bad behavior. If I behaved badly in the army I'd be sent back, which would bring shame on the factory. If my behavior in the army was outstanding and I was awarded second-degree honors, it wouldn't necessarily guarantee me a department job after I returned. They might see it as setting a devil on horseback—pretty risky.

Luckily, I was in love and didn't have any strong urges to join the army anyway, so I never followed up.

The conscription physical took place at the factory, in the infirmary, as you'd expect. Appropriate-age young people from the workshops were sent in groups for their physicals. There were seven or eight of us standing solemnly in the doorway when it rolled around to the mechanical repair workshop's turn. We were surprised when we saw that Long Legs wasn't with us, figuring he must have been disqualified on account of his height. They were probably afraid he wouldn't sleep comfortably on the army cots. Xiao Li had wanted to come, but Chicken Foot put his foot down, saying that the electrician team had been too busy recently. Everyone who showed up was expendable. Some people in the group were wearing glasses, clearly attempting to avoid being drafted.

I walked in but didn't see any servicemen, just two aunties in civilian clothing who I guessed were doctors. They were speaking with pure Beijing accents. Bai Lan stood to the side talking to them, also with her Beijing lilt. Thanks to all my conversations with Bai Lan, I'd learned to speak in the Beijing dialect and could almost be mistaken for a Beijing local. The aunties made me stand up straight, lift my legs, and perform a couple of other movements. They looked pretty pleased with themselves, but I felt anxious. Next we had our vision and hearing tested. The visual acuity in my right eye was slightly off. One of the aunties gave me a sharp glance and said, "Are you faking it?"

"I honestly can't see clearly. There's no way I could fire a gun," I said. "You can send me off to be a military engineer if you want. I could dig out landmines. I'm an electrician and I run really fast, I'll be able to detect the mines—bounding mines, blast mines, or anti-tank mines—none of them scare me."

"Okay, Mister Mine, I think we've heard enough from you."

Bai Lan was next to us, laughing into her hand. She laughed herself into stitches.

I put my clothes back on and swaggered out just as Yuan Xiaowei was going in. I stayed by the door and watched awhile. The aunties looked very impressed by Yuan Xiaowei.

They knew what they were doing: this was the young guy who had trained himself to tear electric wire with his bare hands. A few days later, the news came: Yuan Xiaowei had been chosen. He sat in a car wearing a red flower while the union people beat their drums, and like a bride he was passed over to the army. Chicken Head was devastated and kept saying what a waste it was that such a fine specimen was going to a place where there were only men. He was tempted to hand Yuan Xiaowei over to Auntie Ah Sao to have her way with him first.

"I think you might have just had another dream shattered, Lu Xiaolu," Bai Lan said. "You haven't become a shop assistant, you aren't in the departments, and now the army doesn't want you either."

"But joining the army was never my dream," I said.

"You boys all dream about joining when you're young, playing your fighting games, pretending to be the People's Liberation Army capturing the hills. How can you say this was never your dream?"

I told her she really didn't understand boys. When we were young and playing our games, a lot of us had wanted to pretend to be the White Guard, the Japanese, and bandits because that made it more interesting. It had nothing to do with dreams. I really didn't want to discuss fucking dreams with her again. By this point, I knew I was going to be sent to the saccharin workshop, and I was feeling pretty down. I had zero interest in laughing at myself.

There was a period following this one when factory-wide maintenance and repair work was being carried out. The electrician team was short of manpower, and Chicken Head insisted I stick around. So I lingered there for another couple of weeks. The order to send me to the workshop had arrived, so there would be no getting out of it—I might as well have been drafted. I resigned myself to the inevitable.

There was an accident that fall. A ship transporting methanol exploded on the part of the river next to the factory. In my father's safety instructions, he had warned me to stay far away from pipes, valves, storage tanks, and tanker trucks, but he'd never mentioned ships. This shows that there's always a gap between experience and reality. The ship's cabin was empty when the accident happened. The methanol had all been siphoned out, but the sealed cabin was still full of methanol-infused air. A painter went to do some work in the cabin, carrying a lit light bulb and trailing an electrical wire. He tripped, smashing the bulb. There was a huge bang as the boat exploded. I was at the electrician team station playing chess at the time. All I heard was a sound like muffled thunder, and all the chess pieces were knocked down. Chicken Head put down his teacup, looked up, and gave a deep sigh. "That's an explosion, guys. Get ready to run."

We threw down our tools and ran outside to see what had happened. We couldn't see anything wrong with the factory, but then someone cycled over and said a ship had exploded on the river. It had been really terrible, and none of the crew had survived. The glass in the side of the boat had shattered in the blast, injuring a number of passersby. While the others ran to the scene of the accident, I turned and made a mad dash toward the infirmary—the little red building was close to the surrounding wall, and Bai Lan's infirmary was on the eastern side, close to where the explosion occurred. I ran into the building, seeing everyone clustered around like wasps. I went up the stairs and kicked open the infirmary door. All I could see were the two smashed eastern windows, glass all over the floor, and toppled chairs. Bai Lan sat on the floor with her hands over her cheeks, saying nothing. She looked as if she'd seen a ghost.

I helped her up and got her seated on the examination table. I looked her up and down, but it didn't seem too serious. She had no external injuries, though her clothes were dirty.

"Where was the explosion?" she asked, shaking her head.

"A ship exploded."

She dashed to the window to look out. The area a few hundred feet ahead was in a state of complete disarray. The explosion had split the cargo ship in half, and it was in flames as it sunk into the water. The street was covered in debris, and there were people running all over the place.

"I'd just been thinking I should open the window and let in some air," Bai Lan said. "If it had been a couple of seconds later, I'd have been a mess."

"It would be a crying shame if your face got disfigured," I said.

"You shouldn't stand there," Bai Lan said. "There could be a second blast."

I went back to her side and crouched down, looking up at her. She sat, looking down at me. We looked at each other awhile, then she said, "I'm okay."

"I was scared that if I asked you if you were okay, you might say 'How is that any of your business!' As long as you're okay, that's all that matters."

She laughed and pushed me away gently with one hand. I sat on the floor, then heard Wang Ming's voice outside. "Bai Lan, are you alright?"

I turned and saw him standing in the infirmary doorway, clearly shocked to see Doctor Bai sitting on the examination table laughing while I sat on the floor. It was pretty fucking baffling.

"Lu Xiaolu, what are you doing here?" Wang Ming said.

Bai Lan and I responded in unison: "How is that any of your business?"

The explosion didn't happen in the saccharin factory, so no one was held accountable. No compensation was awarded for the three people who died onboard the ship; their deaths were basically treated as suicide. Other injured parties included the people who'd been walking along the river and sitting in the teahouse I often used to go to, which was completely torn apart. Everyone had to come to terms with what had happened. Bai Lan took a trip to Shanghai around this time. I missed her a lot. While she was away, we received a phone call from the safety department saying they needed a light bulb changed. Xiao Li and I went together and found Wang Ming sitting on his own in the department. I held the ladder without a word while Xiao Li climbed up to do the job.

"Does the whole electrician team misuse manpower like this?" Wang Ming asked solemnly.

Xiao Li asked him what he meant.

"There are two of you changing this light bulb," Wang Ming said, "which is at best a one-man job. Although half a man could probably manage it."

Xiao Li went back and told Chicken Head about this exchange. Chicken Head raced straight to the safety department and asked Wang Ming, "How is it any of your business how the electrician team carries out its work?"

So now even my vile team leader was using the phrase *how is it any of your business*. It was as if we'd all made some tacit agreement to start using it, and for a while this phrase became a popular mantra for everyone in the factory— everyone apart from those whose business it actually was. But for the rest of us, being told constantly that things weren't our business tended to lighten the load.

During my last days on the electrician team, I was careful to stay out of trouble. The night-college semester had started, and as soon as the workday was over, I'd rush off to class. It had been a long time since I'd sat in a classroom. I didn't use to enjoy school at all. Now I felt cursed by my middle-school teacher's words: "Only after you leave school and enter the real world will you appreciate this school desk." He was completely right, but it wasn't just the school desk I appreciated. I came across a female classmate from my middle-school days too. She was a shop assistant at the People's Department Store. She'd filled out somewhat, and from the neck down bore no resemblance to how she used to look. She was very friendly and sat down next to me. The classroom was hot and stuffy, and she took out a little fan that sprayed perfume and fanned my face with it. It felt so cool and refreshing that I nearly fainted. She lowered her head and said, "You were a terror at school, but you seem nice now." I told her about all my ups and downs, how I'd had my sharp edges softened. She listened to my bullshit and actually looked quite moved, saying, "Oh, I know how you feel." During the break, she stumbled down the dark corridor to use the restroom and I sat there quietly feeling proud of myself. I was pretty alright—I'd just had a girl fan me. She'd seemed kind of naive, oblivious to the menial nature of a job at the saccharin factory. I heard her come back to her chair.

Without turning, I leaned over and quietly asked, "Do you have a boyfriend?"

"Excuse me, Lu Xiaolu!" When I heard this cold voice, I jumped out of my seat.

I turned around and saw Bai Lan staring at me. "Wow, you're a smooth operator, aren't you? Will you please come outside with me?"

I trailed behind Bai Lan down the dark corridor, down a dark path, and to the edge of a dark forest. I had an expression of abject misery on my face, but realizing she couldn't even see it, I went back to my normal expression.

She kept walking, so I said, "Where are you taking me? It's the river up ahead."

"I just got back from Shanghai, and I really missed you," Bai Lan said. "I rushed over to see you, but you're already hooking up with some new girl. Don't try to explain yourself. I was at the back watching you for half the class."

"You were checking up on me, clearly. Well, for your information, I wasn't trying to hook up with her. We were middle-school classmates."

"I saw her fan you," Bai Lan said.

I walked over and took her hand. She clenched it into a fist and said nothing. "Let's take a walk," I said. "I won't go back to the class."

I led her away, feeling her hand gradually loosen and her temper start to fade.

Later she said, "The fact that you can have that effect on people actually made me pretty happy. It proved you weren't completely undesirable. But be a little smarter in the future—don't get carried away."

I thought I understood what she said, but actually I didn't have a clue.

The next day when I got to the factory, I was told that Chicken Head and Wang Ming had faced off.

This was precipitated by a straightforward chain of events. The day before, Chicken Head had gone to the bathhouse after work, and Wang Ming had opened the steam valve to heat the water in the pool. Chicken Head felt that the September weather didn't warrant such hot water and went over to close it again. As an ex–tank soldier, Wang Ming felt he had more heat tolerance than an electrician, and he didn't find the water nearly as invigorating when it was cooled. So he went back and opened the valve again. The two of them continued to turn that valve open and closed. But Wang Ming was stronger, and Chicken Head was the first to lie down exhausted. But Chicken Head had his subordinates. He sent for five people—Six Fingers, Xiao Li, and Long Legs among them—ordering them to take turns closing the valve. This valve war went on until Wang Ming lay down exhausted too. Chicken Head was electrician team leader, so Wang Ming wouldn't have dreamed of beating him up, but he glared at him.

"What the fuck are you staring at?" Chicken Head asked. "You're lucky I don't have my fiercest people here today. That crazy motherfucker Yuan Xiaowei, with the biggest dick in the world, isn't here because he's joined the army. And my bravest fighter and most effective defender, Lu Xiaolu, otherwise known as Magic Head, is off studying. If either of them were here, you'd have just dug your own grave."

People who'd been bathing left the bathhouse and immediately started bragging about the big scene they'd just witnessed. Chicken Head was somewhat of a player, and when the gaggle of aunties carrying their bathing materials down the stairs heard what had happened, they were filled with glee. They wanted Chicken Head to get a beating and were disappointed it hadn't come to blows. When Chicken Head was done washing and headed out of the bathhouse, he jumped in surprise. The doorway was blocked by twenty or thirty aunties, all of whom he'd had indiscretions with. They were cheering him, telling him he had to take on Wang Ming.

I was accosted by Chicken Head as I was packing up my tool box. He told me I had to take on Wang Ming.

"I've had enough of fucking fighting," I said with annoyance. "I'm getting transferred tomorrow. Can't you just deal with him yourself? I've got better things to do than run around the bathhouse turning valves like a maniac."

"Fucking hell," Chicken Head said. "Long Legs said you'd been working out so you could give Wang Ming a beating. But you've obviously just been getting yourself ready for the saccharin workshop."

I couldn't stand being disrespected like this. "So how are you planning to take him on?" I asked.

He told me he planned to do the reverse of the day before: keep the steam valve open.

Our gang went straight to the bathhouse after work. Before long, Wang Ming entered. We sat in the pool in a row, waiting for him. The water was chilly. Other bathers had wanted to open the steam valve, but we hadn't allowed it. We waited for Wang Ming to do it. He walked over and opened the valve, and our group exchanged nasty smiles. When the water was hot, Wang Ming walked over and shut the valve. Chicken Head followed him over and opened it again.

Wang Ming smiled and said, "Oh, not scared of a bit of heat today, are we? Team Leader Chicken, I'm not going to lower myself to your level. I've finished bathing. So long."

That wasn't part of Chicken Head's plan. "If you're scared of the heat, Wang Ming, you can't be a real man!" he shouted.

This kind of goading wasn't usually very effective in our factory. The saccharin factory guys would just call you a dickhead and laugh it off. But somehow Chicken Head got to Wang Ming. When he heard this, Wang Ming went straight back to the valve and opened it fully. Then he turned to Chicken Head and said, "If I get out before any of you guys, I'll kiss all of your asses. What do you say, Chicken Head?"

"If we lose, we'll all kiss your ass."

"Yeah, that'll do," Wang Ming said. "And if you go back on your word, I'm going to haul your naked ass out of here and feed you to the aunties."

The heat was on. The water in the pool started to warm from the surface, while our feet still felt a bit chilly. It was a strange sensation, but soon I was no longer able to distinguish between the feeling of hot and cold on my skin. The water temperature rose rapidly, to the level you'd usually want it at in winter. The bathers who'd been there from the start could no longer take it. The department cadres were the first ones to leave, then the workshop operators, cursing Chicken Head as they splashed out of the pool. Six Fingers was beside me. He'd been trying to withstand it but with a sudden yelp, he jumped out. I turned to see that the whole electrician team had gotten out of the pool but were still in the bathhouse, leaning against the wall to cool down. There were a handful of people left in the pool, including Chicken Head and me in one corner and Wang Ming in the one diagonally opposite, all as far away from that fucking valve as we could be in order to last in the pool for a little longer. There were two boiler-room supervisors soaking in the middle of the pool, bona fide bad-asses.

"The water feels great today," they said as they washed.

"Supervisors, you two don't have to stay in. It's not like we're going to kiss your asses if we lose."

The supervisors bathed awhile longer, then said, "Fuck! You're all stupid assholes." They ran over to the steam valve, shut it, then climbed back in, saying, "If you're really intent on killing yourselves, just jump in the pool of sulfuric acid."

They meant well, but all they'd done by closing the valve was prolong the game. If the steam valve were opened again, we'd boil. Even with the valve closed, the water was hot enough to have us teetering on the brink of death.

Chicken Head gave a long sigh and said, "Lu Xiaolu, we can't carry on. We'll just have to bow down to him." He let out a cry and bounded from the pool. He ran toward the shower, yelling, "Quick! Someone turn on the cold tap for me!"

Then there were two of us left in the pool: Wang Ming and me.

The people crowding around us were laughing and saying that one of us had to die to make this worth it. Wang Ming and I were still at diagonally opposite corners of the pool. We continued to stare each other down for a while, but then I no longer wanted to see him, so I dropped my head and looked instead at the flat refraction of my body through the scalding jade-green water. I felt as if my pores were open so wide that if I rubbed my hand along my head, all the hair would slip out. But I could still keep going. Someone opened the fanlight, which made it feel slightly cooler, although I didn't feel the water temperature drop—in fact, the reverse. My body was drawing in all the energy from the hot pool water, overloading like a motor. I took a deep breath. Everyone was probably thinking I was sacrificing myself like this for Chicken Head.

It was only Wang Ming and I who knew the truth, that on the sparkling rippled surface of the water between our naked bodies floated Bai Lan's reflection.

There was a brief interlude to all this when Pu Nani came in to wash. He didn't have a clue what was going on or why the pool was so empty. Common sense should have told him that the water was too hot, but the fact that Wang Ming and I were in the pool confused Pu Nani, and he jumped right in. Then, like a movie rewinding, he gave a yelp of pain and leaped back out.

"What are you two playing at?" he asked.

Neither Wang Ming nor I was capable of responding.

Bai Lan was in the infirmary while this was going on. She'd been waiting for me to finish work so the two of us could go hang out, but she'd been waiting for ages and I still hadn't shown up. Then Little Pouty Lips dropped by and said, "Apparently Lu Xiaolu and Wang Ming are in the pool, seeing who can bear the hot water the longest."

"How boring," Bai Lan said airily.

Factory bets came in all shapes and sizes. I'd seen the biggest bad-asses betting on who would eat a toad, then being rushed off to the emergency room for treatment. There were a lot of oddball practices, and this bathing challenge didn't sound like anything special. Even if she'd wanted to, Doctor Bai couldn't have come inside the male bathhouse to see what was going on. She assumed this was just me being up to my old tricks, trying to win myself a smidgen of glory with this pointless task. She was annoyed and decided to go off on her own. She closed the infirmary door and went to the bike shed. As she was pushing her bike along, she heard a hauler saying gleefully, "It's really fucking awesome. That water is so boiling hot that I couldn't even get my callus-covered foot in it."

Bottom line: she was a doctor. She turned and rode her bike to the bathhouse entrance.

"The emergency services have arrived," people called out. "There are two of them in the pool still."

"Pull them out quickly before someone dies," Bai Lan ordered.

Wang Ming and I were still lucid, but our movements were slow and our bodies floppy. We'd taken the bet this far, and it was no longer important who got out of the water first. Chicken Head didn't want a death on his hands. He said, "Game over. I'll bow down to both of you, will that do?"

Both Wang Ming and I shook our heads and looked grim. I knew I was almost at the point of no return, but I just couldn't conceive that Wang Ming could hold on for more than one second longer than I could. But Wang Ming must have been thinking the same thing. In the end it was Chicken Head who caved in, watching me inch further and further down into the water. He ordered everyone to drag us both out. Back on dry land, I told them I was fine. My whole body was red, like I'd had a once over with a soldering iron; my heart was beating rapidly, and my head was swelling. I stood up and took a couple of steps, feeling okay. Wang Ming stood up on the other side of the pool but proceeded to fall headfirst onto the ground. I gave an involuntary shout: "I win!"

"Do you really think you won?" Bai Lan asked me afterward.

"I didn't really win," I said. "As I recall, we were both fished out of the water at the same time. But he was the one who passed out and only came to when he'd had a bucket of cold water thrown over him. I was totally fine. If we're talking in terms of degree, I held out for slightly longer than he could."

"Do you know why you won?" Bai Lan asked.

I shook my head. I actually didn't know—Wang Ming was in better physical shape than I was.

"You won because you're younger. You're nineteen and Wang Ming is twenty-six."

"That's not a big difference," I said.

"It is a big difference. Games like this can kill you. If you don't scald yourself to death, your heart might explode. I hope that by the time you're twenty-six, you won't be so impulsive, taking risks like that with your life. We might not still know each other, but I still don't want you dying young."

I told her I wasn't really bothered. A little later I said, "I'm actually really happy I beat Wang Ming. Didn't you say you were scared of him? Now you know that he faints from the heat. While they were all pouring cold water over him, they were laughing at him and calling him a stupid dickhead. I admit I was stupid too, and what I did was completely pointless, but at least I held out. Imagine what that was like for him, lying naked on the bathhouse floor having cold water poured on him. After he came to and lifted his head, the first thing he must have seen was a group of naked guys surrounding him, their dicks all pointing at him as if they were all pissing on him. Poor guy."

Bai Lan rolled her eyes. "You've had days like that too, remember?"

"First, I wasn't naked and I didn't have a bunch of dicks pointing at me," I corrected her. "Second, that was last year when I was only eighteen. These situations aren't even in the same ballpark."

I never thought of myself as invincible, which meant that each time I was victorious, I really cherished it. This incident could be recorded in my hall of fame. Afterward, whenever I saw Wang Ming at the factory I felt a huge psychological advantage and got slight delusions of grandeur. Not long after all of this, Wang Ming was on patrol and wandered into the formaldehyde workshop, exposing himself to some gas that caused an allergic reaction. His body erupted in red welts that turned out to be incurable. He disappeared for some time on long-term sick leave. A couple of months later, I was bathing in the bathhouse when I saw a leopardlike figure skulk in and get into the pool, murmuring, "So relaxing."

It was Wang Ming. He never came back to work at the factory, he just convalesced at home. But he still came to the factory to use the bathhouse. Because of his welts, the public bathhouses wouldn't admit him. Our factory bathhouse had to because his condition had been caused by a work injury. When he jumped in the pool everyone else scrambled to get out, myself included. We would be like the women and make do with just a shower, leaving him to soak comfortably all on his own in the pool of hot water. He'd soak to his heart's content, then go home. On the days, he visited the word spread: the leopard's been here today; take a shower, don't soak in the pool. But he was actually fairly restrained and didn't come in every day. Sometimes he'd turn and look at me. I was working in the saccharin workshop by then, covered head to toe in white, and my complexion was terrible. "Lu Xiaolu, why don't you come in and we can bathe together," he'd mutter.

CHAPTER TEN

MY BROKENHEARTED LOVER

It was ten years ago that I stood in Bai Lan's doorway, hugging and kissing her. I'd only made out with one girl before her, but who knows how many since. I certainly couldn't count. These things weren't important to her—what was important was that I said, "I love you." At first I did so very reluctantly; I wasn't used to saying these words. But the more I said them, the more they rolled off the tongue. One day I realized it was always me saying this to her, never the other way around. I asked her if it was an army command and if I were her subordinate. She laughed and tried to say those words back to me, but she couldn't.

I brought a poem I'd had published in the factory newspaper to show her. She was sitting listlessly on the examination table, and she told me that she'd read it. So I asked her in a reserved way what she thought of the writing. She told me she didn't really understand it, but that it seemed fine. It was about camels and birds and so on. Then she frowned and said, "You're an electrician. You should be writing about light bulbs and motors, not camels and birds."

This annoyed me—in her line of logic, zookeepers would be the only ones allowed to write about camels and birds. She wasn't in the mood for a pointless argument. "Bai Lan," I said, "these poems were dedicated to you."

She opened her eyes wide and asked why I hadn't included a dedication to be printed next to them. I said I was afraid people in the factory would gossip, and people used this newspaper to wipe their asses. I didn't want to tarnish her purity. She just laughed, called me crazy, and asked who'd bother gossiping over these poems.

In 1993, the factory got its new head, and one of the major changes was increased discipline. Aunties no longer dared to knit during working hours, eating snacks was forbidden, and washing bras was expressly prohibited. If you committed such offenses, your name would be added to the labor department's blacklist and you'd be next in line for the saccharin workshop. It wasn't long before a new factory doctor joined Bai Lan's infirmary. She was a fat old lady with a huge mouth, a butt as big as a mah-jongg set, and a voice that was deep, low, and commanding. Apparently she was related to the new head. As soon as she started, people were predicting that Bai Lan would be sent to the saccharin workshop too because the infirmary had been a pretty cushy job already, and having two factory doctors was overstaffing, which was completely at odds with the new management style. This big fat old lady gave people the heebie-jeebies. She didn't seem to know much about medicine. An iron filing flew into Xiao Li's eye once, and he was in so much pain he couldn't open it. He rushed to the infirmary for treatment, and Bai Lan wasn't there. The big fat old lady pushed Xiao Li onto the examination table, rolled back his eyelid, and blew into it for ages, to no effect. So she clasped a piece of gauze with her tweezers and pressed it against Xiao Li's pupil. Xiao Li yelped with pain, bounced up from the examination table, and fled from the infirmary with a hand over his eye.

Once the big fat old lady started working at the infirmary, I couldn't really visit Bai Lan there anymore. Whoever visited Bai Lan would have to put up with the big fat old lady standing behind her and peering at you both. Strange ideas would form in your mind, like, should you punch her in the right eye or the left eye? But thoughts like this couldn't be developed into actions, or there would be dire consequences.

"There's a rumor going around that you're going to be sent to the saccharin factory," I told Bai Lan. She smiled but said nothing. I went to find Little Pouty Lips and asked her if the labor department was insane. What were they thinking, giving the factory doctor the three shifts? Little Pouty Lips explained that the factory was short of manpower, which meant that even graduates could get three shifts. The previous rules no longer applied: it had all gone to the dogs.

I told this news to Bai Lan and her response was, "Let it go to the dogs, then."

The factory had a meeting that fall. It was moderated by Hu Deli, head of labor, and all cadres and team leaders were required to attend. Ordinary employees were allowed to stand at the back and listen if they wished. The meeting was held in the big hall above the canteen. It had a stage and a DJ stand. This place was generally used for parties and celebrations or karaoke contests. The old supervisors told us it hadn't always been this way. For years, it had been the site of political struggle meetings, rather than leisure and entertainment activities. Back then, "leisure" meant going home to fuck your wife.

I stood at the back of the meeting to listen with a cigarette between my lips. A group of midlevel cadres sat on the stage. Below the stage, you had low-level cadres at the very front, then section chiefs and team leaders, behind them the advanced workers, and the ordinary workers at the back, cigarettes in their mouths and seeds cracking between their teeth. Not only did the ordinary workers have to stand, but a white chalk line had actually been drawn across the floor that we weren't allowed to cross. This was worlds apart from when leisure activities such as karaoke were held here, when you'd have the workers occupying the front of the hall and the cadres cowering at the back. I saw Bai Lan sitting in the back row, but she didn't turn and see me.

The meeting was running pretty smoothly. First they congratulated themselves for reaching their annual production quota ahead of schedule. Next they celebrated the expansion of the saccharin workshop and the new factory head taking office. Last they reiterated the problem of labor discipline. First Hu Deli criticized a couple of the low-level cadres without naming names—then he criticized a few lazy workers, by name this time. My name was on this list for "taking liberties with girls from the laboratory during working hours." Ah Sao from the pump room was mentioned too, although Hu didn't give details as to what bad deed she'd committed during working hours. At this point the workers started jeering. "Hey, Hu Deli, what exactly did Ah Sao do wrong?"

Hu Deli ignored them and continued to speak into the microphone. A supervisor grabbed hold of me and said, "Lu Xiaolu, were you taking liberties with Ah Sao?"

"Fucking hell, do you have cloth ears?" I said. "I took my liberties with the lab girls, thank you very much."

The people around us roared with laughter and pushed me until I stumbled over the white line. Whenever I tried to step back, they'd just push me again. So I just stayed there on my own at the front, protruding from the crowd. Bai Lan turned around and saw me. I suddenly felt like a person waiting in line for his execution. I was standing there with people looking at me from all directions, cheering, while in front of me I could see my executioner with a solemn expression on her face. My secret love, watching me through the sea of people, and I couldn't tell if the expression on her face was pity or scorn.

Hu Deli noticed me standing in front of the crowd, but to him I probably didn't look like a poor soul about to be shot to death, more like the leader of a labor revolt or a rebel army. Hu Deli yelled into his microphone, "Lu Xiaolu, you are about to be sent to the saccharin workshop, yet you continue to be this antagonistic!" All the workers below looked at each other in dismay when they heard this. Being sent to the saccharin workshop was the most severe punishment available. There were plenty of incidents of taking liberties with girls in the factory, but no one had heard of someone being sent to produce saccharin as a result.

I hadn't planned on saying anything, but after Hu Deli's outburst, I couldn't help myself. I framed my mouth with my hands and shouted, "Stop talking crap, Chief Hu! There are plenty of people from the saccharin workshop present. I, for one, feel that working in the saccharin workshop is an honor!" The workers took a couple of seconds to recover their wits, then one saccharin workshop auntie said, "Fuck you, Hu Deli! We saccharin workers are people too, you know." This auntie was really cute, and if it weren't for the sickly sweet smell wafting from her body, I would have hugged her.

That's when the head of safety stood up and grabbed the microphone. "Get Lu Xiaolu out of here, get him out now!" he said, pointing at me. Two factory police ran over and grabbed my arms. I knew these guys pretty well, and they looked embarrassed to be taking me to task. "Hey, buddy, a smart guy knows when the odds are against him. Let's leave quietly," one of them said.

"I'll go by myself, you don't need to take me," I said. But the workers behind us were blocking the door, laughing raucously, preventing them from escorting me out.

"There's nothing I can do unless you throw me out the window," I said.

The factory police were trying to claw through the crowd when one had the cap snatched off his head. One of the workers had taken it, and it was now being thrown back and forth across the mob of workers. The factory police were embarrassed. We all knew each other pretty well, so they couldn't really get angry with us.

"This commotion is all your doing, buddy," was all they said to me. "You better buy us lunch tomorrow to make up for it."

The two factory police turned around and waved to get the head of safety's attention. The head of safety was still shouting, "Get him out! Get him out!" The factory police were getting agitated now and said, "You fucking come and get him out if you think it's that easy."

The meeting dissolved into chaos. The workers at the back were making a total ruckus, while the cadres and foremen at the front were rolling around in the aisles laughing. The cadres on the stage were the only ones who remained straight-faced. The head of safety was having problems even leaving the stage. He managed to jump down, with the intention of coming over and getting me himself. He was still a fair distance away, so I pointed at him and shouted, "Hey, dickhead, you dare come over here and I'll drown you in the can!"

Everyone laughed their heads off when they remembered about Blind Fang pushing the head of safety into the latrine. "Blind Fang has shut off the electricity!" yelled someone else. The cadres looked alarmed and gazed at the fluorescent bulbs above their heads. They were all still lit; it was only fearmongering, obviously.

Hu Deli grabbed the microphone, summoned all his strength, and shouted, "No more messing around!" Our factory hall had two big speakers, one on either side of the stage. There was a sudden roar from these speakers, followed by a thunderous bang. Everyone in the front of the hall screamed, and a few toppled backward. They all sat back down, and a couple of the cadres pointed at Hu Deli and said, "Hu, you motherfucker! You've deafened us."

Meanwhile, the head of safety was rushing toward me. I'd dredged up his weaknesses, and now he was baying for blood. It was strange how quickly he'd transformed into this imposing figure, as if he'd been taking a heavy dose of steroids. But if he had the time to fight, why would he go for me over Blind Fang? Later Bai Lan explained that I'd given the man no choice but to react in this way. No one wanted their weaknesses displayed publicly—it was only natural he'd want to retaliate. However, I didn't know any of this at the time. I just took my stance and waited for him to launch at me. He was still 150 feet away, but approaching fast when one of the supervisors stuffed his electrician belt into my hands and said, "Whip this in his face. He won't be able to dodge that." This alarmed the hell out of the two factory police next to me. One took hold of my arm, while the other grasped me around the waist.

"What the fuck?" I said. "That guy is coming over to beat me up, and you're both holding me like this. You can't only restrain one person in a fight."

"Put down the belt," the factory police ordered.

I threw it to the ground, but they didn't let go of me. The workers at the back were now rioting too, holding off the head of safety as he tried to storm his way through.

"Please, Lu Xiaolu, we're begging you," the factory police said. "Master Lu, please just get the hell out of here."

All I'd wanted was to get out of there, I told them, but I couldn't leave now that the head of safety was on his way over—he'd think I was scared of him! I wouldn't dare hit any other cadre, I explained, but the head of safety didn't scare me. If you beat the head of safety in a fight, you could just step in and fill his shoes.

"Who do you think our head of safety is, a bandit?" the factory police asked, with irritated amusement.

The crowd behind us was loosening up, and tugging me with all their might, those two factory police finally managed to drag me outside. At that very moment, the head of safety managed to break through the crowd. His body was at a forty-five-degree angle, his fists in a flurry in front of my face. Fucking hell, I thought, he couldn't even have killed a chicken with that boxing.

That's when we heard screaming from the stage. Everyone in the crowd turned to look. All we could see was Hu Deli, soaking wet, his eyes glazed over, and Ah Sao from the pump room beside him, a plastic bucket in her hand. I recognized the bucket; the cleaners used it when they mopped the floor. Ah Sao had made him into a drowned rat, drenched him through and through with dirty mop water. He said nothing. The audience fell into a state of shocked silence. The head of safety and I were so caught up with the Hu Deli drama that we completely forgot about our fight. Auntie Ah Sao broke the silence with the scornful words, "Hu Deli, you're a bastard!" She threw down the bucket, turned on her hips, and walked off under the puzzled gaze of the crowd.

From there, the meeting descended into pure anarchy.

"Lu Xiaolu, you've just completely screwed up your political life," Bai Lan told me outside the hall. Then she changed that from "political life" to "professional future."

My professional future was always going to be as a worker, I told her. Anyway, I knew how to get by. I didn't need her poking her nose in all the time.

"You can't go on like this. Are you trying to get yourself killed?"

Irritably I told her about how I'd read the classic *Dream of the Red Chamber* and there was this character called Aroma who was always making a fuss, just like her.

"You're impossible," she said before leaving.

Later that day, I took part in the workers' karaoke contest. The original plan had been for it to follow the big meeting, but after the meeting dissolved into mayhem, the cadres bailed. The union official didn't know what to do; he thought they should cancel it, but the workers and supervisors disagreed. The day had already been so much fun, the workers enthused, that karaoke would be the icing on the cake. They couldn't hold the karaoke contest now, the union official said. How could they hold a freaking contest when the judges had all fled? Who were the judges? the workers wanted to know. The cadres, of course, the union official replied. The workers and supervisors were up in arms when they heard this: "When we're at work, we're bossed around by them. When we're singing fucking karaoke, do we really have to be judged by them too? This is complete bullshit—we'll judge it ourselves." So a couple of workers volunteered to come up to the podium to keep score, while people carried the television, the sound mixer, and the LCD monitor from the back. I was outside at the time, watching Bai Lan walk away and feeling pretty upset. But then Six Fingers came over, tugged at my sleeve, and dragged me upstairs to sing.

Ten years ago, the streets of Daicheng were full of people singing karaoke. They didn't just sing at home, they did it at restaurants, teahouses, and bathhouses, absolutely everywhere. You didn't get your own private singing room back then, it was too expensive. Often it would be in a big hall, and you'd pay two yuan for a song, taking turns howling in front of a television set. Later, I became a karaoke addict too. Who couldn't learn to howl?

I was dragged up onto the stage and sang "Kiss Goodbye" and "When the Wind Blows Again." Both were met with thundering applause from the workers below, and a couple of randy supervisors pulled aunties into the crowd to ballroom-dance. When I'd finished my two songs, the judges' scoreboard lit up with 9.99! The union official was at the side, clenching his teeth. I raised my right hand above my head, waved at the audience, patted my chest, and gave a farewell bow. This was the interlude between the worker-poet Lu Xiaolu leaving the stage of his day shift and moving over to the saccharin workshop to work the three shifts. When the contest was over, I was awarded second place. I couldn't understand it—how could a score like 9.99 be second best? Six Fingers told me there had been a young auntie up singing before me who'd lifted her skirt a little and held her head high while sticking out her chest and butt. The judging supervisors gawked idiotically and awarded her the full ten points, shunting me down into second place. Second place would have to do; I didn't have the chest or ass for anything better. *Fair enough*, I thought to myself as I went to collect my prize. First prize was an electric rice cooker, and second prize was a thermos. I took my prize and walked off. It was nearly dark outside. A group of middle-shift supervisors rushed into the hall as I was leaving and said to the union officer, "You can't stop it yet—we haven't had our chance to sing!" The union officer almost passed out. I heard that they kept going into the wee hours, crop after crop of workers turning up to sing. It was only when the electricity in that part of the factory was shut off that the whole thing ended. I didn't see any of this, though. I'd already gone back home.

I knew I'd said something to offend Bai Lan after the chaotic meeting, and I wanted to take her out for a meal to make it up to her. It was my birthday, but she didn't know that. I phoned the infirmary, but she told me she was busy that evening and couldn't make it. I sat on my own and ate a bowl of noodles, a portion of spareribs, and two poached eggs. After eating I had nowhere to go, so I cycled to New Knowledge New Village and wandered around there. It was a fall evening, and dried leaves were falling on my head. There had been a big drop in temperature since daytime and, wearing only a thin jacket, I was really feeling the cold. I locked up my bike and sat on the steps in front of Bai Lan's building to smoke.

I considered the fact that I was twenty now and had achieved absolutely nothing. It wouldn't be long until I started the three shifts, producing saccharin. It wasn't the kind of life I'd wanted, but I couldn't say what kind of life I did want. All I could say for certain was that I'd end up where I ended up. What choice did I have? All I could do was take each day as it came. A little while later, Bai Lan appeared on her bike with a guy next to her. I didn't call out; I just hid my cigarette so the glowing tip didn't give me away. The two chatted for a while, then said their farewells, and he left. She locked up her bike and walked over, noticing there was someone sitting there. She took a closer look and gave a start when she saw it was me.

"What are you doing here?" she asked.

"Waiting for you," I said.

She considered this a moment, then said, "Okay, come on up and we'll talk."

I followed her up the staircase in silence. I bumped my knee on a broken box when I was turning the corner. It hurt like hell, but I kept quiet about it and limped up the stairs. We walked into the main room and she pulled the cord for the light, shut the door, and said, "That was a friend from my review class."

"What review class?"

"My graduate studies class," she said. "Please don't mention it in the factory."

She showed me her graduate studies exam materials, a thick stack of notes that looked like another language to me. I asked her when she was going to take her exam. In a month, she said. Once she'd been accepted, she'd get her personal file transferred and go start her new life as a graduate student.

"Where will you go?"

"Shanghai or Beijing."

As her boyfriend, I should have asked why she'd never mentioned any of this to me before. But I forgot. My brain always felt foggy at times like this, like Zhuangzi's dream about being a butterfly—he woke up wondering if he weren't in fact a butterfly dreaming he was Zhuangzi. When I thought back on this whole conversation later, I felt ashamed of my flimsy grasp on reality. Or, in my mother's words: *You wouldn't even dodge a truck driving toward you.* I didn't say anything to Bai Lan, I just pulled open the door to leave. She leaned against the door, stopping me from going. She tilted her head and asked, "Do you still want to be my boyfriend?"

"Sure, why not?" I said. "But now I just want to go home and sleep."

I went again to open that door. This time she didn't stop me. I felt my knee throbbing as I walked down the stairs. She must have been expecting me to leave like last time, leaping down the flights, but instead I walked down without making a sound.

If you rewound time back to that fall, you'd find me in the workshop playing with my utility knife. It had a red plastic handle and a ten-centimeter blade. This knife had been fairly blunt when I got it, but I'd used the grinding wheel in the bench worker team and sharpened it so much that it could have killed someone. I'd wanted to bore two blood groves into it, but the supervisors told me it would lead to an accident and refused to help me do it. That knife came with me to many different cities, traveling in my pocket; no one viewed it as a banned weapon. When it was humid, the knife would rust over, but all you needed to do was dip it in water and rub it against a brick, and it would go back to its former sharp shininess.

I was playing with my knife that day, practicing my knife throwing. I could whirl it in a circle and make it fly off. I could tuck it inside my sleeve and get it to fly out from just above my waist and hit a bull's-eye on anything within fifteen feet. When I finished practicing with my right hand, I'd practice with my left. When I'd trained standing up, I would work lying down. I also did the Rhino Full Moon, the Phoenix Spreads Her Wings, the Young Ghost Knocks at the Door, the Eagle Captures the Chicken, and other such moves. I really wanted to find a living person to practice on. I wouldn't stab them. It would be like the circus: someone would have an apple on top of his head and I'd throw the knife, splitting the apple right down the center. If I damaged even half a strand of hair on his head, I'd be willing to pay with my life. But when people saw my sharpened knife, they'd start to tremble and outright refuse to let me have a try. I was beginning to think that the whole thing was futile and was putting the knife away when I was careless and nicked myself on the webbing between my thumb and forefinger. It didn't hurt right away, but a couple of seconds later the blood welled up, and soon my whole left hand was red and throbbing with pain.

I looked at my hand in disbelief. Even though I could throw my knife like a circus performer, I'd managed to cut my own hand. I threw down the knife and grabbed my left wrist, holding it high, and went like that to the infirmary to find Bai Lan. The blood was dripping down my arm as I was walking, running into my armpit. Everyone I passed assumed that my arm was raised in victory. It was only when they got near that they saw I had a serious injury. It was pretty embarrassing to have this kind of accident, but what did I care—I was about to start producing saccharin anyway.

The big fat lady stood behind Bai Lan as she bandaged me up, which was pretty annoying. I watched as Bai Lan wound the gauze around my hand. I asked if I'd cut through a tendon. She told me I hadn't, then took a towel and wiped the blood from my arm.

"You've lost a lot of blood," the big fat lady said. "Such a waste when you could have donated it."

Bai Lan turned to stare at her.

"People at the chemical factory aren't allowed to donate blood," I explained. "Our blood is toxic."

"Were you trying to kill yourself?" Bai Lan asked.

"No, I wasn't," I said, "I was careless."

"Trying to be like an outlaw?" she asked me.

No, I wasn't, I said. It wasn't either of these things. I didn't know how to answer her.

According to Borges, memory always clings to a certain point in time. My memory clings to the point when I was a twenty-year-old outlaw. The more I return to this point, the less real it feels. The age of outlaws was over. No one even wanted my blood donation; they thought my blood was too dirty. I lived in an age when there was no need for outlaws—I would neither kill nor be killed. I'd just be sent to the saccharin workshop, where a mistake would mean money docked from my wages. That's just the way it was. In this age, the only way I could kill myself would be deliberately or through carelessness, but I refused to kill myself over saccharin or wages, or over love. But I'd be prepared to go and die for no reason whatsoever. That was just the way it was.

I sat in the examination chair in the infirmary. Bai Lan moved a chair over and sat opposite me, and the big fat lady stood between us, looking at me for a bit and then at Bai Lan. I couldn't work out what the fuck she was trying to do, and it suddenly started to seem pretty funny. I smiled at Bai Lan. She looked at me calmly. All of a sudden, I didn't find the big fat lady quite so annoying. I was happy for her to stay where she was. My undecided lover stood silently on the other side of the river, looking at me from across the great divide.

There was an earthquake that fall, which caused a tsunami in the East China Sea. It was nine in the evening or soon after, and I was at home lying out across my bed when I felt the bed frame start to shake, and my mother's vase toppled from the chest of drawers and crashed to the ground. I jumped up from my bed, extricated my mother from her knitting, and ran outside. As we got out to the street, we saw my father running from the building too. He'd been playing mah-jongg at a neighbor's.

The street was overflowing with people, all the houses were lit up, and it was drizzling. It was another mass exodus from Pesticide New Village. But this time it was night and late fall, and no one was running around naked. The people around us started to calm down. They were looking at the houses, making sure that nothing had tilted or toppled. After checking out everything, they declared that there had been no damage and figured it must have been a very small quake. Other people phoned the pesticide factory, asking the on-duty workers if any pipes were leaking. The on-duty workers hadn't even been aware of the quake—the workshop equipment always shook like 7.0 on the Richter scale. Out on the street, I realized I was wearing only shorts and an undershirt. I was freezing, so I went back into the house to put on something more suitable. I was on my way out again wearing warmer clothes as my father came in with a couple of neighbors, and they all started playing mah-jongg. Our apartment was on the first floor, and they figured that if there were another earthquake it would be relatively easy to run back out. Playing mah-jongg was their way of waiting for a second quake.

I changed my clothes, put on my shoes, and took a couple of bank notes from the drawer and stuffed them into my pocket. My ma asked where I was going. To get something from a friend's house, I said. I told her if there was another earthquake, she should take a couple of buns and hide under the mah-jongg table and wait for me to come back and save her. After giving her these instructions, I deserted my ma, got on my bike, and headed toward New Knowledge New Village. The roads were all packed with people, their umbrellas open, raincoats on, washing basins on their heads. The rain was getting heavier. What had been light moisture floating in the air had become ice-cold needles stabbing at my face. A car had crashed into a tree trunk at the entrance to the

Culture Palace. The city was definitely more chaotic than normal, but there had been no power cut on the roads—people were still driving around, and the dim streetlights were reflecting off the road and looked like glowing pools of light. I passed through Daicheng College. The door guard seemed to have vanished. There were tons of students standing on the road, eating and chatting. Someone had climbed up the metal railings and was howling hoarsely. I skirted around the dense crowd and stopped my bike in a narrow little doorway. The door was unlatched, so I kicked it open and went through, seeing New Knowledge New Village up ahead.

The streets of New Knowledge New Village were also very crowded. The intellectuals may not have sung karaoke, but they were as scared of dying as anyone else; cultural accomplishment didn't solve everything. But their earthquake avoidance strategy was pretty ridiculous. There were apartment blocks everywhere, and these people had gathered in between them all. There were so many people packed together that if just one flower pot fell, it would have killed a few.

I scanned the crowd for Bai Lan. I did a circuit of the place before eventually spotting her inside her apartment leaning against the windowsill, watching the commotion with a cigarette between her lips, looking even more nonchalant than I did. Bai Lan beckoned me up. I threw down my bike and ran up the steps two at a time. I went in through the door and looked around. What a strange sight it was. The poor creature was wearing a white silk nightgown, very low-cut. She was sitting at the desk, her feet bare and one of those coffee-colored More cigarettes in her mouth. The most bizarre part of this ensemble was the red-and-green plastic hair curlers she had on her head. I racked my brains for a long time, wondering why I recognized this look, and then it came to me: it was how the concubines of Kuomintang officers dressed in movies.

"There's been an earthquake," I said. "Didn't you know?"

She ignored me, and with her cigarette clamped between two of her fingers, she gestured to the space beyond the window ledge, like a great man pointing at his territory. In a loud voice, she recited, "The Zhongshan storm changes, the color of the sky as a million strong, soldiers cross the river, this city at its greatest a tiger, crouching a dragon, coiled passion, and determination has built . . ."

I didn't know what the hell it was. It sounded like lines from a poem, but I couldn't make any sense of it. She turned to me, and I could smell alcohol on her breath.

"Well, how was that?" she asked.

"How was what?"

"How was that poem?"

"It was very lively. It sounded familiar, but I've forgotten who wrote it."

"Some fucking poet you are. How can you not know it? My father wrote it." She exhaled a mouthful of smoke into my face. "Today's earthquake made me think of my father."

I waved my hand in front of her eyes to test her reaction. She seemed alright, slightly drunk rather than wasted. I picked her up from the waist and carried her on my shoulders. I wasn't trying to take advantage of her—that window ledge was dangerous. A small tremor could have flipped her down off the building. I dropped her onto the bed as her chest heaved violently. I told her there could still be aftershocks, and if this dilapidated building crumbled, we'd both die inside. So were we going to run or not? She looked at me and gave a charming smile. She undid the plastic hair curlers one by one, her gorgeous curly locks tumbling down her face. She took off the silk nightgown; it slid down from the bed onto the concrete floor. She stood up and gave it a kick. Then she started to kiss me.

She told me she'd been curling her hair when she'd heard the commotion. She paid no notice at first, but then the neighbors started running outside, screaming loudly about the earthquake. She wanted to go out too, but she was wearing her nightgown and felt it was too racy. She took a half-full bottle of red wine from the bookcase and tipped some into a glass. After drinking half the glass, her body started to feel hot and her head floated. She'd never been such a lightweight before. She got carried away with the sensation, feeling as if she were floating along a river. She started crying but wasn't sure why. As she cried, I'd been cycling like crazy through Daicheng's streets and lanes, just like an outlaw. It was soon after that when she saw me outside her house and beckoned me up.

She told me that in 1976, her mother had taken her older sister to Tangshan to visit relatives. Her mother had been a doctor too. When the earthquake struck, her mother and sister had both been buried in the rubble. I'd never heard her talk about this before. She asked if I thought her hair looked nice with curls. I told her it looked very pretty. She said, "My ma's hair was naturally curly, mine isn't."

She said her pa had been a language and literature teacher. After the earthquake, he stopped sleeping, stopped speaking. By fall, his hair had turned completely white. She was taken in by a relative and saw him only occasionally after that. She always thought he looked like an unruly tree. "He suffered like this for ten years, but then he couldn't take it any longer and passed away."

She told me she wasn't scared of earthquakes. She wasn't scared of dying randomly. She said she was more of an outlaw than I was, only other people didn't know it. Then she hugged me as a great gust of wind blew in through the window, onto my back and her legs. I felt a shiver run through her body, like death passing by. She let out a soft moan as I entered her, arching her back so her chest rose up to meet me, like a dolphin gliding gracefully up through the water. She gripped me firmly around the waist with her legs, but I didn't feel like a trapped mouse this time—more like a boat floating down the river, her legs the river's banks.

After a while she said, "Let's change positions." So I lay flat back on the bed, and she climbed on top of me. This time her body was upright and her eyes shut tight. She stretched a hand out, her fingers taut like branches. I could see some mold growing on the ceiling just above her head, and this backdrop imprinted itself deeply in my brain.

"Does this feel good?" she asked, her eyes still closed as I thrust up into her.

"No," I said matter-of-factly, "it doesn't."

Her eyes sprung open and she said, "How would you like to do it, then?"

That wasn't what I meant, I said. It was just that if the ceiling crashed through when we were in this position, her head would be cracked open and I'd see her die before my eyes. That would be horrible, and if by some freak chance I didn't die with her, I'd be so emotionally scarred from the experience that I'd be impotent for the rest of my life. I'd rather go back to the position we were in before, so that if the ceiling crashed down it would fall onto my back and I might even save her life.

She laughed and continued to move up and down on my body. She said that my way wasn't any good either; if my eyeballs got smashed out, they'd land in her mouth. She dismounted me and lay face down on the bed, grabbing a pillow from the side of the bed and wedging it under her belly.

"This way is good," she said. "If your brain gets bashed out, I won't have to see it."

So I entered her again, and it felt pretty special that time—her body was no longer wrapped around me so I was no longer the boat in the river, but a motorbike speeding crazily through a heavy mist.

"Damn, be a bit gentler," she yelled, then carried on moaning.

She was very tight down there, and when her body was slightly bent, she was even tighter. She told me I was going too fast, to slow down. She made me lie down and straddled me again, then pulled me up and held my head to her chest. She said this way was good. If the ceiling came down, our brains would be bashed in together.

We went back to our original position after that. I held her legs up in the air. We didn't mention the bashing of brains again because we were feeling a similar sensation, only with a different part of our anatomy bashing together. Just as I was about to come, she gave a forceful yell. I felt the bed frame shake violently, the windows started to rattle, and we heard a commotion outside and people yelling: "Another earthquake! Quick, run!" I launched myself over Bai Lan, covering her body while holding onto the sides of the bed. I was one outlaw and she another, both of us climaxing just as the second earthquake hit. After I'd finished coming, after that cold cruel shudder of death had passed by our bodies, I lay there huffing and puffing like a rusty motor, feeling her still and solid underneath me. I could see the shadow of the room's ceiling lamp swaying slightly, while outside all hell was breaking loose, everyone shrieking and crying. Then the bed frame stopped shaking. With her eyes still closed, she let out a sigh. "Has the earthquake stopped?" she asked.

"There wasn't an earthquake after all," I joked, "just us fucking so hard that the earth shook."

She tittered. "I've learned one thing," she said.

"What's that?"

"It takes the same amount of time for an earthquake to hit as it does for a man to come."

Later we sat on the bed with our backs against the wall and smoked. She had a piece of cloth pinned with thumbtacks to the wall alongside the bed. She smoked her More while I smoked my Hongtashan, the ashtray resting on my stomach.

"You weren't too bad—have you done that before?" she asked.

I told her I hadn't. I'd just seen a lot of porn. She asked if I'd jerked off when watching the porn. I told her I hadn't. I'd watched them with a group of people, so not very conducive to jerking off. I'd go back home, close my eyes, revisit the images from the movies, then jerk off. I'd committed them so deeply to memory that I knew every move those porn stars made.

She admitted with noticeable embarrassment that she'd reached her grand old age without ever having seen a porn movie. *Fuck me*, I thought to myself. That meant all those up-and-down, backward-and-forward positions had been learned from live action. But I didn't really care. Having sex with a girl then forcing her to recount her sexual past really wasn't my style. I told her that most of the porn I'd seen was from the West, and the girls had such deep booming voices, as if they had drums in their chests. Those thick-hipped, large-breasted women weren't really my thing. I saw a Japanese porno once; the girl in it was a nurse with a shapely figure. I told Bai Lan that she and this porno nurse had moaned in a similar way. Like a she-cat mewing in her sleep. I had a real thing about doctors and nurses. Bai Lan slapped me when I said this and it felt good, like we were real lovers; although sitting side by side against the wall like this, smoking our cigarettes, we probably looked more like prison mates.

"We put ourselves in quite a risky situation just now. The ceiling could actually have crashed down and killed us," Bai Lan said.

"If we'd have died, we'd have died," I said. "At least I wouldn't have had to go to work tomorrow."

"I thought you would have run," she said.

"That would have been horrific. Imagine me just on the brink of climax and having run outside naked, jizzing as I went. That would have been too awful for words. I'd rather have died in bed."

"Dying like that wouldn't have been very good either. We'd have been locked together—no one would be able to pull us apart."

"They would have to saw off my dick, separate us that way. My dick would be left inside your body. It would be like leaving you a little memento."

"What if I didn't die? I'd have had to get a small saw and cut your dick myself. I'd find that too gruesome. It's not a good way."

"Sawing off my dick shouldn't be a problem for you—you're a doctor, aren't you? Haven't you cut one of them before?"

"It would be easy if I were a doctor of traditional Chinese medicine. I'd just cut it off and preserve it in alcohol. Every year I'd take it out at the Tomb Sweeping Festival and drink a mouthful for virility."

"You don't need freaking virility," I said. "Save it for a guy to drink, then I can still have sex with you through him."

This thought clearly turned her on, because she moved the ashtray off my stomach and replaced it with her naked body. She gave me a wicked smile and said, "Again."

We did it twice that day, the wind outside becoming more and more blustery as the rain battered the awning outside the window with a rhythmic putt-putting. Apart from that, it was quiet outside. Luckily, we weren't hit by a third earthquake. My nerves couldn't have taken it—I'd probably have fled from the building butt-naked. Lying there, I suddenly had the feeling you get when you hear the first warbler in spring. I felt a surge of faith in life and an affirmation that I did not want to be killed in an earthquake.

I told her I was going to give her the nickname Suction Pump. "Ah, so you finally got around to giving this aging mama a nickname," she said before hitting me.

I jumped out of bed and went over to the window to look out. There wasn't a soul out there; no wonder it had become so quiet. It was completely dark, and the rain falling through the darkness looked like ink. I wasn't sure whether the people who'd been outside the building had run away or gone back inside to sleep. Later I saw the clock. It was three in the morning. The building opposite was lit up, everyone still awake like on Spring Festival eve.

"Don't you want to go home and see your family?" Bai Lan asked. "Is your ma at home?"

I told her not to worry. If the dilapidated houses in New Knowledge New Village were still standing, the dilapidated houses in Pesticide New Village would still be standing too. Besides, I said, my ma was smart. As soon as she felt a slight breeze or saw the grass quivering, she'd be fleeing for her life. That was the drill at Pesticide New Village.

"Won't your ma be worried about you?" Bai Lan asked.

I realized she was right. It would be so much easier if we had a home phone, I told her. There was no way anyone would answer the public grocery store phone at this time. I said I'd wait for the rain to die down a bit, then go back home. By the time I'd said this, she'd put her clothes on. I reluctantly put mine back on too.

"It's so quiet, it's like nothing happened," she said.

"Well, I guess nothing did happen, did it?" I said, then wondered if she'd tricked me into saying it. I turned to look at her. She looked back at me with an expression that was hard to read. I walked around the room sheepishly, thumbing through her books and that thick pile of study material, all those profound subjects written about in a language I didn't understand.

"You won't sober up and regret what happened?" I asked.

"What's to regret?" she said.

"I'd like to do that with you again sometime," I said self-consciously.

She looked at me and gave a sudden laugh. "Do you want some instant noodles? I'm starving."

While we were eating our instant noodles, I told Bai Lan about someone from my past, my cousin's girlfriend. Bai Lan didn't understand why I'd brought her up. I wasn't really sure myself, but later I explained that talking about porn had made me think of her.

It had been with my cousin and his gang that I'd first seen porn. It was all on VHS back then; a couple of us kids locked ourselves away in a room to watch in secret. I was only in junior three at the time, but I'd already hit puberty. I'd gone out looking for my cousin and bumped into him and a couple of his friends, and they let me watch it with them. One day his girlfriend walked in on us while we had it on. She slapped my cousin, saying he was leading me astray. My cousin laughed at this and told her to take me away then, which she did. I wasn't too pleased about this, but I couldn't say anything. I just had to play dumb so she'd be nice to me. I saw her cleavage—it was a deep crack, and it gave me bad thoughts. She didn't have a clue, she just thought of me as an innocent child. Later she patted me on the head and said, "Xiaolu, you mustn't be like your cousin when you're older. You must make a promising future for yourself."

I often thought of her. Other people called her Ah Juan. I did at first, but she didn't like it and asked me to call her "sister." She ran her own clothing boutique. She hadn't had much schooling, but I really loved her all the same. She was very good to my cousin, gave him pocket money and even had an abortion for him. When my cousin's gang and another neighborhood gang got into a fight, she saved my cousin by grabbing a piece of pipe and smashing his opponent over the head. She had her boutique destroyed in retaliation for this, but she said nothing. My cousin hit her after this—in fact, he beat her pretty badly. That was the last straw, and she ran off to Nanjing to start a knitwear business. I never saw her again.

I loved her because she radiated love. I may have had a slightly deviant understanding of love, but that was not the point. This sister gave me pocket money and said that when I was older she'd introduce me to her little sister, who could be my girlfriend. I didn't hang out with my cousin much after his girlfriend went to Nanjing. I thought he was a total bastard. Sometime after, he was stabbed six times in the head; and that time, nobody helped him out.

I told Bai Lan that I found the concept of a "promising future" pretty hollow. I didn't know what "promise" meant—all I knew was that I didn't have any, and that people without promise couldn't be loved. Even so, in my first twenty years on this earth, I'd had people who'd loved me for a long time, and some who'd loved me for a short time, and I would never forget any of them.

After I told her this story, I went home. She'd really wanted me to stay the night but I suddenly started to feel defeated, as if I'd ejaculated all the fluid from my brain as well as from everywhere else, leaving everything empty. In retrospect, I know that what I was feeling was called nihilism, but at the time I didn't know how to describe it. I couldn't understand why all of a sudden I felt so defeated. If I'd known this was nihilism, I probably wouldn't have felt so sad. Nihilism tends to just appear, then disappear just as quickly.

My lower back was aching as I walked down the stairs of her building. This couldn't be kidney failure, could it? If I was twenty and already suffering from kidney failure, I'd be impotent by the time I was forty. Distracted, I tripped on something on the stairs and fell all the way to the bottom. That thing I'd tripped on cried out. I took out my lighter and sparked it, and fuck me, I was among twenty or so people who were all crouched in the corridor, napping. It was no wonder—outside it was still raining, and there was no earthquake shelter. I apologized over and over again, and in so doing woke up the rest of them. They all stared at me. An old professorial man looked at me, tut-tutted and said, "So, it was you up half the night singing karaoke?" I may have been a complete good-for-nothing, but I still blushed when I heard that. These intellectuals were something else; even their insults had artistic flair.

❖

The saccharin factory wasn't affected by the earthquake. The pump room by the river was the only thing that crumbled, and most of the time there was no one inside there. It did crush a lot of rats, however, and the ones that survived ran out to cruise the streets. These rats were all very vicious, and smart too. When they needed to cross a road, one of them would scuttle over to the other side and crouch by the roadside squeaking, and a huge procession of rats of all shapes and sizes would waltz over and join him. We didn't dare antagonize this rat army—we were too scared about what terrible revenge they might plot to take on us.

Bai Lan and I had sex another couple of times after that initial encounter, always at her house. The apartments in New Knowledge New Village were very badly soundproofed. How bad? Well, when squatting in her restroom, I could hear her next-door neighbors pissing in theirs. If it was a woman pissing, I could hear everything—the wall might as well have been a drape. Bai Lan told me that the building was constructed in the '70s and made entirely of precast panels. It might not have been great in terms of privacy, but houses like this were very stable and shockproof, which she'd been glad about when she moved in. At that time, Chinese people were terrified of earthquakes. This fear had been shaken into them, literally.

Unless you were drunk, having sex in a building like this would bring out another kind of fear in you: fear that the next-door neighbors would be propped up against the wall, listening in on your "karaoke." I knew a few different eaves-dropping techniques. The most basic was to put a glass against the wall and put your ear to the opening. Tricks like this were pretty much unnecessary in New Knowledge New Village, though—it was noise-canceling methods you needed. If you didn't want to listen to your next-door neighbors, the most effective trick was to cover your ears.

I told Bai Lan about the snide comment the old man in her building had made to me that morning. She said, "He can say what he wants, who cares?" But next time we were having sex, she started to feel self-conscious and held herself back from moaning. "Is it a letdown when I'm like this?" she asked. I told her it was fine—I liked hearing her holding back, holding back until she could hold back no more.

"Why can we never hear your next-door neighbors fucking?" I asked her after we'd had sex once. "Are they all holding back as well?"

Bai Lan told me it was an old couple living next door. The man had been labeled a rightist and had been forced to hold back his whole life. I asked about the old woman: she couldn't have been a rightist too, could she?

"You're really annoying," Bai Lan said. "Why are you so interested in all of this?"

I told her it was new to me. In Pesticide New Village, it was just rebel factions.

Whenever we had sex after that, we'd keep our voices down, and we always used a condom. "Do you steal these from the infirmary?" I asked. She didn't need to steal them, she said, she could take a handful when she needed them. She kept the condoms in a rice bowl. Sometimes she'd take the lead and put it on me, other times she'd watch me put it on myself. One time she took it in her mouth and put it on me that way. She had pretty great technique—I'm sure not all doctors are this skilled. When we were done, she'd make me hold the bottom of the condom when I pulled out.

There were a few subtle changes after we started sleeping together. If we bumped into each other at the factory, the way we looked at each other was different. There weren't many couples in the factory, and after they'd started dating they usually liked to show off about it, wandering from the formaldehyde workshop to the saccharin workshop together, swaggering from the driver team to the boiler house, all ostentatious. The supervisors would stand at the window and watch them walking over and make a big fuss, saying, "Oh look, how impressive, it's the steamroller!" After that, they'd start finding faults with both members of the couple. I was never subjected to such treatment, essentially because she hadn't been willing to "steamroll" around the factory with me, and also because I didn't feel there was anything that great about whispering your sweet nothings among formaldehyde and saccharin. I didn't even eat lunch with her—she ate with the cadres and I with the workers. We just exchanged glances. We both had big eyes, which made these exchanges lovely.

Bai Lan had been suffering from a toothache when I bumped into her at the factory once, and I asked, "Is it still hurting?" Pu Nani walked out from behind me as I said this, and he turned around and sized me up. Bai Lan made a show of pain, pointing at her cheek and miming that she couldn't speak.

I went to the infirmary later that day when the big fat lady was out. "Can you please be more careful what you say? If people hear a question like 'Is it still hurting?' they're bound to get the wrong impression."

"There won't be a misunderstanding about that," I said nonchalantly. "It only hurts virgins!"

She whipped me across the face with something when I said that, and it really stung. I looked down and saw a rubber glove in her hand. "Is it still hurting?" she asked.

I got really angry then. "We have a really good friendship, then I make one simple joke and you whip me with the freaking glove you use for gynecological examinations!"

"It's a clean one," she said.

My grandmother used to say if a man is hit by a woman, he'll have a run of three years' bad luck unless he hits her back. But a girl like Bai Lan, who'd actually dared to bite a tiger, would hit me back again for sure. We'd just get caught in this cycle of slapping each other back and forth, on and on and on. If we had this much free time, we'd be better off just going to bed and fucking. If there was bad luck ahead, so be it.

Bai Lan and I kept our love a secret from everyone at the factory. Bai Lan didn't want people pointing and talking about her, and I'd already been dealt my fair share of crap because of my poetry and the bra incident. I thought back to when I'd just started at the factory, swaggering around with Old Bad-Ass, no one messing with me. Factory life had one rule: hidden corners were the safest. As long as you stayed out of the limelight, you could muddle along as you pleased for years on end. Unfortunately, I learned this rule too late. I was unlucky and got the three shifts in the end.

There was actually another reason Bai Lan and I kept our relationship hidden from the world: we knew that one day, it would come to an end.

"When we break up, which factory girl will you go for?" Bai Lan asked me once.

I thought about it and said, "Little Pouty Lips. She used to give me a hard time, but she's much mellower now."

"What's tough about that girl?" Bai Lan asked. "She's just a little girl."

"She's a year younger than you—how can you say she's a little girl?"

"Why don't you get Auntie Qin to fix you up then?"

"She's Xiao Li's girlfriend, and you can't steal your friend's girl."

"That's true. I'll introduce you to my younger cousin. She's still at technical middle school."

"I'm only interested if she looks like you."

"That makes it hard," Bai Lan said. "She'd be a movie star if she did."

When I look back to the way we used to joke around, I realize that we were actually hinting things to each other. Back then, I thought that splitting up was so sad that you couldn't talk about it directly. It was like April showers. You couldn't see the individual drops of rain with the naked eye, and from inside you could never tell if you needed an umbrella or not. I felt this sadness, but all we could do was give each other these hints and goof around to comfort ourselves.

Another time, she said, "Xiaolu, I find it very hard to picture the kind of wife you'll end up with. If she's doesn't have a sharp tongue, you'll bully the hell out of her."

"Well, I can't imagine what your husband will be like either," I said. "He'll definitely be very kind, very educated, the type to run away when he sees thugs."

She looked at me with a sassy glint in her eye and said, "I bet when you're thirty, you'll run away when you see thugs too."

I didn't believe her at the time. I thought I'd be a fighter my whole life. I really was immature. According to Bai Lan, I'd turn thirty and find that I was bald with a beer belly, teeth stained black from smoking, bags under my eyes, a sallow complexion, and abnormal liver function from being on the three shifts for so long. I'd ride my bike through the streets wearing my work uniform, and people would see at a glance that I was a poor wretch. The thugs would pick on me rather than Bai Lan's husband.

One time, there was a strange atmosphere between us when we had sex at her house. The graduate study review material was piled up on the desk, and after we finished fucking, she casually picked up a book, turned a couple of pages, mumbled a few of the words, then put it back again.

"Is studying like that in any way effective?" I asked her.

She told me she'd reviewed almost all the lessons already and just couldn't motivate herself to start looking over it all again. I didn't say anything, but I scooped up the book to take a look.

"How's your accounting going?" she asked.

"I haven't started it yet. We're studying advanced mathematics at the moment," I said listlessly.

"Studying advanced mathematics, that's brave!"

I told her that being a bench worker and an electrician had taught me the value of math while leading me to the conclusion that language was a pretty screwed-up subject. Math made people smarter and smarter, while language made them dumber and dumber. I didn't have much of a basis for math, so studying advanced math was fairly tiring, but the class was growing on me.

That was the time she opened the door of the north-facing room, the room that was always closed, that I'd never been in. I saw a row of shelves inside, a gramophone, and how screwed up was this: an actual double bed.

"Look how mean you are. You've had this huge bed here the whole time, and instead you've made me practice my parallel-bars skills on the single bed."

"This was my father's bed."

"I'm sorry, forget I said that. The last thing I want to do is disrespect your father."

She let me take a look at the books, a lot of them novels, many in classical Chinese, and a good number of anthologies too. They were all old books and gave off an even mustier smell than the room itself.

"All these were my father's books," she said.

"You're really lucky to have had access to so many books since you were young," I said, thinking back to my childhood. There had been two big books in the house: *Dong Cunrui* and *The Lady of the Camellias*. Both were incomplete—*Dong Cunrui* didn't have an ending, and *Lady of the Camellias* didn't have a beginning. This was pretty lucky, really. It would have been unfortunate if it were the other way around, and I'd missed out on reading about Dong Cunrui blowing himself up or Marguerite Gautier dying. I was eight when I started reading those books. By the time I was fifteen, I was still reading them. I lingered between revolutionary martyrs and French prostitutes for many years, not sure which one I was more like. Back then, if I'd had as many books as Bai Lan, I wouldn't have been so confused.

"Help yourself to a book you'd like to have," she said. "I'm happy to give you one, as long as you promise never to sell it."

She opened the gramophone and took a black Bakelite record from the closet. She told me it was Beethoven's "Kreutzer," played by David Oistrakh— an extremely precious rare edition.

"Don't go giving me any of this classical music," I said.

She said she wasn't giving away any of her records; she wanted to keep all of them, but she'd let me listen. Nothing wrong with listening to a bit of classical music, I figured, but I listened mainly to Hong Kong pop stars. She turned the handle on the gramophone and the speaker made a rustling sound and then the music started to play. I sat on the big bed and listened quietly to "Kreutzer" the whole way through.

I told her that I wanted to be someone who had love and goodness. Love was sleeping with her, and the goodness was beating someone up for her. For me, these two things were separate. But when she gave me her father's book, it was an act that was both loving and good, so I would remember it forever.

That winter, I found myself sitting on my own in the entrance to a middle school. The graduate-school entrance exams were being held inside. I was sitting on the edge of a flowerbed. I lit a smoke and stared down blankly at my fingers. It was cloudy, and a couple of snowflakes started to drift down, landing on me. The wind blew at my face until it was icy cold, and it felt like forever before I felt the snow on my face melt into water droplets.

The music store opposite the main road was playing Zhang Chu's "Sister." They played it over and over. I listened quietly to the song, and when the manager eventually put on another song, I threw down my cigarette butt and walked over to buy the cassette.

Later I saw Bai Lan walking over from the playground. Her hair had been blown askew by the wind. "Are you on night shift?" she asked.

"No, I took today off. Have you finished your exam?"

"All done," she said. "Shall we go back to my place?"

She hadn't wanted to have sex with me for some time preceding the exam, and she had banned me from her house. I was doing the three shifts at the saccharin factory, swapping so frequently that I felt completely discombobulated, didn't even know night from day—my sex drive had pretty much evaporated, so I couldn't really be bothered to seek her out anyway. We got back to her house. She boiled me a couple of eggs, sprinkling a little sugar on top, and got me to eat them. This was how to repair the body, apparently. Leading up to this exam, she'd been living off instant noodles because they were so easy. She commented that I seemed a bit lethargic, not all there.

I said, "Madam, I came straight to the school from my night shift, I haven't slept yet, of course I'm lethargic."

She seemed slightly disappointed.

"Do you want to have sex?" I asked.

"Meh," she said. "Sleep for a while first."

I did as I was told; I had those two hot eggs inside my stomach, and the drowsiness was kicking in. I fell back onto her bed and immediately started to snore.

It was dark when I woke, and I couldn't work out where I was. I'm always like this when I first wake up. Then I remembered I was at Bai Lan's house, lying on her bed. She was sitting under the lamplight, listening to the tape recorder. She had the volume on very low and was listening with her ear up against the machine.

"What are you listening to?" I asked.

"Your tape," she said. "The other songs aren't that great, it's only that 'Sister' song that's good."

"I only bought it for that song."

"What's that smell on your clothes?" she asked. "It's like a mixture of coffee and burnt charcoal."

"You wouldn't know it," I said. "It's called methyl. It's a raw material we have in our workshop. I am in charge of methyl. The smell sticks to your hair and clothes, and you can't get rid of it."

"It's not such a bad smell," she said.

"That's all I really have to feel lucky about. I might be a thug, but at least I'm not a thug who stinks from head to toe."

I asked her what she planned to do next. She said she'd be handing in her notice after Chinese New Year, then waiting to hear about her university acceptance. Once she'd been accepted, she'd start her life as a graduate student. That was, if things went according to plan.

"What if you don't get accepted?" I asked.

"I wouldn't stay here anyway. The new saccharin workshop will be ready by the end of the Spring Festival holidays, and I've heard they'll be transferring a lot more people over there."

I nodded, saying, "You really don't need that kind of hardship."

"I'm going to give my notice soon, get my file transferred to the district office so the factory won't be able to block it."

I asked her what blocking files meant. She said it meant dragging their heels and not releasing her file. If the new term started and her file still hadn't arrived at the university, they would cancel her admission automatically. This was quite common—work units did things like this on purpose.

"No way," I said. "If they dared block your file, I'd knock their blocks off."
She laughed and shook her head, saying, "Typical."

I yawned and said, "I'm not joking."

I imagined if the factory did block her file. I'd run up to the big department building with a couple of detonators. I didn't actually know which department I'd need to run to, but my detonators would be talking detonators and they'd tell me where to go. She would go off to her graduate studies, and I'd be sent to jail. My behavior was completely sociopathic. I felt animosity toward everything—it was actually probably closer to pathological. As Bai Lan put it: "Lu Xiaolu, you should fantasize less about this kind of thing. Do you even know where to buy a detonator?"

She told me she planned to head north after she quit, take the long-distance train from Shanghai to Beijing, then on to Tangshan. She'd always wanted to visit Tangshan. After that she'd head west to Dunhuang, then Tibet via Golmud. She wanted to spend some time in Tibet, see some friends and then come back to Shanghai via Chengdu, and finally back to Daicheng. She had a map of China on which she'd drawn her square-shaped route.

"By the time I get back to Daicheng, it should be May," she said.

I was propped up in her bed, completely silent, just watching her pointing and squiggling on the map.

"Xiaolu, why don't you come to Tibet with me?" she asked.

I shook my head. "What's so good about Tibet? Anyway, I couldn't ask for that much time off, and I have night college to go to."

She didn't feel she had much to say to me after that. I was feeling more and more like a three-shifts worker. As soon as I woke up, I went to work; as soon as I got home from work, I'd want to sleep, and that sleep was never enough. She cupped her cheeks with her palms and looked at me. I gave a succession of yawns. I wasn't being a smartass. I honestly didn't know what Tibet had going for it. Sometime later, I learned that Tibet was a mecca for young creative types: once in your lifetime, you had to visit. Now I yearn for this mystical place and feel consumed with regret. There are too many things that you don't get to do in your lifetime, and while it's not worth crying over, not going with her to Tibet when I was twenty is something I'll always regret.

"Xiaolu, with all your life experiences so far, what's the thing that scares you most?"

I told her I was most scared of three shifts: your days and nights inverted, working until the point of delirium, having a resurgence of your teenage acne, your skin making you look like someone who'd just crept out of a coffin.

"So the thought of our breaking up doesn't scare you?"

I was puzzled by her question. Breaking up was very sad, but what was scary about it? I thought carefully before answering. "Initially, I'll probably be scared; and after a while, I'll be alright. But three shifts leaves you feeling scared constantly."

She stroked my head and said, "Poor little Lu Xiaolu."

Then she told me that during the mayhem at the saccharin factory meeting, she'd realized she loved me a lot, but that my actions showed I was always looking for trouble. If I stayed on the three shifts for the rest of my life, this aggression was only going to get worse. I said I didn't care, and besides, I wasn't really aggressive—I was actually pretty gentle most of the time.

"As long as you don't give up on yourself," she said.

"I won't."

That winter seemed incredibly long. The sky was always overcast, and I couldn't even imagine what a sunny day might look like. I spent a portion of my time asleep and the rest of it producing saccharin in the workshop. The workshop was very badly lit, and even on a sunny day we were still confined in gray and gloomy conditions. I felt like a person living in the Arctic. I'd heard that the night lights could give people depression, destroy their sex drive, and cause their fertility rates to plummet. These were all the symptoms I was experiencing now. When I got to Bai Lan's place, her bed looked so inviting that I dropped down onto it and fell fast asleep.

Each year before Spring Festival, the factory issued us a ton of New Year's goods. The workers were all very happy, transporting case after case of instant noodles and oranges back home. The best was when they gave us fish, fish more than six-and-a-half feet long. They used a truck to transport them all to the factory, then distributed them to the various teams. There were big fish and small fish. Everyone drew lots, then lined up to choose their fish. I was still on the bench worker team during Spring Festival 1993 and was lucky enough to have drawn the second pick. Good Balls got first pick, and the dickhead decided to do the whole revolutionary martyr Lei Feng thing and choose the very smallest fish. When it was my turn, the bench worker supervisors all stood around staring at me. Feeling timid, I chose a small fish too, a mere three feet long. With no shame at all, Old Bad-Ass, who was next in line, took a huge fish. By Spring Festival 1994, I really wanted to even the score, but I was on night shift the day they gave out the fish. I got to the workshop to take a look at 10:00 p.m., and there was only a tiny fish—not even three feet long—hanging out in the lounge. They told me this was my fish, that they'd drawn lots and I'd come in last. I asked them who'd drawn the fucking lot on my behalf. They told me the others had all picked theirs, and the last one left had been mine. Who knows how many turns they'd all taken for me to come out last.

They gave out rabbits too that year, live ones. Our factory was expanding and acquiring land. It had eaten up a huge area of a nearby village, which happened to be a rabbit farm where they bred thousands of them. The farmers didn't have space for all those rabbits, so they sold them all to the factory. There were more than a thousand rabbits at that rabbit farm with nobody looking after them, dying batch by batch. Dead rabbits were difficult to deal with. You couldn't eat them and nor could you throw them in the trash, as people would think they had died from the plague. The factory couldn't think of a better way, so they gave out the rabbits for the workers to take home, to kill or keep as they saw fit. I cycled home with a live rabbit dangling from my bike basket. I'd tied him with twine, but he wasn't very comfortable, judging from his constant kicking. I'd never eaten rabbit before and wasn't sure I'd like it, but skinning it wouldn't even provide enough fur to make a ruff. I cycled to Bai Lan's house, thinking she must have a rabbit too. If the two rabbits could be together, then maybe they'd find life a little bit easier. But when I got to New Knowledge New Village, I turned the bike too sharply and the rabbit's head was thrown into the wheel. There was a crunch as his neck twisted and broke, and finally he was no longer kicking.

I felt pretty bummed out carrying this dead rabbit up the stairs. It was late at night when I walked into her place, and the first thing I saw was a table piled high with bones and a plate with a couple of pieces of leftover meat on it. She was going at her teeth with a toothpick, saying, "Oh no, you haven't come all the way here to give me this rabbit, have you? I just finished eating one."

"Bai Lan, you're so heartless. I can't believe you ate your rabbit. Who killed it for you?"

"I killed it myself."

I didn't believe that she could disembowel a little bunny.

"I've skinned more rabbits than you've seen rabbits," she said. Then she complimented me, saying, "Lu Xiaolu, you really know the ropes, wringing a rabbit's neck like that."

"I didn't wring its neck," I said. "It got twisted in my bike spokes and broke its neck."

She rolled up her sleeves and said, "Different strokes for different folks, I guess. You got the job done all the same. I'll make another spicy Sichuan-style rabbit stir-fry. I guarantee you'll eat every morsel—even the head."

While I was eating the rabbit, I couldn't help asking, "Bai Lan, would you say you were a warmhearted person or a cruel one?"

She sat beside me, watching me eat. "I'm both."

"I don't think that warmheartedness and cruelty can coexist in one person," I said.

"You're like that as well, aren't you? You write poetry, but you also fantasize about strapping a detonator to yourself. Sometimes you act all lofty, and other times you're violent. Before I met you, I didn't know those two traits could coexist in one person."

I finished the rabbit and wiped my mouth. She pointed to the head on the plate. I told her I was too full and couldn't manage the head. Besides, it looked a bit like a human head. Was it worth puking up rabbit legs to eat a rabbit head?

I'd experienced her warmheartedness firsthand, but her cruelty only indirectly, via that rabbit. I told her I didn't want to be exposed to her cruelty. I felt like one day, she might kill me. I was lying butt-naked under her quilt as I said this, wide awake, not in the slightest bit drowsy. Bai Lan rolled out a rug and covered her legs as she sat on the bed. She smoked a cigarette, saying, "I don't know what you're talking about. It would be pointless for you to want to die for me. Like you just said—is it worth puking up rabbit legs to eat a rabbit head?"

That was the last time we had sex. There were no tender words. I don't know why; I couldn't think of any of those sweet words she loved to hear. The sex wasn't great and was over very quickly. I blamed it on my choppy routine and lack of regular sleep. She seemed pretty sapped too. While we were fucking, she suddenly opened her eyes and stared at me. It gave me a jolt, and I lost control. The way I came felt more like a wet dream. She'd looked at me with the eyes of a killer, but maybe I was just seeing things. Who was I to talk? I basically felt a bit hopeless. She reassured me, saying that this happened to all men: wet dreams, ejaculation, premature ejaculation, impotence. All guys went through it.

A while back, I'd told her that if she ever left Daicheng, I'd be sure to take her to the train station to see her off. She liked this idea, thinking it would be like a scene from a movie. But when she was actually on that train heading north, I hadn't been there. That day I'd been in the workshop producing saccharin, and I'd put the sulfuric acid and water into the reactor in the wrong order. You needed to put the water in first, then the sulfuric acid. But I was distracted and got it wrong, causing the reactor to thunder like a cauldron of boiling water and the smell of sulfur to seep out. All the workers started shouting at once, running for the door. One female worker fell down the stairs as she was running and knocked out a couple of her front teeth. She threatened to have her husband come stab me. Soon after, her husband rushed over and seized my collar. He was a section chief from the formaldehyde workshop. He'd heard his wife was in trouble and was the first to appear on the scene. I allowed him to grab me and watched as he raised his fist, but he didn't actually hit me in the end. The reason? He told someone else, "That boy had murderer's eyes."

They sent me to the safety department, where I wrote a self-criticism and filed an accident report. It was well into the night by the time I finished these and was allowed to leave. I imagined Bai Lan carrying her travel bags and getting on the train alone, and I felt that this scene really did seem to belong to a movie. I couldn't even say if I'd ever seen a sadder movie than that scene in my head. And that was how I missed my chance to see Bai Lan off.

I saw her one more time in May. She came to the factory to do some paperwork and popped into the saccharin workshop to say hi. Her skin was a lot darker, and she was wearing a Tibetan cloak and looking very western. She'd cut her long hair and looked somewhat boyish, while I'd shaved my head and looked like an inmate.

She'd been accepted at a medical college in Shanghai and would start her studies in September. Between now and then, she'd be in Shanghai taking an English course. She touched my shaved head affectionately and asked, "Why did you do this?"

I shook my head and said nothing. Our meeting was brief. I had to pour continuous bags of sodium nitrate into the boiler, my head and face were covered in dust, and it was impossible to concentrate on a conversation with her. Both of us looked like we'd been on long trips. After that she left, and when I went to her place to look for her, there was no one there. I couldn't figure out where she'd gone. I never saw her again after that.

Sometimes when I left work, I'd pass by New Knowledge New Village and stand outside her building and look up. Her windows were all shut, and there were no clothes hanging out to dry on the balcony. She didn't live there anymore. I think this must be the best way to part, the least sad. It was like getting separated from a friend in the fog.

Around the end of June, I received a postcard at the factory. It had been sent from Tibet in April, and on it was written: *For my Xiaolu: I've traveled a thousand miles, but I can't forget you.* This postcard was stuck behind the glass window at the front desk for anyone to see, although nobody bothered to look at it. It was four in the morning, and I was just finishing work when I noticed it. I was feeling pretty dizzy. The postcard had a picture of Potala Palace on the front against a backdrop of blue skies and white clouds. I looked at the writing on the back, then at the Potala Palace on the front again. I turned it back and front, again and again. It was very dark—the only light was an incandescent lamp in the factory entrance, surrounded by swarming gnats. There was no one around on the road. At that moment, the whole world was sleeping soundly. The person I loved was sleeping soundly, having sweet dreams. I momentarily lost it, and my tears fell onto those pencil-written characters that had traveled for thousands of miles.

Sometimes I wonder if Bai Lan had it all planned out. Did she always know that she was going to take her graduate studies exams, have sex with me, give me that book of her father's, and finally hand in her notice and leave Daicheng? I felt like she might have orchestrated it; everything she did was so neat and methodical. Nothing like the way I went about life. But later, I thought it through seriously. I was a nobody who worked the three shifts. I was flattering myself to think that someone would write having sex with me into her master plan. Perhaps all those other things she'd done had been planned, and having sex with me had been the exception. Which meant there was nothing to be too nostalgic about.

She once said to me, "Lu Xiaolu, I really can't work out why I love you."

I found it pretty strange too, the fact that there was actually someone who loved me, who wanted to have sex with me. If word of our affair had gotten out in the factory, no one would have actually believed it. Not even my mother would have thought it possible.

"Do you know what a journey of discovery is?" I asked her. "Yours is to go to Tibet. But I have my journey of discovery too, you just don't know about it." I told her I wasn't sure how much of the road I walked in my life was fantasy, but I was pretty clear about how much was bullshit. That meant everything that wasn't bullshit, I saw as part of my journey of discovery. Thinking about it this way wasn't due to my immaturity. I was trying to tell myself that when this journey came to a close, it would be like waking up from a dream. At least that's what I thought.

I told her that when we'd been taking Good Balls to the hospital, as I carried him on my back into the emergency room, I'd felt as if my heart were about to explode. If I'd actually had a heart attack and died then and there, everyone would have thought I'd died for Good Balls. Fuck, if I'd lived only to nineteen and given up my life for a stupid bench worker team leader. People would have found that hilarious. The truth would have been that I died for my journey of discovery. I'd been like an actor in that heavy rain, and because of her, I'd played the role of an outlaw.

I told her that for a long time, I'd seen myself as someone who couldn't love anyone, so I just had to love myself. I was ashamed of this loving, but on my journey, I couldn't be held responsible for this shame because having nowhere else to go meant it was not my fault. But I didn't want to open my innocent eyes and see her neither on this side nor that side, but in the middle of the river. Most people are damaged by something they experience in childhood. I thought I was damaged from the start. But actually that was an illusion. I'd been soaked by time too, rinsed by it until I was wrinkled and disheveled. It was only when I turned thirty that I took it out of the water and hung it out to dry in my novel.

Never again would I be ashamed about this kind of love, I told myself. At thirty I thought back on it and felt like a bullet had been fired into my head. Unfortunately, she didn't get to see my brain being blasted apart.

In spring of 2000, I was at a hotel in the suburbs of Shanghai when I saw a girl in her early thirties. She wore her hair in a tidy bun and was wearing a Prada skirt and carrying a Chanel bag. We were in the elevator together, and she looked so familiar that I said, "Bai Lan, it's been so long." She looked at me from behind her shades, and after a long time she said, "You have the wrong person."

I laughed and said, "Yes, you're right. My memory's not great." After that, a foreign man walked over and addressed her very affectionately as "Lisa" before giving her a kiss on the cheek. This was a greeting kiss, a public kiss. The kind of kiss I'd never had the chance to express in my youth. Then she got into a Buick minivan with this foreign man.

I once said to Bai Lan that if I ever saw her again in the future, I'd call out her name without hesitating, because I was loving and good and I'd never pretend not to know her. From her midriver position, she'd see me there on the side. "You're a young worker, why do you make yourself feel so miserable?" she asked. Then she told me that in the future, I wouldn't find myself with nowhere to go and so I wouldn't run into her again. These were conversations I'd forgotten. Occasionally I recalled them and felt like there was sludge in my blood, or a clot—and if it blocked my brain, I would die.

I lay in a hotel bed in the middle of the night, answering phone call after phone call from all the hookers. Each time I'd give a cursory couple of sentences and hang up the phone, then wait for it to ring again. I just lay there, running over all the things she'd told me that year. The telephone's ring cut through the darkness again and again, until the wee hours. The last time I picked up the receiver it wasn't a hooker, but her voice. She said, "I checked out, and I'm rushing to get my flight to England."

"When's your birthday?" I asked her.

"Why are you asking that?"

"I didn't know what else to ask, so I came up with a random question. I've never been able to remember your birthday."

I hung up the phone, lit a smoke, and gazed at my fingers, illuminated by the weak glow. I suddenly remembered being in a similar position long ago, watching a cigarette in my hands, sitting on the edge of a flowerbed as I waited for her, listening to Zhang Chu's "Sister" while a snowstorm approached. I just sat like that, glazed over, as if I were the only person left in the world.

CHAPTER ELEVEN

SWEETHEARTS, GO!

Winter was the cruellest season at the saccharin factory. The trees look quite sickly at the best of times, but in winter they looked as if they couldn't wait to die. Like they couldn't stand the place and would rather commit suicide than be there a moment longer. If you wandered around the factory during this season, you'd find withered vegetation, a feeling of lifelessness, and multicolored earth, some sealed over with a solid layer of salt efflorescence. White steam wafted up from the wastewater in the manhole, and people who weren't familiar with the place thought it might be a precursor to a volcanic eruption. The three-shifts workers suffered most during winter, especially those in the saccharin workshop. The formaldehyde workshop had a sealed-off operation room, programmable electronic control, and surveillance cameras inside the reactor. The saccharin workshop was dilapidated and relied completely on workers to operate things manually; if you wanted to monitor things inside the reactor, you had to stick your head in and look inside. I had to do this a couple of times a day. At the beginning it felt totally surreal, like having magma flow toward your face like in a science-fiction movie. When you'd been doing it for a while, it just felt scary, and the hole was so small that my lower jaw would get trapped sometimes and I couldn't pull out my head. The saccharin workshop had a very small lounge where you could go to eat sunflower seeds and chat, but not to smoke, as that could cause an explosion. A steam pipe ran through the lounge, which meant that it was warm there in the winter, but you clearly couldn't spend all your time cowering away in the lounge. When you got back to the workshop floor, it would feel as cold as an icehouse—even with two padded jackets on, it was still pretty hard to take.

The saccharin workshop was enormous. The process, from tipping in raw materials and mixing them up until white saccharin poured out, required a huge number of stages. Each stage was divided into a large number of steps, and each of these steps had a different team in charge. What we called "team leaders" over there, here they called "section chiefs." Our section chief was only a minor official, but you couldn't offend him or he'd make you feel like you'd be better off dead.

Before I was transferred to the saccharin workshop, Long Legs and Xiao Li took me out for a meal. Long Legs started crying and said, "Oh, Xiaolu, it's all my fault."

I was drinking spirits and said, "What the hell's it got to do with you?"

"I took the night college exam, then you tried for it too—and because of that, you got the three shifts."

"You're crazy," I told him. "The reason is because I was caught by the factory head taking liberties with the lab girls. It has nothing to do with you."

But Long Legs was inconsolable; he just continued to cry. Soon we became fed up with his crying, and Xiao Li said, "There's going to be a huge number of people sent to the saccharin workshop next year anyway."

"I'm one step ahead of you guys," I said. "I'll see you both there."

Long Legs opened his eyes wide and said, "I'm not going! I'd rather quit than go!"

I raised a glass and said, "Let's drink to me on my way to sweetness."

Neither of them raised their glasses, so I gulped mine down alone. I felt pretty drunk after that, and I got lost on the way home.

It was winter when I first went to the saccharin workshop to report for duty. I was back wearing the neither-blue-nor-green work uniform. As an electrician, I'd always worn my lapel collar suit to work, but you couldn't wear a suit to produce saccharin, so I had no choice but to get reacquainted with my uniform. I arrived at the workshop that first day, and the workshop manager told me I'd been assigned to front-end production. I didn't know what this meant. She explained, "Front-end production is putting the raw materials in, and back-end production is when the finished product comes out."

"Which is better," I asked her, "front or back?"

"Front-end production is very tiring and very dirty," she told me sagely. "But you won't become sweet. Back-end is more relaxing, but you'll end up sickly sweet head to toe. Which would you prefer?" I told her I didn't mind. She shook her head. "If you're still single, then front-end production is slightly better. It might be more tiring, but you'll still be able to find yourself a girlfriend."

I ran to my work section, where I was received by the section chief, Big Buckteeth Weng. He was wearing a denim shirt covered in patches, the zippers on his clothes were all broken, and he had a length of twine tied around his waist. He couldn't have looked more tragic if he'd tried. Big Buckteeth Weng was squatting on an iron stool. He didn't ask my name or offer me a tour of the workshop. Instead he said, "Hey, little shitface, I want you to haul twenty bags of sod nit."

I hated his fucking tone of voice, so I asked, "What's sod nit?"

Sodium nitrate, he told me, and said I was dumb if I didn't even know that. I did as he said, jogging up to a truck and hauling two bags of sodium nitrate back each time, each one weighing forty pounds. Big Buckteeth Weng watched me from the lounge. He waited until I'd shifted all of them, then said, "Tear open the bags and pour them in the boiler." Without hesitating, I pulled out my utility knife and sliced open the bag, pouring out the entire contents from those twenty sacks. Big Buckteeth Weng said, "Alright, come find me in two hours."

"What should I do until then?" I asked.

"Stand over there and keep watch."

I stood there, surveying the saccharin workshop. The darkness was full of reactors, meandering coils of intestinelike pipes, ice-cold valves, and flanges. There was a layer of soot on the workshop windows; the only panes that weren't gray were the ones that had been smashed. I sat on a pile of raw material sacks, waiting for those twenty sacks of sodium nitrate to turn into something else. Big Buckteeth Weng came over later and told me I had to put my head inside the reactor to inspect it. Don't bullshit me, I told him, I knew how reactors worked: you could put your face up close to check them, but you should never stick your head inside.

"When I order you to stick your head inside, you stick your head inside," Big Buckteeth Weng said. "You got any more bullshit? Go home and tell it to your mother."

So I stuck my head inside reactors regularly to see how those starchy raw materials were reacting. Normally I'd just get a face full of noisy hot steam and couldn't inspect a fucking thing. I knew that Big Buckteeth Weng was giving me a deliberately hard time, but I didn't know under whose directive. The opening of the reactor was very small, and it wasn't easy to squeeze my head in, which was why I decided to shave my head. There was a worker called Four Hairs in this workshop—he was a bit mentally ill. Whenever he saw me slide my head in, he'd take a steel pipe and poke me right in the ass. With my head in the reactor, I couldn't defend myself, and by the time I retracted my head, he'd be running off laughing. I couldn't chase after him, as that constituted "unauthorized abandonment of one's post." One day I caught him off-guard. I saw that he and Big Bucktooth Weng were both in the lounge. I ran in and grabbed Four Hairs by the neck, punching him three times in the face: once in the mouth, once in the eye, and once on the nose. I punched him so hard, he was rolling on the floor. Then I stepped on his head a few times wearing my leather worker boots. Four Hairs was whimpering and yelling. When I'd finished beating him up, I rubbed my hand along my shaved head and looked at Big Buckteeth Weng. He had a toothpick sticking out of his mouth. He looked back at me but said nothing.

I'd told myself that I had no talent for electrical work and no talent for bench work, but you didn't need talent to produce saccharin. All you needed was brute strength and patience. Big Buckteeth Weng used those twenty bags of sodium nitrate to test my physical strength, and then he used Four Hairs to test my patience. Once I'd shaved my head and beaten up Four Hairs, my scalp was an unsightly greenish hue and bulged with a Y-shaped blood vessel. But I had a smile on my face, because Big Buckteeth Weng caused me no more trouble.

My clashes with Buckteeth Weng were all in the daytime. I never saw him during the night shift, which tended to be a bit calmer. But I hated the night shift too, having to leave the house in the middle of the night and work through to the morning, only getting home once it was light outside. I was living the life of a ghost.

One of the workers on my team was a burly guy with sideburns. He was bald while I had my shaved head, which meant that walking around the factory together, we got lots of raised eyebrows. His nickname was Wine Jar Guo; I can't remember his real name. He always carried a bottle of cheap and nasty sorghum liquor in his pocket, and he always showed up at the workshop blind drunk. When sober he could be pretty ruthless with his fists, but when drunk it was the opposite. He didn't care how badly he was beaten. When he was drunk, he'd show up late for work or not at all, but he never left early. He'd have a long sleep, wake up, then stagger home. When this happened, I'd be left with all the extra work. Sometimes he'd sober up and say, "Buddy, I'm so sorry." Then he would pull the bottle of liquor out of his pocket and offer me some.

I spent many afternoon and evening shifts sitting in the lounge, putting up with the reek of liquor rising from his body. I desperately wanted to give him a good beating, to let it all out, but I never beat up drunkards. It's just not what real men do. But coming across him sober was easier said than done.

A woman phoned our lounge once in the middle of the night. I answered and she shouted, "Is Wine Jar Guo there? He promised he was going to marry me today, why isn't he here?" Wine Jar Guo happened to be laid out on the floor, snoring. I kicked him, but he remained completely motionless. "He's drunk," I was forced to tell his jilted bride. "I can't wake him, but feel free to come try yourself."

I waited for him to wake up, then told him what had happened. He slapped himself on the face, saying, "Damn! I completely forgot about the marriage registration." Then he shook my hand and said, "Buddy, you're a hell of a good fella." I didn't know what to say as my hand was being squeezed between his two callused ones. I'd never actually seen him as a buddy, only a talking wine jar.

One day, Wine Jar Guo ran up to me. He was sober. "Xiaolu, I've quit," he said.

"Been fired, have you?" I asked.

He shook his head and said, "I've really quit. I'm rich!"

He saw my puzzled expression and said, "You're my buddy, so this is only for your ears. My old lady got rich playing the stock market, which means I'm rich now too."

I'd heard a lot of stories about people getting rich through stocks and shares. His wife was in the clothing business, and she'd had a little spare cash on hand. She bought a few shares, and that bit of spare cash became a big wad of spare cash.

"How much did she make?" I asked.

"Three million."

I was dumbfounded. There really was no need for him to come back to work.

He patted me on the shoulder and said, "Farewell, buddy. If you have any problems in the future, you come and find me."

Fuck you, asshole, I thought to myself, just running off like that, not even taking me for a meal.

I returned to Daicheng in 2004 to see my ma. I'd been sorting something out that took until late at night. On my way back, I saw a drunk man with his arms around a telegraph pole, vomiting. The wind was very blustery, and I was lost in my thoughts as I walked along the road, not noticing him until his vomit sprayed onto my pants. I was furious and grabbed hold of him, and I saw it was Wine Jar Guo. A girl wearing a skirt ran out of a restaurant, apologizing to me repeatedly. She helped Wine Jar Guo up, shouting, "Chief Guo! Chief Guo!" Wine Jar Guo was too drunk to even speak.

"What's this 'Chief Guo' all about?" I asked the girl. "What kind of company does he run?"

"A real estate firm," she said.

"Fuck me! He's made it big. Can I ask—are you his wife or his mistress?"

The girl blushed and said, "I'm his assistant."

She was very pretty and looked shy, so I smiled and said, "I used to know this dickhead. He was drunk every day. Does he still drink sorghum liquor?"

"He only drinks Moutai," the girl said. "Today he dined with some investors. Chief Guo doesn't drink very often. I'm really sorry. As you're an old acquaintance, why don't you give me your business card and I'll pass it on to him."

"There's no need," I said. I helped Wine Jar Guo stand up straight and took his face in my hand—he didn't remember me. "Armani suit, not bad," I said. "What label's the tie?"

"I don't know," the girl said.

I considered socking him in the mouth a couple of times, leaving him something to remember me by. But I couldn't find the impulse to punch him that I'd had in the saccharin workshop back then. So I gave him a gentle slap around the face instead. Hitting and making love are the same: a debt incurred ten years ago will inevitably need to be written off. I'd wanted to sock myself in the mouth, but I thought about it and decided to just forget it.

That was the period when I was chopping and changing between the three shifts. Late at night, the factory seemed like another world entirely. I walked through it with nobody around. Dim lights fell onto the road, and you could make out the shadowy outline of the storage tank in the distance. Steam illuminated by the lights rose up in a blur and dispersed. The constant rumble of machinery and the sound of motors in the distance made up the factory's particular nighttime calm. If I managed to forget that I was producing saccharin and pretended that instead I was a cameraman, director, or artist, it was a pretty bewitching setting.

I would always arrive for my night shift at nine. I'd ride my bike in through the gate and be in the workshop with my clothes changed before ten o'clock, then go start my shift. I was never late for the night shift because you had to do a handover. If I didn't turn up, the person handing over to me wouldn't be able to leave his station; those were the factory rules. Wine Jar Guo was completely unreliable. There were two female workers in the shift before mine, and making female workers go home in the middle of the night was a shitty thing to do. They might meet a rapist. I may have been an asshole, but I was never going to be an accessory to rape.

The night shift was pretty laid-back. All you had to do was complete three production batches, and you were done. I was in front-end production, which meant I couldn't be held up by those in front—in fact, it was often other people urging me to work quicker. Some people did shoddy work, spending twenty minutes doing what should have been two hours of mixing. But who would ever find out? Even if the products were defective, they couldn't deduct your bonus. The only thing they could do was fire the workshop director. No one gave a shit what you got up to during the night shift, as long as you didn't smoke in the workshop. If you smoked, you could blast everyone into the sky, and no one wanted that.

During our breaks, we'd find a place to put our heads down. We should have been able to sleep in the lounge, but it was too narrow; and it wasn't right for the guys and the girls to be squeezed so close together to sleep. Besides, most of the time Wine Jar Guo was in there, reeking like death. As long as it wasn't freezing winter, you could usually find a corner to nap in—perhaps behind the storage tank or by the side of the power distribution box. These dark, dry places gave you somewhere to sleep and be safeguarded against being caught by the on-duty cadres.

Two cadres were assigned to night-shift duty, stationed in the department building. At midnight, these cadres would pick up their flashlights and come out to patrol, and if they found you sleeping, they'd deduct your monthly bonus. Some cadres were lazy or had a good rapport with the workers, and therefore wouldn't carry out these checks. Then there were the more annoying cadres, like Hu Deli and Pu Nani. When we were on the night shift, the first thing we did was go to the gatehouse and ask which cadres were on duty. As soon as the old doorman told us the names, we'd know whether we'd be getting some sleep that night or not.

Catching sleeping workers was a bit of a game for factory cadres. After leaving the department building at midnight, the first place they'd visit would usually be the power distribution station. Once the power distribution station's duty supervisors had received their inspection visit, they'd phone through to let the fertilizer workshop know, then lie down and have a sleep. The fertilizer workshop supervisors would get this call, then courteously await their inspection visit. When that was over, they'd place a call to inform the formaldehyde workshop located behind them, then they would have their rest. This formed a beacon-style alarm system, telling the workers exactly where the cadres had gone. There was a tacit understanding between the workers and most of the cadres that this was how things were done. When someone like Hu Deli or Pu Nani was on duty, things were more difficult. They would vary their routes, inspecting the formaldehyde workshop first, then the saccharin workshop, then doubling back for a surprise attack on the formaldehyde workshop. They planned their moves with such cunning that not even psychic powers would have helped predict them, and it gave us workers a huge headache. Whenever Hu Deli or Pu Nani was on duty, someone from each workshop would be assigned to stand sentry. If there was no apprentice, an intern would be given this role; and if there were neither, we'd draw lots. The sentry stood in the workshop doorway, and as soon as he saw a shadow he'd shout the code: "What did you have for dinner?" If the person approaching answered, "I had seafood," it was someone from your workshop. If the sentry didn't hear the word *seafood*, he would run along the pipeline, knocking against it with a stick as he went. The sound would travel down the pipe and spread to all areas of the workshop. The sleepers in all the corners would rise to their feet like zombies. It actually looked pretty freaky. Despite this system, bastards like Hu Deli and Pu Nani still managed to catch us off-guard. Sometimes they'd come up from the freight elevator and block off the back route—a desperate measure, as it was insanely slippery back there and you were risking your neck.

Workers caught sleeping by cadres would invariably start to quibble with them. Sleeping could be done in many different positions, and there was lengthy debate about what counted as sleeping. It was only after I was transferred to the workshop that I became acquainted with the study of sleep. As any sleep psychologist knows, it's an infinitely fascinating field of study. The rules were: if you nodded off sitting down and you woke up right away when the cadres shouted at you, it wouldn't count as sleeping, just resting; if the cadres shouted at you twice and you still didn't wake up, then it was sleeping. If you were sprawled across a table dozing and drooling, it was definitely sleeping. Lying on the floor, asleep or awake, would always be seen as sleeping, unless you could prove you'd had an epileptic fit. It never counted as sleeping if you were found asleep standing up, because that was just too damn awesome. Sleeping standing up surpassed human capabilities; it made you a fucking horse!

Wine Jar Guo was the only saccharin factory worker who dared to sleep openly. Not even Hu Deli could take him on. When Wine Jar Guo went to sleep, that was it—he couldn't be woken, not even if there were a hundred cadres shouting at him. When he woke up, he'd have forgotten not only that he'd been caught by the cadres, but that he'd even been drunk. But when it came time for the awarding of bonuses, he suddenly became very clear-headed. One dime short, and he'd smash up the workshop director's office.

I was caught once by Pu Nani. It was four in the morning, and even the sentry had fallen asleep. Pu Nani tiptoed in via the freight elevator. This was total perversion; we'd fulfilled our production quota by then, the machines had all been turned off, and it was perfectly reasonable to be taking a nap. This was the reason Pu Nani had his nickname, the old masochist. He came in the workshop and found a couple of workers sleeping in their various corners, but didn't wake them. Then he spotted me next to the power distribution box. I was sitting on the ground, hugging my knees, my head buried in my chest. My sleeping posture shouldn't have given me away, but I'd shaved my head. Pu Nani was ecstatic. He even kicked me a few times as he shouted, "I've caught you sleeping, Lu Xiaolu!" I popped up like a zombie, waking the other nearby workers, who all got to their feet too. But I was the only one Pu Nani was interested in. "Come with me," he said, pointing. "You're coming to my office to write a self-criticism."

I stumbled after Pu Nani, but it was only after we were out of the workshop that my brain caught up with my body. Fuck, I'd actually fallen into Pu Nani's hands. For years, he'd been mouthing off about what he'd do if he ever got his hands on me. The factory rules stated that if you were caught sleeping, you'd have your monthly bonus deducted, and it would impact your annual and biannual bonuses too. I was feeling pretty distressed, and as I walked along the road, I felt an overwhelming urge to grab a piece of metal pipe and smash it down on Pu Nani's head. I wanted to hit him so hard he got amnesia, but I didn't know my own strength, and it would be too harsh if he ended up a vegetable. It would mean I'd be forced to take care of him for the rest of his life too—and his wife and kid. Smashing his head in really wasn't the best plan. I wondered if I should knock myself out instead.

By the time we reached his office, Pu Nani was brimming with glee. He didn't have a clue what had been hanging in the balance for him just moments before.

"So this is what it feels like to catch you," he said.

"I've been caught tons of times," I said. "Coming to work late, leaving early, taking liberties with girls."

"Yes, but this is the first time I've caught you. You break the law, and I uphold it. Boy, am I feeling fine today!"

"You've wanted to catch me since I was a bench worker, you asshole, that's two whole years. You're actually prepared to admit that."

"You dared to threaten me with a file back then!"

"You made a complaint to the labor department, you asshole, told them I tried to stab you with a file."

He took a stack of paper from his drawer and said, "Write your self-criticism on this and then write your name, otherwise we have no evidence for when we deduct your bonus."

"I'm standing right here—what other evidence do you need?"

"Black characters on white paper is the only evidence that counts," Pu Nani said.

I picked up the pen and slowly started to write my self-criticism. First the ballpoint pen was giving me trouble because the ink wasn't flowing properly, and my writing tore through the paper. Then there were a lot of characters I wasn't sure how to write. I dawdled so much that my self-criticism took over an hour. So long, in fact, that Pu Nani needed to take a leak and went off to use the bathroom. That was just as I'd hoped. As soon as he was gone, I rifled through the pockets of his jacket, which was hung up by the door, and pulled out two hundred-yuan bills and a handful of small notes and stuffed it all into my pants pocket. I quickly finished up my self-criticism, signed it, then waited for him to return. I handed him the sheet of paper and strolled off. Mr. Pu Nani, you take your time and find your evidence for how that money went missing, I thought to myself.

A note about my private life in 1994. It could be covered in two words: *sexual frustration*. It was like a long drought that came after a great flood. If I were still a virgin, I'd have found it easier to cope. Working the three shifts lowered your sex drive to some extent, but it wasn't as if I was a eunuch. Once I got used to my new work routine and spring was around the corner, I started to feel sexually frustrated again. The only difference being that before, the frustration had been fueled by my imagination; now it was fueled by nostalgia.

I was twenty, and by all rights I should have been looking for a girlfriend. But if I found one, I wouldn't be able to have sex with her. All we could do would be to stroll around, watch movies, and talk about dreams. This made me feel pretty sad. I'd been spoiled. A couple of relatives offered to introduce me to girls, but I declined. I had no desire to take another girl for a stroll along the street; I'd had enough of strolling. My ma was pretty worried. "Are the three shifts burning you out? You don't even have enough energy to look for a girlfriend." It wasn't that I was burnt out, I explained. But if I wanted to do my shifts and study at night college, something had to give. My mother was very moved by this, thinking that I was starting to value my time. By way of support, she used to wash my underwear. She never told me I was disgusting, even when she came across very dirty pairs. Because this was the price paid for my not having a girlfriend.

When spring arrived, I was still on the three shifts. Dinner and midnight snacks were always a bowl of noodles in the canteen; not because I loved noodles, but because rice wasn't really an option. All they had by then was rice left over from the day, which had turned hard and cold and sent your stomach into spasms. The noodles were far from great. They were made in the canteen's noodle-making machine. The thick pieces were like chopsticks and the thin pieces like fishing wire, and you never knew what you were going to get when you bit down. But at the end of the day it was hot, and it came in some broth.

I went to the canteen for my noodles one evening, along with a scattering of middle-shift workers. I chucked my enamel bowl through the window with a couple of plastic meal tokens, and a short while later, a bowl of steaming hot noodles appeared. I sat down and started slurping my noodles, but halfway through I noticed a sparerib in the soup. I was puzzled and stared at the rib for a while before finally gobbling it up. The following evening was the same: I found another sparerib hidden under my noodles. I didn't hesitate this time, just polished it off neatly. On the third evening, I'd finished my sparerib and was about to pick up my bowl to leave when Auntie Qin appeared before me.

"Have you been enjoying your spareribs, Lu Xiaolu?" she asked. As soon as I heard this, I knew I was fucked. I dreaded to think what kind of love interest Auntie Qin might have dredged up on my behalf. "Do you know who makes the noodles?" Auntie Qin asked.

I told her no, I didn't know him. Auntie Qin told me it wasn't a *him* but a *her* who made the noodles. I continued to shake my head. I didn't know the girl who made the fucking noodles; all I knew was that they were bland fucking noodles.

"She's the fat one with the short hair and the freckly face. Her name's Kuai Li," Auntie Qin told me. I clutched my head with my hands and tried to remember if I'd ever seen her. I had a faint recollection of a girl standing by the stove and putting noodles in the water, but her whole body had been enshrouded in steam and I hadn't seen her freckles.

"Yes, that's her," Auntie Qin said. "That young girl has been very good to you, giving you all those free spareribs."

"Oh, so she was the one who put the spareribs in the broth? I thought they might have been dropped down from above."

"Don't you play dumb with me," Auntie Qin said. "I'm telling you, Kuai Li is the flower of our canteen, and she's taken an interest in you. What are you? A mere saccharin-producing . . ."

"That's right," I said, "all I do is produce saccharin. What could possibly have made her interested in me?"

Auntie Qin got close to me and whispered in my ear, "Kuai Li saw you during that great ruckus you caused in the hall, and she liked your style." I was shocked and assumed I'd misheard. There were actually girls who were drawn to natural-born killers, you just didn't expect it.

"I've tried reasoning with her," Auntie Qin said, "but she happens to have a thing for your type. What could I do? There really is no accounting for taste."

"Yes, knowing what you like and what you hate has its advantages." But something about it didn't make sense. "Hang on, that happened last year. Why has she only asked you to set us up now?"

"She had a boyfriend then, but he's dumped her now."

I closed my eyes and let the misery wash over me.

"Come now, Lu Xiaolu," Auntie Qin said, "give it to me straight. What shall I tell her?"

Was this really the old lady's matchmaking method? It seemed pretty screwed up. Auntie Qin obviously had a really bad impression of me, didn't think I was worth my salt, not even up to the standards of a girl like Kuai Li. If this had been the '60s, I'd have said yes to any of the canteen girls—but unfortunately for them, state grain reserves were abundant now, and pimping myself to the canteen for the taste of a sparerib really wasn't worth my while. I kept these harsh words to myself, and instead said, "I already have a girlfriend."

"From which workshop?"

I felt my bile rising. "She's not from any workshop. She's studying at a graduate school in Shanghai."

Saying this made me feel pretty low, so I slunk off with my bowl in my hand.

The next time I went again to get noodles, there was no sparerib and the canteen staff were pretty rude to me. I dropped my food bowl in through the window, and after a while it was shoved back at me with a few scraggly strands of noodles and not a morsel of garlic. As I was carrying this bowl of noodles, I thought of Kuai Li, the girl who knew what she liked and what she hated. If she were to place rat poison in my bowl I'd be finished, kaput. So for a while I had to eat outside the factory, which basically meant baked flatbread. While working the night shift I couldn't even get hold of those, so I had to bring in my own meals. After a few months of this, I was just skin and bones.

Later I realized that a miserable life is often unperceived by the one who's living it. It's only via specific events or people that it is revealed. These things serve as a pair of glasses that cast light on this misery. Of course, there were plenty of people in the world who were suffering more than I was, and I knew I shouldn't be taking my troubles to heart.

When I was young, sadness and misery were always distinct from each other. Sometimes you felt miserable but not sad, other times sad but not miserable. Only through Kuai Li and Auntie Qin was I able to see a reflection of myself as sad and miserable. How had they managed to convey the truth of this sad, miserable state of affairs? Had some supernatural power taken over their bodies to pass the message to me? It gave me a strange feeling and left me confused for some time.

I met another girl that year, at a poetry reading. One of my night college classmates gave me a mimeographed leaflet and told me it was a meet-up for Daicheng's young poets. The leaflet listed a few of the attending poets, gave the time and location and an incredibly flowery paragraph of which I've forgotten every word. This classmate worked at the Fourth People's Hospital as a gardener, not a doctor. His main duty was to turn soybeans into a kind of fertilizer and pour it under the flowers and trees. He taught me a lot about different ways to make fertilizer, regardless of whether I seemed interested or not. My fellow night-college students came from all different trades: there were salespeople, butchers, flight attendants, workers, and low-level office workers, but he was the only gardener. Like me, this gardening classmate would also write the odd poem, and he also got them published in the evening paper supplement.

He'd often bring in a copy of the *Daicheng Evening News* and point to a string of characters, telling us it was one of his poems. The fact that he had a pen name—more than one—made his story less credible, and people assumed he was bullshitting them.

One day this gardener-poet said, "I'm going to take part in a poetry reading soon." Then he took out a leaflet, waving it in front of my face so I couldn't read it properly. I had to take it from him and scrutinize it before I understood that it was a gathering for young creative types. He suggested I go with him, and I accepted. I'd never been to a poetry reading and was eager to see what it would be like. That afternoon, the gardener-poet called my workshop and told me something he'd eaten had upset his stomach, and he had the runs so badly his legs had turned to jelly. He would have to pull out of the poetry event.

That evening, I ventured out on my own. I made my way to the west of the city, to a factory recreation center. There was a dance hall I'd been to once before. I strode in and saw lots of long-haired boys sitting there and a lot of young girls, all clustered together smoking and drinking beer. The lighting was dim, and a number of candles had been lit. Someone was onstage reciting a poem loudly into a microphone. It was quite a familiar scene, and if my ears were covered I'd think I was watching someone sing karaoke. I snuck a few looks around but didn't see Hai Yan from my factory, so I found a corner and leaned against the wall. No one paid me the slightest bit of attention.

That's when I met this girl. She was standing next to me and asked, "Would you be so kind as to keep an eye on my things for a moment?" I hadn't come across such a polite girl for a long time, and I blushed slightly as I nodded and was handed her coat and bag. It was a red camelhair coat, lovely to the touch, but its collar was a little scuffed. She made her way onto the stage and took a piece of paper out of her pocket. She read her poem in a very quiet voice, took a bow, then left the stage. There was no applause, not even from me. She walked back to where I was leaning, and I handed over her things. She stuck her tongue out in a show of exasperation.

"Was my poem awful?" she said.

"You were too quiet—no one could hear you," I explained.

"Okay, I'll remember that for next time."

There was a pretty lively atmosphere at the poetry reading. One guy ran up onto the stage and read something like ten poems, each one as long as *The Divine Comedy*. Waiting for him to finish his poems felt like waiting for a bus. When another guy had finished reading a couple of his poems, he dug a lighter out of his pocket and set fire to the paper they were written on. Some people applauded loudly at this, while others voiced disapproval, and a minor tussle broke out. That's when the presenter jumped onto the stage and said to the people below, "Hey, we're all young, let's enjoy ourselves!" A disco ball started to spin, and music started to pump from the speakers. A group of people filled the dance floor. I watched the lights flashing on this shadowy crowd, making them look like a cluster of demons coming back from the dead. I was still leaning against the wall in the corner, not to look cool but because I seriously had no idea how to dance to disco music.

The girl was still next to me. At the start she had looked very excited, pointing to the poet on the stage and saying, "That's Big K!"

"What's he, a baseball player or something? Is Babe Ruth here too?" I asked. She laughed and said, "You must have just wandered in off the street if you haven't even heard of Big K. He's a famous poet." She pointed to someone else, saying, "And that's Feng Ma. He's been to Tibet!"

My mood slumped as I was reminded that if it hadn't been for the three shifts, I'd be in Tibet.

"I really want to go to Tibet," the girl said.

That remark worried me. The last thing I needed was another girl trying to entice me to Tibet. That would just be too fucking ironic.

Soon all the poets were dancing, and I told the girl I was going to head home.

"Let's leave together," she said. "I'm not one for dancing either."

We followed the dark corridor outside. We were in a gold-processing factory, and the ground was covered in iron filings and bits of wire. On the way, she took my hand lightly, clasping my fingers with her small ones, but when we got to the lit road, she put her hand back in her pocket. Again I noticed her collar and the tiny hole in it; it was as if all her gentleness was nestled there.

I saw her back to her place. On the way, she told me her name was Xiao Jin, and she was a department employee at the flour factory. She asked about me and I told her I produced saccharin at the saccharin factory, just a lowly worker. But I hadn't just wandered in off the street to the poetry reading, I explained. I wrote a little poetry too.

"Let's see one of your poems," she said.

I told her I hadn't brought any but that I'd let her see another time.

"Recite one you know by heart."

"I don't know any by heart—another time."

I walked her to her front door. Her house was a long way away, in a new village in the suburbs. We exchanged mailing addresses, and she thanked me for escorting her home. I told her she was very welcome. Then I watched her go into her house like a small cat might. It took me a whole hour to ride home. The flour factory was near my house, and the thought of such a gentle, kind girl having to spend two hours a day getting to and from work pained me.

About a week later, I received some mail from Xiao Jin. It was a document envelope, and inside were her poems. Her handwriting was really beautiful. Next to one poem, she'd written in red pen: *This poem was published in the* Star Poetry Journal. I picked up the poem and spent a long time reading it before putting it away in my drawer.

I never wrote back to her.

One spring day, I was finishing the early shift at 2:00 p.m. when I saw a huge crowd of people standing around the factory's bulletin board. Usually pictures of exceptional employees were stuck up here, which served mainly to make us all laugh, but that day the board was surrounded by a group of people looking anguished, some even crying. I stopped my bike and ran over to find out what all the fuss was about, and I saw a sheet of blood-red propaganda paper with a list of names. It was the list of employees who were being sent to produce saccharin. The brand-new saccharin workshop was nearly complete, and this red sheet of paper was a public announcement of the first batch of people to be sent down. The oddest thing about this list was the words *Listed in no particular order.*

This list destroyed lives. A girl who worked in the storage room explained that she was pregnant and would rather die than work the three shifts. The factory didn't back down; the factory office manager told her that if she didn't go on the three shifts, she'd be let go. When she heard this, she head-butted him in the chest and knocked the wind out of him. She ended up having a miscarriage. Around this time, the factory slogan changed from *Go to work happily, return home safely* to *Follow the bureau's orders, strive for advancement* and *If you don't work hard today, you'll be working hard to find a job tomorrow.* They were just shy of slogans like *One worker's job lost, a whole family's glory gone.* The workers shit their pants when they saw slogans like this. The slogan *The working class leads everything* from years before could still be seen on the little red building, like memories of a teenage dream.

A few fights broke out that day. "Zhang Wei" was one of the names on the red piece of paper, but there were five men in the factory named Zhang Wei. Three of them were already working the three shifts, and of the remaining two, one was a canteen chef and the other drove for the driving team. Neither of them should really have been getting the three shifts. The two Zhang Weis stood there, each claiming the name on the red paper wasn't his, until a fight broke out between them. Someone from the safety department ran over saying, "No fighting allowed! If you carry on like this, you'll both get the three shifts!" So they stopped fighting. Telling someone they were getting the three shifts was just like putting a curse on them; it was pretty fucking effective.

I joined the crowd to watch the drama. I was the most relaxed person there. I'd been touched by that curse a long time ago. I didn't see Long Legs' name, which I felt pretty pleased about. Later Xiao Li walked over, pale-faced.

"Have you been transferred?" I asked.

Xiao Li shook his head, then whispered into my ear, "Little Pouty Lips has been sent down to the workshop."

I couldn't believe it. Little Pouty Lips was a labor department employee, and she always behaved herself. How the hell had she been assigned the three shifts? A few of us ate dinner together that evening. Little Pouty Lips looked pale as well. She ate two mouthfuls of food before putting down her chopsticks and bursting into tears. Long Legs and I were at a complete loss. Xiao Li tried to console her, but she continued to cry.

"Aren't you a cadre?" I asked her. "Can cadres get the three shifts too?"

"They're transferring a lot of people this time," Xiao Li said. "The factory doesn't have a large enough labor force, so they're transferring a bunch of low-level cadres as well—to serve as examples."

Little Pouty Lips' face was streaked with tears. "That's bullshit," she said. "The factory head has a relative who wants to work in the labor department. That's why I've been transferred!"

"Yep," Xiao Li corroborated. "That's the other reason."

All I could do was to urge her to think positive. I was working the three shifts, and you did get used to it.

"We're not the same, you and I!" Little Pouty Lips said. "Since being in the labor department, I've offended so many workers. Now they're going to bully the hell out of me, aren't they?"

I was surprised she had this small amount of self-awareness.

"Well, why don't you quit?" Long Legs suggested. "If they transferred me to three shifts, I'd just quit."

"At least you can fix pipes," Little Pouty Lips said as another stream of tears welled up in her eyes. "I can't do anything."

Xiao Li explained that Little Pouty Lips had studied business management as a secondary-school diploma. Neither the qualification nor the subject was worth shit in a factory. Foreign enterprises even had their college students in the workshops, working on assembly lines. In our factory, we actually had it better.

Xiao Li and I went out to take a leak. As we were standing against the wall, he said, "What if Little Pouty Lips marries a department head? That way she won't be sent to the workshop."

"You're talking crap," I said. "There are no what-ifs in real life."

"It's not a what-if," he said. "It would be pretty easy to make that happen."

I had a lot of daydreams around that time, such as: what if I were an outlaw; what if I had money; what if Bai Lan hadn't left me; what if Xiao Jin and I had gotten together. You think about things in that way, and it might make you happy or it might make you sad. But I wasn't prepared to start asking what-if about the three shifts. Those kinds of what-ifs were completely pointless. An ideal should not be so lofty that it encompassed saving all of humanity, but nor should it be so base as to focus on not having to do the three shifts. If a female department head asked me to marry her in exchange for reinstating me to day shifts, fuck! I'd rather produce saccharin for the rest of my life. So what if you had no goals, as long as you didn't degrade yourself because of it, going off in search of some bullshit and coming back with it raised in triumph. This was my bottom line, and I wasn't going to lose sleep over it.

Little Pouty Lips came to the saccharin workshop as a manager. This meant checking the meter and answering the phone, so it was pretty laid-back work. The only arduous part was having to actually do the three shifts, but at least she didn't have to produce saccharin. On the floor beneath the workshop, there was a filthy control room that served as an office for the managers. The desks in there were completely black, and if you were to lick one you'd find it had a sweet tinge, because everything did. Little Pouty Lips soon became a sweetie, too. I used to call her "sweetheart," which made her smile. Little Pouty Lips changed quite dramatically around this time. She dropped the attitude she'd had in the labor department. When she saw me, she'd shout "Supervisor Lu" as if I really were one. I asked her if she was thinking of splitting up with Xiao Lu and marrying a department head or something. "Ha!" she replied. "Why don't I just marry the mayor? Then I could get the factory head transferred, have him produce saccharin." I really liked her tone of voice—it reminded me of a certain factory doctor who used to speak quite similarly.

Little Pouty Lips became nimble and feisty. We all found it very strange. I thought she'd be like Lu Xun's tragic character, Mistress Xiang Lin, walking around day after day with tears streaming down her face. Later I learned that when some people were provoked, they secreted a pituitary hormone that caused them to change dramatically.

But Little Pouty Lips didn't seem bothered by the way she'd changed. She rode her bike in the production zone at top speed, the short hair on her temples sticking out like pine needles. You weren't allowed to ride bikes in the production zone, but she didn't care. Sometimes she'd see me walking along the road and race toward me yelling, "Supervisor Lu, I'll carry you for a block!" I'd jump up onto the bike rack, and she'd cycle for a bit before shouting, "You're too heavy. You peddle, and I'll hold the handlebar." We looked like a circus act cruising along to the workshop like that.

Xiao Li was pretty jealous when he heard. "Whose girlfriend is she, anyway?" he asked.

"Of course she's still yours," I told him. "It's not just me she takes on her bike, she's carried Long Legs too—ask if you don't believe me!"

"Forget it, forget it, I have no say in what she does," Xiao Li said.

Not only was the girl riding her bike brazenly around the production zone, but Little Pouty Lips was learning to drive a forklift on the sly. Whenever the forklift supervisor saw her, he gave her a thumbs-up. She had no forklift license, so that was in violation of the rules too, but no one in the production zone gave a shit. I was itching to try it, so I leaped up onto the forklift and drove it in a semicircle before knocking down a small tree.

"Supervisor Lu, you're terrible! You have zero talent for this," Little Pouty Lips said.

"Oh, and you've discovered your natural talent is driving? I really couldn't tell."

"I don't care if you believe me, but I learned to drive a forklift truck in five minutes."

A note about genius: I've already mentioned that I couldn't fix water pipes or climb telephone poles—now it was proved that I couldn't drive a forklift either. I could have given her a bashful look and explained that my talent was for writing poetry, but saying something like this to a female forklift driver was just asking for trouble.

"It's enough that you're my sweetheart," I told her. "Who cares about driving forklifts!"

We both worked the same shifts, and although we couldn't actually work side by side, we finished at the same time. At the beginning, Xiao Li would come pick her up at the end of her middle shifts. But Xiao Li worked the day shift, and having to go back to the factory again at night was giving him a nervous breakdown. Once when he went to fix an electric circuit, feeling a bit out of it, he touched the electric gate and nearly died. He invited our group out for a meal not long afterward and said, "Since my girlfriend drives you to work, how about you take her home—you're on the way anyway. I'll be forever indebted if you do." No problem, I told him, I'd look after Little Pouty Lips as if she were my own girlfriend. After I said this, the three guys gave me a frenzied beating.

It was about that time that we got to know about a pervert in the neighborhood. He rode a twenty-eight-inch bike and followed the female workers as they left work. The female workers had bikes with small wheels, which meant they couldn't outride him. He didn't actually do anything to them: if the girl rode fast, he'd ride fast; if she got tired, he'd slow down too, always maintaining a three-foot distance from her. The freakiest thing was that he wouldn't chat with the girl or tease her when he was doing this, he'd just look very intent. This proved that he was a pervert, not a thug. The female workers were all scared to death. Little Pouty Lips may have been nimble and feisty, but she was still afraid of this pervert. So I'd head to her place on my way to work, wait outside her building, and we'd cycle to the factory together. When we finished our shifts, I'd be sure to see her to her door. After doing this for a while, I started to suspect that I liked her. It wasn't long before I realized that I really did like her. But I kept it to myself.

Little Pouty Lips never had a run-in with that pervert, but another pervert came out of the woodwork: Big Bucktooth Weng from the saccharin workshop developed a thing for her. Big Bucktooth Weng was a widower. No one knew how his wife had died; some said he'd killed her, others said that she couldn't put up with him any longer and killed herself. All the rumors about him hinted toward his perversion. Big Bucktooth Weng worked the day shift when there were lots of people around, which didn't give him many windows of opportunity. To facilitate an encounter with Little Pouty Lips, he volunteered to work overtime for free. On the middle shift, when there was no one in the office, he lunged toward her and crouched in front of her with a toothpick in his mouth, giving her a lecherous grin. Little Pouty Lips absolutely detested him. Blurting out some excuse, she ran up the stairs into the workshop and raced to my side. Big Bucktooth Weng followed her to me. Little Pouty Lips pointed at him and said, "He's harassing me." I picked up a crowbar and whirled it around, then hit it against the reactor, which gave off a series of sparks. Sparks could cause explosions, just as cigarette butts could. Big Bucktooth Weng was too scared to approach; he just pointed at me and left.

"Lu Xiaolu, who is she to you?" the workers asked. "Why are you sticking up for her?"

I hesitated.

"He's my boyfriend!" Little Pouty Lips announced loudly, still hanging onto my arm.

I didn't deny this wild claim. I bit the bullet and shouted, "Big Bucktooth Weng, if you harass my girl again, I'll round up ten people and we'll break your front teeth!"

I warned Little Pouty Lips that she'd made a bad move. First, Xiao Li was going to get the wrong idea and think I'd stolen his girlfriend; second, my reputation was so terrible that if the factory thought we were dating, they'd probably make her produce saccharin alongside me.

"You're taking it too seriously," Little Pouty lips said. "I'm being transferred out next week."

"Transferred where?"

"To the water authority."

"Good for you," I said.

"You're really sweet, Xiaolu," Little Pouty Lips said. "Thank you for picking me up and taking me home all this time."

"It's called love and goodness—we can't let our brothers down."

"I don't want you to see only Xiao Li and Long Legs as your brothers," Little Pouty Lips said. "I want to be your brother too."

"Then brothers we are. For life," I said.

There was something adorably cute about Little Pouty Lips right then. People are only at their cutest for a limited spell—they can't be consistently cute throughout their whole lives. The fact that I got to be Little Pouty Lips' brother when she was at her cutest truly was my good fortune. I really wanted to see her and Xiao Li get married. I could be best man, and Long Legs would be a bridesmaid. The scene was like a painting in my mind. If we'd all just stayed that way forever we'd have all gone on being cute forever, maybe too cute for this world.

One evening that summer, when Little Pouty Lips was soon to be transferred, I went to the bathhouse for a soak. I soaked until my whole body was red. I felt very relaxed after my wash and headed out in the direction of the bike shed, carrying my towel and my bar of soap. That's when I saw the ambulance driving in through the factory gate. This was handover time between the middle and night shifts, when you didn't tend to see work accidents. "Lu Xiaolu," a saccharin workshop auntie shouted to me. "Go and see! Your girlfriend's had an accident." At first I didn't react. When I realized she was talking about Little

Pouty Lips, I threw down the towel and ran like crazy. The ambulance got to the scene of the accident before me, and by the time I arrived, all I saw was a group of people lifting a body into the ambulance, the door banging closed, and the ambulance roaring away.

I stood there, freezing cold. The workers around me looked over sympathetically and said, "Du Jie's over." *Over* was our slang for ruined, finished.

"Dead?" I asked.

"She won't die—unless she kills herself."

Little Pouty Lips had finished the middle shift and was riding her bike toward the bathhouse. She rode over a manhole that was usually covered, but that day a migrant worker had been dredging it and had forgotten to cover it back up. The manhole was pretty shallow, and the mouth was pretty small. A strapping guy like me would never have been able to get inside, even if I'd wanted to. It was the middle of the night when Little Pouty Lips rode her bike over it, and her front wheel knocked against the manhole, flipping her off her bike and into the hole. She was so petite—the circumference of that manhole seemed to have been tailored to fit her body. The poor girl dropped right into the hole, which was flowing with boiling discharged workshop water.

Everyone commented on how unlucky she'd been. If only she hadn't been riding her bike. If only the migrant worker had put the cover back on the manhole. If only she hadn't been so petite. If only it had been winter (in winter, the boiling water would have been steaming, and she would have seen it). If only, if only, but life doesn't have what-ifs or if-onlys.

Having fallen in, she cried out loudly and was fished out by a couple of supervisors who were walking past. By the time they got her out, she was completely disfigured. "There was nothing wrong with her face, but from the chest down she was a write-off," someone told me. I went and peered into that deep black hole. Had it been a smokestack, I'd have smashed it with a hammer. But it was a manhole, deep in the ground, and save for filling it up with earth, there was nothing I could do. I had no way of venting my anger. After kicking the lid back into place, I cycled to Xiao Li's to tell him the news.

A word about Little Pouty Lip's accident: the factory's final judgment on the matter was that she'd been riding her bike in the production zone, which meant that the responsibility for the work accident was hers to bear. The factory would not give one cent in compensation. Little Pouty Lips' ma came into the factory crying, saying that the least they could do was buy her an air-conditioning unit.

The girl's body was covered in burns, and her treatment required her to wear rubber clothing. Being bound up in that during the July heat was an experience that most people wouldn't even be able to imagine. She was in sweltering-hot, itchy agony, and each day she'd scream that she didn't want to keep living. The factory backed down. They said they'd help her out this one time. They tore down the old air-conditioning unit in the labor department and let her mother take it back home.

Her mother walked off crying.

That whole year for me felt like it was the last day of the world. All the things I loved had turned to dust, and I stood like a fool on my own among all this dust. I acted like kind of a dick when I was young, and I had built up a lot of bad blood. If anyone crossed me, they'd have to pay for it. This bad blood could be resolved with either a brick or a wooden stick. But when it came to the situations with Bai Lan and Little Pouty Lips, you could have given me a machine gun, but I wouldn't have had a clue who to fire it at. The way I saw it, people who couldn't find anyone in the world to love could just love the world itself. But not being able to find anyone to hate left you with a vague feeling of antipathy toward the world, which was absurd.

In 2004, I went to an internet café in Daicheng. The first thing I saw when I walked through the door was a telephone pole of a guy lodged in a chair playing *Counter Strike*. This telephone pole was using an AK47, and even though his shooting was crappy, he wasn't losing lives. Dodging, turning, jumping, moving, he was all over the place—three enemies surrounded him, but still they couldn't kill him. I found it hilarious to watch. Ten years ago, he was forever being surrounded by supervisors, and a decade later he still hadn't forgotten this martial art. Finally, he ran into a dead end. He wanted to turn but wasn't quick enough, and he was blasted to bits by a machine gun. I remembered the way he used to look when he'd been caught, like a sad-faced Don Quixote. When the plumbing-team supervisors saw this expression, it triggered their maliciousness, and a dozen or so of them would start slapping him around the face. Watching him playing *Counter Strike*, I had the urge to give him a good pummeling too.

He turned around and saw me but didn't recognize me right away. If I'd had a towel in my hand, that might have jogged his memory—I could have whipped it at his dick. He'd have known me then. Once it clicked, he leapt up from his chair to hug me.

"Fucking hell, Long Legs, stop groping me," I said.

"Don't call me Long Legs," he said. "No one's called me that for years."

He dragged me toward the front desk and thumped down on it loudly. The female boss poked her head out from the back. She looked the same as before: small face, thin eyes. The only difference was that her lips were no longer pouty. As soon as she saw me, she let out a shriek and ran to the desk, grabbing my arm. I saw she was wearing a pair of black gloves. "Sweetheart! Let's go for a drink!" she said.

The three of us had drinks at a restaurant. Little Pouty Lips told me my timing was awful—Xiao Li had just taken their son to Nanjing.

"Why aren't your lips pouty anymore?" I asked. "Did you have plastic surgery?" As soon as I said the words, I wanted to slap myself.

But she wasn't angry, she just said, "I'm thirty now. If I were still pouting, my mouth would probably look more like a beak."

"That's going to cause problems. I'm so used to calling you Little Pouty Lips, but now you're no longer little or pouty-lipped."

"Just call me 'sweetheart,' then," she said. "Don't you speak English every day now?"

"Don't mock me. The only words I say daily are fucking curse words," I said.

"Long Legs, are you still fixing pipes?"

"Fuck off," he said. "I'm an investor at the internet café where you found me, and the boss of a computer business."

"I think fixing pipes is better. You could be a household plumber, go into people's houses, fix their pipes—and get laid if you're lucky."

"I don't want to get laid," Long Legs said. "If you get laid, you don't get your fee."

"You can play hide-and-seek with the women in their houses," I said. "We all know how good you are at hiding."

"Don't tease Long Legs," Little Pouty Lips said. "He's just had his heart broken for the first time."

"A thirty-year-old having his heart broken for the first time?" I asked.

"Fuck, it's hell!" Long Legs said.

"Long Legs fell in love with a female entrepreneur, boss of the clothing boutique next door," Little Pouty Lips said. "He really worked hard to pursue her, but then the woman suddenly shows up with this young kid, tells him it's her son, and says if Long Legs wants to marry her, he'll have to step up and take care of the child."

"What's the problem?" I asked.

"Do I look like someone who's ready to be a father?" Long Legs said. "I'm still thinking things through—I just had my heart broken!"

I told Long Legs he should step in as this kid's pa; it was a noble thing to do. After all that dick-whipping back in the day, he was probably infertile anyway. Long Legs lunged at me and grabbed me around the neck. Having a man in his thirties touch me with his ice-cold, slender hands made me break out in goose bumps.

Then we got drunk. Long Legs was the first to slide under the table. Little Pouty Lips and I looked at each other stupidly.

"You weren't brotherly enough toward me," she suddenly said. "You never came to see me after my accident."

"I was too much of a softie—I couldn't bear the thought of seeing you in that state. Anyway, you two never invited me to your wedding."

"We didn't have a ceremony, his parents were against our getting married," Little Pouty Lips said. "After we married, we went to Shanghai for my medical treatment, and when we came back to visit the factory you were gone."

"You must forgive me. I couldn't stay any longer."

"I always knew you were in love with Bai Lan. I thought you went to look for her."

"I did, but she was gone."

"Where did she go?"

"Overseas," I said. I didn't want to talk about Bai Lan anymore. "Back then I thought that if Xiao Li didn't marry you, I would marry you instead. Only the asshole was too obstinate."

"I wouldn't have married you anyway," Little Pouty Lips said. After she said it, she slipped under the table too.

I received Bai Lan's last letter in 1994. It was very brief, a bit like a telegram. She said she'd been given an opportunity to go abroad, so she was dropping her graduate course. She wished me farewell. In the past, her habit had been to add a few words of encouragement before saying good-bye, but that time there were none. Perhaps she felt they were superfluous.

I wanted to go to Shanghai to look for her, but I didn't have time. The factory was rushing to meet its production quota. I heard they'd signed a contract with an overseas enterprise, and if they didn't produce enough saccharin for export, we'd all be sold to Malaysia as piglets. This was obviously just the workers talking shit. By fall that year, the new workshop was up and running and the conditions were pretty good. There was a program-controlled operating room, air-conditioning and central heating, plus restroom facilities on both floors. But I still had to work in the old workshop, which was dirty and dilapidated. The only reason it still existed was to give troublesome workers a reason to reform. I'd probably spend my whole life reforming in there. The two saccharin workshops were both running at full throttle, and the production targets were bearing down on us so heavily that we didn't have a moment to breathe. A team was sent down from the workshop to supervise operations, one cadre to oversee each section. Whenever I wanted to take a leak, I had to report it. The cadre actually told me that for the sake of their production quota and for China's foreign exchange, I should be drinking less water.

"Fuck it, why not get me to piss straight into the reactor, you wouldn't be able to taste the urine in it anyway."

"Do you think you're playing a part in *Red Sorghum* or something? Stop being so dramatic," the cadre said.

I'd also had a run-in with a female cadre who was in her forties and looked quite austere, but she was actually pretty intimidated by us gang of roughnecks. When we were working, she couldn't just do her own thing—she had to pace up and down the workshop in silence. I raised my hand and asked if I could use the restroom.

She looked at me very carefully and asked, "Is it for a number one or a number two?"

"Number one," I said.

"Come back quickly in that case," she said.

This exchange prompted laughter from the surrounding workers, because it made us sound so intimate.

I came across Wei Yixin in the saccharin workshop too. He still had his stammer. I thought he'd have risen to cadre level by now, but here he was producing saccharin too. That degree course in mechanics and electrics had obviously been a complete waste of time—he'd actually been demoted since graduating.

"Can't you still mend water pumps?" I asked him. "How are you being forced to produce saccharin too?"

"D-d-don't don't b-b-bring it up." He stuttered a string of words before I understood what he was saying. It turned out workers were being drafted from every team, and the bench worker team had been asked for one member. Supervisor Wonky Balls had the weakest production skills on the team, so it really should have been him to get the three shifts. However, when the saccharin workshop cadres heard his name, they all just shook their heads; they weren't interested. Wei Yixin happened to have just started dating a girl who was a saccharin workshop manager. So they sent him to produce saccharin and put them both on the same shift. They were told that this was the factory's way of looking after them, as it would allow them to be together twenty-four hours a day. If they were put on different shifts, they'd hardly have seen each other—in fact, they'd have had to use a complicated mathematical formula to work out an opportunity to meet.

"Lu Xiaolu, I'm ev-ev-even unluckier than you," Wei Yixin said. I didn't understand. "Y-y-you've committed so many wrongdoings and finally got the three shifts. I-I-I haven't done anything wrong, but I end up getting the three shifts anyway." Hearing this bothered me. Later I remembered a story my ma once told me, about a group of criminals in prison who became really happy when they saw that a political prisoner had been brought in too. I was like those criminals, so coming across a political prisoner like Wei Yixin should have made me happy.

I was on night shifts once and hadn't slept for two whole days. I couldn't take it at work on that third night, and after finishing the day's production quota, I wanted to find somewhere to catch up on sleep. There was a cadre on site, so I couldn't sleep in the lounge. Nor could I sleep in the workshop. So I said I was taking a leak and made my way to the raw material heap at the bottom of the freight elevator. This was basically a mountain made from sacks of raw material. It was very dark, and people would tuck themselves up behind it and nap unseen. As soon as my ass hit the ground, my eyelids came together and I didn't even notice the bad smell. I'd only meant to have a short nap and get back up. Instead I fell into a series of dreams and slept like the dead. The next thing I was aware of was what felt like water being poured over me and flowing down my neck. I'd been sleeping like a baby, but this made me wake up immediately. I opened my eyes and saw a shadowy figure standing on the sacks of raw material, pissing right onto me. "Fuck you!" I shouted out, scaring whoever it was half to death. He gave a strange yowl and started to run off, his dick still in his hand. I couldn't let him get away; I jumped aggressively to my feet, leapt over the heaped-up sacks of raw material, and grabbed the guy by the back of his neck. It was Wei Yixin.

Wei Yixin was taking care of finished product in back-end production, but he had run off to take an urgent piss. He didn't have enough time to get to the can and back if he wanted to fulfill the production quota, so he ran to the sacks of raw material instead. It was the middle of the night, and he was woozy and didn't notice a certain Lu Xiaolu asleep behind these sacks. This incident was forgivable, although that wasn't my mindset at the time. I'd had my head pissed on. If news of this got out, I'd be a laughingstock, and pissing on my head would be seen as fair game. "You're not going anywhere!" I shouted. I grasped hold of Wei Yixin's belt, preventing him from tucking his dick back in. I wasn't actually planning to hit him—I just wanted to safeguard the crime scene, and his exposed dick proved he was the culprit.

Wei Yixin was terrified. He thought I was going to attack him and chop off his balls. He struggled like crazy, yelling for everyone in the workshop to come save him. Everyone rushed out, and when they saw what was going on, they laughed so much they fell over, some of them nearly passing out. Wei Yixin's girlfriend rushed over to protect him. She seized his belt as well, and tried to yank it away from me. I was not prepared to release my grip. This girl was a bitch, and I bet that when she did manage to drag him back home, he was definitely not going to be getting any action. This was the scene: I was pulling Wei Yixin's belt with Wei Yixin and his girlfriend pulling it against me, making it into a tug of war. Wei Yixin's dick was hanging there pitifully between these six pairs of hands. All three of us were loath to brush against it, thinking that to do so would be pretty inappropriate. So we all avoided touching it as much as we could. The workers around us were laughing the house down—they'd never seen such entertainment, so they kept egging us on.

The most ridiculous part of this whole fiasco was when I loosened my grip. I did it because I thought it was starting to get ridiculous. I was fighting with these jackasses, and it looked as if we were all trying to grab his dick. I'd had enough of it and thought I should let Wei Yixin tuck his dick back in, and the two of us could go outside the factory for a real fight. I didn't give them prior warning before I released him, however, and in line with Newton's first law of physics, the force exerted by Wei Yixin's and his girlfriend's hands produced a strong inertia. With a loud and bitter cry, Wei Yixin covered his lower body and crumpled into his girlfriend's arms. This incident had huge educational value, namely: whether you love or hate a person, you should always bear in mind Newton's first law of physics. Suddenly letting go of someone can be a lethal move, sometimes even more lethal than a squarely landed punch. I learned a new term that year: *testicular contusion*. Had the Wei Yixin situation not familiarized me with this term, I'd have thought I was hearing the words *discussion* and *conclusion*.

I went to the safety department the next day to report what had happened. I explained emphatically that the whole thing had been Wei Yixin's girlfriend's fault. I'd seen it with my own eyes. I told them that the bitch had clamped her hand around Wei Yixin's nether regions (I didn't use the word "dick" in the safety department). Everyone just laughed, thinking I was trying to frame her and that I needed my head checked.

The head of safety invited me in to discuss it. This was a new head of safety. Apparently, my altercation at the big meeting with the last one had caused his downfall. The new factory head had deemed him overly aggressive, had not been impressed, and arranged for him to be transferred. This new head of safety was pretty courteous toward me, and rightly so: he wouldn't have landed his job if not for me.

"What were you doing behind the heap of raw material, Lu Xiaolu?" he asked. "Your job doesn't require you to be behind the heap of raw materials." I hadn't expected such detective work from him, and it flummoxed me. He just laughed and said, "If you report this as a fighting incident, you and Wei Yixin will both be punished. You hit someone, and he pissed on our production materials. Your offense would be aggressive bullying, and his would be damage to property."

We were the only two in the department at the time. I knew what he was saying.

"How do you suggest resolving this, sir?" I asked.

"If it's reported as a work incident, nothing needs to be done," he explained. "You'd be responsible for his medical fees, but being pissed on you'd just have to put down to bad luck."

"Let's do it that way, as you've suggested," I said.

He patted me on the shoulder and said, "Go back home and say hello to your father for me. Lu Daquan's son, eh."

It suddenly all made sense. I rubbed my shaved head in bemusement as I walked out. I went to see Wei Yixin after that, carrying a basket of fruit.

"Lu Xiaolu," Wei Yixin said. "I-I-I didn't rat you out, I did-d-d-d-d didn't say you were sleeping."

I felt a moment of sadness pass through me. I wanted to tell him he was kind, and to thank him. But before I got the chance, his girlfriend came in and shooed me away. I didn't blame her for being petty—I'm sure if I'd had a girl-friend and my dick had been written off, she'd have been just as mad.

My father took his retirement early, long before 1994, due to worry about fac-tory buyouts and privatization. He received his five-hundred-yuan monthly pension and spent monotonous hours at the mah-jongg table day in and day out. Soon he started sprouting white hair and his back problems flared up. Gradually he became like an old man with a stooped posture. I hadn't expected him to age quite so quickly. He was like a tree in fall, his appearance changing almost overnight. I imagined I'd be the same when I was old. Or as Bai Lan used to say: I'd get prematurely senile, and that way I wouldn't have to deal with sudden aging. When I was young, my father would beat me and I'd just have to take it. Later I started fighting back. When he got older, I stopped fighting back. I never laid a hand on my father again.

Before my pa retired, he sent a message to the saccharin factory's head of safety, who was a former colleague. The head of safety agreed to transfer me to the gatehouse, where I could work as a factory policeman. I rejected this offer. Bai Lan once told me: "Whatever you do in the future, Xiaolu, don't let them put you on the gatehouse." I asked her why, and she said, "That really would make you prematurely senile, and it would break my heart."

The head of safety said that if I didn't want to be a factory policeman, that was fine—he'd put me on a temporary transfer to the defense team, which was an even more relaxing job. I rejected this offer too. The defense team had been making a bad name for themselves lately.

I found the time to go to Shanghai that year to look for Bai Lan. All I had on me was an address. I boarded the train and took the Huning line east. By the time I got to Shanghai, it was midday. I sat on a bus that took me to the medical college, where I looked around for Bai Lan. The people in the dormitory told me that she'd left the week before, and none of them knew where she'd gone. I lost my sense of purpose and didn't know where to go. I didn't know what to do with myself except stroll around the medical college campus, taking in the place, trying to understand her dreams. I walked for a long time—every road seemed familiar, as were the leaves on the ground, and I remembered something she'd said: every dry leaf would crunch underfoot, and this was an echo of the sound of the wind left behind from summer. She was such a poetic person. What a shame that being poetic is almost a human defect. It felt like a couple of lifetimes since I'd seen her.

I walked down a dark passageway with no one else around. Both sides of this passageway were lined with bottles, all filled with specimens of human organs. As I moved forward, I saw tons of freak specimens, like fetuses so distorted that you could hardly bear to look. They were all hideous, but I felt there was someone summoning me forward. I walked until I got to a door. It was locked, but I looked in through a small window and saw a couple of human corpses lying there, covered with cloth. They looked so peaceful, and it was as if I had walked to the edge of the world. I was suddenly overwhelmed with horror. I turned around and ran like crazy. A laughing voice came out of the silence, telling me that my journey of discovery ended here.

I went back to the train station that evening to go back to Daicheng. In the North Plaza, I bumped into three guys and we had a minor scuffle. Then, without any explanation, the three of them surrounded me and started to beat the shit out of me. They had me in their grip; I couldn't break free. I heard one of them speaking in a Daicheng accent, and all my anger burst forth. During the fight, one of my molars was knocked out and my face was beaten to a pulp. The three of them ran away, and I was too much of a mess to run after them. I just plodded into the train station and washed my face in the washroom so the police wouldn't stop me. When I looked in the mirror, I saw that half my face was so swollen that it looked like a pig's face. My face had lost all its charm and looked no different that the strange specimens I'd just seen at the medical college.

I got on the train. I only had a standing ticket, and the car was packed. I was feeling dizzy from the beating and I couldn't stand steady, so I made my way to the buffet car and asked for a cup of their eighteen-yuan green tea, which allowed me a buffet car seat. I desperately wanted to sleep, and I felt as dizzy as if I'd been riding a carousel, but I was too scared to go to sleep in case I missed my stop.

"Where are you going?" the girl sitting opposite me asked.

"Daicheng," I said.

"Sleep awhile. I'll wake you when we get there," she said.

I opened an eye and looked at her (the other eye was too swollen), and she smiled at me. She was a plump girl with big eyes. *Just as long as I don't die, I'll make you my girlfriend*, I thought. So I lay my head on the table and fell asleep. I'm not sure how much time had elapsed when she tapped me on the shoulder and said, "We're at Daicheng."

I woke with a splitting headache. I stood up and was about to leave the train, but she hadn't moved. "Aren't you getting off here?" I asked.

"I'm going to Nanjing. That's where I'm from," she said.

I stumbled from the train feeling utterly confused, thinking this was how I lost the love of my life. I will remember this Nanjing girl for the rest of my life.

Many years later, sitting on the curb in Shanghai, I told these stories to Zhang Xiaoyin. Later, when she was my wife, I'd tell them to entertain her. I decided to tell her a little bit each day, but I'd already finished telling her the ones from the factory. All stories have to have an ending, even if you have a *One Hundred Years of Solitude*–style start. The ending might still be garbage, but it's always better than no ending at all.

I told Zhang Xiaoyin that I'd done a lot of bad things in my life. After being beaten up at the train station in Shanghai, I went back and joined the defense team. I wanted to find that gang and beat the fuck out of them, maybe even jab them with an electric baton. But instead the defense team armed me with a flashlight, and although it was electric, it would be in no way as effective as a baton. I carried this flashlight as I wandered the streets, feeling very out of sorts. My ma was pretty worried and begged me not to put my job at risk.

"What are you scared of?" I asked her. "The defense team only gives decent people a hard time."

I remember being out on early-morning street patrol once, eating break-fast and joking around with a couple of colleagues, when a vegetable-selling auntie ran over and said, "There's a man acting indecently over there!" We ran over to take a look and saw a young migrant worker sleeping on the sidewalk. All he was wearing was a pair of underpants, and his morning glory was poking out of the leg hole and pointing at the sky. It was chunky and red and shiny. The girls who caught a glimpse of it as they crossed the road all looked very embarrassed and took a long detour to avoid him. We didn't really know what to do. "Aren't you responsible for these rural types?" the vegetable-selling auntie asked. We were at our wits' end. We had no choice but to kick the migrant worker awake, arrest him, and take him into the defense team station on the grounds of public indecency. I didn't know why I was arresting him, I had nothing against this man: no animosity, no hatred. What right did I have to interrupt his erotic dream? I find things like this difficult to talk about.

I remember standing out in the street at night shouting, "Watch for thieves! Watch out for gas! Remember to lock your windows!" Nowadays this is done via loudspeakers with recorded messages on a loop, but in those days we just shouted them. They told me that being awarded second prize at the karaoke contest meant that I was the most qualified to shout out these messages. We came across a thief who'd once stolen a bike. He fled when he saw us, but five or six of us from the team chased after him. I fucking well tumbled to the ground, ripping my pants. Clearly the defense team wasn't just for show, and once we'd apprehended our thief, we were very pleased with ourselves. As pleased with ourselves as when we were carrying home our New Year's goods. By the time we arrived at the station, the thief was so scared he was crying. I grabbed a copper-buckled belt and threatened him with it. Then we marched him through the street, shouting that we'd caught a thief. His voice had been so pitiful, and I wondered if the people in that neighborhood had heard it and thought they'd been having a nightmare. I didn't know what the point of all this was. Could I really transform my life by whipping a thief with a copper-buckled belt?

Zhang Xiaoyin told me my defense team stories were hilarious. I told her she was right, and I really could have made them sound hilarious, like skits in the Spring Festival gala show. But I didn't find them hilarious. I didn't think there was anything the slightest bit funny about these stories.

"So how did you decide to quit in the end?" Zhang Xiaoyin asked.

I told her it happened like this: one evening a stray dog showed up near the factory, and a kid from one of the residential houses called it over. The dog thought it was about to get some food, so it went up to the kid—but instead the kid took a metal stick and poked the dog in the ass. The dog went crazy, biting the kid and tearing a clump of flesh from his butt. I was on duty at the time, a smoke stuck between my lips as I loitered in the street. The kid's mother ran over, grabbed me, and dragged me to her place. The kid was on the ground, crying loudly. "You're on the defense team," the mother said. "Beat that rabid dog, it's bitten my child!" I looked in the direction she was pointing and the dog bared its teeth at me, looking pretty scary. "Are you going to do something about it?" the mother asked. "Aren't you the defense team?" Clenching my teeth, I picked up a branch, but the dog was smart: it turned around and fled. "Chase after it! Chase after it!" the mother yelled.

I pursued the dog along the river. It ran at lightning speed. When I started to lose it, it stopped a moment, as if waiting for me to catch up. When I started chasing it again, it raced away once more. I chased it past the main gate of the saccharin factory, where a couple of workers were squatting down to smoke. They cheered loudly and said, "Lu Xiaolu, are you chasing a dog? Dog meat for dinner, is it?" I ignored them, too focused on chasing this dog. After running for half a mile, I managed to drive the dog onto a small pier. It wasn't going to get away now unless it jumped into the water. I gave it a malicious smile, wanting to force it into the river. I'd heard that rabid dogs were scared of water. The dog looked at me, and I realized it wasn't a rabid dog after all—at least at that second he wasn't. But he still didn't seem eager to go in the water. The river water was so dirty that swimming in it would probably give him skin disease. He howled and suddenly flew at me, biting my calf.

I was scared shitless. I'd been bitten by a rabid dog. That meant I was going to turn into a rabid dog myself. I ran away, the dog chasing madly after me. When we passed the main factory gate this time, the workers were in hysterics. "Lu Xiaolu, which one of you is on the defense team, you or him?" they shouted. Again, I ignored them and continued to run. I ran up to the child, and his mother said, "You wimp! How have you allowed the dog to chase you back here?" I turned to see that the dog was tiring too. He was crouched a way off, watching me.

I grabbed a length of steel pipe from a nearby bike stand. "Fuck you, I *will* beat you to death," I said. The dog really was smart. As soon as he saw the steel pipe, he turned and fled. In what world was this dog rabid? Raising the steel pipe above my head, I followed on his heels, chasing him yet again past the main gate of the saccharin factory. This time, there were forty or fifty people gathered around to watch me chase the dog. He didn't run onto the pier this time but trotted down the road. Then he turned around and looked at me. At that moment, the dog and I were of one mind.

He was asking me: "What the fuck are you doing?"

"I'm trying to beat you to death," I told him.

He followed that with an even more profound question: "What the fuck are you living for?"

I couldn't answer that one. It was a question posed to me by a rabid dog; I was no longer sure which one of us had rabies. I threw down the steel pipe. I didn't know what I was living for either, running back and forth through the world in this ridiculous way.

Handing in my notice is another ridiculous story. I ran up to the labor department and slapped a small piece of paper onto the desk: my letter of resignation. That's when they told me that I was a contracted worker. I'd signed a five-year contract, so what I was doing could not be called "handing in my notice" but rather "breaching my contract." Instead I had to write an "application to breach my contract," then wait for the factory to consider it and make a decision. I decided that if the factory didn't approve it, I just wouldn't come to work anymore and then they'd fire me.

Unfortunately, I didn't get to see Hu Deli at the labor department. After giving my notice, I picked up a three-sided scraper and jogged into the bike shed, where I found Hu Deli's bike. I used the scraper to scratch up his tires. I didn't find it very cathartic, so I stripped the tires off the bike completely, leaving the two metal rims. Then I went home. The next day I went back to the labor department and was told that I had been granted permission to breach my contract. They talked to me very politely. I didn't get a glimpse of Hu Deli this whole time.

I went back home and lay on my bed. My ma sat by my bedside. "What do you plan to do now?" she asked.

"I'm just going to take it easy," I said. "Let me be for a while."

She sighed. I thought she was going to start grumbling, but she surprised me by saying, "Washing is going to be a problem for you in the future."

"What?" I asked.

"You used to wash every day in the factory. Now that you've quit, you only have the public bathhouse. That's five yuan a wash. There's no way you can afford to go there every day."

"So what will I do?"

"You can wash your butt and feet daily, the same as when you were at school," she said. "Personal hygiene should be your priority. Girls won't give you a second glance if you're grubby."

I laughed loudly when I heard this. I've looked at astrology some, and my ma was a Sagittarius. This meant that she was a silly lady who was extremely optimistic her whole life. Because of her, I saw the world as a comedy. My good fortune was my destiny to be born to her. Many years later, I went to Shanghai on my own to find a job. My ma saw me to the front door. I was pretty upset to be leaving. Her parting words were, "You mustn't take advantage of young girls, Xiaolu." I was speechless. Then she added, "Of course, you mustn't let them take advantage of you either!" With those words, she ushered me out into the world. She raised her son just as one might raise a dog, scared that I'd catch fleas or get into trouble with the opposite sex. I love my ma like I love all of this world's fresh flowers and white clouds.

EPILOGUE

BABYLON

I used to write essays when I was young. When the teacher asked me to describe Daicheng, I said it was located between Shanghai and Nanjing, and all its citizens had a few relatives from Shanghai and some had relatives from North Jiangsu. You could ask the Shanghai relatives to buy you sewing machines and wool coats, while the North Jiangsu relatives could bring you salted duck eggs. That's what I wrote in my essay. The teacher was not impressed. He thought I had a chaotic mind and that I'd made Daicheng sound like a wretched place.

Daicheng is a great city, this teacher of mine said. It was built in the great spring and autumn period of Chinese history. One day, a king came to the area with his beloved concubine. They stood on the mountain and looked over the kingdom. His concubine pointed at a plain between the junctions of the rivers and said to the king, "You must build a city in that place." The king sent huge numbers of slaves and large numbers of troops and many talented architects to build the city. They built wide, imposing watchtowers, enchanting bridges, and quaint secluded gardens. He and his royal concubine lived in the center of this city. Sometimes they would go on excursions out of town. They would go to a nearby mountain where there was a well. The beloved concubine peered into the well and saw a face of unparalleled beauty reflected back at her. She didn't know that the corpses of large numbers of slaves were buried behind the mountain.

Like countless numbers of leaders of their time, this king and his beloved concubine enjoyed their power. They would look down from their watchtower at the slaves cheering below, and they would watch as the expeditionary forces returned triumphant. It was like this until one day when another king and his troops stormed the city. They killed the former king, and his beloved concubine was rolled up like a spring roll and thrown into the river. As the story goes, this city holds on to an eternal sorrow, like someone who lives to be a thousand but can only pine over a long-lost love.

Later, lots of factories were built in this city. Huge numbers of cargo ships passed along the rivers, shipping out silk, rice, vegetables, and tea leaves, and, of course, my saccharin. This was 2,500 years later. My Daicheng was a city that a concubine bought with her beauty. She was killed in the end, and the city was taken over by someone else, and her beauty was relegated to the water. It's a very poetic legend, but if you think about it too much it gets boring.

When I was twenty, someone from the Institute of Literature and History announced that Daicheng would be 2,500 years old that year, and we should hold a celebration. I had no real concept of so many years. This wasn't a Roman city, it wasn't Jerusalem or Athens. It lacked any evidence of its origins: none of the original palaces, watchtowers, or bridges were still in existence; all that remained was the legend. There were still a few dilapidated buildings from the republic era, and if you looked down at the city from high up, you'd see those buildings dotting the area of the old city. They were old and dark and ramshackle, with rats and cockroaches running amok. None of these houses had restrooms, and they could catch fire at the drop of a hat. There really wasn't any evidence of that 2,500-year history, but the place did look a lot like a coffin.

They marked this anniversary with a tourism festival that attracted a lot of Japanese people. The factory gave each local person a badge and asked us to pin them to our chests. These badges were made from aluminum and were designed with the Great Wall as it appears on a map, with a woman's profile in the middle—that beloved concubine, apparently. She sold herself so that we, her successors, could enjoy the city. She even lost her life for this project. So it was only right that we would commemorate her. I pinned the badge to my chest. One bungling supervisor was too forceful when attaching his, and the pin went straight through his nipple. He was sent directly to the infirmary for treatment.

Tourists came to visit Daicheng and took home some of our local special-
ties. One of these was a cake made from date and rapeseed. It was deadly sweet,
completely unsuitable for diabetics. When the sellers were shouting it out, they
shortened the name to "date-rape cake," and as a result the salespeople were forever getting into fights with customers. But the name couldn't be changed. The
tourists had to take a slice of date-rape cake home to show that they'd visited
our city.

I muddled along in Daicheng for many years. I don't like the place, but it's
full of evidence of how I spent my twenties. If I wanted to erase this evidence,
the only way would be to bulldoze the city. I realized that there was no need
for such radical action; no one gave a damn about the evidence of my youth. I
wasn't the beloved royal concubine who'd sold herself, and I wasn't worth level-
ing a city for. As long as I can remember these years, that's enough.

Later I moved to Shanghai, where I got together with Zhang Xiaoyin. We
first met in a dilapidated factory near Fudan University, which is now used only
to host rock concerts. It looked like a very ineffective factory with no workers
to speak of, iron wire and iron filings piled up like hillocks, and rust glinting in
the moonlight. It made me think about my old factory. I was nearly thirty. The
sweat poured out, soaking my back as I crouched there listening to rock music,
surrounded by girls and guys who were all in their twenties. When I was young,
all there was to do in Daicheng was sing karaoke—there was no rock music
whatsoever. I crouched there listening to the rock, doing the things I didn't get
the chance to do when I was their age.

I'd never been as quiet as I was recalling my Daicheng and my journey of
discovery.

I was almost thirty when I took that train to Shanghai to find work. I was
thinking about the other time I'd been to Shanghai, going to the medical college to look for a certain someone. Recalling those past events felt like lifting
my head and smashing it against a pane of glass. The train passed a section of
road and I could see the saccharin factory, the steam pumping out of its roof.
That's where I'd been standing, many years before, watching a train bound for
Shanghai.

The weather was good that day. The train was pretty empty, just me and one
other person in the whole car. He looked about twenty and was wearing glasses.
He sat in front of me to the left, leaning back against his seat and looking out
of the window. For no apparent reason, he took off his glasses and wept. I sat

there looking at him, unable to comfort him. He was crying with such sorrow and such anguish. I felt the sorrow from when I was twenty dripping out along with his tears and falling all along the tracks.

No one is curled up sleeping

On the high luggage rack

And no one has thought

To lie down on the rushing train's floor

Fields fly past along with trees and clouds

And it all seems too much like a tragedy

Those people running alongside the train

They're the ones who die young as they frolic in the water

It all seems too much like the start of a tragedy

The train attendant strolls along the train as it travels at fifty miles an hour

Unhurriedly

The fish in the torrent is now docked on the shore

Naked and bright

The tragedy passengers are woken from their nightmares early the next morning

The attendants who wake them are only seventeen

They have candy in their hands

Their uniforms have long been crooked

In the dark

Will old age creep up a little slower?

ABOUT THE AUTHOR

Photo © 2013 Fei Teng

Lu Nei, formerly Shang Weijun, was born in 1973 in Suzhou, in east China. He is the fiction moderator for the "under-literature" section of the website sickbaby.org. He has held a wide range of jobs, including factory worker, shop assistant, salesperson, warehouse manager, radio announcer, and creative director for an advertising agency. He lives in Shanghai.

ABOUT THE TRANSLATOR

Photo © 2014 Sophie Baker

Poppy Toland studied Chinese at Leeds University, UK. She lived in Beijing for four years, working as an editor for *Time Out Beijing* and field research supervisor for the BBC's *Wild China* TV series. She is now based in London, pursuing a PhD in translation studies at Bangor University, and working as a freelance literary translator.